SKULL OF DISGUISES

MEMENTO MORI ⧗ TREASURE LIFE

PRAISE FOR SKULL OF DISGUISES

Michael Karpovage once again successfully weaves factual history into modern day fiction to create an intricate mystery of murder, mayhem, witchcraft, and lost treasure. His descriptive writing style gives the reader the impression they are right there in the scene of a movie. In SKULL OF DISGUISES, he presents two parallel plots that eventually intertwine with unexpected twists keeping the reader on the edge of their seat until to the very end.

   —Gene Conrad, reviewer, Berkshire, NY

This book has Clive Cussler-like plot lines that make for staying up way too late reading page after page. The writing was so descriptive, the characters even found ways into my dreams. SKULL OF DISGUISES is a great read for fans of historical fiction and a special treat for all Brothers of the world's oldest fraternity.

   —Brother Billy Gould, reviewer, Cabul Lodge No. 116, Green Cove Springs, FL

Another Karpovage masterpiece! He grabs you on page one and never lets go. Reading his book is like watching a movie.

   —Robert Brian Miller, reviewer, Alpharetta, GA

Authors of genius create alternate universes that you never wish to leave. Karpovage's third book in his Tununda Mysteries universe is another that stays with you forever as the scenes replay on the screen of your mind. SKULL OF DISGUISES is a Rubik's Cube of betrayal, inhumanity, honor, bravery, and adventure set against the historical backdrop of WWII and a Freemason's legacy. For men of the Craft like myself, you'll be reminded why you first chose to walk as a Freemason as Karpovage exemplifies the core Masonic principle of brotherhood through his characters and plot. This book goes on my forever bookshelf!

   —Brother Timothy S. Yarbrough, reviewer, Northwest Lodge No. 1434, Spring, TX

If you like stories that are so well written that you can't put the book down to go to bed or to work, start this when you have a day or two free! This is the third book in the series (be sure to read the first two to understand the backstory). Michael Karpovage has done it again – thorough research, terrific characters and storyline, which turns into a very believable tale. It will keep you guessing and cheering for the good guys right to the end!

   —Linda S. LeCroy, reviewer, Brandon, FL

Warning: SKULL OF DISGUISES will grip you tight like the jaws of a gator. It will then consume you. Not every author has this ability. Michael Karpovage does it by weaving little-known facts with fiction to create a totally believable plot. This book is an absolute must-read. Definitely a 5-Star rating!

   —Paula Howard, reviewer, Indianapolis, IN

MICHAEL
KARPOVAGE

/MichaelKarpovage

THE TUNUNDA MYSTERIES
  Book 1: *Crown of Serpents (2009)*
  Book 2: *Map of Thieves (2014)*
  Book 3: *Skull of Disguises (2018)*

KarpovageCreative.com

This is a work of fiction. Names, characters, places, and incidents either are the product of the author's imagination or are used fictitiously, and any resemblance to actual persons, living or dead, business establishments, events, or locales, is entirely coincidental.

Published by
Karpovage Creative, Inc.
5055 Magnolia Walk
Roswell, Georgia 30075
www.karpovagecreative.com

ISBN: 978-0-9856532-6-2

Printed in the United States of America
First Edition

Cover / interior book design, maps, and illustrations created by
Karpovage Creative, Inc.
designer • map illustrator • publisher
www.karpovagecreative.com

To my mother, for giving me a strong foundation.
I miss you, RoRo.

AUTHOR'S NOTE

Skull of Disguises is a work of fiction based on pure speculative narrative, and all present day characters are creations of my imagination. But some of the historical figures in this book are real people. They existed and left records of themselves, some more abundant than others. I tried to be faithful to their actions and encounters as best I could determine from historical sources. Some sources are recorded, others come through individual oral histories. These 'facts' combined with speculative 'fiction' are the basis for each book in The Tununda Mysteries.

There's also major theme that acts as the foundation to these novels: Masonic brotherly love and protection – especially in the heat of battle. Meaning: the loyalties of a Mason outweigh the loyalties to a country or an army. This core tenet of Freemasonry is time immemorial and the most fascinating aspect of Masonry for me personally. And also, by extension, for Jake Tununda. This unwavering rock solid foundation, a man-to-man oath, is what binds together the oldest universal fraternity in the world – a fraternity that has outlived armies, governments, and nations.

In *Skull of Disguises,* Jake's loyalties and inner convictions are put to that test once again: breaking the rules to do what's morally right versus following the letter of the law. What would you do if confronted with similar circumstances?

For a breakdown of the historical facts versus the embellished legends used as the backstory within this novel, be sure to read the end notes of this book under *Fact or Fiction?*

Visit **KarpovageCreative.com** for author interviews, book signing events, newsletter subscription, photos, and more.

— *Michael Karpovage*

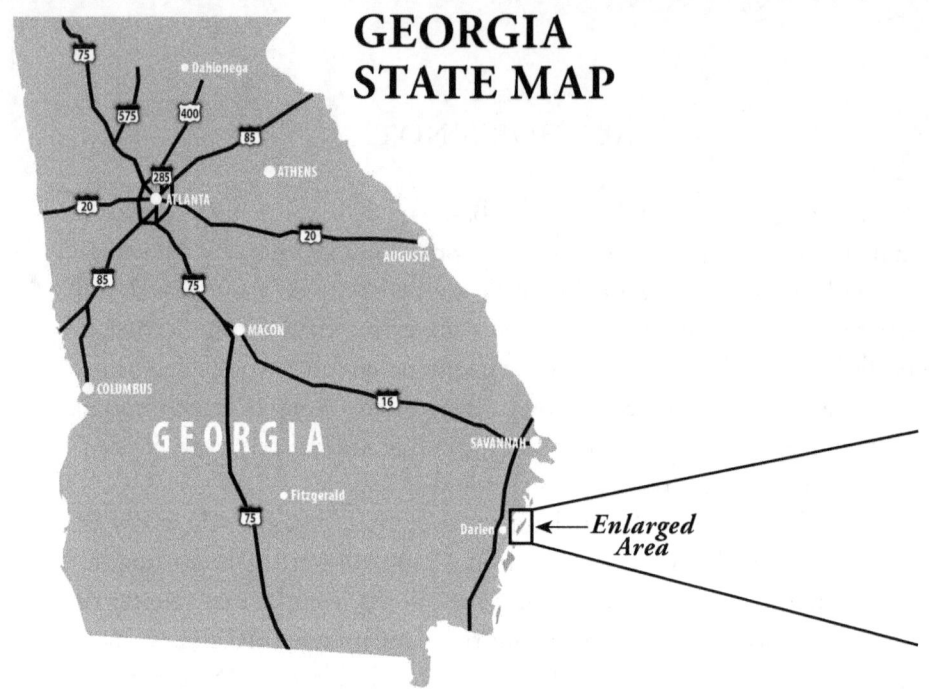

GEORGIA STATE MAP

GEORGIA

← *Enlarged Area*

U-Boat Type XXIII *(Elektroboote)*

Diagram by Michael Karpovage
©2018 Karpovage Creative, Inc. • KarpovageCreative.com

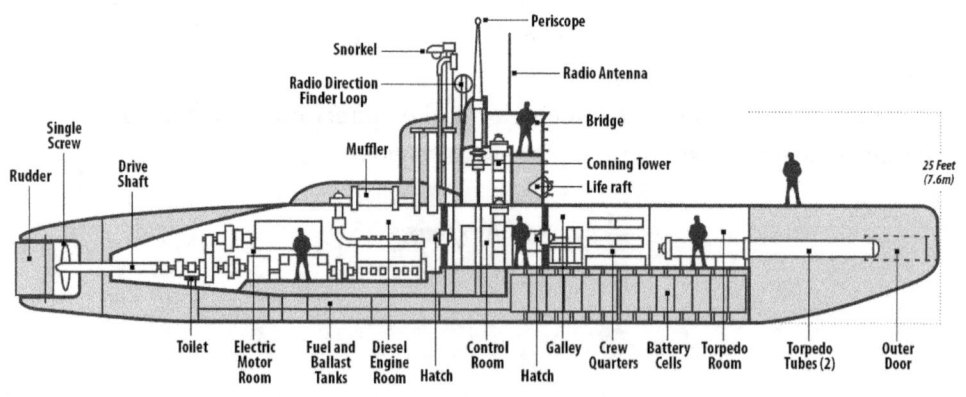

Periscope

Snorkel

Radio Direction Finder Loop

Radio Antenna

Muffler

Bridge

Single Screw

Drive Shaft

Conning Tower

Rudder

Life raft

25 Feet (7.6m)

Toilet | Electric Motor Room | Fuel and Ballast Tanks | Diesel Engine Room | Hatch | Control Room | Galley | Hatch | Crew Quarters | Battery Cells | Torpedo Room | Torpedo Tubes (2) | Outer Door

STERN

AMIDSHIPS
114 Feet (34.7m)

BOW

SAPELO/BLACKBEARD ISLANDS MAP

PROLOGUE

September 17, 1945. 7:15 a.m.
U-2370 Elektroboote
Blackbeard Island, Georgia

A SHARP CRACK JARRED GERMAN *KAPITÄNLEUTNANT* Werner Witte from his deep concussive slumber. His eyes fluttered open to semi-darkness as the penetrating sound echoed in the back of his skull. Somewhere far away, a strange man's voice pleaded over and over again: *"Outta da watah! Outta da watah!"* Another loud report followed. The captain flinched, blinking with heavy lids, head throbbing as he slowly swam back to the surface of consciousness.

A third blast. He squeezed his eyes shut, the pain ricocheting in his head. As a veteran of war, that sound was all too familiar: rifle fire.

A man then screamed in abject terror, followed by another crack of rifle fire. And another. *Must be a dream, a horrible dream,* thought Witte.

Then all went completely silent.

Captain Witte blinked and the darkness before him turned to blurry light. Sunlight, it seemed. Something he hadn't seen for days. The air he gulped was beyond the stench of oil, smoke, sweat, and vomit he had become used to. Focusing from blurriness to clarity revealed he was inside of a cylindrical tunnel dripping with water. He looked straight up at a curved ceiling with long, metallic condensation-caked pipes and a wafting gray haze of smoke. Clumps of smoldering electrical wire dangled from damaged conduit tubes. Handwheels, gears, valves, and smashed glass faces of gauges lined the walls. As the cobwebs in his mind drifted away, it finally hit him.

He was still inside his U-boat.

Covered with splintered pieces of wood paneling and dressed in rain gear with a yellow life vest, he lay in a heap amidships near the crew quarters. Slowly turning his head, he glanced toward the bow. One of the two torpedo tubes was barely visible behind a torn curtain. Panning his eyes in the opposite direction, just past the open bulkhead hatch, he could see inside the control room, now basked in glorious rays of smoky sunlight.

But a strange feeling enveloped him: a complete lack of motion, as if he were floating.

Is this finally my iron coffin? he thought, unsure if he was alive or just another ghost crewman finally joining his fellow dead submariners of the *Kriegsmarine.*

Blinking to adjust his eyesight, feeling the numbness of his body slowly turn to pain, he soon realized he wasn't dead after all. He wasn't floating either. His U-boat was grounded.

But Witte had fully expected to go down with his ship – to share the fate of his comrades in service of the Fatherland. Every time he'd heard one of his sister U-boats was lost at sea, he felt that ever-present, agonizing survivor's guilt.

Of all German wartime forces, U-boat men suffered the heaviest casualties. Out of a force of fifty-five thousand, over thirty thousand didn't survive the war. Life expectancy was a mere sixty days on missions to the North American coast where his boat had operated in his last days.

Only tough-as-nails veterans like himself knew how to keep their crew – half of whom were on their first mission – alive during those last deadly days of the war. They were a *Schickalsgemeinschaft* – a group of men sworn to each other, dependent on each other, and bound by fate.

I beat the Gods. Again, Witte thought.

He now knew his desperate gamble of jamming himself inside the galley cabinet had saved his life when the sub wrecked. Ultimately, though, it was his tough little U-2370 that won the real battle; the U-boat he'd killed with and surrendered with under the German flag, but then was forced to commandeer under the enemy's flag.

But whose flag was the real enemy?

Closing his eyes, he flashed back to how he'd gotten here and the dreadful last death throes of his doomed sub.

At just 114-feet long, Captain Werner Witte's Type XXIII submarine was the shortest, lowest-profile U-boat in the German fleet. Only two bow torpedo tubes were fitted and there were no deck guns. Its small size meant it was so crammed with equipment that there was virtually no room for his crew. But all that technologically-advanced equipment gave them the edge they needed to win in battle.

With an operating complement of just fourteen compared to the more common Type VIIs and their crews of almost sixty men, the Type XXIII was a sleek, agile, and highly stealthy killing machine – a 'miracle work' dubbed by German engineers. Because of its high-capacity battery cells fueling the electric motor for maximum undersea operations, it was officially called an *Elektroboote* by the *Kriegsmarine*. Mostly used in shallow, coastal patrols to interdict Allied shipping, she could rapid crash-dive in nine seconds.

At the end of the war, in a last-ditch effort to re-establish the U-boat offensive in the Western Atlantic; his U-2370 was assigned to *Gruppe Seewolf*, the last wolfpack of the Atlantic campaign. U-2370 was the only one in its class to make the unprecedented desperate journey across the north Atlantic from its Norwegian port. Refueled and resupplied along the way by larger class U-boats, once they reached the coast of North America, Witte and his crew went to work relaying information to other attack boats in their group.

Whenever his U-boat submerged to avoid detection, Witte would try to employ the revolutionary new snorkel system to circulate fresh air within the sub. Long gone were the days of running out of breathable air and having to resurface only to be pounded by enemy warships and planes. His crew survived fully submerged for unheard-of lengths of time. With the high-speed electric motor and a hull covered in an anti-sonar rubber coating, his sub easily outran the fastest warships the Allies threw at him.

While hunting together with U-546, a big war horse Type IXC/40

U-boat – Witte used that same quiet cloak of invisibility to help make the *Kriegsmarine's* last kill of the war. On April 24, Witte's U-2370 made contact with a destroyer off the coast of Newfoundland. He relayed the location to U-546 and together they attacked.

Witte launched both of his bow torpedoes. One missed, the other hit on the port side, forward, causing an explosion. U-546 fired a stern torpedo and made its mark amidship. The destroyer jackknifed in two and was sent to the bottom of the ocean with 115 men. It was the destroyer escort USS *Frederick C. Davis*, the last combat sinking of a U.S. Navy vessel in the Atlantic Theatre. Only 77 survived.

Five other destroyers then hunted the pair of U-boats down. After enduring ten bone-jarring hours of depth charge attacks, the deadly game of cat and mouse claimed a victim. A heavily damaged U-546 was blown to the surface and then stitched with gunfire. Only 33 crewmen escaped before the U-boat rolled over and went down, taking 26 men with her. Witte's U-2370 managed to escape in a southwesterly course at maximum depth running silent while using only its electric motor.

Soon after, on May 8, Witte received a radio transmission from *Kriegsmarine* Admiral Karl Dönitz with orders to surrender under a black flag to the closest Allied ship or port. Dönitz had been elevated to *Reichspräsident*, Hitler's successor as head of state, after the death of the *Führer* and in accordance with his last will and testament.

For Witte, the war was over. But his brutality had just begun.

On May 16, Witte surfaced his ship undetected just 600 yards from a completely surprised American destroyer 100 miles off the coast of Boston. He was the first one on the bridge hoisting a black flag. Being fluent in English, he shouted their surrender through a bullhorn as the destroyer closed in. His U-boat was immediately boarded, all of his crew off-loaded, and taken as prisoners of war.

Command of his sub was given to an American officer and a prize crew hand-selected from the destroyer. The destroyer escorted U-2370 west to the Portsmouth Naval Shipyard island in the state of Maine, where it was placed in dry dock and studied by Navy engineers because of its treasure-trove of stealth technology.

Witte and his U-boat men were then housed at the notorious Portsmouth Naval Prison, a Navy brig on the island. The German prisoners of war learned the brig was nicknamed the "Alcatraz of the East" because it was virtually escape-proof and housed the worst convicts of the U.S. Navy and Marine Corps. It also held several other POW U-boat crews who had just surrendered, too, including men of U-234, U-805, U-873, and U-1228.

Naturally, he and his crew were treated harshly. Hardened American inmates hurled every imaginable insult at them, along with urine, feces, and garbage. Muscular Marine prison guards, commanded by aggressive officers, manhandled the crewmen, some as young as eighteen. They were punched, slapped, kicked, and beaten with rubber truncheons. Their personal possessions were looted as souvenirs. Stolen were diaries, personal letters and photographs, watches, rings, badges, awards, binoculars, cameras, wallets, and almost 3,000 Swiss francs. One massive Marine guard even stole Witte's captain's hat. But these indiscretions were nothing compared to the private interrogation sessions.

The Office of Naval Intelligence (ONI) and the Office of Strategic Services (OSS) had interrogators question the POWs to gain information about German weapons technologies. Anyone who didn't comply was harshly beaten by the Marine guards – all behind closed doors. Captain Werner Witte learned the hard way after he endured a round of severe facial slaps by the same Marine who'd stolen his hat. A swollen black eye and busted lip brought him back in line to answer questions properly. That's when he was forced to reveal he had helped sink the USS *Frederick C. Davis*. The Marine then gave Witte the worst beating of his life using a rubber truncheon. Witte ended up in the prison hospital for two weeks.

The captain of U-873 wasn't so lucky. *Kapitänleutnant* Fritz Steinhoff was assaulted by the same burly Marine during another interrogation session. Two days later, after being transferred to a Boston jail, he bled to death from a sliced wrist, apparently self-inflicted from broken sunglasses. Suicide was the official cause, but a crewman from U-873 whispered it was the Marines. That crewman warned Witte he might be next.

After four months of brutal treatment and constant physical and mental abuse from the Marines and inmates, Witte's luck finally changed when he was snatched from his cell and made an offer he couldn't refuse.

The OSS wanted U-2370 back in service and for him to train an American crew as part of a secret mission.

As added incentive, his original thirteen crewmen of U-2370 wouldn't be beaten and tortured. If the German captain was a good Kraut, they had promised, then his sailors would be transferred to a POW camp where humane treatment under the Geneva Convention was honored. If not, they'd be beaten some more for good measure and then shipped overseas to a Russian POW camp instead. The choice was rather simple: Witte would do anything for the well-being of his crew to keep them out of the hands of the vengeful Russians, which would surely result in their deaths.

In early September U-2370, with an American skeleton crew of just eight men, including himself, went back into service, this time under the American flag. The man in charge of the operation was an OSS agent who went by the name of Mr. Baker. The hand-picked crew was made up of former U.S. Navy submariners who had been pulled directly from the prison as part of the mission.

All because they were expendable – especially Witte.

For the American convicts, each serving long prison sentences for heinous crimes, and for Witte, it would be their first mission of many as a clandestine U-boat crew – or so they were told. With his fluency in English and being a highly experienced submariner, Witte's role was the translation of the German-labeled machinery and the training of the American captain, first officer, and chief engineer on how to operate the technologically-advanced U-boat. A mechanic, helmsman, and radar operator rounded out the crew, all of whom were commanded by agent Baker.

The first leg of their mission was to get the sub from Portsmouth to Bermuda where they would receive new orders and take on cargo. Witte was initially treated like shit during those first few days. The American captain was undisciplined and the crew would have been uncontrollable if not for OSS agent Baker laying down the law. After several crash dives under Witte's command, running submerged and silent, the Americans soon respected the German as their de facto commander.

After all, their lives depended on him, for he was also tasked to show this crew how to avoid detection from their very own forces on patrol in the air and on the sea. Those hunter-killer groups of U.S. Navy and Civil Air Patrols included ships, planes, and even blimps – and they had gotten quite good at sinking U-boats over the course of the war.

Successfully arriving at the U.S. Naval Operating Base at Ordnance Island, Bermuda, U-2370 received her new orders and was subsequently stocked full with secret cargo destined for the United States. It departed with one new passenger who was introduced as Mr. Bosch, making for a total of nine men. Dressed in a neatly pressed black suit, the VIP was a slight, wiry, middle-aged German who also spoke good English.

The OSS agent and the American captain revealed to Witte only generalities in their orders so he could plot navigation. They were to transport the passenger and cargo to a small, restricted Navy airfield at Harris Neck on the Georgia coast, just beyond Sapelo Sound.

However, during the loading of the cargo, while sitting hidden on the toilet at the very aft of the boat, Witte unwittingly eavesdropped on the chief engineer and mechanic. Drunk already, their loose lips revealed key details about their new mission.

They said once the boat reached Harris Neck and off-loaded their goods, they'd refuel, reload, and smuggle back to Bermuda booze, cigarettes, chocolate bars, silk stockings, smut magazines, and any other contraband items of worth. From Bermuda, that cargo would then be flown to occupied Germany by OSS planes, and eventually sold on the black market. Apparently, it was all cover for their real mission, something they called *Operation Overcast*.

The two American crewmen even joked that once Witte sufficiently trained the crew, he wasn't going back to prison. He was destined for Davy Jones' Locker, they'd said. Witte had learned this phrase when he studied at an English college for an eight-month stint in 1937.

From Bermuda, the single-propeller, diesel-driven engine of U-2370 made great surface speed traveling at night, while running deep and silent during the day on battery power. It avoided all U.S. air and sea patrols because of its sophisticated *FuMO 65* radar and radar detection technology.

No matter; theirs was still a doomed mission to the U.S. coast.

· 7 ·

Disaster struck just twenty miles off the coast of Georgia.

It was a moonless night with distant thunderstorms and increasing winds from a massive hurricane traveling north up the Atlantic coast of Florida. Although they'd heard radio reports that the hurricane had destroyed the Homestead Army Air Field down in south Florida, U-2370 was still due to beat the storm and take safe haven at Harris Neck.

The American crewmen and even agent Baker, though, had gotten utterly complacent, figuring those last miles would be a breeze. Below deck they were either drunk or dozing off at their stations. Witte himself had fallen fast asleep in a hammock, having been up for eighteen hours straight. But the most crucial crewman of all, the radar detection operator, was occupied on the head with a severe case of diarrhea. Without a full operating contingent onboard, no one could replace him. His absence was their Achilles' heel.

Up on the bridge, the American captain and first officer were scanning the skies and waters for contacts. With no forewarning at all, an undetected U.S. Navy PBM-5S2 Mariner bomber, using advanced microwave radar technology, dropped from the clouds at enormous speed. It drenched U-2370's bridge with daylight from its forward spotlight and blinded the two night watchmen. All they could do was duck behind the bridge shield.

Despite all U-boats having been ordered to surrender by German high command back in May, which the overwhelming majority did, Allied patrols still knew there were some that defied the order. Just the previous month, U-977, a Type VIIC U-boat, surrendered in Argentina after making a 99-day voyage to escape Europe.

The Mariner pilots visually identified this surface contact as a German U-boat, and with shoot-on-sight orders, had the nose turret gunner open up with his twin .50-caliber machine guns. The sub's bridge lit up in a rain of hot lead. The American sub captain and first officer were killed instantly.

Making its low level pass, the Mariner then simultaneously dropped two, 500-pound depth bombs. One of the bombs bounced off the starboard saddle tank leaving a dent. They were preset at a shallow depth of only 25-feet, so it was just seconds before they sank and detonated. One was a dud, but the other created an incredible blast.

The underwater explosion lifted the small boat out of the water. Two more crewmen lost their lives in the engine room: the radar operator on the toilet and OSS agent Baker, who had been sifting through some cargo. Both died from blunt force trauma when their heads were bashed against machinery from the bomb blast's underwater concussive wave. Everyone else suffered severe migraines when their brains were rattled like Jell-O.

But the depth bomb failed to crack the tough hull and sink U-2370.

As quickly as it had appeared, the Mariner disappeared back up into the clouds. The bomber, previously suffering an engine malfunction and flying on nothing but fumes after a long-distance patrol, could ill afford to swing back for another attack. Instead, they radioed the sub's location for other coastal patrol units to follow up.

Scrambling up to the bridge, Witte found the shattered bodies of the American captain and first officer. The captain caught a round that had blown the top half of his head clean off. The first officer's body took several rounds and was torn to pieces. The periscope and snorkel up top were both shattered and useless, while the radio aerial was split in half. Witte immediately flew the American flag in the hopes it would deter any more attacks since now the sub was nothing more than a sitting duck. He left the bodies where they lay.

Below deck, floor plates were askew and covered with hand wheels, broken glass, and pipes that had been blown from their mountings. The mechanic reported that the hydroplanes had jammed, the ballast tank had split open, and the diesel engine was inoperable with severe oil and hydraulic leaks. Plus, the sub was taking on water in several places. All that remained functional was the electric motor powered by battery cells, which had already been depleted by three quarters before the attack.

Worst of all, they were unable to submerge to escape further attacks.

The civilian Bosch, trying to help, said the radio was so damaged there was no way to communicate to Harris Neck that their mission was now a bust and they needed rescuing.

With a severely damaged and hapless submarine, the five survivors, distraught from the air attack and deaths of four crewmen, begged Captain Witte to save them. Under his direction, they made as many repairs as they could. It was frantic non-stop work. They exhausted themselves so much the chief engineer passed out from the effort. They were successful, however, in keeping the ship afloat and moving again under electric power.

But Hell had soon unleashed a new fury upon them.

They were now on a collision course with the oncoming hurricane.

Secured with a metal belt, clothed in rain gear, goggles, and a life vest, Witte tried his best to navigate the sub while up on the bridge. As the weather became violent, he called down gyrocompass bearings and orders to the acting helmsman below who made the proper rudder adjustments to keep up with the shifting winds. The electric motor was barely a match for the monstrous waves that soon overtook them. Keeping her headed in the right direction, let alone making any significant speed, was difficult enough. Once the batteries ran out, they'd be powerless and adrift.

Witte watched in dread as mountains of waves rose from the sea. The white-capped ridges seemed to rise to enormous heights as if meshing with the slate-colored pulsating clouds above. He had never been caught in a storm of such sheer magnitude. The constant flashing and bolts of lightning streaking to the sea and the heavy booms of thunder like an artillery barrage were never-ending. He remembered thinking it was like the fists of the sea god Poseidon smashing the fists of the sky god Zeus while everything in between was crushed in their wrath.

The boat pitched high in the air as it rode one towering wave after another, only to be swamped by tons of water as it descended deep in the troughs, losing all visibility between the breakers. Cascades of water poured over the bridge and down the open hatches below, drenching the remaining men in the control room. The nightmare never let up. They were literally stuck inside a bottle being violently shaken in every direction.

Long washed away in a massive wave were the bodies of the American captain and first officer. The boat shook, shuddered, and vibrated, seemingly ready to fall apart. Every man had lost his meal. The swinging and listing were constant, but Captain Witte had managed to keep her from going sideways and literally rolling over.

Sometime during the storm, Witte spotted faint lights he hoped were navigational markers into Sapelo Sound. If so, their final destination was close: Harris Neck Outlying Landing Field (OLF), a highly-restricted, remote, auxiliary anti-submarine air patrol base that had been transferred over to the U.S. Navy from the Army Air Force several months back. Closed to all air traffic except on prior approval, it was where the Mariner bomber that attacked them had made an emergency landing when her fuel ran out.

Harris Neck was located beyond Sapelo and Blackbeard Islands, across the deep natural harbor of Sapelo Sound, and just up the South Newport River where they were supposed to have been escorted in after radio contact. The tiny base was completely surrounded by salt marshes in an unpopulated area miles away from prying eyes. Witte felt he'd gotten his sub on the right course to Sapelo Sound, but it was down to pure luck if it would actually make it into the harbor refuge. Three times he desperately shot off red flares, but the hurricane gobbled them up within seconds.

Pressed against the metal bridge shield by 120-mph winds and thick sheets of sideways rain, he was overcome with sea sickness almost to the point of passing out while vomiting until he had the dry heaves.

The milky, frothy foam of whitecaps lashed him like whips in a torture chamber until he could take no more. Struggling to close the bridge hatch against the howling winds, he slid six feet down the ladder into the conning tower and fell exhausted to his knees inside the tight tube. More wind and rain entered this chamber as it, too, was riddled with holes by the air attack.

Climbing down through the conning tower hatch and clamping it shut above him, he slid the rest of the way to the control room. Under a red glow of light, he could not believe the sight before him. No one was there. The boat was pilotless, abandoned.

Witte clutched the ladder to hold himself in place. His feet lifted off the floor weightlessly, then slammed back down in ankle-deep water. Water sprayed everywhere from burst pipes and valves. The combined sounds of the outside storm and the destruction within were unbelievable.

Items not tied down became free-floating, banging against anything in their path. Anyone inside who had not secured himself in time was certain to be mangled to death. Witte caught a clipboard in the mouth that chipped a tooth. Soon he tasted warm, salty blood.

Something heavy slammed into his legs, almost knocking him over.

It was the chief engineer. His battered body was being tossed about like a rag doll, broken limbs flailing, twisting unnaturally into strange angles. The engineer's head repeatedly clanged against the deck plates every time the sub rose and crashed down, his neck obviously broken. Eyes wide open, face blanched, bloodied, and battered, he hadn't been dead that long. Witte realized he would end up the same way if he didn't take refuge.

The stern bulkhead hatch to the engine room was sealed shut, but the forward door was still clamped open. Where the helmsman, the mechanic, and Bosch were, he hadn't a clue since there wasn't much room to maneuver because of the amount of cargo crammed within. He yelled for the remaining crewmen over the high-pitched whistling of the winds outside. No response.

The battle was over, he realized. He had lost. The remaining men were either dead or fending for themselves. If the sub went down, that was that. He'd done everything he possibly could. He knew he'd die in a matter of minutes if he didn't find a secure spot to brace himself. That's all he could do at that point – take cover and pray. The Gods would make the final decision.

He knew exactly where to shelter: the galley cabinet right around the corner just fore of the open door. Pulling himself through the forward bulkhead door, he hung onto a handle to support himself for another rollercoaster ride on yet another tremendous wave. Next to the two-burner countertop stove, the five-foot high wooden galley cabinet had already ejected its inventory. Both doors banged open and closed.

Splashing about on the water-covered deck plates below it were broken porcelain dishes, utensils, pots, and pans along with provisions of flour, beans, bread, and bottles of wine. While still clutching the bulkhead door handle, Witte kicked at the shelving inside the cabinet until it broke free. Now he had room to crawl inside as soon as the boat leveled out.

A hammock supporting suitcases over the crew cots suddenly broke free and spilled luggage across the deck. One of the suitcases flipped open and spewed piles of foreign currency. When the sub dipped into the next trough, high denominations of Reichsmarks, French francs, British pounds, and American dollars floated about like confetti in a parade. Unsurprised, he realized the Americans were smuggling loot back to the States. Witte had no time to even care.

It took several lunges, but once inside the galley cabinet he was able to brace himself and hold on to ride out the storm.

But the nightmare refused to let up.

The last thing he remembered was feeling the sub caught in a powerful current. The boat surged ahead and the hull banged against underwater objects until the bottom seemed to suddenly drop out.

Witte felt a massive impact. The collision flung the entire cabinet from its wall mounts – with him inside – and smashed it to bits against the far wall. He suffered a severe concussive head wound and his world went black.

Another rifle crack outside his wrecked U-boat jolted *Kapitänleutnant* Witte from his memories and brought him back to reality.

His resurrection was about to begin.

MICHAEL KARPOVAGE

1

Present day. Friday. Late October
Tununda's Military Menagerie
River Street. Savannah, Georgia

RETIRED ARMY LIEUTENANT COLONEL ROBERT 'Jake' Tununda stood behind an empty, sawdust-covered lobby display case, its top strewn with construction tools. He was a reading a surveillance system sales brochure on how best to monitor the old warehouse that would eventually house *Tununda's Military Menagerie,* his valuable military artifact collection.

A warm dusk breeze off the Savannah River swirled in from the front door left ajar from the last of the renovation crew who had kicked off for the weekend. Jake glanced up at the tourists passing by against the fading light, reminding him that he, too, needed to call it quits and lock up. Tossing the brochure aside, he skirted the counter and headed toward the entrance.

A black male teenager stepped inside.

"Sorry, but we're still under construction," Jake announced with a raised voice. "Probably open next month." The old battle scar on his left forearm tingled a warning that no state-of-the-art security system could ever pick up.

The five-foot-eight, well-built teen, dressed in denim shorts, a white t-shirt, and basketball sneakers, completely ignored Jake. Instead, he slammed the door behind him shut. Chest heaving, head down, a hand plunged deep into his front pocket, he now strolled toward Jake.

Already with a firm grip on his holstered firearm concealed under his loose work shirt, Jake backed up behind the counter and was at the ready should things turn to shit. He wasn't about to be the next victim in the rash of armed robberies, assaults, and homicides plaguing Savannah's famous historic district.

Just last week, the shop owner of *Books 'N Booze*, right next door to Jake's place, had a gun put to her head. Luckily, she survived when a bibliophile with a concealed pistol intervened and shot the robber dead.

But so far this year, 50 people hadn't survived. Everyone in the city knew who the culprits were since most fit the same profile: young black males. Drugs, gangs, joblessness, poor education, and non-existent parents all contributed to the destructive cycle that created these lawless wolves. These predators were not only killing fellow blacks in their own neighborhoods, but they also targeted the wealthy downtown historic district, murdering its residents, business owners, and tourists that swarmed the streets.

It sucked that he had to racially profile these young men, for the vast majority were just the opposite, but Jake knew what the reality was if you wanted to survive in virtually every big inner city across the United States. He knew firsthand how dangerous these deadly gangbanger wolves could be when his own life was almost snuffed out in Atlanta's Historic Oakland Cemetery over a year ago.

"Something I can do for you, son?" Jake asked, focusing on the kid's hand as he pulled it out of his pocket. No weapon, just a closed fist holding a yellowed, folded piece of paper. Jake relaxed his pistol grip.

The boy looked up and took a deep breath. He had pleasant brown eyes and youthful chin hair. He unfolded the paper and read from it. "Yaas'suh. Are you Mr. Ton-Ton-oonnda?" he asked, struggling to pronounce Jake's American Indian last name.

Not ten feet away, an attractive woman with auburn hair, leaning against the wall texting on her phone, let out a little snicker.

Jake's eyes wandered over to her for just an instant before falling back on the teen. He replied with a smirk. "Close enough. Yeah, that's me."

The kid opened his hand revealing a thick silver ring. He delicately placed it on the counter top.

Jake raised his eyebrows, knowing instantly it was a WWII-era German

SS *Totenkopf* or Death's Head ring. He leaned his five-foot-ten inch frame over the ring to get a closer view of the raised skull and crossbones in the center of the band.

The kid continued to read from his paper. "Can you please axe-axe-ssess the market value of this, um, this Toe-tin-cop ring, suh?" He said it in a strange, almost Creole-like accent mixed with a deep Southern drawl that Jake had trouble understanding. "I'd like to sell it because I read in the newspaper you're a military art-art-artifact collector looking to buy stuff. Supposed to be worth a whole lot of money." When he was finished, he looked up with nervous, pleading eyes.

Jake tried to summarize what he had heard just to be clear. "You'd like me to assess the market value of this SS *Totenkopf* ring?"

"Yaas'suh."

"You think it's worth a lot of money, and you're offering to sell it to me, is that correct?"

"Yaas'suh," replied the teen, still gathering his breath. Beads of sweat hung on his forehead. He stole a glance at the front door.

Jake couldn't help but follow his gaze. It was a typical heavy wooden warehouse door with a small window full of iron bars. No one was there. He kept an eye on the teen's hands, though. So far so good. He detected no threat from the youngster.

Jake picked up the ring and rolled it between his fingers. He'd only seen these in a select few collections over the years. These rare rings were, hands-down, the most-sought-after item of the Third Reich and most certainly were worth a lot of money, especially if you could match the ring bearer's name engraved on the inner band with that of the history of the SS officer who it once belonged to. This ring *looked* authentic and had the correct rune markings, but he wasn't taking any chances. He needed to compare it to other genuine assessment photos found on the internet. Plus, he had met a military expert from Charleston he could compare notes with, too.

On the flip side, he knew full well there were tons of fakes out there and it seemed strange that a teenager even possessed one of these rings in the first place. "How old are you, young man?"

"I'll be eighteen in two days, suh," the boy said, proudly.

"That's great. Now I need to know where you got this from," Jake held the ring up. "Who had ownership of it, how you obtained it? It's called provenance and it adds to the overall value of an artifact like this."

"I understand pro-ven-ance," said the teen. "You're talking about its history of possession. My great-grandpa gave it to me. All's he said was he got it way back in 1945 at the end of the big war. He was one of them Buffalo Soldiers. Told me it'd be worth good money, suh. You see, I'm trying to raise capital funds for investment, suh."

Jake cocked his head, impressed. In the corner of his eye, even the woman raised her eyes from her phone. The boy was obviously very well-educated. And certainly respectful, too, in using the term "sir," Jake thought appreciatively. Simple manners went a long way and now he was feeling like a dolt at profiling the kid in the first place.

Still, it was kind of difficult to decipher the way he pronounced his words. It definitely wasn't the trashy Ebonics, ghetto talk the local thugs used. The boy's language was more of a French, sing-songy tongue with a tinge of West African if he wasn't mistaken.

"Buffalo Soldier, huh? Happen to know which division that was and where your great-grandpa fought?" asked Jake, as a test, knowing full well the history of this segregated, all-black unit being the only one of its kind to see combat in Europe during the war.

"The 92nd, suh," replied the boy. "Fought in Italy along the Gothic Line, he told me."

Jake pursed his lips, pleased at the right answer. "Correct."

While he inspected the ring closer, he heard the boy blurt out, "Oh shit!" He looked up and followed the kid's line of sight to the front door. He was staring at the silhouetted figure peering in with cupped hands from outside the little window.

The boy flinched. As if on cue, the door flew open and a tall, muscular black man with a ponytail of dreadlocks entered. The scowl on his face meant he was pissed. He wore a stylish pork pie straw hat and was dressed rather nicely in casual, yet expensive-looking clothes. Jake couldn't help but notice an oversized gold and diamond Rolex watch on his wrist. And what he thought looked like a thin branch from a tree clutched in his hand.

In a gruff voice, the man barked out some indecipherable angry words in the same dialect as the kid's while making a beeline to the youngster. Before Jake knew it – and hardly even saw it – the man cracked the boy on the back of his bare legs with the switch.

The boy gritted his teeth, absorbed the pain, and stood his ground. "Two more days and I'm done with you," he defiantly spat to the man,

"What the fuck are you doing?" yelled Jake, dropping the ring on the counter, fury in his eyes.

"Stay the fuck out of my business, bro," the man replied, pointing the switch at him, the tip of it not a foot from Jake's aquiline nose. "Dis boy be *my* property. I'm his guardian and dis be *discipline*." He then wound up and whipped the kid again in the same spot. This time the boy howled in pain. The man grabbed the kid by the neck and shoved him toward the door.

Jake scampered from behind the display case and followed. "You okay, little man? That true what he said? He's your guardian?"

"Leave it alone, bro," warned the guardian.

The kid turned and nodded, embarrassed, eyes wide and teared-up. "Yes, he is. He's my uncle. I gotta go. Sorry to bother you, suh."

"Get back on the boat, little *beeatch*," the uncle growled. He smacked the kid in the back of his head, then pushed him toward the door again. He turned to say something to Jake, but found a finger in his face.

"Touch him again and I'll shove that stick so far up your ass you'll be tasting bark."

"Try it muthafucka," snarled the brute "and I'll shove six up yo' ass." He lifted his shirt to show Jake a silver revolver tucked into a waistband holster.

An authoritative woman's voice erupted from behind Jake. "And I'll shove seven up yours, *muthafucka!*" It was the woman who had been texting – Jake's new bride, Rae – a force to be reckoned with when a threat loomed, especially against her new husband.

She had pulled her Glock 42 .380 pistol out of her concealed carry purse and now clutched it in the firing position. Dressed in jeans, knee-high boots, and a button down blouse, she advanced on the target.

A restroom door near the front entrance then kicked opened behind the stunned man. "And I'll add eight more, *bitch!*" another woman yelled.

Dreadlocks, already shocked at the sight of the white woman with the pistol bearing down on him, turned around to face the new threat. She was a heavyset black woman in a white dress. He couldn't believe his eyes. She was aiming a compact pistol at his chest at point blank range.

That was Becky Holden, Rae's closest friend in Savannah. They were headed out for happy hour drinks, but she had become rather preoccupied in the bathroom due to a stomach illness.

"Now get the fuck outta here!" ordered Jake, his 1911 pistol at the ready, about to put two .45 ACP rounds in the face of his target.

Dreadlocks immediately dropped his switch and raised his hands. "Y'all just chill now, ya hear? Crazy-ass, mo-fos. We're leaving. We're leaving." He slowly backed away toward the open door, hands still up. But then he paused as he was just about to exit. He stared at Jake, nostrils flaring.

"Go ahead, trip my fuck-it switch," Jake challenged.

But the kid grabbed his guardian's shirt and pulled him outside.

Jake jumped at the door, slammed it shut, and bolted it. He, Rae, and Becky watched through the window as the man and boy ran across the famous cobblestone River Street. They reholstered their weapons, the threat now gone.

"What in the hell was *that* all about?" Becky asked in her deep Southern drawl as her eyes followed the fleeing pair cross the tourist-filled plaza.

"The kid wanted me to assess a ring," said Jake, eyes focused on the duo while they jogged beside the old electric power plant, now turned into a luxury hotel. In an instant, they made it to the river's edge at the newly-built docks, ran down a gangway, and jumped onto a black-painted, hardtop antique speedboat.

"And then his guardian uncle comes in and whips the boy like he's his damn runaway slave or something," Rae added. "Said the kid was his *property* and he was disciplining him. The kid didn't do a damn thing wrong. I saw the whole thing."

"I heard that poor boy pitchin' a fit out here," said Becky.

"I know," said Jake. "The piece of shit then flashes his piece at me when I warn him to stop beating the boy."

They all watched as the kid was whacked hard in the back of the head as he struggled to release the boat's mooring lines. Jake shook his head and sighed. Dreadlocks planted his ass in the rear seat of the boat as if he were some VIP, while the boy manned the helm and fired up the boat. It pulled out into the main channel then headed down river. Quite noticeable was a black flag on the stern. When it unfurled in the draft, it displayed a pirate's skull and crossbones.

"Christ, I need a drink," mumbled Jake, turning from the window. He grabbed the discarded switch, snapped it in half, and shoved it in a trash bin. Back behind the display counter, he reached underneath for a hidden flask.

"Thanks for covering me, ladies," he said. "I swear to God, I had less attempts on my life when I was deployed overseas in war zones. Maybe this River Street location was a mistake? Probably should have picked a quiet spot down near Tommy's place." He unscrewed the flask and took a shot of High West whiskey, his latest favorite spirit. He offered the flask to the ladies. Rae shook her head, but Becky's eye's lit up.

"Gimme some of that," Becky said, nodding. "I ain't never done that before, taking my gun off safety, and aiming it at someone. Bout shit my drawers." She took a long swig. "Again."

Jake and Rae burst out laughing, the nervous tension from the near-shooting dissipating like a balloon losing air.

"Jake," said a still smiling Rae, hands on hips. "This is Savannah's main strip. We've got the river literally out our front door. We landed a gold mine location here the day we bought this little warehouse and started renovating. And we paid a pretty penny for it, too. High public visibility is what your collection requires to be successful. We're going to meet veterans, history lovers, and fans from all over the world. Plus, with my office right upstairs, it's a great location for what I'm doing, too."

"Don't let them bad apples turn you off," agreed Becky. "*Tununda's Military Menagerie* would be lost down near ol' Tommy's place. Besides, y'all are popular here in Savannah. Kinda like celebrity status. And with all them fans from your old TV show, y'all got a really unique brand name in Tununda. You'll make a killin' at this location."

"Yeah, I know," conceded Jake.

'Ol' Tommy's place,' that Becky referred to, was the late Tommy Watie's Cherokee Rose Manor near Forsyth Park, a primarily residential area on the southern edge of Savannah's historic district. The home and all of Watie's possessions had been willed to Jake and Rae upon his passing over a year ago for them helping Tommy fulfill his lifelong dream. Unselfishly, the couple then immediately sold the manor to Becky for $1.00 since she was Tommy's caregiver in his last years. To honor Tommy's legacy, Jake kept the old man's Civil War collection that once filled a room in that house, and was planning on featuring it as one of his main exhibits in his new museum. Since then, he and Rae had made some serious life decisions back up North in their home states of New York and Pennsylvania.

Jake requested and was released from the Army with an honorable discharge, full pension, and benefits. He still kept close ties, though, to the staff at the Army's Military History Institute where he had worked as a field historian. But given the amount of publicity – good and bad – he had generated in his various exploits, the army he had served in for well over twenty years of his life couldn't wait to part ways.

Top Pentagon brass never liked Jake's notoriety with his and Rae's now defunct *Battlefield Investigators* show on the American Heroes Channel, nor their hero celebrity status for acting in self-defense and gunning down an assassin in broad daylight in Savannah. Jake had, in turn, tired of the brass's politically correct bullshit under the hold-outs of the previous liberal administration anyway, so his retirement had been a divorce of mutual agreement.

But it was his link to the death of a Congressman from Atlanta who was connected to the widely-publicized theft of the West Point Museum items last year that became the final nail in the coffin of his military career. One of those stolen items – a Civil War general's hat – Jake had even recovered to return to the museum. The other two items were still missing, though: the famous Lilliput golden pistol of Adolf Hitler and an ivory baton of Hitler's second in command, *Reichsmarschall* Hermann Göering.

The very first thing he did after leaving the Army was propose marriage to Rae. They tied the knot at a romantic, all-inclusive, adults-only resort in Costa Rica. Their close friends, Alex Vann and Marissa Morgan, were also married that same day, each couple acting as each other's witnesses. No family, no drama, no drunken bachelor or bachelorette parties with strippers, no big gaudy weddings. After what the four went through last year, and their near-death experiences, they all knew what they wanted and cherished. They wasted no time in locking up their partners for the rest of their lives.

With an incredible amount of wealth bequeathed to them from Watie, plus vast treasures safely hidden away both in Georgia and New York, and recently becoming silent partners in the Vann's new mining company, Jake and Rae decided to pursue their dreams in better climates. They kept Rae's small cottage in the Finger Lakes region of New York so they could have access to their underground secret bunker in the Seneca Army Depot, and also as a summer retreat from the humidity of the South. Since they both fell in love with Savannah, her eccentric and friendly people, her history, and the fact that they were sick and tired of the long cold winters up North, they decided to make their permanent residence in the Savannah coastal area.

Jake's dream of having a military artifact collection and research office came to fruition when his Savannah lawyer contacted him wanting to sell an old abandoned two-story warehouse dating back to the early 1900s. He'd always wanted a large exhibit room for his relics after seeing *Highlander*, one of his favorite boyhood movies, when the lead character Connor MacLeod strolled into his own antique military trophy room. And this warehouse fit the bill.

When the Tunundas discovered its prime location on the far west end of River Street in the new Plant Riverside District under the shadow of the Talmadge Memorial Bridge, they snatched it up before it even went on the market. Not only was it a keen real estate investment, but Rae also saw her dreams fulfilled with a new upstairs office for her private detective business. She quickly earned her private investigator license in Georgia and had already solved cases for several prominent Savannah clients: two involved cheating spouses, the other an embezzlement case. But her hottest job now involved contracting with the U.S. Army's Criminal Investigation Division (CID) out of Hunter Army Airfield, not a half hour away south of Savannah.

While Becky, a registered nurse, both lived and worked at Cherokee Rose Manor – her new assisted living business – Jake and Rae chose to make their residence out on quiet Skidaway Island, one of the coastal barrier islands not twenty minutes southeast of Savannah.

Skidaway was home to the exclusive golf resort community called The Landings. It was the largest gated community in America, comprising some 7,000 residents living in homes ranging from modest on up to massive mansions. They even had their own security department. The Tunundas purchased a 5-bedroom, Spanish style, 7,000 sq. ft. villa on five acres of land fronting the Moon River side of the island. It was their dream home come true. They even had a private dock where Jake captained a brand new 32' offshore power catamaran. Sometimes their work commute consisted of boating up through the river system and docking right in front of their new building.

Jake and Rae lived the good life in Savannah: everything they owned was top quality, money was no issue, and their dreams had just begun.

Life was completely grand – until that teen walked in.

Jake grabbed the flask from Becky and threw his head back for another shot of the fine straight rye whiskey. Looking back down, he rolled his eyes. "Dammit! The kid forgot to take his ring. I don't even know his name or where to return it."

"You gonna do as he asked? Find out how much it's worth?" asked Becky.

"Yeah, I need to. Immediately," said Jake. "I owe the boy that much for making the effort to come here and getting his ass whooped for it. I'll get online tonight and consult with Erhardt Hoffmann. He's a military historian Rae and I just met in Charleston. One of the foremost experts in Third Reich militaria. Plus, he's a fellow Freemason. If the ring proves to be a fake, then I'll confiscate it, but if it's the real deal, then I need to return it to him somehow."

"Hmm, what's this?" whispered Rae as she bent down to pick up a folded piece of paper by the display case. She unfolded it and noticed it was rather aged with yellow and green stains. It was no bigger than a typical 3 x 5" index card. But it had some newer scribbling in pen on one side. She read Jake's surname – her new last name – and a sentence asking for an assessment on the market value of a ring.

She flipped the page over and a startling graphic of an elaborately designed skull stared back at her. The strangely mysterious black and white design had an immediate powerful impact. The symbol on the forehead especially caught Rae's attention. Her eyebrows furrowed. "Hon? You may want to take a look at this." She handed Jake the paper.

Jake first read the kid's practice speech on the back, then flipped it over.

The swirling hypnotic design within the raccoon-like eyes sucked him right in. He then shifted focus to the large symbol centered on the forehead. At first he saw two Xs, then he squinted and saw something else: the Freemasons square and compasses, the symbol of the oldest fraternity in the world.

Of which he was a member.

"Lemme see that," said Becky, snatching the old paper from his hand. Her eyes widened, her lips smacked, and in a low voice she muttered, "Oh

Lord, I haven't seen this skull in a long, long time." She went for the whiskey flask sitting on the counter.

"Huh?" said Rae as she watched Becky tip the flask to take a pull.

As the alcohol slid down the back of her throat, she closed her eyes and shuddered. "Y'all don't want no part of this. Uh uh. No, siree," she warned, holding up the paper.

"Do tell," demanded Jake.

Becky glanced at Rae with wide eyes and received a nod of approval. "Alright, but I'm warning y'all." She took a deep breath.

"This here is a *skull of disguises*," she said, touching the image on the paper. "It has many hidden meanings, they say. On the surface, it was used as a label for some legendary moonshine called *Doctor Blackbeard's Elixir of Life*. The skull's black beard gives it away."

"Moonshine?" interrupted Jake, head tilted. "*Elixir of Life?* And they use a skull as its logo, the symbol of death?"

"Uh-huh. That's right," said Becky. "Part of the disguise. My grandma said it was the best-tasting, purest, white lightning corn whiskey she's ever had in her life! And trust me, she's emptied many a jar of the stuff over the years, let me tell you."

She winked and smiled. "I remember one of her sayings: *Make your eyes twirl 'round like they was on fire, like they was full of life*. My family is Gullah-Geechee from Shellman's Bluff in McIntosh County and that 'shine is legendary down there. The whiskey you got, sugar," she gestured toward his flask, "is really good, but Doctor Blackbeard's stuff is tons better. They say it had some secret ingredients in it that made it so powerful. And why it was in such high demand. But expensive as hell and almost impossible to get. Yup. Best quality liquor around these Lowlands for many, many years. Some tried to imitate it, but if you didn't see that skull of disguises, then you know the stuff you was getting was shit. Or worse – poison."

Rae snickered. "Sounds like this was probably a family tradition, huh? That you might have had a drop or two of this moonshine yourself?"

Becky's smile was all teeth. "Girl, I've been known to partake in a shot or two. Or three. Or four. And then I'd hit the floor!"

Laughs all around again.

In his best English pirate accent, Jake tried to add to the humor, "Arrrrr, matey, where exactly was this *Doctor Blackbeard's Elixir of Life* made? On a pirate ship?"

Becky didn't bite. She instead gave Jake the eye.

Rae cracked Jake on the arm. "She's being serious, let her finish."

Jake felt like a dope at the failed joke. His eyes rolled, embarrassed.

"Nobody ever put a label on moonshine because it was bootlegged and illegal. Word-of-mouth and a handshake was trust enough. But after some forty poor blacks died in Atlanta in one week back in 1951 from drinking poison, disguised as moonshine, then some of the makers started adding a stamp or a secret mark or a label to their glass jars and kegs. This guaranteed the customer was getting the best quality 'shine, and not that shit poison that left people dead, dumb, blind, and paralyzed so they could make a fast buck off poor blacks."

"Another disguise," she continued, "is in all the skull's symbols pointing to where the 'shine was made. It's like a code. Supposed to be some secret, well-protected location near Blackbeard Island. Sand dollars, starfish, and a nautical star. Also notice the alligator teeth instead of human teeth? Notice the snakes around the border? Signs to keep away."

Jake and Rae looked at the label again. Becky was right.

"Doctor Blackbeard was an ol' Saltwater Geechee, but he's not the kind of doctor you're thinking of, I bet?" Becky locked eyes with Jake.

"This doctor could put a hex on you. He was a root doctor, doing all that ancient magic Hoodoo stuff brought over with the slaves from West Africa. Supposedly, that was part of his secret ingredients. That's what I'm warning you about. That shit is real, y'all. You don't mess with Hoodoo."

Jake's face grew serious. He knew exactly how real and deadly the paranormal world was – that spiritual realm that exists beyond our physical, material forms. It's a realm he wholeheartedly believed in.

And feared.

"If I remember some of the history correctly," said Becky, "my grandma said this 'shine dates all the way back to the Reconstruction period after the Civil War. The recipe and the process was a closely guarded secret and handed down through many generations of Doctor Blackbeards. Like a family inheritance. But then through the Prohibition years . . ."

"1920 to 1933," Jake chimed in.

Becky nodded. "Yup, when it was being bootlegged along the coast is when the demand for whiskey skyrocketed. It was a favorite of both the poor, Gullah-Geechee black folk, and the rich white folk in all their posh private resort clubs in Savannah and the Sea Islands. That's where America's wealthy elite came down to play. Grandma said that the politicians and celebrities, and even some Presidents who visited down here, all loved Doctor Blackbeard's brew."

Becky directed her eyes back to Jake. "And then during World War II the military boys really started getting a knack for it. Grandma told me stories that it was even being shipped overseas to Europe! Crazy. Some connection about that ol' military base out in the middle of nowhere down the coast. Umm, what's it's name?" She tapped her foot and it came to her. "Harris Neck. Yeah, that's it. It's just across the sound from Blackbeard Island. Well, lots of corruption happened down there. Anyway, not even the law caught up to the Doctor. Ever. He had special connections it was said. People protecting him."

"Perhaps it was Freemasons?" asked Jake. "That symbol on the forehead is very Masonic in nature."

Becky shrugged. "Looks like two Xs to me, Jake. Might simply advertise how good quality the 'shine was. Two Xs usually means double-distilled whiskey."

"You know your whiskey," Jake smirked.

"It is a *hobby* of mine." Becky replied with a wink while wetting her lips. "Like I said, there's lots of disguises and everyone sees things differently. You might see something on the surface, but once you go down deeper then you get the real meaning."

She sighed before talking again. "His 'shine just stopped flowing one day. Just up and disappeared altogether. That was back in the late 1980s, I reckon. Some say Doctor Blackbeard died and he had no one to pass his secrets on to. Some say Doctor Blackbeard never dies, that he's like a zombie wandering the island looking for his lost moonshine still. Who knows for sure? Y'all just take this here skull as a warning is all I'm sayin', okay?"

"Where's this Blackbeard Island anyway?" asked Jake. "Is it near here?"

Becky waggled her head. "Kind of. It's down next to Sapelo Island, where there's a marine college and where that rich, tobacco magnate Richard Reynolds Jr. once had his big ol' mansion and estate."

Jake and Rae both shook their heads, unaware of the place.

"I'd say it's about an hour boat ride south from your home on Skidaway." Becky instantly knew she said too much and glanced at Rae apologetically.

"Hmmmm," murmured Jake, with a raised, mischievous eyebrow. "That's it? Might have to do some exploring Sunday when the Vanns arrive. Alex and Marissa will love the trip."

"No, Marissa and I already have our day booked at the spa. Why, Jake?" asked Rae with an edgy tone. "What for? Why do you need to go *exploring?*"

"To return the kid's ring to him, if it's real. I just can't keep it."

"What's the rush?" asked Rae, getting a little snappy. "Just let him come back for it. He'll know he left it here soon enough. Just wait for a phone call. It's none of your business trying to find him. Didn't you hear what Becky just said. This skull is a warning." She pointed to the label.

"Listen, Rae . . . ," said Jake.

"No," interrupted Rae, "don't *listen* me. I'm not an idiot. I know you. You've got that fever again. You've been bored and frustrated lately with all these renovations. Your curiosity is piqued. You take these risks all the time and it almost gets us *killed*. Like that damn tornado we were in last year!"

"And it led us to a tunnel of freakin' gold!" countered Jake. "Besides, Alex and I already had plans to go out fishing tomorrow down near St. Catherines anyway. Talk some business, too. We'll just do a little recon to those islands and see if we can spot that speedboat is all. Just pinpoint a location. Nothing more. Don't worry about us."

"Don't worry about us. Pfft!" said Rae. "Last words."

Becky made a noise with her throat to break the tension. "Jake, those islands are totally remote. Sapelo is off-limits to the public without special permission from the college or from one of the island residents. Last I heard there's only about 35 people that even still live there and it's like the size of Manhattan! And Blackbeard is nothing but a big wildlife refuge with some trails. If you don't know those waters around it, the tides, the currents, the shoals, then you're in for trouble."

"I'll do my homework before I go. I won't go off half-cocked."

Rae angrily sighed and stormed off toward the rear entrance, hands flailing, knowing full well Jake was going to do what Jake was going to do. "Come on Becky. I'm the one who needs a drink now!"

2

NATHAN KULL, AKA PHOENIX, HAD STRUCK AGAIN. This latest theft was on a luxury cruise ship in Alaska and one of his easiest scores yet over an exceptionally prolific career as a master thief. And one of his most lucrative. Since the age of seven when he stole his first bag of Gummy Bears because his mother refused to buy them, he had spent his entire lifetime refining his craft of *wealth redistribution*, as he liked to call it.

Redistributed into *his* deep pockets, of course.

The 38-year-old multi-millionaire was playing at the top of his game, bursting with narcissistic self-confidence. Although very successful running his own legitimate security consultant business under his real name, he favored his alter ego as a thief much more. It was the challenge of the next score that had him hooked. So much so that he had long since rationalized his habit of stealing from others as completely acceptable behavior – and without the slightest bit of remorse.

He knew he had a high-level addiction as a kleptomaniac and embraced every facet of it: how no two jobs were the same; the intense patience and logistical planning involved; the vetting and manipulation of people; the thrill of the break-in, the action, the adrenaline-rush at the moment he pocketed his stolen goods; the mental challenge to elude capture, outwit security, and law enforcement; and most importantly, how it all fed his enormous ego. His many talents and skills got him to where he was today, but he also knew he was becoming a bit complacent with every successful new job, that he needed more and more self-discipline to counteract his abject cockiness.

A master of disguises, an exceptional actor, and a convincing con man – not to mention his Brad Pitt-like blue-eyed, shoulder length blond-haired GQ model looks – Kull sometimes thought of himself as a Batman-like character, but for all the wrong reasons. Sure he was selfish and shrewd, but he also knew how to own a room with charm and poise as if playing one of Pitt's lead roles in a movie. It was that self-gratification of defeating every obstacle thrown at him which kept him going back for score after score.

Operating out of his luxury New York City condo as a much sought-after thief-for-hire, the whole world was his playground for crime, adventure, and the good life. But he kept his criminal life completely separate. No physical evidence of any kind linking him to his illegal activities was left in his home. Instead, he kept his tools of the trade and stolen goods in a handful of storage lockers, three in the U.S. and two overseas.

He was the epitome of a criminal who got away with it all. Never once arrested, never working with a team, and never opening his mouth to brag to strangers, Nathan Kull would have been one of the top ten most successful thieves in history if anyone could ever Google his name.

Except he used a slew of fake identities, some stolen, some backed by official paper records even in other countries. No one knew this thief by his real name. Not his nefarious clients, nor their brokers who hired him for jobs. Not even the FBI. All they had in their Next Generation Identification (NGI) database were fingerprints he unwittingly had left behind at several high profile, unsolved burglaries. If they ever connected an actual name to those prints, it would be his almighty undoing.

Early in his career, he had been dubbed "Phoenix" by investigators because of his ability to seemingly disappear and rise again with a different criminal modus operandi. Whether it was stealing irreplaceable heirloom jewels or rare works of art, he baffled detectives on the details about how he pulled off his scores. After reading of the nickname in a newspaper, he vainly adopted it as his for-hire brand name on the black market of the Dark

Web. It made him legendary and in high demand.

In fact, Phoenix was the man responsible for the widely publicized theft of a Civil War general's hat and two Nazi trophies at the West Point Museum over a year ago. He conceived, reconned, and flawlessly executed that notorious heist in just two days time. But it was the delivery in Atlanta where things went off the rails and he almost got caught.

The general's hat had ultimately been recovered by a U.S. Army military historian named Jake Tununda, who had stolen it back from the client who commissioned the job: late Georgia congressman Tom Black.

Phoenix's cunning, though, allowed him to escape Atlanta with the remaining two Nazi items after framing another man to take his fall. An FBI task force took the bait. After a SWAT house raid, they insisted they had terminated Phoenix for good.

In reality, that dead man was an illegal alien Sureños-13 gang enforcer whose crew took his stolen Nazi items after Phoenix was carjacked in Atlanta. To regain his loot, he had to cross the line of being a non-violent criminal all of his career. He had to meet violence with violence. And he did it with flair.

First, he kidnapped, then brutally interrogated, and ultimately stabbed to death a 14-year-old gang member as part of his scheme. Then he firebombed one of the gang's drug labs in a residential neighborhood killing a man inside after the house blew sky high. Once he regained his Nazi relics, he subsequently buried the two artifacts in a south Georgia cemetery.

Since the West Point job, both FBI and Army investigators had frozen their cases, deeming the culprit neutralized, and the recovery of the two remaining World War II-era items not high enough on their priority list to pursue further leads.

In the end, Phoenix had gotten away with it. As he always did.

Having just pulled off another great theft, he leaned back in his seat at the American Airlines departing gate, ran his hands through his long hair, and crossed his arms behind his head. Closing his eyes, he recapped the last 24 hours. A wry grin stretched across his face.

The firm he was hired to target was the Compass Fine Art Gallery, a mainland-U.S. based gallery which catered to the wealthy onboard a luxury cruise ship of 3,000 people. Little did anyone know, their operation was one of the most notorious scams afloat.

Compass's onboard art gallery shared a percentage of their sales income with the cruise ship in a special concession contract. Both entities targeted ignorant retired couples with excessive amounts of disposable income. It was very well known in the industry that fleecing guests while they were onboard the ship brought in more sales revenue than the mere cruise ticket fee itself. It's why 24-hour casinos, all-day games of bingo, and onboard shopping malls chock full of glamorous wares were now the norm for every cruise ship.

With round-the-clock, all-you-can-eat buffets, high-end specialty restaurants, endless entertainment, and bottomless alcoholic drinks abounding, guests easily parted with enormous sums of cash as they were taken in by the luxurious atmosphere. Repeat VIP guests were even mailed special invitations, their cruise ticket prices comped, just to get them back onboard. They received a tour of the bridge from the captain himself and preferred dining at his head table in the ballroom. They were also hounded the whole trip to attend the art auctions because the cruise company and the gallery both knew those pampered guests would be spending tens of thousands of dollars on the artwork. One elite VIP even racked up sales of over $500,000 in art purchases alone during her 10-day cruise.

Compass held an art auction every day, advertising one-of-a-kind originals they claimed were purchased from galleries and estate liquidations all over the world. Their main show room was strategically located adjacent to the high traffic, grand spiral staircase in the middle of the cruise ship. Beautiful, colorful paintings of all sizes and styles, framed in gold, silver, and black, lined the red-draped walls of the auction area, while even more stunning artwork sat on easels throughout the room.

Rows of more artwork were stacked upright, frame-to-frame, in the gallery's storage room one deck below. When it was locked, a keypad code allowed entry to the windowless room. There were no surveillance cameras inside or outside the door at all.

Before the auction began, the charming auctioneer, a scholarly looking middle-aged man with a lovely British accent – and one of the three owners of the gallery company – would work his magic. Along with his four-person staff of college-age, attractive males and females dressed in expensive suits, they made their attendees feel like royalty. The staff and auctioneer doted on would-be art collectors with special attention in creating an unforgettable experience.

They poured free champagne, chit-chatted, stroked egos, and gave away free raffled gifts of watches and necklaces to keep their guests occupied. Typically, the younger staff members were just revolving-door seasonal help, there as eye-candy to schmooze, to pre-sell the artwork, and to lug the framed pieces up and down the stairs. They had no idea of how the company's scam really worked.

The pre-auction highlight and the "wow" moment of the company's operation was showing off their half dozen, *real,* one-of-a-kind, original paintings that were truly purchased direct from big name contemporary artists, other galleries, and art auctions all at top market value. These were the real-deal, premiere offerings of the auction and the most valued investments of the company.

However, besides the real paintings, there were a good seventy five pieces of other artwork on display that were nothing but elaborate prints or forgeries the owners purchased on the black market. The auctioneer and his cohort partners had, in some cases, even forged artist's signatures themselves. Plus, they added thick brush strokes of paint that gave the paintings a three dimensional effect. By adding these nuances to the artwork they could claim, if a guest asked, that the art was truly a one-of-a-kind original since an embellishment was indeed made.

Buzzed on champagne, the guests gawked at the mix of originals and so-called originals with dreams of grandeur in possessing them. Since no photography was allowed, no video, no jeweler's loupes, and no touching of the artwork, detection of the forgeries was guaranteed to be missed. All guests could do was place their trust in the gallery company's convincing promises. And that's exactly the kind of gullible customer Compass preferred.

Once everyone was seated, the auctioneer would take his place behind the podium. At the sound of the gavel, the Compass Fine Art Gallery scam commenced.

To provide provenance and authenticity to their artworks, the three principals of the company had pre-forged Certificates of Authenticity. They even falsified appraisals with fake company names based on real experts' reputations. Sometimes the other two owners even sat in the audience to place fake bids to falsely increase prices and hype the excitement.

As the auctioneer began opening bids, he seduced the attendees with his keen knowledge of art styles and techniques. Lesser art pieces started at a mere $500 and went well up into the high tens of thousands as artwork flew off the auction block at remarkable speed. Fast-talking and gaveling behind his podium, he plied the high pressure and sold one piece after another at exorbitant prices. What his customers didn't know was that he was nothing more than an extremely talented salesman who obtained his knowledge of art history from several junior college courses. His real skill was in preying on ignorant people who wanted entry into the special world of owning art so they could vainly show it off to their friends back home. Some were even suckered into thinking they were making a financial investment that would reap them a huge profit in the years to come.

As soon as the auction ceased, the final con was put in motion. After paperwork was finalized, credit card payments authorized, and delivery within four weeks assured, all purchased artwork was taken a deck below and put back in storage for so-called security purposes. The customer never saw it again for the duration of their cruise. Instead, they turned into giddy braggarts, unable to contain themselves until receiving their artwork back home once their dream vacation had ended.

Some 4-6 months later, when, and if, their artwork arrived, it was usually damaged, the cheap replacement frame broken or chipped, the protective glass usually cracked. Customer service, through phone calls or emails, was virtually non-existent, and refunds or repairs were all but impossible.

The icing on the con cake was that the artwork they purchased wasn't even the genuine originals the gallery advertised and displayed. Instead, they were mostly Giclée (zee-klay) reproductive digital prints made on canvas with a very expensive 12-color inkjet printer back at the gallery's mainland office. They were mere high resolution copies of the real original works of art the gallery owned, and also of its many forgeries. They could be sold again and again, endlessly generating profit with every new cruise.

The Giclées were of such amazing technological quality that without a microscope to detect the inkjet spray pattern of almost imperceptible droplets, a layperson couldn't tell the difference between a real painting and a forgery. There was no other reproduction method or printing process resulting in such fine color accuracy in the world. Even some of the best art experts and auction houses had been fooled.

The customer was none-the-wiser, too, when they received their art. And the gallery and the cruise line that much richer in the end. For in reality, each Giclée print was worth a mere $75 to produce. It was a classic, bait-and-switch con.

If somehow the customer did detect that the artwork they had purchased was just a copy, as many had, they had very little legal standing for retaliation because the gallery covered their asses in the fine print on the invoice. When the customer purchased the artwork onboard the ship – signing the paperwork associated with the sale, and of course never ever reading it – they doomed themselves legally. The barely readable small print said: *"I further state that no verbal representations have been made or relied upon by me in connection with my purchase."* That statement alone absolved the gallery of any fraudulent sales misconduct made during the pre-selling process before the auction began, and while the auction took place.

In the five years the gallery had operated, the three owners had taken in over $12 million dollars in illicit sales based on their scam.

As it happened, several months ago, one of the seasonal female staffers, an attractive, savvy, fine arts student from the Rhode Island School of Design, got wind of the scheme. She had worked the summer cruise ship auctions and thought the claims of originality the auctioneer made to guests during pre-sales quite peculiar. She was hired based on looks alone and not for her technical art knowledge. Her education is what did the company in. She had a wealthy aunt in the art business back in New York City, in whom she confided her doubts.

That aunt's name was Maya Levana, aka Mona Lisa – Phoenix's top fence for his art and jewelry thefts.

And the only woman whom he got close to in a serious relationship.

Phoenix had dated many other women for a fling here and there, but Mona was more than just a friend with benefits. Her independence and cunning attracted him as much as her sexual prowess. He found himself coming back to her time and again, even confiding in her during pillow talk the details of some of his biggest scores and how he pulled them off, including the West Point Museum theft. The very attractive cougar, in her mid 50s, was so much on his mind that he even thought about revealing his true name to her, a risk that excited and petrified him at the same time.

With the intelligence gained from her niece, Maya, an art and antiques expert herself, had then sailed on her own cruise specifically to attend one of Compass's auctions as a test. Her reputation and credibility preceded her once the gallery owners knew she was onboard and looking at artwork to purchase for her own gallery. Knowing in advance what painting she would bid for, she made deliberate gestures in hyping her desire for it. It was the gallery's most valuable investment: a 14 x 22" painting that was a one-of-a-kind original by the French Cubist artist Fernand Léger. It had a starting price of $250,000. Online research conducted before the auction showed Maya that the value of the painting was legit.

Her niece was still one of the auction staffers on the cruise, but never let on about their relationship. Acting in her role of a mere assistant, but secretly Maya's lookout, she gave up the keypad code and allowed her aunt private unfettered access to the storage room where she knew the Léger painting was stored. The gallery's other most valuable legitimate paintings were also in the same room. While the auctioneer and the rest of the staff were several decks away having lunch, Maya went about her business.

Armed with knowledge of unique distinguishing features of the Léger painting itself based on provenance, and closely examining the front surface as well as the reverse of the canvas with her high powered jeweler's loupe, Maya determined it was the original and not a forgery or a Giclée print. All was in order. She then made a secret scratch mark in a corner of the painting with her fingernail, and took a cell phone snapshot of that same mark.

At the actual auction a day later, Maya was one of a handful of people to bid on the costly painting. Another man that her niece had pointed out as one of the silent partners of the gallery also bid the price up on purpose. He backed down and Maya ultimately purchased it for $350,000. With $50,000 down on her own credit card and the rest financed in a two-year payment plan, she signed the proper papers and ecstatically pranced away. The rest of the cruise she was treated with celebrity status once word had gotten out of her purchase.

Upon receiving the painting in the mail – some six weeks later after repeated phone calls – she inspected it again, this time under a microscope. She found the distinct Giclée droplet pattern instead of real texture and brush strokes. Her secret nail scratch was missing from where it should have been. On the reverse side of the canvas, along the edges where the painting brush strokes had bled over in the original, she instead found a clean straight edge further indicative of the print process.

As expected, the gallery had sent her a fake.

Revenge and repayment was now her mission. The niece, having already gone back to college, told her aunt the company never changed the keypad code to the storage room in all the time she had been employed. That's all Maya needed. That laziness proved to be the company's Achilles' heel.

Maya's next act – now as Mona Lisa – was to call upon Phoenix to steal her the original Léger she was entitled to. She passed the keypad code onto him, but now it was his mission to work out the details of the actual theft.

When Phoenix arrived on his cruise not two months later, lo and behold, the gallery had the audacity to display the same original Léger painting up for auction again. They figured in a fresh set of cruise guests another one would play the sucker role. Sure enough, a wealthy older businessman from Japan purchased the same Léger painting that Mona did – for much less even – and the gallery placed it back in storage until the cruise ended.

After observing the auctioneer and his staffers' work and off-work habits over several days of the cruise, he made secret entry in the storage room late at night to inspect the Cubist painting. Under a flashlight, he found Mona's scratch mark in the exact same place as her cell photo indicated. The painting was the authentic one.

He then found and secretly marked each of the other five original paintings owned by the gallery that the niece and Mona also had identified.

The actual theft one night later was laughable by Phoenix's standards.

On the last morning of the cruise, while everyone onboard was still sleeping, Phoenix slipped back into the storage room with his duffel-style luggage bag, found the Léger, and removed it from its frame. He did the same with the other five originals, then rolled them up and stuffed them in the bottom of his bag.

Pulling out three bottles of 100-proof vodka he had purchased at the ship's duty-free store, Phoenix poured the contents of each bottle over the remaining rows of framed forgeries and Giclées stacked upright on the floor. He made sure the surface of each painting was thoroughly doused. The empty bottles went back into his duffel bag.

Quietly exiting the room and checking to see if anyone was about, Phoenix lit a piece of paper soaked in the alcohol. He tossed it back into the room and it instantly ignited in a wall of blue flames. By using alcohol, the room didn't explode at once like other flammable liquids, but merely spread quickly enough to give him time to shut the door and scamper off.

Message from Mona Lisa sent. She was not one to be played with. Ever.

While the contents of the room burned behind the locked door, Phoenix was already outside on the deck in the darkness dropping the three empty vodka bottles to the sea below.

He then nonchalantly made his way back to his room to await the inevitable fire alarm. Ten minutes went by before the ship's alarm sounded and the captain made an announcement that a fire had broken out in the art gallery, but that it was already contained by the crew with fire extinguishers. As a precautionary measure, all guests were asked to remain in their rooms until further notice when the ship docked at their final port in Anchorage.

A couple of hours later, as Phoenix was lined up with the other guests to depart the ship, duffel bag slung over his shoulder, the crew had moved the crowd back to allow the onboard doctor and his medical staff to push a gurney through. Strapped on was a blanche-faced, middle-aged man that Phoenix recognized as the auctioneer/owner for Compass Fine Art Gallery. Someone murmured he had a heart attack after learning his entire stock of art had gone up in flames.

Phoenix's thoughts snapped back to the present as he heard the First

Class pre-boarding announcement for his flight back to New York. He opened his eyes, got up, had his boarding pass scanned, and walked down the ramp to enter the plane.

By that night he was in bed with Mona at a posh New York City hotel, champagne on ice, and the canvasses of six valuable original paintings spread across their bed sheets.

By the end of the week, the originals were slated to be sold on the black market to a businessman who lived on Long Island. Secretly, he was a member of the *Vory v Zakone*, or Thieves in Law, an organized crime group based in Russia. As one of Mona's long-time customers the "Vor" would have the paintings shipped overseas to Europe to resell to even wealthier private art collectors. As the mastermind of the plot, Mona stood to pocket a majority of the two million dollar profit, and Phoenix would get a commission of $800,000. Even Mona's niece was slated to bag $80k in cash for her role.

Mona and Phoenix lived the good life in New York City: every hotel they hooked up at was top notch, every meal they shared was gourmet, money was no issue, and the future of their adventurous thievery and fencing saw no end.

Life was completely grand – until Mona's phone chimed a notification.

She touched the screen and took a minute to privately read a new email from her secret Dark Web account. Only select trusted individuals knew her in the circle of black market contacts. One of them was now expressing interest in the two Nazi items Phoenix had stolen from West Point Museum.

After several promising inquiries over the last year – but none ever advancing beyond a few back and forth emails – this one looked like pay dirt. And she liked who sent it: the broker who commissioned the museum job in the first place.

3

WITH FELLOW RETIRED ARMY BUDDY, NOW business partner, Alex Vann, onboard, Jake accelerated his new ArrowCat 32RS offshore power catamaran up to 35 knots or 40 mph and softly sliced through the Atlantic Ocean paralleling Ossabaw Island. He named his boat *Lizzie* in honor of his Seneca tribe clan mother Miss Lizzie Spiritwalker. She had a profound influence on his life a few years back just before she finally 'ate her strawberries at sunset' at the age of 103. On the stern of *Lizzie*, Jake flew a yellow Gadsden flag, the coiled rattlesnake shouting out his famous phrase of 'Don't Tread On Me.'

They had departed from Jake's Skidaway Island home and were headed south some 20 nautical miles following the shorelines of several remote, unpopulated sea islands. Their destination: Blackbeard and Sapelo Islands. Their mission: recon for the pirate-flagged speedboat of Dreadlocks, but do not make contact.

Though still early in the morning, both men had cracked open a cold beer while Jake explained the purpose of their trip. Alex, tossing the skull ring up and down in his hand, was all game as expected. The guy thrived on spontaneous adventure as much as Jake.

After a GoToMeeting session with famed Germania military collector Erhardt Hoffman, and comparing a genuine SS ring in his own collection against the one left in his shop, Jake felt confident in the authenticity of the boy's ring. To play devil's advocate, though, Hoffman logged onto a well-known internet forum on SS honor rings and learned what signs to look for in fakes. They uploaded close-up pictures of the ring and heard expert opinions from all across the world that the boy's ring was definitely the real deal. Many of the members even made offers on the spot. Hoffman finally appraised the ring's worth at seven to ten thousand dollars, not knowing the original ring bearer's engraved name nor its provenance. He showed Jake the rarest ring ever on another collector's website. It belonged to Josef "Sepp" Dietrich, the infamous SS officer responsible for the Malmedy Massacre. His ring alone was priced at $235,500.

At the very least, Jake's goal was to return the boy's valuable *Totenkopf* ring and present his findings. He was excited about its authenticity and wanted the boy to share in the thrill of the discovery. He was totally prepared to offer him cash, too, having taken from his home safe a stack of crisp Benjamins totalling $10k. And he wanted to find out more about the Buffalo Soldier great-grandfather who obtained the ring in the first place. The story behind this rare object was essential to its value. He was hoping to make this a win-win all around. The kid could invest his money and Jake could land yet another rare battlefield artifact for his growing collection.

Finding Dreadlock's black speedboat with his pirate flag would be the key to finding his nephew in order to return the ring. But Jake knew he needed to avoid a confrontation with the man and to keep the boy's ring a secret. It was obvious that's why the abused kid had separated from his uncle to seek Jake out in the first place. Dreadlocks had him on a short leash. However, just in case things truly went south, Alex was there as his back up. Both men were licensed by the State of Georgia to carry personal sidearms. In fact, they packed just about everywhere they went – the smart thing to do in a world with people perpetually at each others' throats.

Inside the closed cockpit of *Lizzie*, the two men chatted while tracking the boat's progress through both an in-dash GPS navigational system as well as a laminated nautical chart. The time it would take to reach Sapelo and Blackbeard Islands had also allowed them to catch up on recent business decisions. Past events had unexpectedly pulled them together a year ago up in Atlanta. Ever since, they had turned into the best of friends.

Both men had strong Native American blood coursing through their veins: Jake was of Iroquois ancestry, specifically of the Seneca Nation, having grown up on the Tonawanda Indian Reservation in western New York; while Alex was from the Eastern Band of Cherokee in western North Carolina. Alex was also a direct descendant of the famous Chief James Vann, one of the richest men in the early 1800s.

In past lives, Jake and Alex would have been arch enemies from two of most powerful American Indian empires in all of North America. Or perhaps they might have fought against each other in the American Civil War. In fact, generations of men and women from their respective families fought in most of America's wars since the inception of the nation. Their shared pride in their military service to their country strengthened their trust in one other even more.

They were muscular men with chiseled features sculpted from a lifetime of physical activity in their combat careers. They were warriors in every sense of the word, having experienced war up close and personal. Both had meted out various forms of justice that could never be discussed publicly – especially Alex, a former Delta Force operator deployed around the world doing Jason Bourne shit and capping dudes for Uncle Sam.

In Jake's case, back in his younger days as a U.S. Army infantry officer with the 10th Mountain Division, he had engaged in a hand-to-hand fight to the death with three armed Taliban in a blown-out prison basement in Afghanistan. Jake smashed in the first soldier's face with his rifle butt, knocking him unconscious. The second, he popped three rounds into the man's chest at point blank range. The third sliced Jake open with a combat knife, but then Jake wrestled it away and thrust that same knife into his enemy's heart. And then, in an act of adrenaline-filled loss of self control – as if a past Indian warrior had possessed his body – Jake let out a blood-curdling Indian war whoop and had scalped both dead men. The legend of Jake Tun.unda, Seneca warrior, was born on that dark day. The army awarded him a Silver Star – officially for the prisoner he dragged out, who turned out to be an American Muslim traitor.

To these men, there was no glory or romanticism in war, only carnage, confusion, horror, and survival. After seeing bodies literally blown to pieces, and innocent men, women, children, even infants, beheaded by human monsters, it was difficult to keep their own heads on straight. Fighting off their personal demons was tough enough. It's why they liked each other's company in case things got muddy in their minds. They had no intention of ever stepping back onto the battlefield and all the ugly shit that came with it. It's why Jake spent the last years of his service working as a field historian for the Army's Military History Institute before finally retiring.

As diehard, patriotic Americans, Oathkeepers of the U.S. Constitution, protectors of all they cherished and who they loved, they truly believed that their sheepdog mentality was what kept the wolves at bay in an ultra-violent world. They despised weak-kneed, snowflake extremists on the left of the political spectrum who got their rocks off burning American flags and kneeling for the National Anthem. Instead, Jake and Alex supported the military, police, firefighters, and medics – those who risked their lives and made sacrifices every day so the rest of the law-abiding, hard-working citizens could live in peace and safety. Jake and Alex were men's men, badass to the core, and respected by many.

Jake still wore a close-cropped, military style haircut now tinged with gray at the temples. He was dressed in shorts and a black t-shirt with 'Army' stenciled across his chest. A necklace with a small silver and wampum shell medallion-like brooch sat on his chest. It was his protection amulet. He and Rae both wore them after becoming secret guardians of the *Crown of Serpents* hidden back in New York deep under the Seneca Army Depot.

The younger Alex, also dressed in a t-shirt and shorts, had long, shoulder-length, raven-black hair pulled back into a braided ponytail. A black hat with a white Punisher skull logo sat atop his head, backward.

Both men also had several tattoos up and down their thick arms with one in particular they now shared. This tattoo was inked as a badge of honor and marked entry into a secret society that a rare few men even knew existed. This tattoo was of a golden eagle, wings spread. A shield on its chest depicted a skull crest. This was the mark of a Witch Killer, a warrior who destroyed one of the most evil spiritual entities in American Indian lore: the feared Raven Mocker.

Jake and Alex had hunted down, battled, and ultimately destroyed one of these murderous beings in north Georgia. Their reward was discovering a secret Cherokee Indian tunnel filled with gold bullion along the Etowah River that the witch was protecting. One of the most prized possessions inside that tunnel was a book of Spanish maps that pinpointed ancient lost mines of rare earth metals dating back to the 1500s. This *Map of Thieves*, as they dubbed it, was what old man Tommy Watie had been after all of his life. Upon his passing, the map formed the impetus for the formation of Alex Vann's new mining company near Blood Mountain, Georgia. Jake and Rae agreed to become silent partners and capital investors.

The conversation soon switched to Alex updating Jake on mining operations he and his wife had undertaken in the last year.

"All in all, we're on track with our short-term objectives," said Alex. "Marissa and I have discovered six out of the nine ancient mine sites on Blood Mountain so far. Three of these sites are on private property adjacent to the Federal lands, so we've managed to persuade the owners to sell – at highly inflated prices I might add. Next time you guys come up we'll give you a tour of the new properties. Our prospects are looking good, my friend. It's all looking very good!"

"Incredible! Great news," Jake replied, standing at the wheel, guiding the boat. He was protected inside from the wind and a light rain shower that peppered the helm station windows. "We're gonna have to start deciding on mining and extraction equipment next, I would think? Whether to lease or purchase. Can't believe how fast this is moving. I honestly thought this would take years before we actually started moving dirt."

Alex took a swig from his beer. A coolie with the beaming face and signature blond hair of the president was wrapped around it. A slogan underneath the image said: *'Make America Great Again.'* "With the President's pro-business, America-first agenda, everything has changed. I'm anticipating our mining permit will be approved in just three months time since he stripped all regulations. It used to take fifteen years under the fucking enviro-Leftists running the shop. I meet with Commerce Department officials in D.C. on Tuesday and then Interior on Wednesday. If we can get the mining sites on that Federal land, then we are good to go."

"Helluva job you're doing Alex. I can't stomach politicians. No patience."

"We've been busy beavers up in them thar hills getting things ready once we get the go-ahead."

Jake caught Alex's reference to the famous saying of finding gold in the hills up in north Georgia. "Speaking of which," said Jake. "Did the melting furnace get delivered yet?"

Alex nodded. "Sure did. Two days ago. And that's the last thing I was going to report. Meant to call you but got sidetracked. It's sitting on a pallet in the warehouse on the Etowah River property. We've got to schedule a weekend to get her all set up. I really need your help. And don't worry, Marissa and I have got that tunnel at maximum security, concealment, and even booby-trapped. So, we're all good until you get up there."

"Cool," agreed Jake. "The sooner the better. Mine and Rae's three hundred and fifty pounds of gold bars still sitting in that tunnel has *got* to melt and disappear. Into our bank account, that is."

"Tell me about it," nodded Alex. "Marissa and I have hardly even touched our portion of the treasure. Been so damn busy. We'll get her done, though. Don't worry."

"What's she been up to? I heard she's got a nice speaking gig in D.C. when you're up there."

"Marissa is a non-stop ball of energy," Alex chuckled. "While I'll be busy meeting with *bureaucrats*, she'll be speaking at the Smithsonian's National Museum of the American Indian on the subject of my Cherokee ancestor James Vann. Then she's staying up there the rest of the week doing research at the Library of Congress and the National Archives."

Alex's phone chimed with a new text and attached photo. He looked at it and grinned like a big Cheshire cat. "Speak of the devil! Dude, check this out." He showed Jake the message.

It read, "See what you're missing, boys? Cum back soon," and showed a picture of their wives, Rae and Marissa. The beautiful women were dressed in white spa robes with white towels bundled around their hair. However, both their robes were deliberately and provocatively parted, teasing their oiled nakedness underneath as they each displayed a long slender leg, bare hip, and cleavage. On Rae's chest, Jake glimpsed her matching necklace and silver amulet.

"Holy shit!" said Jake, zooming in on the photo. "Man, I gotta tell ya, we hit the lottery with our brides."

"You ain't kidding. They look like spitting images of Maria Menounos and Halle Berry. Fucking hot. What should I write back?"

"Here, get a picture of this," Jake said with a shit-eating grin. Placing the boat on autopilot, he stepped out of the cabin to the rear deck and grabbed a fishing rod. Holding it up against his crotch with two hands, he pretended to reel in a fish. Alex snapped a photo.

"Type in: 'See what you're missing, girls?'," said Jake.

"Perfect," Alex laughed as he hit the send button.

The men definitely cherished their wives. Certainly drop-dead gorgeous and physically fit, both women were also highly independent and intelligent, humorous, self-confident and financially astute, while wholeheartedly passionate about what they did. They also knew how to throw a punch, pull a trigger, and take a shot — of whiskey.

As *Lizzie* motored further south and caught the tip of St. Catherines Island, the rain petered out, the clouds parted, the sun came out, and blue skies opened up. Jake switched off the windshield wipers and their field of vision ahead improved tremendously. They spotted a massive container ship many miles out to sea, headed north, in their opposite direction, on its run to the Port of Savannah. Some sailboats, luxury yachts, and smaller fishing boats were out and about, too.

A pod of bottlenose dolphins suddenly appeared on their port side and decided to tag along for the ride. He cut the speed down of his twin 250 horsepower engines so the dolphins could catch up. Four of them leapt out of the water, dove, and skirted around both sides of the dual-hulled boat. The men cracked open two more beers and watched as the slick beasts played. It was a great feeling to be out on the water in such nice weather, detached from the rest of the crazy world. No cell phone service. No news distractions. It was an escape they needed from the fast-paced events that dominated their lives. Silence soon took over, each man lost in his serenity.

"I've got something to tell you, man," said Jake, a few minutes later as he watched a pelican cut across his vessel's wake. "It's about the stolen pistol and baton from the West Point Museum."

"Really? The friggin' media coverage on those artifacts is nonstop, over-the-top, sensationalized. What, did you finally find them?"

"I wish, I wish," said Jake, sitting down in his captain's chair. "But things are getting hot. Sergeant Marco D'Arata caught a witness break and persuaded Criminal Investigation Division brass to reignite the case."

"No shit?"

"Yeah, the witness was that airplane pilot," nodded Jake, adjusting the throttle to a higher speed. "He was the very last one to see Phoenix, the real thief – the one who Marco thinks is still alive and got away with it – not that Sureños-13 gangbanger the FBI killed in their raid in Atlanta."

"Really?" said Alex.

"You see, Marco took surveillance pictures of the pilot and Phoenix together when they flew out of Atlanta after the BOLO went out on him. But of course when the Air Force boys forced the plane down in Florida, this Phoenix guy had already disappeared. Remember, the pilot claimed he never even had a passenger?"

"Oh, I remember."

"After that he lawyered up."

"This whole time?" asked Alex. "What's it been, well over a year?"

"Yup," said Jake, eyes glued on the waves ahead. "Until just last week when the pilot shows up out of the blue at CID headquarters over at Hunter and meets with Marco."

"Whoa. So, what happened? What did the pilot say?"

"Marco said all of the Nazi media hype out there finally got the best of him," replied Jake. "Go figure. That he had to get his story off his chest. Was making him physically ill, the guilt of being an unwitting accessory to the crime. Plus, living in pure fear. He came out and admitted he *was* transporting a passenger as a last-minute favor to the late Congressman Black, but had no idea who the guy was and asked no questions. And then he said he was basically hijacked in midair."

"Wow!"

Jake turned his gaze toward Alex. "Yup. And get this: he said Phoenix pulled Hitler's gold pistol on him and stuck it in his ribs while they were flying. The pilot begged for his life and said he had kids and grandkids. That was his first mistake. Guy was scared shitless and said too much. Phoenix then threatened to hunt down his family one by one and kill them if he didn't follow orders."

"Ah, so that's why he's been shittin' bricks this whole time."

"Yup. It was Marco's smoking gun, though. Literally. Having this witness placing Hitler's pistol there with Phoenix vindicated his supposed fuck-up when they forced an empty plane down." Jake placed the boat on autopilot again, sat back in his captain's chair, and swiveled to face Alex. His face was a knot of seriousness.

"Even though it's still hearsay evidence and not definitive proof – one person's word against another – it's the first time we clearly have Phoenix in possession of the stolen items. He then forced the pilot to land at a remote airstrip in some tiny, south Georgia town called Fitzgerald. Rips out all of his radio cords so he has no communication. The pilot said a car was waiting at the end of the runway with a dark-haired, white female and Phoenix jumps in. The pilot then takes off and flies on to Florida as he was ordered before the Air Force caught up to him. That's it. That's the last he saw of our thief. In Fitzgerald, with some woman." Jake took a long slug of beer and emptied his can.

"Another?" asked Alex, holding his beer can up.

"No, I'm good for now."

"So that's how the fucker got away," Alex said, scratching his chin. "Had it all planned out, even his extraction."

"Oh, he's a clever one," nodded Jake. "Fucking brilliant, in fact." He swung back to the dash board to check the nav system. Still on course, he turned back to Alex. "The pilot gave Marco a great description and made a positive ID that it was Phoenix who he departed with back in Atlanta on Marco's surveillance photos. Plus, he also matched Phoenix to the guy they caught on camera at West Point, from the hotel he left. Great detective work. It was Phoenix all along, the original prime suspect, a true professional master thief who's made a career of it and who's never been caught. This guy is a legend. Not that dead Sureños-13 illegal alien. We still don't know the connection there. Perhaps a fence gone wrong? Who knows?"

"Okay, so where's the case going from here?" asked Alex, standing up, arms crossed. "Knowing that Phoenix still exists and the Nazi trophies are with him. Or at least *were* with him. Hell, they could be long gone by now, tucked away in some neo-Nazi's private collection never to be seen again."

"But," said Jake, shaking his head. "They're not. Let me explain. Marco has already brought in and interrogated the guy who dropped Phoenix off at the airport in Atlanta."

"Really? He's moving quick," stated Alex.

"Yup, Antoine LaMar. Attorney from Atlanta. The dude immediately cut an immunity deal once Marco showed him all the charges he'd face. Sang like a canary. Admitted he drove Phoenix to the airport to escape. Marco has already used him undercover as a point of contact in the same role he performed for the actual theft: being the broker."

"Broker?"

"Yeah, it's kinda complicated," Jake explained, waving a hand. "But think in layers. Layers of deniability to cover your ass, as Marco explained it to me. Congressman Tom Black of Atlanta wanted the Civil War general's hat stolen. He was the client who funded the op. He ordered his chief-of-staff to find someone who could make that happen. The chief-of-staff called on this corrupt attorney LaMar who acted as the broker. He, in turn, called on his contacts and found an art dealer from New York City who trades in the black market. She is known as Mona Lisa. She, in turn, hired Phoenix, who executed the job. All parties earned their cut when the Congressman paid up in the end. The problem is Phoenix was supposed to steal *only* the fucking hat. He broke protocol and shit spiraled out of control."

"The guy went rogue," said Alex.

"Right. LaMar told Marco that when he spoke to Phoenix as he delivered the hat to him in person at the Congressman's party in Atlanta, that he asked him why he stole the two Nazi items, too. Phoenix said this: *'A man's gotta have insurance if you're messing with Uncle Sam. If you're going big, might as well go over the top.'*"

Alex pursed his lips. "Insurance? Against what? Getting caught?"

"I think so," nodded Jake. "He was stealing from the Federal government, so if you're gonna do the job for a freakin' hat, then why not grab the crown jewels in the process, is what it sounds like. I mean Hitler's pistol is now estimated to be worth $60 million alone!"

"Okay, okay, so you've got this broker LaMar now working for you . . ."

"Right. LaMar has turned. He already made contact with Mona Lisa just this last Friday afternoon via the Dark Web and we've already confirmed the two items have *not* been sold yet!"

"Ahhh, so that's how you found out."

"Exactly," said Jake. "LaMar told Mona Lisa he was representing a client who is a descendant of Göering and offered three hundred grand in upfront cash for a no-return deposit. Counterfeit of course. That's the bait we dangled and she bit on the hook. Next step is to reel her in and turn her, too, not spook her. Then hopefully we land the white whale of Phoenix. Essentially, Marco wants to con the cons."

"Nice. Give 'em a taste of their own medicine," scoffed Alex.

"And to show them that our so-called client is serious, we're bringing in a real military artifact expert to inspect the Nazi items and confirm their authenticity. We don't want to be conned ourselves by the cons." Jake winked. "If all goes well, we'll get our trophies back and arrest Mona Lisa and Phoenix red-handed."

"Are you gonna be that military expert?"

"I can't do it because my face was all over the news. They'd recognize me and pull out instantly. But Rae spoke to a retired senior FBI investigator who worked on their Art Crime Team. He, in turn, recommended a guy they've used in the past for authentication jobs like this. Marco, Rae, and I already did a face-to-face in Charleston a few days ago and he's good to go undercover for us. This expert is a big time German militaria collector. One of the legends in the business. Like an Obi Wan Kenobi. Name is Erhardt Hoffmann. Same guy I consulted with to verify the skull ring."

"Is Rae in on this?" Alex asked.

"Actually, it's a CID show. They want the credit to rub the FBI's faces in it, but she's under contract assisting Marco," said Jake, glancing at his friend. "She's jacked up. Wants this as much as I do. Misses cases like this when she was a state police investigator back in New York. I'm in the loop, but staying mostly at arm's length because I know I tend to get a bit aggressive and impatient, I guess you could say."

"Noooo, you don't say? Kinda like when you pitted the cock maggot Congressman's limousine?"

"That was a brilliant move," said Jake. "We got the hat back didn't we?"

"Yes," Alex admitted begrudgingly. "And then you fucking stabbed him in the ass with a pen!"

Jake guffawed at the remark. "Yeah, well I had to make my point, huh? Any way, it's happening tomorrow afternoon – the big sting in Charleston. That's the proof of life meeting when the two trophies are supposed to be revealed. Marco's got everything under control. He needs this after everyone thinks he fucked up in Florida."

Jake checked his nav system again and saw they were located in the middle of Sapelo Sound. The wind had picked up and the boat started bouncing on larger waves. He switched off the autopilot, regripped the wheel, and cut back on the throttle for a smoother ride. A large shrimp boat, nets down, was the only other traffic in the sound.

"Okay, task at hand," announced Jake, eyes glued to his navigation system. "We're just a couple of miles away from Blackbeard Island. That's it over to our starboard side." He pointed to his right. "I'll swing in close to shore once I skirt past some shoals. Here's your job, mate: I want a briefing of what this brochure say about the islands."

He picked up a rack brochure on his cockpit dash and handed it to Alex. Jake had grabbed the literature at the Delegal Creek Marina on Skidaway Island when he fueled up, and barely had any time to skim it over.

While Alex flipped the brochure open, scanned the map as to their location, and started reading, Jake turned the boat to port on a new heading out to sea to avoid the dangerously shallow Concord Shoal that jutted out from the northern tip of Blackbeard Island.

"Blackbeard Island National Wildlife Refuge," started Alex, reading from the publication, "has over 5,600 acres of forest, ponds, savannahs, beaches, and marshlands. Got its name from Edward Teach, alias Blackbeard the Pirate, in the early 1700s. Legend has it that he buried his treasure on the north part of the island near a place called The Boneyard. Apparently, he wrapped a heavy chain around a large oak tree to mark the spot." Alex paused, read to himself for a minute, then smiled.

"Gotta love this shit, man: he claimed he was the Devil's own brother and only he and the Devil knew where his treasure was buried. And the one who lived the longest could have it. Blackbeard's life ended in battle with the British Royal Navy. A brutal death. He had five bullet holes in him and over 20 stab wounds after hand-to-hand combat. The Brits then lopped off his head and stuck it on the bowsprit of their sloop as a warning to other so-called *evildoers*. Alex let out a low chortle. "You could say he was well-despised."

"The Islamic State would have been proud of those Brits," said Jake, facetiously.

"And listen to this," said Alex. "His skull was later ornamented with silver and used as a rum punch cup. This trophy is still supposed to be in existence today."

"Would be a lovely addition to my collection," said a still flippant Jake.

Alex continued. "But not a single coin of his treasure has ever been found on the island. Guess only the Devil knows where it is now. Oh, and you'll love this: wildlife refuge visitors are *reminded* that artifact hunting is a federal violation. That means you, Captain Tununda."

"Who me?" said Jake, clicking his tongue. "I've never gone artifact hunting. Don't know what you're talking about, young man."

Alex read on, more serious now. "Between 1880 and 1910, the island was the South Atlantic yellow fever quarantine station for the government. All ships entering the Georgia ports needed to be fumigated with sulfur gas to kill any mosquitoes, which transmitted the disease. If anyone was infected, their ships would be turned back. Facilities included: a surgeon's hospital and twelve buildings along Blackbeard Creek on the south end of the island. At the north end, some eight miles away by boat, was the main disinfecting dock, cleaning station, storage facilities, and a crematorium. A big hurricane and a massive tidal wave in 1898 totally destroyed every single building except the crematorium. It can still be seen today just off a hiking trail at the north tip. Apparently, that's all that's left."

"Burn the dead," mumbled Jake. "Make 'em disease-free."

Alex took a sip of his beer, inspected the map some more, and finished reading the brochure overview about the island. "Blackbeard's been in federal ownership since 1800 when the Navy Department took it over to lumber the live oak trees for shipbuilding, but there are portions where it's still virgin forest. It's run by the U.S. Fish and Wildlife Service, but there's no permanent Ranger on duty at the information booth dock on Blackbeard Creek. Says here it's open to the public seven days a week, sunrise to sunset only; no overnight use or camping is allowed, no fires, leave no trace, watch out for alligators, and bring vast amounts of insect repellent. Did we bring any?"

"Yes," said Jake. "Vast amounts. One thing about living here on the coast is the bugs are brutal. I should buy stock in the manufacturer of Deep Woods Off."

Alex spoke again. "Umm, also says here that access to the refuge is by private boat only. Basically, the island is popular with birdwatchers, wildlife photographers, and hikers. That's about it."

"Okay, and what about Sapelo Island. What's the story there?"

Alex read in silence for a minute. "Sapelo's the opposite. Has highly limited access. Prior arrangements must be made for planned visits. The public can't just come over on the ferry or their private boat. You need to make an appointment, pre-register, and get approved by the ferry captain. We're pretty much screwed from mooring and making landfall."

"Damn! Becky was right," said Jake, smacking the steering wheel. "She said there's some college there, some old mansion, and only like 35 residents left on the island."

"Yup, pretty tight," said Alex, perusing the list of restrictions on the brochure. "Only way to get on the island is to book a sightseeing tour with the University of Georgia's (UGA) Marine Institute or one of the private companies run by residents. Or you can make reservations for a group stay at the Reynolds Mansion or at the Cabretta campground." He glanced at the map to find their locations, then read some more. "The other option is being a visitor of one of the residents where you can rent a room at one of the small lodges that cater to tourists. Or if you're doing business with the State or one of those private residents." Alex paused to finish his beer then cracked opened another from the ice cooler.

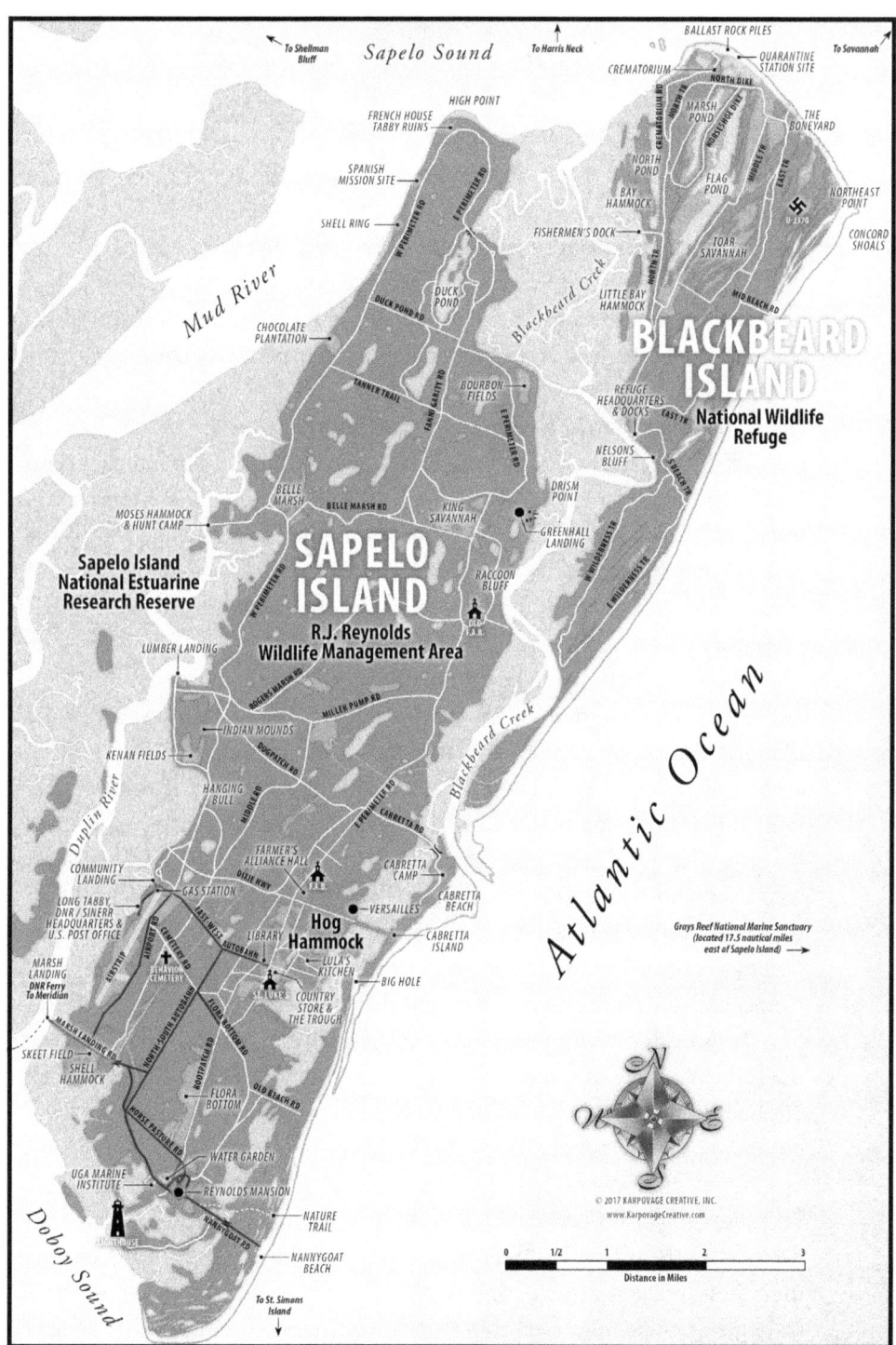

To Shellman Bluff
To Harris Neck
To Savannah

BALLAST ROCK PILES

Sapelo Sound

CREMATORIUM
QUARANTINE
STATION SITE
NORTH DIKE

HIGH POINT

FRENCH HOUSE
TABBY RUINS

MARSH
POND
THE
BONEYARD

SPANISH
MISSION SITE

NORTH
POND

FLAG
POND

NORTHEAST
POINT

SHELL RING

BAY
HAMMOCK

FISHERMEN'S DOCK

TOAR
SAVANNAH

CONCORD
SHOALS

U-2378

Mud River

Blackbeard Creek

LITTLE BAY
HAMMOCK

DUCK
POND

CHOCOLATE
PLANTATION

DUCK POND RD

BLACKBEARD ISLAND

National Wildlife Refuge

TANNER TRAIL

BOURBON
FIELDS

REFUGE
HEADQUARTERS
& DOCKS

BELLE
MARSH

BELLE MARSH RD

KING
SAVANNAH

NELSONS
BLUFF

MOSES HAMMOCK
& HUNT CAMP

DRISM
POINT

GREENHALL
LANDING

Sapelo Island National Estuarine Research Reserve

SAPELO ISLAND

R.J. Reynolds Wildlife Management Area

RACCOON
BLUFF

LUMBER LANDING

Atlantic Ocean

MILLER PUMP RD

Blackbeard Creek

INDIAN MOUNDS

KENAN FIELDS

HANGING
BULL

Duplin River

FARMER'S
ALLIANCE HALL

CABRETTA
CAMP

COMMUNITY
LANDING

GAS STATION

CABRETTA
BEACH

LONG TABBY,
DNR / SINERR
HEADQUARTERS &
U.S. POST OFFICE

VERSAILLES

CABRETTA
ISLAND

Grays Reef National Marine Sanctuary
(located 17.5 nautical miles
east of Sapelo Island)

LIBRARY

Hog Hammock

MARSH
LANDING
DNR Ferry
To Meridian

LULA'S
KITCHEN

BIG HOLE

SKEET FIELD

COUNTRY
STORE &
THE TROUGH

SHELL
HAMMOCK

FLORA
BOTTOM

WATER GARDEN

UGA MARINE
INSTITUTE

REYNOLDS MANSION

NATURE
TRAIL

LIGHTHOUSE

Doboy Sound

NANNYGOAT
BEACH

To St. Simons
Island

N

© 2017 KARPOVAGE CREATIVE, INC.
www.KarpovageCreative.com

| 0 | 1/2 | 1 | 2 | 3 |

Distance in Miles

"Well, that's what we're fixin' to do. Some business with the kid."

"Fixin'?" asked Alex, incredulously. "Man, didn't take you long to acclimate to the South."

"A Yankee has to fit in or else get eaten alive," Jake chuckled.

"Correction. You're a damned Yankee. Know what that means?"

Jake shook his head with a smirk, waiting for Alex's wise-ass reply.

"A damned Yankee is one who makes a permanent residency here in the South. Damn you, Yankee!"

"Don't make me bitch slap you," Jake retorted.

"Pfft!" Alex snickered, looking back down at the map brochure. "Looks like Sapelo is a helluva big island. Some 18,000 acres. 11 miles long and 4 miles wide. Says here it's bigger than Manhattan Island. But 97% of the land is owned by the State of Georgia and enforced by the Department of Natural Resources. They have arrest power for trespassers. Armed DNR Rangers."

"Ooh, I'm shaking," Jake deadpanned.

Alex read some more from the brochure. "The remaining 3% of the island is owned by private land owners mostly clustered in a tiny black community named Hog Hammock near the south end. The residents are Gullah-Geechee, one of the last island-based communities of its kind in America. They're direct descendants of the indigenous West African slaves who lived and worked on the Thomas Spalding plantation dating back to the early 1800s when he brought 385 slaves over. After the Civil War they became freedmen and land owners. Says here Hog Hammock and Behavior Cemetery were placed on the National Register of Historic Places in 1996."

"Maybe Hog Hammock is where the boy lives?" Jake speculated. "If all the residents live close to one another, then surely Dreadlocks would stick out like a sore thumb with his flashy boat and pirate flag. We just gotta look around, discreetly, that is."

"Problem is," countered Alex, "looks like Hog Hammock is land-locked. I don't see any direct boat access according to this map." He showed Jake the map inside the brochure. "See? It's located over four miles inland from the main ferry dock at Marsh Landing. We don't have ground transportation, let alone permission to even step foot on the island. The only other docks I see on this map that he might have access to are along the Duplin River on the west part of the island. And it looks like all those creeks and salt marshes are owned by the state, too, under the Sapelo Island National Estuarine Research Reserve System."

"Crap," uttered Jake.

"Says here the northern two thirds of this island is all just one big wildlife refuge. Used to be the hunting grounds for R. J. Reynolds Jr. when he owned the island. I think we're pretty much gonna be confined to the boat today with our dicks in our hands." Alex tossed the brochure back on the dashboard.

"Shit," said Jake, just as frustrated. "Maybe we're just on a wild-goose chase. Maybe Rae was right. What's my rush?"

"Don't tell her that, though," Alex laughed.

"Yeah, she'd lop off my head and fly it from this boat!"

"I'd treat your skull right, though. I'd have it ornamented in gold and would drink Doctor Blackbeard's moonshine from it in your honor."

Jake shook his head with a grin. "Ha! In my honor."

After a minute, he sighed. "Sounds like all we can do is circle the islands and do some sightseeing."

"Yup."

"We'll take a slow ride all the way around Sapelo, hit as many docks as we can find, then turn around. Just keep the beer low in case the DNR Rangers are out and about. So, mate, grab the binoculars, kick back, and let *Lizzie* reveal the way."

"Copy that, man."

❖

Sunday. 2:00 p.m.
Blackbeard Creek

Some three hours later, having boated all the way up the Duplin River, deep into the salt marshes through the 6,100-acre Sapelo Island National Estuarine Research Reserve, Jake and Alex still hadn't spotted Dreadlock's boat, let alone any other watercraft. They went up the river as far as they could before the tall *Spartina* grass-filled marsh narrowed in on them and they almost bottomed out in a muddy shoal. Not even the Georgia Department of Natural Resources (DNR) Ranger vessel was out on patrol. It had been still moored at Long Tabby with a few other smaller boats when they ventured down a tributary to check out that dock. If not for the slew of wildlife flying and swimming all around them, it was rather an uneventful tour around the west side of the island as far as their objective was concerned.

They hadn't spotted a single soul along the shoreline either, even at the passenger ferry dock facility and pier at Marsh Landing. All that was visible when they approached was a small parking lot with a handful of rusted old cars and pick-up trucks from the island's residents who had presumably taken the morning ferry over to Meridian.

Sunday was a time for residents to get their grocery shopping done on the mainland, or worship at one of the two churches in Hog Hammock. The few businesses on the island were closed, along with the college, the post office, even the gas station. The ferry wasn't due back until 4 p.m., so activity at the dock was non-existent. The already isolated island was down to virtually no visitors this time of year anyway as public island tours weren't even offered on Sundays, let alone in November, the start of the off-season for tourism.

The only thing alive at Marsh Landing was their cell phone service when *Lizzie* puttered near the docks. Having been out of range the entire time since leaving Skidaway, their respective iPhones kicked in with dings, beeps, and pings of various notifications. In fact, it was one of the rare locations on the island that their AT&T service provider was even available. Having texted their wives that all was going well on their day trip, they started on their last leg of the recon swinging past the lighthouse and around the south end of the island to head back north along the beaches. They would be making a detour up Blackbeard Creek, the tidal river separating the two main islands, before returning to Skidaway.

Just past Cabretta Beach, Jake swung his boat into the mouth of the creek, then cut his speed for more controlled maneuverability. He stayed in the middle of the channel as the creek curved around like a massive water serpent. They soon passed the highest section on Sapelo Island on their left: Raccoon Bluff.

Once a thriving inhabited section of the island before all of the residents were moved down to Hog Hammock, all that remained now of Raccoon Bluff was the original First African Baptist Church. Some fifteen feet above sea level, the bluff was a dense wall of loblolly pine, cabbage palms, and gnarled live oak trees dripping with long festoons of Spanish moss. The undergrowth looked to be an impenetrable barrier of bright green palmetto and rust-colored resurrection fern. The few sections that were visible through this bank of forest only revealed a shadowy black world beyond.

As the main creek curved away from the bluff and took them back into the salt marsh, they spotted a narrow tributary off to their left. Like many other spidery channels through this marshland, they wouldn't really have paid it much notice except for a pole sticking above the golden *Spartina* grass. Attached to the pole was a limp, sun-bleached, tattered black flag. Next to the pole was a large white sign with the image of a surveillance camera.

In bold red letters, a warning read: *No Trespassing, Private Property Protected By Video Surveillance, Trespassers Will Be Prosecuted.* A quick look around and they didn't see any cameras.

Must be bullshit, Jake thought. Another smaller sign showed the symbol of a gun, indicating the property was also well-armed against unwelcome intruders. Further back was a rusty old gate across the entrance to the tributary, with a faded wood sign in hand-painted capital letters reading: *GREENHALL LANDING – PRIVATE.* The gate stood open.

A gust of wind suddenly caught the black flag. When it unfurled it revealed a skull and crossbones.

4

A CTING AS PHOENIX'S DEALER TO MOVE HIS GOODS, Mona Lisa had posted his two stolen Nazi relics for sale through her Dark Web art auction network shortly after he stole them over a year ago. Since then, with all of the non-stop media hype fueling their ever-increasing value, she had incrementally jacked up the black market asking price to where they now stood at $10 million for Hitler's pistol and $6 million for Göering's baton. Real world auction houses were estimating the items at $60 million and $40 million respectively, so the bargains one could obtain on the criminal Dark Web were huge. It would be her biggest sale ever if she could pull it off, and she could retire off it, living her expensive Upper Manhattan lifestyle to the day she died.

When she received the email inquiry from Antoine LaMar down in Atlanta, asking if her "side dishes" had been eaten or not, she was thrilled to reply back that they were "still yummy as ever," code for the two items still being available on the market.

A few more emails were exchanged on Saturday and Mona pressed LaMar as to who his client was, but LaMar said the person must remain anonymous. The most he could reveal was: *"A wealthy German descendant of Hermann Göering living in a South American country. Has dealt in black market before. Client wishes proof of life inspection to confirm authenticity before proceeding. Offering $300,000 down payment in cash just to secure* *items from other bidders."* He told Mona that if the deal doesn't close for some reason, then she gets to keep the money for her troubles, the client was that serious.

And that wealthy, she had thought.

Mona showed Phoenix the email exchange and they mutually agreed this was their best inquiry to date. That they really had nothing to lose and were guaranteed a quick $300k in cash if the deal fell through. Plus, Phoenix had met LaMar in person and had his help escaping Atlanta during the FBI manhunt. He knew he could be trusted. Mona knew he could be trusted, too, because he was the one that had originally contacted her to get the Civil War general's hat stolen from West Point in the first place.

The proof of life meeting was scheduled for Monday at 2 p.m. LaMar's client wanted to move fast on the deal before anyone else made any offers or the price went up further.

Phoenix had flown down to Georgia to retrieve his buried treasure. He arrived in Atlanta in the late afternoon, and according to the last call she had received on her cell phone, was already headed south down I-75 in a rental car. Destination: rural Fitzgerald, Georgia and the cemetery where he had stashed the two items.

He'd have to wait until nightfall to dig them back up, though. She told him when he was done to simply head east to Charleston, South Carolina as she was still waiting on a meeting location with LaMar and his military expert for tomorrow. She said she booked a room at the White Point Inn, a historic waterfront mansion overlooking Charleston Harbor. Her flight left in three hours and she'd check-in first and wait for his arrival.

Sitting at a computer desk in her luxury New York City brownstone, the petite Mona checked her luxurious diamond and gold wristwatch and saw she still had time before a taxi would whisk her off to JFK International Airport. She was looking forward to another successful business transaction that would bring her and Phoenix a very serious payday, their best ever. But equally important was another romantic rendezvous with the master thief himself. She just couldn't get enough of him. It was almost getting to the point of obsession. *Or was it love?* Shaking her head, she couldn't even remember the last time she fell in love. It certainly wasn't with her first or second husband, both marriages ending in divorce – with hefty settlements in her pocket. *Maybe three's a charm,* she thought.

She knew Phoenix definitely had deep feelings for her and that's all that mattered in her personal life. Business-wise, though, she knew he certainly didn't give a shit about the history of the Nazi items he stole. He only cared about his pay-off to maintain his highfalutin lifestyle – more than likely with a few other women besides just herself.

It was she who was responsible for the business transaction and needed to be on top of the provenance of his stolen Nazi artifacts in case the authenticator was someone other than who they said they were. LaMar did provide her a name for this expert they were using and after doing an internet search on him, she was satisfied he was legitimate. This relieved her uneasiness somewhat.

His name was Erhardt Hoffmann, a well-known German militaria expert from Charleston, South Carolina. He was all over the web, having published many articles on German war relics. On his website he displayed countless German collectibles for sale, along with glowing testimonials from customers who commissioned him for authenticity assessments. He even wrote a book on the subject and had many public speaking engagements listed on his book tour calendar. Plus, he was also a frequent guest appraiser on the highly popular television program *Antiques Roadshow*, where he was called on for his expertise. Under the site's bio tab, Mona also found it quite fascinating that his German parents were from opposing sides of World War II.

She read that his father was a combat officer in the U.S. Army who eventually was responsible for finding entertainment acts for the officer's clubs throughout the American sector in occupied Germany, including booking gigs for Army Private Elvis Presley. His mother was a young teen in the Hitler Youth during the war, but eventually worked as a secretary for the U.S. Army engineers during occupation in the mid-1950s. The couple met in a park in Heidelberg and were later married in Switzerland. When they moved back to the States, his father took up teaching history at The Citadel military college in Charleston. They remained married the rest of their lives.

Mona always loved a feel-good story of opposites attracting. It would make a nice conversational piece she could ask Hoffman about at their meeting, a strategic scheme to establish a positive relationship with a member of the potential buyer's representatives.

The other burning question she wanted to ask him is why, given his seemingly successful background, he would involve himself with stolen goods? She suspected the same reason why she was in the black market business, and everyone else for that matter: the money, the glory, the excitement of not playing by society's rules. He would probably earn a fee for two hours worth of work equivalent to what he'd make in two years.

To while away the hours before her flight, she had been browsing bookmarked Nazi history websites and YouTube documentaries on her home computer. She had to commit the provenance of each item to her memory for tomorrow's meeting with the client's authenticator.

Starting with Adolf Hitler's pistol, she clicked on a PDF article published in 2009 by Ron Laytner, a world-renowned photojournalist and book author who interviewed the last owner of the pistol after it was sold to West Point Museum. The headline of the article read: *Hitler's Lost Treasure*. It described how, in Munich, Germany at the end of World War II, a combat sergeant with the U.S. Army's 144th Division was billeted in The *Führerbau* or The *Führer's* building and discovered what was most likely the most historic and most valuable set of loot plundered by a private individual during the war.

This unidentified soldier, who told his story years later on a tape recording, was one of three survivors of a platoon that had been decimated throughout the war. The platoon was replaced twice in the three years it had taken him to get to Germany from his 1942 landing in North Africa. Looking for souvenirs in the already ransacked building, this veteran ventured down to the flooded basement. There he found a large box being used as a stepping stone so the soldiers wouldn't have to get their feet wet. When he broke the box open, it contained Hitler's treasury of his most personal belongings. It was as if the box was packed and meant to go with Hitler on an escape he never made.

Within that chest, the sergeant found an inventory of priceless treasures, each taking their own journey of ownership over the years. The inventory consisted of: a diary with 'A H' on the cover and pages of handwritten words in German that the sergeant tossed in the water thinking it of little value – never to be seen again; a large gold pistol with the initials 'A H' engraved on the ivory handle – subsequently sold to the sergeant's captain for $500 after a heated, greed-filled argument; a velvet-lined wooden box containing a smaller gold pistol – the same pistol later sold to West Point Museum; another small box containing a gold watch with the initials 'A H' engraved on it – later lost in a Pittsburgh public restroom after the sergeant removed it to wash his hands; several dozen ancient German gold and silver coins in mint condition and a set of silver cutlery engraved with 'A H', all of which he later gave away to friends and family; a small oval painting of Hitler's mother; a framed photograph of 'Blondi,' Hitler's famous German shepherd; a large swastika banner from a Brownshirt Nazi regiment; an iron cross and eagle medal presented to Hitler in 1935; a decorated plate made of 800-point silver and ambergris presented to the winner of a Nazi pistol-shooting match in 1939; a small silver globe that, when opened, revealed a thick gold and platinum ring with rubies set in the shape of a swastika; an elaborate book with an eagle and swastika on the cover which outlined a state visit by Italian leader Benito Mussolini; the March 13, 1933 edition of *Time Magazine* that for the first time featured Hitler on the front cover; and finally, a tiny box of cut diamonds.

When he was due to ship home from Germany, the sergeant ended up trading all the diamonds to his lieutenant in return for smuggling the rest of the treasure in that officer's foot locker. There was no other way the loot would have made it through customs officers conducting searches as troops re-entered the United States.

The sergeant said in the recording that all he knew was that his lieutenant was involved in a wider smuggling ring that flew loot to Bermuda. From there, he had no idea how the goods made it back to the mainland.

After arriving in New York City during the summer of 1945, the sergeant took a train down to Savannah, and then a taxi farther south to a remote naval airfield surrounded by marshes. He said, *"it was on the coast of Bumfuck, Georgia where the Southern drawl of all them Negroes was so thick I had no idea what the hell they were saying."*

After identifying himself at the main gate, he asked for the name of a certain Navy Master-at-Arms (MA) officer. This was the contact name given to him by his lieutenant. The MA allowed him in, and drove him to a wooded section on base where a large storage bunker was partially hidden underground. There, the MA retrieved the foot locker, allowed him to confirm that all the locker contents were accounted for, and then escorted him back to the main gate. From there, the sergeant rode the taxi back to Savannah and went on with his life.

Afterward, the box of Hitler's personal possessions sat under his bed for some 29 years until he sold his treasure collection to a retired millionaire from Nevada named Ray Bily, an American cheese manufacturer. That wealthy Nevada businessman kept it in a bank vault for his own private viewing and satisfaction. Years later he sold Hitler's gold pistol to the West Point Museum because his wife was afraid of guns.

The palm-sized, gold-plated, Lilliput Model I, .32-caliber, semi-automatic pistol was housed in a small wooden box where it sat nestled in a molded, black velvet-lined interior. Also inside the box were an extra gold-plated magazine with six bullets and a gold cleaning brush.

Bily died in 1994 and the rest of the treasure's whereabouts are unknown to this day. It was a jaw-dropping story that fascinated Mona Lisa. She was sure to remember the main details to quiz the military expert.

Hitler's pistol sat in the same display case at West Point Museum next to his second-in-command, *Reichsmarschall* Hermann Göering's, diamond encrusted ivory baton. The baton was presented to Göering in 1940 by Hitler himself when he created the position for Göering.

Göering held many positions of power within the German government. He was commander of the *Luftwaffe* – and a veteran WWI fighter pilot ace himself; he was also titled the Prussian prime minister; the *Reichstag's* president; the founder of the *Gestapo*; and Hitler's right-hand man and designated successor. But the egocentric, morphine-addicted Göering would also hold a more infamous title: the greatest art thief of WWII.

The bulk of his confiscated artwork came from Jewish victims of concentration camps. More came from private collections, pilfered museums, libraries, churches, and Masonic lodges. His vast collection numbered in the thousands and included: paintings, drawings, altarpieces, tapestries, rugs, statues, jewelry, ornaments, and many other objects of high value.

At the end of the war when the Russians closed in from the east, and the rats were fleeing the sinking ship, Göering emptied Carinhall, his country estate near Berlin, of his entire art collection and loaded it onto a fleet of private trains. All of his ill-gotten treasures were evacuated south to Berchtesgaden in the German Bavarian Alps. He then had his estate destroyed by a *Luftwaffe* demolition squad so it wouldn't fall into the hands of the Red Army and be used for propaganda purposes.

Some treasure trains reached their destination and the goods were unloaded into secret underground bunkers and caves on the German/Austrian border. The bunkers were sealed with 18 inches of concrete that, upon discovery, took American soldiers three days to chip through. Once inside, the contents were so unbelievable they dubbed it 'Aladdin's Cave.' Many soldiers of the U.S. Army then helped themselves to the treasures before the scene could be secured.

The other Göering treasure trains were intercepted by the Allies or abandoned on the tracks, some looted by locals. The captured trains were then diverted to Munich and the contents inspected, inventoried, and partially pillaged, again by U.S. military men seeking war trophies.

In 1945, the *New York Times* pegged Göering's collection at $200 million.

When he knew the war was completely over, Göering fled across the border to Austria before making his way to the American lines where he expected more favorable treatment as opposed to the Russians. He turned himself in on May 9, 1945 and surrendered his foot-long ceremonial baton to officers of the U.S. Seventh Army.

The baton weighed about five pounds. The shaft was made of white elephant-ivory embossed with twenty gold eagle insignias and twenty platinum German Iron Crosses. The solid-gold cap ends held bands engraved in platinum and were encrusted with 640 diamonds. It was a priceless relic.

A year later, Göering committed suicide by biting on a cyanide pill secretly smuggled into his prison cell following his conviction and sentencing to death by hanging at the Nuremberg trials in 1946. Lieutenant General Patch, Commander of Seventh Army, brought the trophy baton back to the

U.S. and presented it to the West Point Academy, where it had remained in its collection ever since.

That is, until Phoenix stole both the baton and Hitler's pistol.

And now Mona would be selling those two prized relics back into a Nazi-lover's hands, the cycle of possession about to come full circle.

5

S AMPSON 'SAMMIE' GREENHALL SAT IN A MOLDY white plastic chair reading a paperback book titled *Nazi Gold*. At his feet on a wooden dock, under a large conch shell, was a week-old newspaper from Savannah. It was opened to a display ad for *Tununda's Military Menagerie*, an upcoming new River Street business soliciting the purchase of military artifacts. The ad had been circled with a yellow highlighter.

Sammie wore a wide-brimmed straw hat, sunglasses, and denim overalls with no shirt underneath. He had strategically positioned himself in the shade of two cathedral-like six-hundred-year-old live oaks standing sentinel over a long dock at his family's salt marsh landing. With a constant breeze blowing in off the Atlantic Ocean, the head of the dock – at the gangway on the bluff – was the ideal place of refuge to escape the nuisance of sand flies and mosquitoes. He breathed in the distinctive, briny, exquisite aroma coming off the alluvial mud flats at low tide. It was perfume to his nostrils, the smell of home.

A purring feral calico cat that Sammie named Cleo brushed up against his legs. It was one of many that roamed the island where people lived; to be near the few people that were left. This particular cat always knew she could get a quick bite to eat from the young man. Sure enough, Sammie dipped into his box of Cheez-It crackers and tossed one on the dock to her.

At the end of the one-hundred-foot dock, at its floating section, a 9' Zodiac inflatable boat with both a 20 HP outboard and a trolling motor was moored. It was Sammie's very own boat given to him by his late father who got it for a steal off eBay when Sammie, an only child, had turned twelve. He used it all around the island for fishing, clamming, hunting, recreation, and utility. On more than one occasion, the DNR Rangers called on him to rescue stranded fishermen stuck in muddy areas where their larger craft couldn't reach.

In the middle of the dock, along its permanent elevated section, was an old wooden boat house and lift that protected *Doctor Blackbeard*: a 22-foot, black-painted, 1955 vintage Chris Craft Continental Hardtop Cadillac speedboat made of African mahogany. It was his great-grandpa Duff Greenhall's most prized possession, gifted to him from R. J. Reynolds Jr. himself, the wealthy owner of the island from 1934 to 1964. The boat was now captained by Sammie and no one else.

As an irreplaceable, high value family asset, it was also his responsibility to keep it in pristine condition given how quickly the corrosive saltwater environment could damage it. After each use, Sammie would wash it completely with fresh water and dry every nook and cranny. He would raise it on a cradle inside the boat house and store it covered under a tarp. Once a year he'd even drain the fuel from the motor, flush the system, and remove and clean the batteries. With a protective maritime paint and a heavy duty shellac on the external surfaces, *Doctor Blackbeard* was just as good as the day his 93-year-old great-grandpa had received it.

Sammie nicknamed his great-grandpa 'Pappy,' but older folks on the island secretly knew him as 'Doctor Blackbeard' – the legendary root doctor and moonshine king of coastal Georgia. However, the general public only knew him as Corporal Duff Greenhall thanks to an NPR News report many years ago during Black History Month. That segment introduced him to people all across the United States as one of the last surviving Buffalo Soldiers from the U.S. Army's all-black 92nd division in World War II. Since then, reporters would come calling on him for the same feel-good stories of survival, resiliency, and no-nonsense advice on life's many challenges.

Duff would revel in the interviews and soaked up the fame. He was quite the character, always conducting interviews in his rocking chair throne on the elevated house porch overlooking the ancestral land of his family: WWII veteran's baseball cap on his head, beloved cigar between his lips, jar of moonshine at arm's length, and a German MP40 submachine gun in his hand with a gleaming SS *Totenkopf* ring on his finger. When a reporter once asked about the ring, all he said was it was a trophy of war.

He was an instant hit with conservatives, military supporters, and patriots on the right of the political spectrum who compared his strong, self-sufficient war-fighting generation against the self-righteous, entitled, liberal progressives of the left. Many internet memes popped up on social media showing a picture of Duff with his gun, 'shine, and cigar against the backdrop of an American flag – opposite a bearded millennial man wearing a knitted purple pussycat hat holding a Starbuck's coffee and a smartphone against the red flag of socialism. The contrast was startling and spoke volumes on the state of manhood in America.

Sammie was present at many of the interviews, deciphering what came out of Pappy's mouth because his Gullah dialect was so thick the reporters could hardly understand a complete sentence. Gullah was a blend of 18th century English, Scottish, Creole, Jamaican patois, and African tongues with modern black English. The replay of his interviews even included captions. Pappy spoke in Gullah to honor and perpetuate the heritage of Sapelo Saltwater Geechee. But Sammie knew he simply liked to mess with the reporters, too, as Pappy could speak perfectly good English if he so desired, depending on who his guest was.

After the passing of the island's legendary matriarch and griot, Cornelia Walker Bailey, in 2017, Duff Greenhall became the de facto griot and respected elder for the island's few remaining black inhabitants. His knowledge of history, flare for storytelling, and unwavering devotion to the land exemplified the struggle to preserve Sapelo's Saltwater Geechee identity.

When Pappy unexpectedly gave Sammie that same SS *Totenkopf* ring off his finger a few weeks back, the teen had plunged into the history of the Nazis, something his public education glossed over in just a couple of days due to political correctness rampant in public schools. It was why he now firmly clutched that thick, dog-eared book, *Nazi Gold*, in his leather-like workman hands. The book told a tale how, at the end of World War II, the Allies committed what the Guiness Book of World Records called, "*The greatest robbery on record*," referring to how $2.5 billion in gold, currency, and jewels hoarded by the Nazis simply vanished.

More than halfway through the tome, Sammie was stunned to learn how rampant the black market looting of Nazi treasures was. Pappy even confirmed that all levels of the U.S. occupying forces were involved, from the lowly army private to rumors of the Military Governor of Germany himself, Army General Lucius Clay – more specifically, his wife.

She was alleged to have traded deep in the black market and had her ill-gotten gains secretly shipped home on the general's personal plane. That overseas flight, from Berlin to the old Harris Neck Army Airfield not fifteen miles away, made multiple departures listed as a 'classified mission' to specifically avoid U.S. Customs. It turned out none of those flights were actually logged with the Army Air Corps. That example of corruption and theft was one of many eye-opening stories Sammie had come across in the book so far, making him turn page after page.

While reading, he leaned down to scratch a burning wound of broken skin on the back of his leg. Bending over, his sunglasses slipped down his nose revealing a swollen black eye. His wounds were courtesy of his court-appointed temporary guardian, Uncle LeShaun Greenhall, the fake-dreadlock wearing, snazzy-clothed, piece of shit slave driver he hated with a passion.

Sammie labeled him 'Buzzut,' the Gullah word for 'vulture' when he swooped in after Sammie's mother, father, and grandparents all died in a fiery wreck five years ago on I-95. An illegal alien who was texting and driving lost control of his vehicle, crossed the median, and crashed head-on with the family's van as they were returning from a wedding in Savannah. Like the carrion bird, LeShaun tore away at Sammie and Duff's lives just weeks after they had lost their loved ones.

This latest physical abuse was one of many injuries Sammie had received since his uncle had taken control of his life five years ago. Buzzut had given him these last marks just two days ago up in Savannah; which reminded him that he'd have to get back up to the city somehow to retrieve his SS ring from that military man's shop. *So wish they all would have shot him*, Sammie thought fleetingly with no remorse.

He loved that his uncle got his ass handed to him. It was the first time he'd seen anyone stand up to the bullying thug like that. A little satisfactory curl formed at the corner of his mouth. It hurt a little to smile because of a cut lip, but he turned his attention back to his book and read some more about corrupt American servicemen.

That particular paperback was one he had recently picked up for just fifty cents at a used book sale at the Hog Hammock Public Library down in the main part of Sapelo Island. The tiny library, located in the former two-room schoolhouse and run by one of the sweetest women on the island – a historian in her own right, named Beulah Brown – had been his lifeblood to furthering his public education during his school years. Books enabled him to reach beyond the minimal academic requirements and propelled him into worlds the average school kid in McIntosh County, Georgia would never have known. Books shaped his dreams and aspirations. Books were his salvation. They helped him enhance his vocabulary, but not necessarily in *how* he pronounced his newly learned words. The Gullah language and its distinct accent he grew up with on Sapelo often confused people over on the mainland.

Despite all the physical abuse and loss of his family, Sammie ultimately graduated as one of the smartest in his high school class at McIntosh County Academy just last spring. He had even earned a year of college credit in the process by excelling at AP level college courses. Now he considered pursuing a college degree, but Buzzut always brushed off higher education as being "too damned expensive." Instead, Sammie had to find part-time work doing odd jobs on the island.

Although Buzzut was a temporary guardian to Sammie, he was granted permanent guardianship of old man Duff and conservatorship of all family assets. After the death of all his family members, the elderly man became a shell of himself. He couldn't take care of his own basic needs, he refused to eat and wash himself, lost weight, drank moonshine like it was water, and mumbled that he just wanted to die. He was prescribed anti-depressants and moped around like a drunken zombie frequently wandering away on the island for miles at a time, sometimes even in the pitch black of night. Several times he took the Zodiac over to Blackbeard Island where U.S. Fish and Wildlife Rangers searched for him after he was declared missing. But he was always found in the vicinity of The Boneyard at the north end.

For these wanderings and his mental state of depression, Buzzut had easily convinced a local probate court that frail Duff Greenhall was incapacitated and partially disabled and therefore needed someone to act in his best interests. Despite his uncle's past criminal background in the state of Florida, Buzzut persuaded court officials that he was rehabilitated and reformed, and the only person capable of caring for the older man and being a father figure to Sammie. They ruled in his favor. This gave Buzzut complete control of all assets within the Greenhall estate. He became power of attorney, executor of the estate, and de facto owner of the land and home. He had access to all the money left in the deceased member's accounts, including close to a million dollars in life insurance payouts. It soon became evident what Buzzut's true intentions were: to ride a personal gravy train while only shelling out a measly weekly allowance for Sammie and his great-grandpa to survive on.

And so, cheaply bought books were a large part of Sammie's intellectual and social entertainment. He didn't have a flat screen TV, a computer with the internet, a social media network, nor an Xbox gaming system. His late parents didn't believe all that mumbo-jumbo technology was needed to live a happy life. Nor did his late grandparents who originally built the four-bedroom house back in the 1970s. His grandparents were lucky enough to have gotten a telephone line and eventually a utility line so they could have electricity at their property. When that happened, they did splurge on one luxury item that made their lives so much better: air conditioning. But even that old system had stopped working in the last few years.

Buzzut even refused Sammie's requests for a cheap new stereo system to play CDs. All Sammie had for entertainment in his late parent's house were more books, a chess set, a piano, an old radio, and many, many conversations with the only other person that lived there: Pappy. He'd moved in when his old home, just through the woods, became uninhabitable.

Pappy's now locked-up, abandoned, one story house, built in 1940 and set deep in the heart of the Greenhall family estate adjacent to where the farm fields once were, had been neglected for many years after the old man's wife passed. It was in decrepit structural condition, rampant with rodents, and packed with every imaginable item his hoarder late wife had stashed away. Access to it was virtually impossible, too, since the undergrowth had so overtaken the old road leading to it.

When the old telephone line at the newer house had been severed in a storm a few years ago and the telephone company refused to repair it due to costs, Buzzut didn't even offer Sammie a cell phone, citing bad service up on the Greenhall estate. When Sammie protested and said he'd need one when on the mainland, he got slapped. The most his uncle allowed the boy was a handheld, two-way radio with a 38-mile range so he could keep dibs on him and the old man. But Sammie soon caught on that his uncle used the other handheld radio for more nefarious purposes, like contacting boats out at sea when he unwittingly heard him talking in some sort of code on another channel.

He'd never known his uncle at all growing up, never had met him, not once. All he heard was that he'd been an uncontrollable menace to their community when he was a teen. Caused a lot of problems with the people down in Hog Hammock. Created a lot of resentment between the Greenhall family and the folks down there. Apparently, he did some heinous things that were unforgiveable still to this day. After he got out of a juvenile detention center, LeShaun had fled down to Miami. The feel-good story was that he was going to college. Pappy once said that the only education LeShaun got was in prison. What for, he never did tell.

LeShaun only showed up back on Sapelo after the family will stipulated that the next of kin take over legal guardianship and temporary custody of the only child: Sammie.

That's when the black sheep returned and stomped on Sammie's world.

Buzzut never held a job, but remarkably found a big, rich man's house in Hog Hammock with all the bells and whistles of modern technology. He also hired a gaunt black woman who looked like she was always high on drugs. Her name was Keisha Tyler and she came across on the mainland ferry twice a month. Rarely spoke to others. She brought supplies, did his laundry, cleaned his home, and performed other services on him that he desired, or so it was whispered by Hammock folk. Beulah Brown even overheard she was an ex-stripper from Atlanta.

For food, Buzzut had appointment-only meals freshly cooked and delivered two days a week by the island's only restaurant, *Lula's Kitchen*. He tipped handsomely as a valued repeat customer. After all, he once told Sammie they made the best barbecue ribs he'd ever tasted. Sammie couldn't disagree there.

Buzzut also owned a big Lincoln Navigator he kept at the Marsh Landing ferry parking lot that he allowed his maid to use for bringing supplies back to his house. For more rugged island transportation, he bought a brand new, $15,000 Bad Boy Stampede 900, 4×4 Utility Terrain Vehicle, the most expensive on the island. He used his UTV to make the trip up to the Greenhall estate to check up on Sammie and Duff, albeit rarely. Sometimes he'd bring white men along who seemed to take an interest in the house, the dock, and the surrounding land as if Buzzut was giving them a tour. Other times he brought suspicious looking Latino men. Usually Pappy would run them all off with a nasty look or a waggle of his finger. If they refused, he pulled out his German submachine gun. One time he even shot it off in the air, which sent Buzzut and his visitors scattering off the estate.

Pappy never liked Buzzut from the get-go. Spoke disparaging of him on most occasions, but also let him get away with things he really shouldn't have. Bottom line, it was because Buzzut had legal authority over him and frequently threatened that he'd move him off the island into a nursing home. Buzzut was simply jealous and resentful of the old man and all of his life experiences. To rub it in, he rode around in Pappy's vintage boat as if he owned it himself, which technically he did.

In fact, since Sammie had gotten his captain's license in his early teens, Buzzut forced him to be his personal captain when he boated to different remote locations along the coast. Mostly though, Sammie acted as a designated driver when Buzzut would be high on drugs or boozed up. And if Sammie didn't comply with even the simplest of orders, then he'd get whipped with his guardian's switch, something his uncle always seemed to have at his side – his *wand of discipline*. If Sammie dared open his mouth, Buzzut threatened to hurt Pappy, sometimes even threatening to kill him.

Despite all the abuse, Sammie took it upon himself to keep the boat in pristine running condition. He knew how much Pappy loved it. When the waters were calm he'd take Pappy out on rides and they'd laugh, smoke a cigar, sip some 'shine, and soak up the sun.

Buzzut's needs, though, always took precedence. He would park his Bad Boy UTV at Greenhall Landing when he wanted Sammie to boat him to nearby islands, Savannah or other private locales on the coast. Sammie definitely knew his uncle was running drugs from Sapelo, though he could never prove how he obtained them in the first place. One time when Buzzut was drunk as a skunk and had fallen asleep on the trip up to Savannah, he noticed hundreds of little baggies of a white substance in his backpack. They had a small red skull logo stamped on them, but the skull had horns like the Devil. Also in the backpack were heavy stones.

Sammie wasn't dumb. He knew if for some reason the authorities flagged down their boat that Buzzut would simply sink the backpack in the water. On their return journey, that same backpack fell open in the boat when Buzzut passed out again. The drugs were gone. Inside were dozens of rolled-up wads of $100 bills. Sammie grabbed two rolls for himself and Buzzut never even knew they were missing. Those thousands of dollars allowed him to stock the house with months worth of much-needed food and staples for himself and his great-grandpa. Plus, he bought two new window air-conditioning units for each of their respective bedrooms.

This was the pattern with Buzzut. A backpack or two full of drugs about once a month, and a boat ride to some obscure location on the coast where Sammie would drop him off. Buzzut would then return onboard with the contents swapped out for loads of cash. Sammie never opened his mouth for fear of a beating; or worse if Buzzut ever used that shiny revolver of his. Being a virtual slave and an accessory to crime was a far cry from the happy days of growing up as an innocent, happy Saltwater Geechee child.

Sammie's childhood was spent exploring all around the tropical woodlands and marshes of Sapelo and Blackbeard Islands. Having the run of the islands gave him the greatest thrills. He and his friends would frequently swim or boat across Blackbeard Creek to the mysterious Blackbeard Island and explore the dark interior or walk the ocean side beach. They'd crack open oysters with a pocketknife and eat directly from the shell. It was a different world for a young black kid on the Sapelo compared to those on the other side: the mainland. He considered his home to be like a giant dangerous playground, given all the freedom he had.

He'd go wherever his feet led him and talked to whomever he encountered – for the residents looked out for their own – whether it was the traditional black folk or the outsider white property owners. Crime was non-existent. Doors remained unlocked. Keys stayed in vehicles. Kids could be kids, free from human predators who sought to harm them. Life was carefree and simple. It was the epitome of peace and quiet.

It's why the island was so popular with tourists longing for a similar escape. Those fed up with the rage, the divisiveness, the whirlwind pace of mainland society, retreated to Sapelo to slow down, to rejuvenate, to experience true freedom. But that flow of tourists, some 30,000 annually, had to be highly regulated so the island wouldn't become overrun. Tourism brought in a decent amount of money, and for some residents of Hog Hammock was a main source of income creating what few jobs there were. Unfortunately, the lack of good-paying jobs had almost pushed the Geechee people off the island for good. Mostly left behind now were the elderly folk fighting the extinction of their tiny black community.

Sammie's family never relied on tourism money, though. Going back many generations, they lived the true 'Salt Life' of fishing, crabbing, clamming, shrimping, and oyster harvesting. On land they hunted, trapped, lumbered, and farmed. They took what God offered and carved out a living.

Including moonshining.

Each member became independent at an early age and was expected to contribute to the family's well-being. It was the Greenhall way: the exact opposite of the safety-obsessed, overprotective helicopter parents who coddled their kids in mainstream society. One day on the Nannygoat Beach nature trail, he even saw a pathetic tourist family with small children all wearing safety helmets in case one of them fell down. God forbid.

Sammie missed his late parents and grandparents dearly. They truly were a fun loving close-knit family. Heck, he never needed a safety helmet when he hiked in the woods. His parents even taught him how to drive the family pick-up truck as soon as he could see over the steering wheel.

Since there were no police on the island and no speed limits either, his parents never gave a care. Nor did anyone else for that matter. As long as he didn't abuse the privilege, he could drive anywhere he wanted. Most of the time his father would let him drive the eight miles all the way down to Marsh Landing to catch the 7 a.m. ferry for school on the mainland. But the roads weren't like the paved roads on the mainland. Sapelo's roads had been around since 1868.

Every road on the north end of the island was a one lane, bumpy, muddy excuse for a road. The only paved roads were on the south end of the island near Hog Hammock. Even those didn't have any street lights. When it got dark, you either slowed down or you'd end up kissing a tree trunk.

And forget about getting a road repaired. McIntosh County government services were just about non-existent for the residents trying to eke out a living on the island while paying exorbitant property taxes. There was no door-to-door trash pick-up or mailman delivery services. If you wanted to get rid of your garbage, a drive to the big trash dumpsters in the middle of the island was in store. From there, a garbage truck would transport it to the Lumber Landing barge back to the mainland. If you wanted your mail, a drive to the post office over by the airstrip at Long Tabby was in order.

There was no ambulance on call. If you were seriously injured, EMTs from the mainland were 1-2 hours away depending on the weather. They would either come by helicopter or boat. If your house caught fire, the response was hit or miss. There were only three fire trucks on the island: one at the DNR headquarters, one at the UGA Marine Institute, and one in Hog Hammock. Everything depended on if the fire trucks were in working condition and enough volunteers could be raised to man them.

If you ventured out on your own on either Sapelo or Blackbeard Islands, you had to contend with poisonous eastern diamondback rattlesnakes and copperheads, bobcats, feral bulls, wild boars, and hungry alligators. It's why just about everyone had some kind of firearm in their home or carried one on their person. Being armed on Sapelo was truly self-defense, but not against other people.

Most of the remaining black residents in rustic Hog Hammock weren't rich. Most had trouble making ends meet. Growing up on the island was tough. Well into the 1970s they didn't have the modern staples of gas heat, electricity, air conditioning, plumbing, or telephones. The first telephone on the island came in 1972 and was in Hog Hammock. A man was on standby to answer it and took written messages to people who lived nearby.

Although life was hard for many, it also created a culture of self-sufficiency and perseverance. They hunted, they fished, and each had their own garden for food. Some even farmed their own cattle. A few cows and bulls escaped many years ago and now lived in the forest as nasty-looking, tick-infested feral beasts. It wasn't unusual to encounter them meandering along one of the dirt roads or trails or grazing alone in an open field. When a tourist would see one it just added further to the island's lore.

Some black folks couldn't bear the lifestyle and moved off the island for the city life with all its modern comfortable conveniences. The population on Sapelo continued its steady decline as a result.

But the Greenhall family was one of the few exceptions.

Growing up independent in the face of adversity was how they survived generation after generation dating as far back as the original slave family freed by Union General Sherman's troops during the Civil War. Through a partnership of former slaves in The William Hillery Company, in 1871 the Greenhall freedmen purchased one of the first 33-acre tracts of waterfront property just about a mile north of Raccoon Bluff near Drism Point.

The 'Bluff,' as everyone called it, was once an important port for the farmers on the north end of the island, especially during Reconstruction. Most had private docks leading down from the higher land to the shore of Blackbeard Creek, as well as boats to transport their various crops directly to the mainland for sale at large markets. Back in the old days, the Bluff subsequently turned into a separate thriving community of some 190 people complete with their own constable and a mailman. Women even had their own midwife to call on. There was a church, a school, a general store, and always a Greenhall root doctor – whether male or female – to cure ailments or inflict punishment. At one time it was the largest Geechee settlement on the island, rivaling Hog Hammock and the other enclaves. But the Bluff community slowly died out in the post-World War II period. The only structure that remained from the old town was the church, used just three times a year now.

During the 30-year reign of tobacco heir R. J. Reynolds Jr., when he owned most of the island and wanted to turn it into one big resort golf course, he persuaded most of the Gullah-Geechee families to resettle south to Hog Hammock. He had enticed them with land swaps and the luxury of new electrical service lines. Every family moved except the Greenhall family. They were the sole hold-outs.

In 1963, right before the sickly Reynolds left the island for good and moved to Europe, Duff Greenhall received the antique speedboat as a gift. He renamed it *Doctor Blackbeard*. No one knew the exact reason why Reynolds granted him such a luxury item given that Duff had bucked Reynolds and refused to give up his land. Others quietly had their suspicions, though, revolving around Reynolds being an excessive drinker who required a constant supply of his "medicine."

Since then, the surviving Greenhall tract of land had become the most isolated section of this most isolated island. Not one other permanent neighbor existed anymore. All of the other private citizens on the island – the mere 35 that now remained – lived down in Hog Hammock, some five miles away down East Perimeter Road. Sammie and his great-grandpa were the only two permanent residents left in Raccoon Bluff. Assessed at nearly $500,000 an acre, because of its Blackbeard Creek access to Sapelo Sound and the Atlantic Ocean, that original 33-acre tract of Greenhall estate was now worth well over $16 million. To the locals it was a mystery how LeShaun could afford to pay the annual property taxes every year.

Land had always been the most coveted asset on Sapelo dating back to the plantation colonial times. Both the black natives who could trace their ancestry back to the 1790s and the newer white residents who now owned homes all lived in harmony off the land. But some of those residents resented the mainland McIntosh County government for trying to turn their age-old holdings into mass tourism developments. The DNR and the UGA Marine Institute staff, however, respected the resident's use of their lands, their unique culture, and even employed many of the people who lived on the island.

The residents felt there was always a looming threat for higher tax-yielding resort hotels, golf-courses, or massive luxury vacation homes. The main reason why they resented the county government was that the island people paid full taxes on their lands but were afforded none of the services the mainlanders received. It was a matter of fairness and equality.

In 2012, the county slammed property owners extra hard when they re-assessed their land values after a fifteen-year hiatus. Anger and lawsuits ensued. The property tax of long-time residents increased 800% in some cases before the issued was finally resolved. The largest home in Hog Hammock, a secluded, massive compound across the marsh from Cabretta Island, had to be abandoned and foreclosed upon because the once-rich white owners had gone bankrupt and couldn't make payments. That's when Buzzut swooped in and purchased it off the market for dirt cheap: using the Greenhall family fortune as if it were his own ATM.

Now Buzzut's land alone was worth some $800,000 for just the three acres. His home was worth even more. Locals derogatorily named his house 'Versailles' because it was so big, gaudy, and out of place compared to their smaller cottage-like homes or trailers. What the locals really despised was the inhabitant within: LeShaun Greenhall, who lived like a king in their eyes. They considered him a cancerous tumor to the island ever since he slithered back home like the snake that he always had been.

Duff Greenhall, though, still kickin' at 93-years-old, was loved by just about everyone else. Since the tragic accident that took the rest of his family, Duff relied on young Sammie for most of his day-to-day needs. As the sole caregiver for the old man – without any help from his court-appointed permanent guardian LeShaun and rarely from others on Sapelo given their remote location – Sammie had it extra tough. The old man could still dress and bathe himself and frequently liked to make meals, but most of all he looked forward to the Wednesday night free community dinner.

Sammie would drive them in their old rusty pickup truck down to Hog Hammock just about every week for the traditional potluck dinner at *The Trough*. All the people in the community, black and white, even tourists and

UGA and DNR staff – with the lone exception of Buzzut – would gather in the one-room bar. They'd have a feast of barbecue ribs, fried chicken, pork sandwiches, scrumptious potato salad, spicy gumbo, and the island's own signature red peas, rice, and peppers dish. While kids played outside, people drank adult beverages and danced to music inside. The old timers, like Duff, took up many a card game, too. The party would last two to three hours until the friendly phrase, "get gone already," would be shouted for people that had to leave and get to bed for work.

After the younger folk left, leaving behind but a couple of Duff's old Masonic brothers, is when he'd break out his famous black flask. On it was a skull label of *Doctor Blackbeard's Elixir of Life*. The contents had come from a seemingly never-ending stash that he had kept hidden when he was distilling the liquor back in his prime. Only Sammie knew where the cache was located – a deeply held secret that men have died over.

Duff would pass the flask until it was empty. His saying was, 'sip it and pass it, brotha.' Sammie would imbibe, too, but limit himself since it was his responsibility to drive them home safely.

For the last five years of loyalty and caregiving that Sammie provided, his great grandfather frequently gave him cash to help out with groceries and supplies. Sammie's Pappy even recently rewarded him with the valuable skull ring and told him to cash that in for his future. If he was successful in selling it, he said he'd give him more rings. The boy didn't even know the full story himself of where the rings originally came from, but he was warned to never tell anyone. Ever.

Especially LeShaun.

It's why Sammie covertly met with the military collector and ended up getting himself in trouble. He broke orders and left the boat docked on River Street while LeShaun and some whore had dinner at one of the rooftop restaurants. By the time they boated back to Sapelo, Buzzut had whipped and slapped Sammie enough that he needed three Ibuprofen PMs just to get to sleep. Buzzut even threatened to kill that military collector and his two bitches for publicly disrespecting him like they did.

When Sammie pushed back again yesterday, telling his guardian he would take his beatings no longer – that in one more day he'd be a free man and in control of his own life – Sammie received the black eye.

Now today was that day of his emancipation.

For it was his eighteenth birthday, and according to Georgia state law, his abusive temporary guardian lost all rights to governing him. Sammie was now his own man. He would now have access to all the money he'd saved up over the years, totalling some $6,000 that went directly into his savings account.

Things were about to change for the good for him and Pappy. He just needed to approach Buzzut in a non-threatening manner to ask for his savings account information to be officially turned over to him so he could access his own money. That final showdown was scheduled for later on that night when he had unexpectedly been invited to a birthday dinner down at the big house, Versailles.

For now, though, he'd sit on the dock and enjoy the peace and quiet of the rest of the day. Sundays were his personal escape. He'd already checked on Pappy, who had been taking a midday nap back up at the house, so a bit of free time entailed. While most others on the south end of the island attended the two churches or did their chores on the mainland, Sammie liked to sit alone amid the ocean breeze and read. It was slow living, at one with the island. And this day of his birth would be no different.

Feeding Cleo another cheese cracker, Sammie perked up at the low hum of a powerboat making its way across the salt marsh. He gazed toward the wide tidal river of Blackbeard Creek, some 700-yards away, and barely saw the top of a boat cabin just above the tall *Spartina* marsh grass. Obviously, the creek was at low tide, down a good nine feet, as he'd usually be able to see the hull. Pleasure craft and fishing boats were a common site on the saltwater creek so he put his head back into his book.

A few minutes later, the sound of the cruising boat got a bit louder. This was unusual. He glanced up again. He could now see the boat slowly maneuvering up their little tributary, spooking a great blue heron.

Don't they know this is private property? There's a big No Trespassing sign at the junction, Sammie thought, getting angry. *Nobody comes up here. They know better.* Then he realized, he must have forgotten to close the gate upon returning from Savannah. Probably because Buzzut was whacking him so much.

Sammie stood up, threw his hat and sunglasses in his chair, and jogged down the dock to the old boat house. He went inside, then quickly emerged with his great-grandpa's beat-up, antique, .22-caliber, bolt action hunting rifle with a short scope and sling. He pulled back the bolt handle and made sure a round was jacked in the chamber, then raised the scope to his eye to see who was making the unwanted visit.

⬡

Sunday. Same time
Greenhall Landing

Jake eased his boat up the tidal tributary entering someone's private property. As captain, he made the decision to deliberately ignore the 'No Trespassing' sign. He figured he'd come all the way out here to the islands, spent all day looking, and the pirate flag was the best clue they'd found. Wouldn't hurt to simply take a peek.

While keeping his boat centered in the narrow, winding channel, his eyes flicked down to his depth finder dash display to make sure he didn't bottom out. There wasn't much room left. The digital display blinked at a mere four feet. Fortunately, his pontoon craft had a shallow draft, sitting higher in the water than most boats. Still, the low tide and the unknown of what could lie around the next bend made him somewhat jittery at becoming stuck in the mud on someone else's land.

The channel's width had been reduced significantly at low tide, making only a tight corridor for navigation. Viscous, dark-brown, oozy pluff mud banks sloped down from the *Spartina* grass on the top layer of the marsh prairie and exposed a moving world of tiny critters.

As he maneuvered his boat around yet another bend, he spooked a massive great blue heron. The blue-gray wading bird took flight and formed its slender neck into a tight 'S' shape, long legs trailing under its tail, wings beating a deep drumbeat to make its escape.

After admiring the bird for a moment, Jake glanced down at the pluff mud again. Swarms of fiddler crabs were dancing about, giving the illusion that the mud was pulsating. Wave after wave of these crabs scampered over large clumps of oysters and mussels that kept parts of the banks solid, like mortar in a stone wall.

While the boat putted along with Jake at the helm, Alex was busy as lookout, standing tall inside the enclosed glass cabin, powerful binoculars pressed to his eyes. He panned up the channel toward the tall bluff at the island's edge.

"Got something," he warned. "Dock with a boathouse, Zodiac boat tied up. Range 100 yards."

"Gotcha," Jake replied.

"Contact," Alex calmly stated, not ten seconds later after seeing an individual. "One on the dock. Black male. Overalls. Just came out of the boathouse. Armed with a hunting rifle. Uh oh, he just charged it . . . a-a-and . . . he's aiming at us. Shit! We've been made."

"Damn," said Jake, still pressing forward at a mere 5 mph. He opened a glove compartment in front of him on the dash and pulled out his handgun. Alex scampered to the rear of the cabin, found his backpack and took out his own sidearm.

"Hey man, take the helm, keep us in the middle of the channel," said Jake as the two switched sides. "Lemme see those binoculars."

Before even getting the binoculars up, he heard the distinct crack of a rifle report. A thin plume of water appeared in the creek ahead of them about 10 feet from the bow.

"For fuck sake! He shot at us," Alex shouted, ducking below the dash.

"Warning shot across our bow. Don't go any further!" yelled Jake, now looking through the binoculars and frantically trying to focus in on the man with the gun. He lost his balance as Alex throttled back to idle. Binocs back up, Jake finally zeroed in on the shooter just as he raised his head from his scope and pulled back the bolt handle of his rifle to chamber another round. Jake instantly recognized him.

"Shut it down, shut it down! Kill it!"

Alex turned the ignition key to the off position and the boat's dual props bubbled to silence. Jake turned around inside the cabin, went over to the dining area, and wrenched open a drawer above the mini-refrigerator and counter top with sink. The contents spilled on the floor. He picked up a white dish towel then pushed open the cabin's rear door and stepped outside onto the open stern deck.

Immediately, he raised the white towel and waved it in the direction of the dock. The binoculars were back up to his eyes and he noticed the young black man lower his weapon. Jake dropped the towel and cupped his hands around his mouth.

"It's Jake Tununda from Savannah!" he yelled as loud as he could. "I'm returning your ring!"

The boy waved his hand in a friendly gesture to approach. "Okay! Come on in," he yelled back to Jake, his voice easily traveling across the water. "Sorry to shoot at you, suh!"

Jake exhaled and shook his head with a smile, thinking how polite that kid is – even after shooting at them.

"Fire us up, Alex. Bring her in slowly. We found the boy."

𝕲

UPON MOORING *LIZZIE* AT THE GREENHALL Landing dock, the young man with a rifle, now slung over his bare shoulder, held out his hand and introduced himself. He said his name was Sammie Greenhall. He apologized once more for taking a warning shot at them, and asked bluntly how Jake found out where he lived.

"First, let me return your ring to you," said Jake handing over the SS *Totenkopf* ring to Sammie's outstretched hand. He immediately noticed Sammie's busted lip and black eye. "Not only did you forget *that*, but you also left *this* in my shop when your uncle showed up."

Jake fished from his pocket the crumpled piece of paper with the skull logo on it. "It was the only clue we had to try and find you. The black woman who came out of the bathroom with the gun, her name is Becky Holden. Well, she recognized that skull logo. Said it was for some famous moonshine made around Sapelo and Blackbeard Islands."

Sammie interrupted and started laughing. "That was great," he said in his thickly drawled accent. "My uncle didn't know what hit him. He thinks he's so bad-ass. I thought he was going to piss his pants when y'all pointed your guns at him."

"That was one close call." Jake grinned back, but he suddenly frowned. "Are you doing alright? You've got a nice shiner there. I figured that wasn't the first time he's hit you. I was about to knock the living shit outta him."

"Suh, I so wish you would have. Don't matter now. As of today, he's no longer my guardian. Today I turned 18-years-old and I am *emancipated*." Sammie straightened up and stood proudly, hitching a thumb in the shoulder strap of his faded overalls.

"Well, happy birthday to you, Sammie," said Alex. Jake offered the same congratulations.

"Thank you both."

"He live here on the island, too?" Alex asked. "That uncle of yours?"

"Buzzut?"

"Who?" Alex asked.

Sammie smirked. "I call him Buzzut. It's Gullah for *vulture*. His real name is LeShaun Greenhall."

"He live here with you?" Jake asked.

"No, just me and Pappy live up here all alone. Buzzut only comes up here when he wants me to boat him around the coast. He does live here on the island, though, down in Hog Hammock. The biggest home there is. We call it Versailles."

Jake pointed at Sammie. "He ever messes with you again, we'll take care of him. You just give us the word, okay, son?"

"Yaas'suh."

"Okay, you gotta stop calling us, sir. That's an order," Jake said with a wink. "Alex and I are retired out of the Army. Just call us by our first names."

"Okay, Mr. Jake," Sammie said, saluting as if he were one of Jake's enlisted men. He had no nervousness about him like their first meeting in Savannah. He was happy just to talk to someone.

"Come on, let's get y'all out of the sun. Follow me." Sammie led the way up the dock.

When he passed the boathouse, he told both men to hold on as he returned the rifle inside. Jake popped his head in and saw the black antique speedboat with the pirate flag lifted up out of the water.

Up the gangway and onto the head of the dock, Sammie gestured to several dirty plastic chairs under the shade of two massive live oak trees covered in spider-web-like Spanish moss.

"You know," said Jake, leaning back in the wobbly chair, "we would have never found this place except for the pirate flag down there at your gate. Same one on that old speedboat you got in the boathouse. I spotted you and your uncle taking off in it. That boat is what we've been searching for all day long. We went all the way up the Duplin River and checked-out every landing there was. We were about to head back home, but figured we'd come up Blackbeard Creek as a last look. Then saw the flag and the little creek here and decided to check it out since the gate was open. You got some big gonads taking a potshot at us!" Jake said jokingly.

"That's because ol' Pappy Duff Greenhall, my great-grandpa, taught me how to deal with you trespassers," said Sammie giving it right back to Jake. "Just kiddin'." He laid his *Nazi Gold* book on the dock next to him then replaced his straw hat on his head and took a seat. Out of nowhere a calico cat strutted up to Sammie's side and rubbed against his leg. Sammie reached down and scratched its back, sending its tail straight up.

Jake took curious note of the book Sammie was reading, but said nothing. Seems everything revolved around Nazis these days. From hyped up documentaries on Hitler, to books on the Monuments Men, to new war movies, and stolen Nazi trophies from West Point. Hell, even the President was routinely called a Nazi by hate-filled Leftists.

Leaning forward, elbows on knees, Sammie continued speaking. "He's the owner of *Doctor Blackbeard*. That's the name of the boat in there. And that's the secret name only a handful of folks know him by. He was moonshining here on the island way before I was even born. This here," he said, holding up the yellowed paper with the skull logo, "is his moonshine jar label. There's a bunch of these laying around the house." He flicked a thumb over his shoulder and Jake and Alex saw a modest, haint-blue painted, one-story, wrap-around porch style house with a rusted tin roof. It was about 75 yards away, framed by grand live oaks and a wide garden plot. "I use em like Post-It Notes."

"Did you say Duff Greenhall is your great-grandpa's name?" Alex asked.

"Yaas'suh. Err, I mean, yes, Mr. Alex."

"He's one of the last surviving Buffalo Soldiers from World War Two, isn't that right?" Alex asked.

"Mm-hmm," nodded Sammie.

"I've read about him, watched some of his interviews," said Alex. "One helluva man. One helluva soldier. A real legend."

Sammie nodded again. "I'd introduce you to him. He'd like that since you're both Army soldiers like him, but he's taking his nap now. Usually sleeps all afternoon. He needs it at his age. Hasn't been doing well lately."

"That's okay. Maybe another time," Jake said. "We don't want to impose more than we already have. Thanks for not having us arrested." He winked.

"There's no police on the island to do the arresting," Sammie stated. "It's why we shoot first and ask questions later, as Pappy taught me."

"I like this kid!" said Alex, cracking Jake on the arm.

"Can I ask you about that logo?" said Jake. "I'm really curious. You see that double 'X' on the forehead?" He watched Sammie squint at the symbol. "Is that symbol supposed to be similar to this one here on my ring?" Jake held out his right hand and showed Sammie his large gold and ruby Masonic ring with the square and compasses icon.

Sammie's eyes went wide and he immediately said he had seen that same symbol for sure. "Pappy has a ring just like it. He's a Freemason."

"Freakin' knew it," exclaimed Jake, slapping his knee.

"A Prince Hall Mason," Sammie explained. "My late father was one, my late grandfather was one. I was hoping to be one, too, someday, but the lodge they belonged to stopped meeting a long time ago. Used to meet in the Farmer's Alliance Hall in Hog Hammock. There's a Mason symbol there up on the second floor."

"I see," said Jake softly. "I'm sorry about the loss of your father and grandfather."

"Thank you, Mr. Jake. Lost *both* my parents and *both* my grandparents in a car wreck five years ago."

"Oh God, son, I'm so sorry," Jake lamented again. "I lost both my parents, too, in a car wreck. They were drunk driving. I feel your pain, Sammie. I really do. Only time heals and time is so damn awfully slow."

"Not a day goes by I don't think of them," Sammie said, eyes distantly staring off to the horizon on the ocean. "Some illegal alien was texting and driving, crossed the I-95 and hit the church van they were all riding in. Head on." He sighed deeply. "I don't understand God sometimes. Everyone in my family died and the illegal guy lived. He never even got deported. That's when Buzzut became my guardian. Don't know why I deserved all this punishment."

It became very quiet. Only the wind blowing through the tops of the trees could be heard.

"You said he's the one that gave you the ring, right?" Jake asked, deliberately changing the subject. "Duff, that is?"

Sammie nodded and pulled the *Totenkopf* ring out of his overall's chest pocket. He held it in his hand.

Jake explained the reason they were seeking him out. That the ring was in fact confirmed to be authentic by experts. He told him it was worth a lot of money. "I'd like to purchase it from you if you're still offering it for sale."

Sammie sat back, stunned. "Sure. Okay, Mr. Jake. I would like to sell it. I really need the money."

"How much do you want for it?" Jake asked, assuming the young man already had a ballpark figure of what they were going for.

"How much do you think it's worth?" Sammie countered, either seemingly unaware of the market value or feeling Jake out for his price.

Jake didn't answer. Instead, he reached for a thick envelope in his cargo pant pocket.

Sammie seemed kind of rattled at Jake's non-answer. He blurted out, "I guess I'd take $500 for it, if that's okay with you?"

Jake's eyebrows lifted and he looked at Alex.

"Sammie, you have any idea how much that ring is worth?" Alex asked.

Sammie looked down, dejected, and shook his head.

Jake stood up and turned his back to Sammie. He opened up the thick envelope and counted out a bunch of $100 bills. Once he was finished, he held out the stack of cash to the boy. "Sammie, will you accept *seven thousand, five hundred* dollars instead?"

"What?" Sammie shifted in his old, crappy plastic chair and one of the legs twisted. With a crack, it snapped. He fell backward and collapsed on the dock, flat on his ass.

Jake and Alex couldn't help but belch with laughter. Sammie busted up, too, giggling uncontrollably. They helped the kid up and straightened his crooked hat. When they had composed themselves, Jake held out the wad of cash again.

"I'm not kidding you," he said in all seriousness. "These SS rings are worth a lot of money the world over. Extremely rare to find one. They range in value from seven to eleven thousand dollars. I'm prepared to offer you seventy-five hundred in cash right now since I don't know the ring bearer's name, nor the provenance of where or how your great-grandpa obtained this ring. Will you accept my offer?"

"Y-y-yes, Mr. Jake, I will," Sammie stuttered, still shocked at the unexpected value of the ring. He immediately gave Jake the ring back and gladly accepted the most money he's ever held in his hands in his entire life.

Jake placed the *Totenkopf* ring on his index finger. He witnessed the thrilled expression on Sammie's face as he fanned the cash out in his hands before stuffing the wad deep in his pant pocket.

It was that 'wow' moment that rarely happened in someone's lifetime and Jake had just made it happen for this young man. Right then and there is what he knew to be the core reason why he wanted to share his artifact collection with military history lovers: to give them their own 'wow' moment. He patted the young man on the shoulder, then held out his hand for a final shake to seal the deal. An ecstatic Sammie gladly accepted the handshake with a huge smile on his face. Sammie also shook Alex's hand.

"Now, I've got one question to ask before we get going," said Jake. "You mentioned back at my shop you were going to use this money for capital investment. What are you investing in exactly?"

"It's an old family business that has been around for generations." Sammie pulled out the skull logo card from his breast pocket. He handed the card to Jake. "Here, you keep it. This business has been asleep for many years and I'm going to wake it up."

"You're kidding me?" said Jake.

"Nope," said Sammie, taking off his straw hat and holding it in his hands. "In my senior year of high school, I took an AP course and was taught how to write a business plan. The teacher wanted us to use something or someone in our family history as the basis for a hypothetical business. That's what the assignment was. The only thing I knew our family was famous for was illegal moonshining."

"That's what I've heard, too," Jake said. "Some famous moonshine."

"Uh-huh," said Sammie, continuing. "My dream is to revive *Doctor Blackbeard's Elixir of Life*, legally, that is. I want to start a moonshining distillery open to the public right here on the Greenhall estate. I want to distribute that 'shine to the mainland, all across the South. I have Pappy's blessing and he's been schooling me in all the new distilling equipment I'm gonna need to get started, new buildings to construct, new dock, new boat, all the costs involved and employees I'd need to help me run it."

"Wow!" said Alex.

"Next step is figuring out all the government permits and regulations and fees and stuff I don't even know yet. I hear it could take years to cut through the red tape. But in the meantime, Pappy's been tutoring me in his secret ingredients and techniques that made him a legend. We've got a little kitchen distillery set up in the house we run tests with." Sammie grinned. "I've been studying and writing everything down so it'll never get lost again. You could say I'm in the exploratory phase of my business plan."

"From what I've heard," Jake said, "that *Elixir of Life* was the best moonshine ever made along the entire Gold Coast. That back in the day even some Presidents drank it when visiting the rich island resorts. I hope I have the honor to taste it one day when you open up your business."

"You will, Mr. Jake," Sammie said, all fired up, his passion on the topic quite obvious. "My goal is to revive the Greenhall estate back to a working farm the way it once was and make jobs for the locals on the island. I guess the term for it these days is 'agri-business.' Pappy said moonshining needs three ingredients to be successful: One – corn for the corn meal that creates the mash. Two – a pure water source. Three – secrecy.

"Well, we've got 33 acres of land here to grow corn on like the family did years ago. We've got a natural artesian well on the property with the finest drinking water on the island that Pappy used when he was moonshining. *And*, we don't need secrecy anymore since I'm going to make this a legal business and not break the law. So, I've got what it takes, I just need the money to make it all work. *Lots* of money."

Jake and Alex were transfixed by the kid's story. It was like they were listening to an experienced adult businessman. They knew what he was going through since they had just started their own businesses for the first time in their respective careers, as well.

"As part of the business course, I had to interview some of the locals who've lived on Sapelo all their lives," said Sammie, now in motor-mouth mode. "These elders taught me the history and how this island was once a really successful farming community of black freedmen after the slave plantation days. And how moonshining was an integral part of the culture. Just about everyone did it. There's many stories of the white revenuers coming on the island trying to arrest them. Even the first Doctor Blackbeard. But they never could. These elders also taught me how important it was to keep this here Greenhall property sacred and always in the family and to never let it be sold off or confiscated by the government like all the rest of the land on the island was."

"That is so true," said Jake. "Preserving your heritage is paramount."

"Well, there's no one really left in my family anymore. I mean I got relatives far away in other cities, but they take no interest in the land. They're outsiders and look down on us. Pappy's gonna be gone soon and I'm it," he said sadly. "He said I'd be the official caretaker and would inherit the land. Taught me what the word 'legacy' really means. I don't ever want to move away either because this is all I know, so I've got to do something to save this land and all the property taxes owed on it year after year."

"That's a huge expense," said Alex.

"That asshole Buzzut was responsible for running the family finances and paying all the taxes out of my mama's and papa's savings and even my grandparents. They had nice life insurance policies that really helped out. But, I don't even know if there's much money left anymore. Now all that responsibility is gonna be on me. I'm the man now. I gotta own up to it. And since going to college doesn't look to be in my future, then I've gotta shoot for something else: a business."

"Son, you are going to be very successful, I can already tell," said Alex, placing a hand on Sammie's shoulder as he offered encouragement. "You're a very smart young man and years ahead of some of those college snowflakes out there. You're educated in *real life*. You're gonna make this happen one day. And like Jake said, I'm also looking forward to having that first drink of moonshine with you."

Jake caught Alex's tone that they needed to leave. "Listen, Sammie, thanks for sharing your dream with us," Jake said, looking at his wrist watch. "You've got all the character traits and initiative needed to meet your goals. I want to wish you all the luck in the world and I hope that cash you've got there will help out. But I've gotta get back home to Skidaway Island and Alex and his wife need to catch a plane tonight for a trip up to D.C. Is there any way that you can get me the full story from your Pappy Duff on how he obtained this ring?" Jake held up his index finger with the *Totenkopf* ring on it.

"Yes, Mr. Jake. No problem. I'll talk to him when he wakes up. How do I reach you? We don't have a house phone or even a cell phone."

"Got email?" asked Alex.

"No, we don't have the internet up here either," said Sammie, looking embarrassed. "I suppose I could ask someone down in Hog Hammock to borrow their phone. Or I can use the computer at the library to email you."

"What you need to do," blurted Alex, "is use some of that money there and buy yourself your own cell phone and a laptop computer. You're going to need both for business."

"Yes, Mr. Alex. I'll do that."

"Here's my card," said Jake, handing him his *Tununda's Military Menagerie* card from his wallet. "My cell phone is my personal and business phone. One and the same. Call me anytime with that information, okay? Or if you have any more problems with that uncle of yours, Buzzut."

Sammie agreed and thanked them both again. "Please do come visit again sometime. If you drive down, I can get you authorized on the ferry, no problem since I'm a resident. Or if you want to boat in again, you can dock here anytime you want. I promise we won't shoot at you!" This time the kid winked back at Jake.

He then walked them down the length of the dock to help them shove off. "Looks like the tide is already coming back in. It'll be much easier getting out."

He unraveled their line and Jake and Alex jumped back onto *Lizzie*. Soon she was fired up with Jake at the helm. As he turned the boat around to head back down the tributary, Sammie dashed back into the boathouse. He emerged with something shiny in his hand and ran back down to the end of the dock.

He reached out as the boat passed and handed Alex a Mason jar of moonshine with the Doctor Blackbeard skull label attached to it. A small white object floated around on the bottom of liquor jar.

"Enjoy!" Sammie said. "It's aged about 30 years. 120 proof. Plus, you got a rare jar with an alligator tooth in it. Just wait until you get home to drink it. Trust me!"

Alex slipped inside the cabin and showed Jake the parting gift. They switched spots and Jake stepped out onto the stern deck as they pulled away for the dock. He raised the moonshine jar and waved to Sammie his thanks.

"Oh, I forgot to tell you, Mr. Jake," shouted Sammie. "Pappy says he's got more rings where that first one came from. Would you be interested in buying some more?"

Jake's jaw dropped, speechless. The rings were rare enough as it was and now there were more available? He nodded his head up and down like a bobblehead doll. Finally, he blurted, "Yes! Give me a call when you've got them. I need to know the full story behind them, okay? Talk to your Pappy for me."

"Will do." shouted Sammie. "Godspeed!"

7

DARKNESS FELL QUICKLY OVER THE RURAL cemetery just outside the quiet south Georgia city of Fitzgerald. That meant it was go-time for Phoenix to retrieve his stash. Having already driven in and walked about the cemetery during daylight hours, he knew exactly which grave slab he'd go to at night. He'd thoroughly scouted the area and devised a plan of entry that would minimize the risk of being seen by some of the nearby residents. It was a far cry from when he first arrived here with Mona Lisa over a year ago and had to hastily jump a farmer's fence and deal with a noisy flock of Burmese chickens.

Those brightly colored chickens had the run of the city. It was one of Fitzgerald's claims to fame, the result of an agricultural project in the 1960s that had gone terribly wrong. Now they were somewhat of a menace anywhere you went in town. He hoped to hell they wouldn't show up for a return visit tonight. The good thing was they were nowhere to be found during his walk-through just hours before.

The next decision was where to park for his getaway. As in any job, getting away safely was his number one planning priority. Phoenix parked his Honda Accord rental car directly across Evergreen Road from the cemetery's main entrance at the now empty Bryant Theological Seminary's paved lot. Earlier in the day, the parking lot was full with students and staff of the tiny, four-building Bible college and conference center. With dense trees and brush providing extra cover along the backside of a long rectangular, one-story brick hall, Phoenix figured it was the least conspicuous place to park, given he didn't have many other choices. When it was dark enough, he had merely crept down the length of the building until he reached the two-lane Evergreen Road.

Once clear of passing cars, he dashed across the road and up the tree-lined entrance to the cemetery's closed main gates. Dressed all in black, from a black winter cap to black gloves and black boots, even with a black backpack strapped to his back, he was a just another shadow against a cloud-filled, dark canopy.

A five-foot high, ornamental iron fence with spiked tips lined the perimeter of the cemetery. Although he could scale the fence to enter, he didn't want to take the chance of injuring himself. Instead, he crept toward the main iron gateway. Brick columns with gradual heights and eight-foot brick walls stood on each side of the gates. Where the spiked perimeter fence met the shortest of the brick columns, he merely had to find the right foothold and climbed his way up and over the column to land on the soft sandy soil of the cemetery below.

Within a minute of walking, he reached General W. J. Bush Avenue where he made a right. Just up the gravel road on his left he came to the Bush family plot, the most visited grave in the cemetery and one of the other claims of fame for Fitzgerald. Here was the horizontal grave slab of General William Joshua Bush, the last of the 368,000 Georgia Confederate veterans of the Civil War to die. Engraved on his headstone was a Masonic symbol and the years his life spanned. He was 107-years-old when he died in 1952.

Phoenix had picked this grave to hide his treasure simply because it would be easy to remember. He knew nothing of the history, nor even cared, of the occupant interred within. Extracting a black foldable military shovel from his backpack, he got down on his hands and knees and immediately began digging at the head of Bush's grave.

After a few minutes of turning soil, he shined a long-handled black Maglite onto the disturbed ground. Still didn't seem deep enough, still hadn't hit the metal ammo container he'd stashed the two Nazi trophies in. Keeping the flashlight on, but angled down into the hole, he continued the dirty work.

A minute later he heard the beautiful sound of metal on metal. Phoenix now dug frantically with gloved hands. An olive green ammo can, thick as a college textbook, revealed itself. More digging and it loosened up in the soil. He grasped the top with both hands and tugged until it came free.

After cleaning dirt off the metal locking clasp, he flipped open the top and pointed his flashlight inside. His items were there. Pulling out a long cloth wrapped into a tube shape, he unfolded a portion of it to expose Hermann Göering's ceremonial ivory baton. He slipped it back in the can.

Next he pulled out a small wooden box, lifted the cover and saw Adolf Hitler's gold-plated pistol still sitting inside with a spare magazine and cleaning brush. Phoenix smiled, shut the box, and also placed it back in the can. He stuffed the can inside his backpack along with the shovel, but held the flashlight in case he needed it.

Exiting the cemetery the same way he climbed in, he dashed across the road and again snuck behind the long hall at the seminary. As he turned the corner to the parking lot, he froze in his tracks.

There, parked behind his rental car, was a black and white cop car, headlights ablaze on his rental. Phoenix stood still, not ten feet behind the cruiser. The cop was still inside. Panic crept over him and his breathing increased. He slowly backed away behind the building again and looked around the corner, hoping the cop didn't see him in his rear view mirror.

The cop suddenly got out of his patrol car. Phoenix held his breath. The cop then left his door open, flicked on a flashlight, and walked toward the rental. Phoenix exhaled. In the headlights, Phoenix saw that he was a tall, wide-hipped, white man with close-cropped gray hair, a gray mustache, and uniformed in dark blue.

Phoenix started to sweat. He didn't know what to do. That cop stood between him and his only means of escape. And more than likely another damn cruiser would show up within minutes. He had to act.

Emerging from behind the building Phoenix ducked low, then crept right up to the rear bumper of the cruiser making sure his footsteps weren't too heavy on the pavement. He noticed the cop was now peering into the rental's interior with his flashlight.

Phoenix's hands shook. He grasped his own heavy flashlight in his right hand like a club. It would have to do, he decided.

He could now hear the cop speaking with a deep Southern drawl into his portable radio microphone clasped to his chest. He heard the cop tell police dispatch that he thought the vehicle might have been left behind by one of the seminary staff or students since it looked brand new. The cop then started walking back to his patrol car as the radio chirped again. He said '10-4', but then stopped at his driver's side quarter panel and turned to face the rear of the rental lit up in his headlights.

At that very instant, Phoenix thought the cop was going to rattle off the tag number of the rental back to dispatch. This would ultimately trace back to who rented the car. He couldn't let that happen.

He stepped out from behind the cruiser and took long, light strides toward the unaware cop. He raised the flashlight as he approached and then will all his force swung it upwards like a batter going for a high pitch.

The heavy blow struck the back of the cop's skull with such force it shattered the lens in the flashlight and caused Phoenix to stumble forward, trip over his own feet, and crash to the pavement while losing his knit cap. Upon impact of the flashlight, the cop was knocked unconscious while still on his feet. The blow spun him around and he fell backward like a chopped tree. He bounced the back of his head on the pavement like a bowling ball being dropped. The sound was sickening.

Taking deep breaths, Phoenix got to his hands and knees. Sweat covered his face, ran down his neck, and soaked the ends of his long blond hair. He crawled over to the prone cop and wasted no time in pillaging the cop's sidearm from its holster, figuring he might as well arm himself. He also snagged two spare magazines from the cop's utility belt, and stole his portable radio, too. His eyes then drifted over to the cop's eyes. They were open, unblinking, fixed in a deathly stare.

"Shit!" Phoenix took off his gloves and placed two fingers on the carotid artery at the cop's neck. No pulse. "Fuck! Fuck! Fuck!"

The double blunt force trauma to the back of the cop's head had instantly killed the 20-year veteran. The first blow landed on the lower part of the back of the skull where the pons and brain stem are located, knocking the victim out where he stood. When his head then smashed on the pavement in the same traumatized area, the brain herniated down the spinal cord causing irreversible damage and death.

Phoenix tried to find a pulse on the cop's wrist next. Still nothing. He placed his hands over his own eyes. "Oh God, what have I done?"

Exhaling deeply, he got up and stumbled to his car. He fumbled with the keys to open it, and got in. Tossing the cop's pistol, mags, and radio on the front passenger seat, he then shed the backpack and placed it on the passenger floor before firing up the Honda.

Peeling out of the parking lot, he knew he had to head east per his pre-planned escape route, so he turned left onto Benjamin Hill Drive, then hit a red light at the intersection of Evergreen Road. Looking both ways to make sure no cars were coming, he stayed on the gas and blew through the red light, turning left again in a wild fishtail of screeching tires.

Not ten seconds later, police dispatch came over the portable radio with a young, female voice in a Southern accent. *"Dispatch to Car-215, sorry for the delay. That Georgia tag number you gave us is registered to Avis Car Rental. We're on the line now with their state office to find out who it's rented to or if its been reported stolen. Over?"*

"No! No! No!" Phoenix shouted, realizing the cop had already given the tag number to dispatch way before he assaulted him. He knew he was fucked now and pounded the steering wheel.

"Car-215, you copy? Over?"

Phoenix grabbed the portable radio, took a deep breath, and keyed the mic. In his best Southern drawl, he replied, "10-4, Dispatch. I copy." The 10-4 sounded like 'tan-fore.'

Thirty long seconds after that, Dispatch radioed again.

"Car-215, that Honda Accord is rented to a Nathan Kenneth Kull. K.U.L.L., out of New York City. Rented it from Hartsfield-International this afternoon. Over?"

Phoenix's eyes glazed over. He stared down the dark road ahead of him. His car slowly drifted over the center double yellow line. He grew dizzy.

The police radio crackled again, snapping him out of his trance. He swerved back into his lane.

"*Car-215, you copy last? Over?*"

Phoenix held the mic in his hand, blinking uncontrollably. Confusion overtook him. Couldn't think straight. Hearing his own name on the police radio simply blew his mind. Bile rose from his stomach.

He knew he'd fucked up royally using his own name and credit card to rent the car, and not one of the alias identities he'd brought. He'd become complacent with his own rules thinking the retrieval of his stash would be a cakewalk. Cockiness had cost him everything. Once they found that cop, there would be a massive manhunt out for him. Not for Phoenix, the master thief, but Nathan Kull, security consultant. And cop-killer.

"*Car-215, what's your status? Over?*"

Kull dropped the mic on the seat. A different image now flashed before his eyes: the teenage Sureños-13 gangbanger he had beaten and stabbed to death in Atlanta. His name was Flaco. That dead boy unwittingly stumbled upon Nathan Kull's true identity, too, and paid the price.

And now Flaco's battered and bloody face laughed at him, telling him he wouldn't get away with murder again this time.

"*Dispatch to any available unit. Car-215 is not responding. Please proceed to last location at Bryant Theological Seminary. Corner of Evergreen Road and Benjamin Hill Drive. Over?*"

As Kull sped down Evergreen Road, he topped a small rise and saw headlights coming toward him. Suddenly, blue flashing lights appeared on top of the oncoming vehicle. His eye's went wide, he took his foot off the gas, and unconsciously held his breath. Flaco's laugh echoed in his ears.

"*Dispatch, this is Car-325. I've got that call. Two minutes out. Over.*"

"*10-4, Car-325.*"

The lit-up cop car tore past Kull. He exhaled.

Driving in a paranoid daze for the next two minutes, he finally heard the dreaded words he knew would come.

"*Officer down! Officer down!*"

8

LESHAUN GREENHALL PULLED THE LIMP, STEAMING
hot dog from the microwave and slapped it into a semi-defrosted
bun sitting on a cheap paper plate. He then rudely splattered some liquefied
ketchup over it, stabbed it with a white birthday candle, and lit the candle.

Specially prepared and delivered for him from *Lula's Kitchen* was his
own dinner. On a lovely porcelain plate sat a full rack of barbecue ribs,
baked beans, and cornbread. He strutted into his sprawling dining room,
placed his scrumptious dinner at the head of his dining room table next to
a glass of red wine, and walked the candlelit hot dog to the other end where
he slid it in front of his nephew, Sammie.

"Happy eighteenth birthday, mutha fucka!" He slapped Sammie upside
the back of his head, then took his seat and dove into his ribs.

Sammie just sat there, looking on the verge of tears. LeShaun laughed
at yet another one of his blatant demeaning provocations. He hated this
kid, hated the whole damn Greenhall family ever since he left the island
when he turned eighteen himself. He wanted nothing to do with Geechees.
He loathed this poverty-stricken community, its pathetic people clinging to
their so-called African cultural lifestyle. All his nephew and the old man
were good for was a boat ride and a free source of income for the last five
years. Now he was forced to abdicate his gravy train.

Regardless, as the executor of the estate, the power of attorney, the conservator, and legal guardian of both Sammie and Duff Greenhall, he had milked the pair for all they were worth. The old man had made a fortune in his lifetime back when he was making moonshine. Greenhall kinfolk also worked themselves to the bone in various hard labor jobs most of their lives, but all they did was just sock their earnings away. They hardly spent a dime of it – only on the essentials of life. They also had this strange philosophy to never let their family ancestral lands fall into an outsider's hands. Sure LeShaun kept up with the high annual property taxes and used the Greenhall money to pay for Duff and Sammie's needs, but he also blatantly broke the law and used the family fortune for his own means. He justified it by saying he *was* family after all.

All the same, he knew the day would come where Sammie had to be let go. And even though he was still Duff's permanent guardian, he knew the incapacitated older man wouldn't live long anyway. He needed to look out for his own future and to establish a new source of income preying on others. It's why he went into a secret new business over a year ago.

Walking Nannygoat Beach when he first arrived, he'd noticed a family visiting the island playing with a toy drone. As that drone flew up and down the beach, it kept passing over a blurry image on the horizon: a massive container ship. A seed was planted.

Night and day these freighters quietly passed by. LeShaun knew full well that among the thousands of the steel containers stacked on their decks a select few held illicit goods bound for American ports. And because of the sheer millions that came in on an annual basis into ports like Savannah, only a small fraction of those containers actually got inspected.

With the ongoing construction of the formidable border wall with Mexico, coupled with aggressive law enforcement, the flow of drugs across land routes was drying up. Just about every land transportation means available had already been tried previous to the wall: cargo planes, buses, rail cars, tractor trailers, automobiles, tunnels, and even human mules. Drone smuggling over the wall was also tried, but with limited success due to the saturation of border patrol agents and surveillance. Plus, they could only smuggle small amounts of contraband and drugs, and the drones used were small, poorly-made, off-the-shelf consumer brands.

Now, the majority of drugs smuggled in from the big Mexican and South American cartels were moving by water again just as they had during the 1980s. Squeeze one area with law enforcement, and the cartels had enough money, technology, and manpower to expand their operations somewhere else. It was like a big water balloon that would never bust.

From the smallest sailboats and private pleasure craft, to fishing boats, luxury yachts, narco-subs, and the largest container ships, drugs were still flowing into America to quench its consumer demands. Everyone in the supply chain was making loads of hard cash, and LeShaun wanted a piece of the action. But his idea would prove ingenious – literally flying above the competition.

LeShaun wanted to start a Georgia maritime trafficking and distribution network based on off-loading goods from container ships with larger workhorse narco-drones *before* the ships hit major ports.

The most important observation he made was that the U.S. Coast Guard and other federal and local maritime law enforcement agencies were virtually non-existent in this remote stretch of the Georgia coastal islands. Instead, they had their hands full in the Savannah port area and popular beach resort islands like Tybee and St. Simons.

Even the lone Georgia Department of Natural Resources (DNR) conservation ranger, the only law enforcement arm on Sapelo, was seldom seen since no crimes ever took place. He instead rotated from island to island enforcing hunting and fishing regulations. In fact, the last major crime that took place on Sapelo was an older resident who was caught smuggling sea turtle eggs off the island via the ferry. He sold them on the black market for $25 each as "party favors" to mainlanders looking for a mythical aphrodisiac. The dumb ass spent almost two years in federal prison for the poaching offense – his second bust for the same crime.

With no other state or McIntosh County law enforcement on the island, the opportunity to smuggle drugs in was ripe for the picking. The fear of getting caught was merely an afterthought. You didn't even need an FAA permit to fly a drone if you kept it under 400 feet.

LeShaun's idea soon became an obsession. He started buying various civilian drones to learn how to fly. With small drones that fit in the palm of his hand, he gradually worked his way up in size and complexity. Finding a remote stretch of beach on the south leg of Cabretta Island, he trained in obscurity, flying the machines up and down the coastline.

His skills improved dramatically as he flew in harsher wind climates over the ocean and at greater distances. He enrolled in drone flying lessons with a remote controlled aircraft hobbyist club on the mainland and soon became one of the best student enthusiasts, even entering in several drone races using a First Person View (FPV) video goggle headset.

At one time, he became so consumed with drone technology that he even stole a firefighting drone prototype developed by a start-up company who was putting on public demonstrations for Sapelo Island's DNR fire management program. Aimed at improving wildlife habitat and reducing the chances of wildfire, the dense underbrush typically went through a rotation of prescribed or controlled burns. But on Sapelo, manpower was limited and the safety of firefighting personnel venturing into remote, inaccessible areas was paramount. Instead of sending a man in on foot to light a fire and possibly getting trapped in it, the start-up company developed a drone that would drop 'Dragon Eggs' into areas to be burned.

Using ping-pong ball sized orbs, the drone had an on-board mechanism that injected a liquid into the plastic spheres to start a delayed chemical reaction which allowed the balls to fall to the ground before igniting with ground fuel of brush and grass. The drone even had a thermal imaging camera to detect heat signatures.

LeShaun was so impressed with the potential for other sinister uses, he knew he needed to grab one of these drone units for himself. And this he did one night, breaking into the company's storage trailer as it sat in the parking lot at Lumber Landing waiting for transport back on the barge. A subsequent criminal investigation into the theft almost nabbed him when someone said they thought they saw him in the parking lot that night. He played the classic 'don't know nuffin' card and the case went cold. The company took the loss while LeShaun had a future toy hidden away inside his compound.

With his acquired drone flying skills, keen knowledge of the technology, and observations of law enforcement practices, LeShaun felt confident enough to take the biggest risk of his life. It was time to make a proposal and find an investor. And why not go for broke?

Calling on his old drug dealer contacts in Miami, he eventually received an audience with a regional VP of the Mexican Sinaloa Cartel – the Southeast boss responsible for distribution. Being the most powerful drug smuggling, trafficking, money laundering, and organized crime syndicate in the world, the Sinaloa Cartel, or Blood Alliance as they were called on the streets, were always willing to thwart their competitors or law enforcement with new ideas. Staying ahead of their enemy's practices in the multi-billion dollar illegal drug smuggling industry was a constant battle.

LeShaun proposed using the latest drone delivery technology just like UPS, FedEx, and Amazon were doing, but his maritime narco-drone would travel only by night, blacked out, and would elude all the latest surveillance technology from law enforcement.

Plus, his drone would be capable of carrying larger loads up to 40 lbs and at higher speeds than normal ones. The beauty of it all was that it would be remote controlled and authorities could never prove who exactly was flying the aircraft. They could never identify a live human being with direct evidence of drug smuggling. No one would go to prison for a crime. And if a drone was ever lost at sea it could easily be tracked by GPS and retrieved since it was light enough that it wouldn't sink. The Miami boss loved the idea and so it went up the chain of command eventually getting LeShaun instant buy-in with top officials of the cartel. They decided to bankroll his project and turn him into a franchise.

Soon that initial seed of thought on Nannygoat Beach took physical fruition. Engineers on the cartel's payroll started building and testing a maritime narco-drone prototype. They consulted with LeShaun closely and had him visit Mexico on numerous occasions for test flights.

Ultimately, they developed a giant quad copter delivery drone system piloted with FPV goggles and capable of high speeds, flips, and even flying upside down if need be. It was lightweight and could be lifted easily by one person. Their drone performed extremely well in windy conditions, nighttime operations, and even on autopilot landings on moving boats.

LeShaun even became a bit of a celebrity within cartel management. They had high hopes for him as a pioneer in a new avenue of distribution. It was a crucial investment they were banking on for future profits. If successful, his idea to utilize offshore mother ships and swarms of drone deliveries by select smugglers all along the southeast coast would prove an advanced technological leap for the cartel.

LeShaun's maritime narco-drone then finally went into operation. While the regional boss and his security contingent took the island ferry over and rented out Reynolds Mansion for several days under the pretense of a corporate retreat, other cartel members secretly delivered the drone by boat. At night they met LeShaun up a tidal creek location called Big Hole at the end of Cabretta Island – his secret launch pad site. The Southeast cartel VP soon witnessed LeShaun's maiden flight. He mentioned that the drone sounded like a bumblebee. The name stuck and soon became LeShaun's radio ID.

Communicating on his handheld, two-way radio directly with a cartel-controlled container ship passing through the shipping lane off the coast of Sapelo Island, LeShaun flew a watertight bin of Greenhall family cash outbound. A half hour later he received his first shipment inbound: 15 kilos or 33 lbs. of cocaine. It was a highly successful and impressive round trip. The regional boss even threw a party at the rented Reynolds Mansion the next day, with everyone indulging in some of the same cocaine that was flown in by Bumblebee.

Over the next few weeks, using the island ferry and with his personal vehicle, he delivered the goods to trusted mainland distributors also on the payroll of the Blood Alliance. In the end, he netted a massive profit.

LeShaun's next drone shipments became even more profitable, but deadlier, for the consumer. He was landing 'Fire,' heroin cut with fentanyl; 'Flakka,' a synthetic drug like bath salts; 'Liquid O,' black tar heroin in water-based form; and 'Devil's Breath,' which literally created zombies out of people whose actions could be controlled and who would answer any question truthfully. They all came neatly packaged and labeled, like a pharmacy on wings. All he had to do was disperse it to his dealers.

His shipments alone proved to be responsible for hundreds of overdose deaths once they made it to the streets. Not only did his products saturate the coastal lowland population, but eventually they reached much larger cities up and down the Eastern coast. Cities like Jacksonville, Savannah, Charleston, and even inland to Atlanta.

But LeShaun didn't give a shit where his product ended up. Wasn't his problem. Consumers demanded it. In 2016 alone, there were over 64,000 people killed from opioid overdoses, more than all 58,000 American military deaths in the 12-year long Vietnam War. Hell, he even remembered growing up in the 1980s in McIntosh County when there were more slaves to drugs than there were slaves to whites during the plantation days. Back then, drug dealing went on at hidden juke-joints, private clubs, and bars. The same places where his family's famous moonshine flowed all night. The night clubs had been covers for the highly profitable drug businesses. Drugs came in on shrimp boats, speed boats, you name it. All he aimed to do was keep that life long trend continuing as a renewable source of steady income.

But off-loading the drugs to his mainland distributors was the weak link in his delivery system. Using the island ferry was a huge risk since the ferry captain had every right to inspect any bags he saw fit. Plus, getting pulled over on the mainland in his own vehicle for a simple traffic infraction would prove disastrous.

To remedy the mainland transportation risks, LeShaun got ahold of his grandfather's – ol' Pappy Duff's – precious luxury speed boat and then pressed ignorant young Sammie to be his boat captain. Now he was making boat trafficking runs to coastal stops in his secret network. As long as he stayed away from the more populated waterways, he rarely saw any maritime law enforcement patrols.

At first Sammie asked questions, but after whipping him on the back of his legs with his ever-handy *wand of discipline*, the teen kept his mouth shut and followed orders to the 'T.' Then back home to Sapelo they'd boat, LeShaun's backpack stuffed with wads of cold hard cash.

His one-man, maritime narco-drone smuggling business provided more money than he'd ever fantasized about. It was a far cry from what he made as a low-level dealer selling in Miami's Little Haiti. He made so much money so fast it put him in a quandary. Currently, he had $4 million stashed away in the box spring of his king-sized bed. He simply didn't know how best to store it and protect it from theft. He couldn't put it into a bank account. The Feds would swoop down on him in an instant. A bank's private safe deposit box was enticing, but that was like sticking a prized hen who laid golden eggs inside the fox's den. With a search warrant from law enforcement, he'd lose everything in the box.

A large floor safe he'd purchased on backorder was finally supposed to be delivered on the island barge next week. Once that arrived, he'd have an almost impenetrable combination lock system to secure his cash, and his immediate storage worries would be over.

But for protection, even a police-linked security system was out of the question because there was no police presence on the island to respond to a break-in. Plus, he'd never let a cop into his home anyway. That'd be suicide. He even considered guard dogs. At the very least, they'd get rid of the infestation of damn feral cats around his yard – but then he'd have to train, feed, and take care of the dogs – too much work for his lazy bones, he deemed. He had to settle on high resolution exterior surveillance cameras that he could monitor himself.

He had plans to have a high brick wall constructed around his property, but even that was still in the planning phase. And he'd also bantered around the idea of bringing in a two- or three-man live-in security or bodyguard force, but couldn't really trust anyone. Plus, he didn't want to share his home with simple street thugs for hire. Until the floor safe arrived, the only thing he could do was keep his cash stashed, doors locked up tight, video cameras rolling, and his weapons handy.

The only person he did trust was his heroin-addicted maid from the mainland. Keisha Tyler, his thin, little ex-stripper bitch. She kept his house sparkling clean, clothes washed and ironed, and fuck sessions frequent. She had no idea what he did for a living other than he paid well and provided her enough heroin to last a couple of weeks until her next servicing.

Unbeknownst to anyone else, he was already the wealthiest single resident on Sapelo Island. Soon he'd increase his wealth by secretly cashing in on the most lucrative piece of land left: the Greenhall family estate. Once that deal finalized and he reaped the profit from the sale, he'd be the new

R. J. Reynolds Jr. of Sapelo, he reckoned. After that, he could build his own mansion as big and bold as he wanted, and live like a fucking king with a staff of servants and a team of bodyguards.

Even Scarface, from his favorite movie, would have nothing on him.

"Go ahead, make a wish, little beeatch. Your future be bright," LeShaun taunted, chewing his rib meat like a horse. He licked his fingers then washed the food down with a gulp of red wine.

Sammie placed his index finger and thumb on each side of the birthday candle flame and pinched his fingers to snuff it out.

"You didn't make a wish," said LeShaun, shoving a square of cornbread in his mouth.

Instead, Sammie reached inside his overall's breast pocket and pulled out a thin black candle. Holding it in his fist, he lit it up with a Bic lighter. LeShaun cocked his head, wondering what the fuck his nephew was up to.

Sammie then closed his eyes and bowed his head. LeShaun noticed the kid's chest heaved several times, and his lips move as if speaking. Even when the hot candlewax hit Sammie's hand, he didn't flinch. LeShaun just kept chewing away and smacking his lips. He grunted loudly on purpose and remarked how good his dinner was. He wanted this birthday dinner to make a lasting impression of the disdain he felt for his nephew and for his own grandfather, who the kid worshipped like a hero figure.

LeShaun flung his dreadlocks over his shoulder in arrogance. As he lifted a forkful of baked beans to his mouth, he kept an eye on Sammie, thinking if that little fucker dared talk back to him, he'd backhand his bitch-ass mouth again, no problem. Maybe pop him in his other eye, too. *Gotta keep that boy in line now that he thinks he's his own man. Gotta keep the fear in him. Keep him down to be tamed. Show him who's boss on this island.*

Sammie calmly raised his head and slowly opened his eyes. His nostrils flared. He stared down the table with unwavering rage at LeShaun. His normally submissive brown eyes had turned coal black.

When LeShaun caught Sammie's stare, he lowered his fork.

"What? You light another candle because you want me to sing happy fucking birthday to you, huh, big man?" he mocked, mouth full of beans. He looked down at his gold wristwatch. "Hurry up and eat, I ain't got all night. Shit, I's gots work to do." He resumed chewing loudly.

Sammie didn't waver. He never blinked. He stuck the burning candle into the hot dog, then raised his index finger and pointed at LeShaun, locking eyes with him. His uncle's chewing stopped. Sammie mumbled unintelligible Gullah under his breath. His outstretched finger drew a small circle in the air around his uncle's head. Still not blinking, he then jabbed the center of the invisible circle.

Finally, he blinked. His eyes turned back to a normal color, but the rage was still present. He stood up, seemingly taller, chest wider. "Give me my savings account information right now and I will leave you alone. *Forever.*"

LeShaun wasn't exactly sure what had hit him, but the stare-down and finger jab from his nephew actually caused a chill to run through his body.

When he was about 10-years-old, LeShaun once saw his grandfather Duff make the same gesture to a nasty DNR worker on the island who was harassing LeShaun's now-deceased brother. That man had a tree fall on him two days later, breaking his legs. He was evacuated from the island and was never seen again.

People said it was a hex that Duff laid on him. That when someone finger jabbed you in your face it was called the 'dog finger.'

Did Duff teach Sammie that same Hoodoo magic just to fuck with me? Did he just put the 'dog finger' on me and curse me right before my eyes?

That made him think of another childhood nightmare, also courtesy of old Duff. When LeShaun was twelve and got caught breaking into a building on the UGA campus, he slapped his own mama who was reprimanding him for his actions. Duff then stepped in and whipped him with a switch as punishment. That old Hoodoo doctor son-of-a-bitch then threatened to conjure up Yahoodi, the island's feared boo hag, to steal his breath while he slept if he ever laid a finger on his own mother again.

The boo hag was the undead evil spirit of a woman that fed off of living humans, like a vampire witch, stealing the energy of people while they slept. The Gullah-Geechee people feared her above all else. It was ingrained in their culture. Toddlers were kept in line at the mere mention of her name. She would only come at night, though, shedding her skin and appearing bright red in color with blue bulging veins covering her body.

From what LeShaun remembered of the stories, this hideous looking woman would sit on your chest while you slept, riding you like a horse, stealing your breath and energy to sustain herself. If you woke up feeling completely exhausted after a long sleep, locals would say you had been ridden by the boo hag. Another sign that she gave you a visit was if your bedroom smelled like a rotting carcass of a dead animal.

On Sapelo, the legend revolved around one ugly boo hag in particular who had been roaming the island for ages. Her name was Yahoodi and people said she was a Guale Indian priestess who presided over the Shell Ring rituals on the northwest side of the island below High Point. The Spanish missionaries who lived at the Raccoon Bluff garrison in the 1600s had converted many of the natives to Christianity, but she was a defiant hold-out who ultimately murdered a Spanish priest during a brief uprising. She was captured, beaten, and skinned alive, then burned at the stake.

Her defiant soul never made it to the afterlife. Her spirit was confined to the island forever. But in order to survive among the living on Sapelo, she had to steal a person's skin. This enabled her to wear it like a set of clothes and roam among the living without arousing suspicion. Many people over the years thought they'd caught a glimpse of her hiding behind trees, roaming deserted roads, or standing in the marsh grass like a scarecrow.

As an out-of-control youth, most physical discipline didn't work on LeShaun, but his grandfather's threat of calling Yahoodi to visit him in his sleep did. He never lashed out at his mother in anger again. It didn't stop him from committing more crimes on the island, but it sure made him respect and fear Duff up until the time he left for good.

It was a threat that LeShaun never forgot, something he resented the old man for. It was his own personal ghost in the closet staring back at him for years into his adulthood. The nightmares were the most terrifying. Many times he woke up feeling exhausted and swore he saw the bitch riding on top of him. It's why he always slept with a light on in his bedroom and consistently relied upon sleeping aides and drugs to suppress any dreams.

Will Yahoodi make a visit tonight for all the wrongs I caused this kid and the old man? No, not a chance, LeShaun thought.

Regardless, there was something different about Sammie's demeanor that gave him pause. So much so that LeShaun felt compelled to walk over to his office just off the living room. While he opened a desk drawer, his handheld radio, charging in a stand on the desktop, squawked a loud static-filled message: *Bumblebee, this is White Lotus, time to get your nectar. Over?* LeShaun snatched the radio and keyed the mic. "Copy that, White Lotus. Bumblebee taking flight, ETA thirty minutes. Over?" A reply came back: *Copy, thirty ETA.*

LeShaun replaced the radio and grabbed a thin folder from the drawer. He tossed it on the dinner table in front of Sammie and resumed his seat to continue his meal.

"Your savings account statement is in there," he said, taking a bite of cornbread. "Ain't much left since I had to pay for all your *shit* the last five years. Hey, but you're a big man now, so get a real job and start saving again. Oh, and know this: you and Duff's days are numbered on this island."

LeShaun then stood up, swallowed his food, and placed both hands on the table. "Now get duh fuck outta my crib! Ain't never step foot on my property again or I will fuck you up sumpin' fierce, *boy!*"

Head held high, Sammie picked up the folder, glanced at the burning black candle, blew it out, and walked toward the door. Just before exiting he turned and said, "Have a good night, Buzzut. Sleep tight and don't let de boo hag ride ya!" With that he bolted out the door and bounded down the back steps into the night.

LeShaun almost had a heart attack. He jumped up, knocked the table, spilling his wine glass over, and made for the door to catch the little asshole. Just before stepping outside, he snatched up his handy switch leaning next to the door, intending to whip Sammie's ass to oblivion once he caught him.

Outside, he was too late. Sammie spun the tires of his pickup truck among a scattering of feral cats, and fish-tailed it out of the gravel driveway. LeShaun was the one left steaming hot now. All he could hear as Sammie's truck faded down the road were the loud ominous hoots of an owl perched on the roof of his house.

✸

Same time

Sammie couldn't help but smile at the pissed off look on Buzzut's face before he escaped his uncle's house. He checked his rearview mirror for headlights to see if he would pursue him, but then remembered that Buzzut was in a rush for other business – that of which he spoke on his radio – and wouldn't waste his time to further abuse him.

This got him thinking. Maybe he should sneak back and find out what his uncle was really up to once and for all with that radio code language. It had something to do with drugs, that much he knew for sure. There were other times at night when he overheard Buzzut speaking to those unknown persons on his own matching radio he kept back at the Greenhall house. The same Bumblebee name had come up then, too. And then the very next day his uncle would order Sammie to captain *Doctor Blackbeard* for a secret backpack run to the coast.

Not fifty feet ahead Sammie saw a cut in the woods on his left and swung the truck in, hiding it behind a tree. Decision made. He cut his lights, grabbed his scoped .22 rifle, and trudged back up the road.

Sammie didn't dare go close to the house because he knew his uncle had several exterior surveillance cameras set up to cover his property. Camped out in the dark quiet woods across from the well-lit house, though, he observed through his rifle scope an owl hooting from the peak of the roof. Sammie had an eerie feeling of something bad happening, for it was well known in Hoodoo that if an owl hoots atop your house it was a sign of death to come. The curse was already working. Panning his rifle, he caught LeShaun running about gathering items, including his handheld radio.

All of the lights suddenly went dark and the ground level remote control garage door started rising. Sammie saw two headlights shining back at him. It was his uncle's Bad Boy UTV. The utility terrain vehicle pulled out of the narrow one-car garage, motored across the back lawn, and backed up to a 5x6' enclosed cargo trailer hidden just inside the treeline. Sammie had never seen the trailer before.

Once hitched up to the trailer, LeShaun turned out of his driveway and headed east toward the ocean. *But why?* Sammie thought. The road was a dead-end at the marsh's edge. Sammie bugged out of his hiding spot and jogged down the road after him.

Now it was making sense why his uncle bought the UTV, for he didn't stop at the end of the road. Instead, he drove it straight ahead down a narrow seagrass-filled causeway over the marsh. Once the only road over to Cabretta Island, it had been abandoned for well over twenty years when the bridge over a wide tidal creek had collapsed. This causeway was all but forgotten to most residents on the island and completely off limits to the public because of its dangerous conditions and the threat of alligators. The only public route to get across to the little two-mile long island was Cabretta Road at the north end. That road provided vehicle access to Cabretta Camp where people could spend the night and take a short trail to the beach.

As Sammie jogged up to the dead-end where it met the old causeway, he caught his breath and watched through the rifle scope as the red tail lights of LeShaun's UTV bounced along a good half mile away. He saw its headlights again as it turned onto Cabretta Island and started heading south. Soon it disappeared as the dense live oak forest swallowed it up.

9

A FTER KULL'S MELTDOWN AND SUBSEQUENT DEATH spiral of his real identity, his alter ego Phoenix emerged with renewed focus. The calculating career criminal now thought rationally in devising an immediate getaway plan. Any chance of a second life depended on drawing from his experience of eluding capture.

It was imperative that he ditch his rental as soon as possible since he knew the police had the make, model, color, and license plate number. The exact description was soon announced over his stolen radio with a BOLO (*Be On The Look Out*) for all units in the vicinity.

More chatter followed, including his name as the prime suspect. They said his name frequently and angrily, further hammering home the reality that the life of Nathan Kull was truly over. At one point, he even heard they had captured his assault on the deceased officer's video dash cam. Then soon after, he heard the phrase, "Skip rope, Jack and Jill," several times and all went silent. It was an obvious code, knowing he had stolen the radio and was listening in on communications. A switch to other channels revealed silence, too. They were probably using personal cell phones at this point, he all but assumed.

Where to drop his rental was now the key question as he drove on. He only had a small window of opportunity, knowing full well a warrant would be issued for his arrest and his face would be plastered all over the media. He needed to make tracks into another county or state by separating himself from the scene of his crime. But he was in rural farm country of southeast Georgia. For a city dweller like himself, it was like a foreign country. He couldn't just blend in and easily disappear among the masses. Unlike New York City, any new face that popped up in these little rural towns, where everyone knew everyone, would surely stick out and be remembered.

The first step was to put Nathan Kull out to pasture for good. He needed to dump any evidence that linked him to that name. First, he needed to take care of his New York City residence where the FBI would surely get a search warrant to raid. He pulled over on a secluded dirt road near a swamp and cut his headlights. Using his regular smartphone, he tapped a one-of-a-kind, three-phase app that he wrote himself. No one else knew it even existed. The graphic icon of the app was a little cannonball with a lit fuse.

After logging in, the app made an encrypted remote access connection to his laptop computer sitting on a desk in his condo. Among the many legitimate work-related files on his laptop, there was one hidden folder of documents. One secret folder, but a treasure trove of incriminating digital evidence on Phoenix: from the locations of his storage lockers full of stolen loot, to passwords of his secret overseas banking accounts, to a master listing of all the jobs he had pulled off. He even had a file on Mona Lisa – Maya Levana – having found out her real name after he trailed her one day in the city. She was a very well-known high society art dealer and gallery owner. If the authorities ever got ahold of that folder, he'd lose all the monetary gains that he'd accumulated over his entire criminal career. And Mona would go down with him.

Next, he typed a special code in the app that triggered a doomsday software program on the laptop that he'd written specifically in case of a catastrophic event like this. The program was designed to immediately upload that one specific folder to his secret Dark Web cloud account. This would then enable him to easily download that same data in the near future once he established his new life. Flipping to another app on his phone, linked to his Dark Web account, he held his breath to see if the data exchange was actually working.

With a loud exhale, he flung his shoulder length hair from his face, tipped his head back, and smiled. It was running smoothly. Not a minute later, the folder was sitting in the cloud where he could access the files.

Now came phase two of the doomsday program: erasing all data off his laptop. A mere five minutes later his computer was scrubbed clean.

Lastly, phase three was implemented when a tiny spark inside the motherboard ignited a combustible material that melted the components. Phoenix knew the laptop was destroyed when he lost connection. He was quite pleased at the results. Any vestige of Phoenix's digital connection to Kull's name had now completely disappeared into the cloud. The FBI would have shit to go on.

He quickly dismantled his smartphone, broke the SIM card that carried its unique identification number and data, and rendered the device inoperable. He tossed everything into the murky swamp. He would now only use his untraceable burner cell phone for future communications.

After that, he removed from his wallet any IDs and credit cards under the name Nathan Kull. They, too, were scattered in the water.

With Kull's identity now floating away, a new destination spurred him on: a strategically rented storage locker in Pooler, Georgia at the I-95/I-16 interchange. It was his Southeast storage unit he had rented years ago while pulling jobs in the region. It held all the resources he needed to go on the run and exit entirely from the United States.

After a rendezvous with Mona in Charleston to drop off the Nazi trophies, he planned to escape the U.S. using an Uber-like, on-demand, private charter jet service based out of Turks and Caicos that he frequented on his criminal endeavors. The trusted owner/pilot, Dean Kennedy, a forty-something expat from Halifax, Nova Scotia who had served a stint in prison for money laundering, was always on time wherever Kull needed him. And he prided himself on client discretion. Kull always paid in cash with an over-the-top gratuity to make sure of that.

His final destination would be Saint Lucia, a sovereign island nation in the Lesser Antilles of the Caribbean Basin. It's where he already owned a luxury home and an anonymous shell corporation where he had been laundering all of his ill-gotten gains.

He had purchased a lifetime citizenship many years ago for $750,000 as part of the nation's citizenship-by-investment real estate program and, most importantly, was even issued an official biometric passport, and a driver's license under a brand new name. It was a highly discrete and completely confidential application process. He didn't need to visit in person, nor be interviewed. His residency wasn't even required after he gained his passport, but he liked to spend vacations there at least three times a year. Plus, with his passport, he traveled visa-free to many other countries across the globe where he committed even more thefts. The passport and driver's license were the only two forms of ID that remained in his wallet now. They went wherever he went, just in case he needed to officially bug out of Nathan Kull's life.

And that time was now.

Kull's premature retirement stared back at him in his rearview mirror. The new person that Phoenix would soon morph into would be Frank Alan Mason: the Saint Lucia name he'd chosen. It was fittingly based on three role models he studied in depth throughout his criminal career. In his opinion, they were the greatest con men and master thieves that ever lived: Frank Abagnale, Alan Golder, and Bill Mason.

As a citizen and legal resident of another country, albeit under a different name, he wouldn't have to worry about being hunted down like an international fugitive. It's what he'd planned all along when he decided to leave his life of crime behind.

Consulting a Georgia state map he picked up at the airport rental agency back in Atlanta, he figured out what road he was on and what backroads he'd have to take to get to Pooler. Staying off the I-16 was paramount, though, as there were surveillance cameras, and, most likely, Georgia State Patrol vehicles with license plate readers just waiting for him.

If he could get to one of the larger towns south of the I-16 corridor, he'd ditch the car – the main connection to his crime – in a parking lot and then set up other means of transportation. For the next hour, it was a slow, nerve-wracking zigzag of paved, dirt, sand, and gravel roads cringing at every car that passed him in the darkness. To top it off, his gas tank showed he was near empty and he needed a place to take a piss, find a pay phone, and a local phone book.

As he approached Daisy, Georgia on US Route 280, the police radio began chirping and ultimately ran out of battery life. He threw it out the window as he passed over a creek. Coming into the tiny municipality, he noticed a Dollar General store, a Dairy Queen, and a disgusting old gas station with, sure enough, a rare public phone booth.

It was a place where a group of local jackasses smoked cigarettes not ten feet from a customer pumping gas. The kind of place where, when Phoenix ventured into the men's restroom on the side of the building, he found a clogged toilet with a smorgasbord of intestinal items in a rainbow of lovely colors. He had used his foot to kick open the door in fear of contracting a disease if he touched anything with his hands. Finding the women's bathroom unoccupied and less dirty, he relieved himself then ventured over to the public phone.

While occupying the phone booth, some obese specimen of a woman with blue and purple hair and missing teeth walked up to him and asked him for a ride in a deep manly voice. At first he thought she was a she and not a he, but, then again, he didn't want to assume its gender in case it got *offended*. He shook his head and thought to himself: *'Merica!*

In the phone booth, he quickly rifled through the phone book to the taxi cab category where he noticed an advertisement of the only company around. He immediately placed a call to the taxi service using his burner cell phone. Arrangements were made for a pick-up in fifteen minutes.

While waiting in his car, Phoenix changed into a different shirt, put his hair in a ponytail, and placed a black baseball cap on his head. It was the best he could manage in such a short time. He stored the backpack with the Nazi trophies inside his travel duffel bag and stuffed the cop's stolen gun into a side pocket. The damn gender-neutral thing, now smoking a cig, watched him the whole time.

Soon the taxi arrived and parked in front of the gas station.

He exited his rental, leaving the keys on the seat, the window down, and the door unlocked.

"Hey sweety," he said to the large person as he passed it by. "Still need that ride?" It nodded. Phoenix pointed to his rental. "Free transportation. Keys are on the seat. Have fun." It looked at him in disbelief.

Phoenix then hopped in the back seat of the taxi driven by a sketchy-looking Hispanic. He explained he needed transportation to Pooler – that he was already running late and needed to go now. He flipped the driver $200 in upfront cash and watched as the man's eyes grew large. The taxi immediately pulled out of the gas station and headed east at a good clip. In the rear window, Phoenix watched as the gender-dysphoric individual waddled over to his rental, started it up, and took off in the opposite direction. The person was in for a rude awakening if it ever got pulled over.

The taxi driver folded the wad of cash, and tucked it into his breast pocket with a smile. He never even started the fare meter. For Phoenix, it was a cheap investment in a fellow man with loose morals. The driver would keep his mouth shut if he happened to recognize his face when the murder went public. After all, aiding and abetting a fugitive could get you a nasty prison sentence.

The beauty of his transaction was that, unlike alternative taxi services like Uber or Lyft, no credit card was used, no GPS tracking app, or even a smartphone was needed. Plus, no identification was required. It was old school with the shake of a hand and a flash of some cash.

About 45 minutes later, after passing four state police patrols, he was dropped off at a Waffle House next to the Mighty Eighth Air Force Museum at Exit 102 off the I-95. After the taxi departed, Phoenix promptly walked over to a storage facility company, entered his security code to unlock the gate, and headed over to his small storage garage. Another security code gave him access to his unit where he slipped in unnoticed, flicked on a light, and opened up a cabinet next to a black, crotch-rocket type motorcycle. Inside was a theatrical special effects kit.

He immediately went to work changing his appearance. He needed to match the picture on his Saint Lucia passport and driver's license taken five years ago when he was quite tan and wore his hair shorter with a matching brown goatee. He could not afford to have anyone make any remote connection to the Nathan Kull being hunted by police.

Using scissors to chop off his long hair, and an electric clipper to trim the sides of his head, he soon had a close-cropped businessman haircut. With his makeup kit, he then applied a fake bronze tan with several layers of foundation to any exposed skin. Since he was clean shaven at the moment, he needed to apply a dab of glue for a pre-made brown goatee in his selection of fake beards. Donning eye glasses with an amber tint and a silky black button down shirt with black jeans, his attire was complete. He was confident his new face and alternative legal identity would be enough to pass muster if anyone happened to give him a double-take.

Next, he slipped on a black leather riding jacket, his backpack, and a helmet with a dark visor. He fired up his stolen Ducati Monster 1200 and motored out of the garage. Soon, he was on the road north to Charleston and an awaiting Mona Lisa.

Two hours later, he parked the bike on South Battery in front of White Point Inn near White Point Garden at the tip of peninsular historic downtown Charleston.

Phoenix spotted Mona Lisa waiting on the raised porch of the historic home, having a glass of wine in a rocking chair. He walked up, took off his bike helmet, and said hello to her in a fake British accent. His new disguise worked perfectly. Mona didn't recognize the tanned man with the short hair, goatee, and glasses. She asked if he was looking for the main office to check-in.

"Mona, it's me. Something bad happened," he said in his normal voice.

She gasped, then looked at him closer, now recognizing features of the man she knew intimately. Mona then stood up and got in his face. "Well, if it isn't Mr. Nathan Kenneth Kull," she whispered with a hiss.

She held up her cell phone screen to Phoenix showing a news website and a breaking alert headline: *"Police Launch Manhunt for Nathan Kenneth Kull After Cop Killed in Fitzgerald, Georgia."* He saw his own headshot from his New York State driver's license photo – albeit how he looked with shoulder length locks and devoid of all facial hair.

His chin dipped and he turned away.

Mona kept her voice low, but was still livid. "What the *fuck* happened? I can't be an accessory to this."

Phoenix kept silent, his back turned.

"You at least got the two *items?*" she asked quietly in his ear.

Phoenix gave a slight nod and tapped his backpack.

He turned around slowly, lowered his glasses, and met her eyes. He spoke in a barely audible voice. "Don't worry. I'm leaving the country. *Permanently*. I have to. Nathan Kull is a dead man if I stay."

"What?" Her mouth fell open in disbelief.

"These things are cursed," he said angrily, smacking his backpack. "Listen, I'll scout out where the meeting place is tomorrow and hand off the goods when you give me the cash deposit. Then you close the deal yourself. It's what you do best. I've got to get the fuck out. Wire my share to my account and never ever mention you saw me here in Charleston."

"Oh God," Mona said, tears filling her eyes as she collapsed in her chair. "Where, where are you going?"

"Where Phoenix can never rise again."

10

AFTER A WILD EXHAUSTIVE ROMP IN BED, WITH a few shots of *Elixir of Life* moonshine in between, Jake and Rae lay happily asleep in each other's arms. They had missed each other all day long on Sunday doing their respective activities with their close friends Alex and Marissa Vann. Once they had dropped the couple off at the Savannah airport to catch their late night flight to Washington, D.C., Jake and Rae had wasted no time in returning to their waterfront mansion on Skidaway Island and stripping each other's clothes off.

A few hours into their slumber, Jake's iPhone chimed with a new text message that woke him up. The phone's screen also lit up in the darkness of their bedroom. Jake grunted and squinted his eyes, turning his dizzy head to his nightstand not an arm's length away. If he leaned over to grab it, he thought, he'd disturb Rae cuddled up on his shoulder. He chastised himself for not putting his phone on mute earlier. His eyes then grew droopy and he closed them, deciding to simply ignore the phone. Thirty seconds later the alert chimed again as a reminder.

He flinched awake. "Jesus H–"

Rae stirred in his arms. "Just check the damn thing," she slurred before rolling over and nestling herself into a pillow.

Jake picked up the phone. It was a message from Special Agent Sergeant

Marco D'Arata of the Army's 3rd MP Criminal Investigation Division (CID) out of Hunter Army Airfield in Savannah. It read: *"You up? See news? Phoenix killed a cop in Fitzgerald, Georgia. Got his real ID. Call me."*

"What the –?"

"What is it?" asked Rae, rolling back around to face him.

Jake reread the message for her, then tapped a news app. He held the phone so they both could see the screen. Across the bright red breaking news banner at the top, it read: *"Georgia Cop Killed, Manhunt Underway."* Below was the lead story along with a driver's license photo of the suspect and dash cam video stills of the same man.

A manhunt is underway for the murder of a Fitzgerald, Georgia police officer Sunday night. The search for Nathan Kenneth Kull, 38, of New York City, began after he was positively identified by dash cam video from the slain officer's cruiser and by his driver's license from the car he had rented.

Sergeant Everett Jenkins, a 20-year veteran of the force, married with three kids, was fatally attacked as he was inspecting a car parked outside a closed seminary in the south Georgia town. A police department spokesman said that Jenkins was able to call in the tag number before being attacked from behind. Dispatchers were able to trace the car as a rental out of Hartsfield-Jackson Atlanta International Airport driven by the suspect.

Kull fled in the vehicle, a 2017 gray Honda Accord with Georgia license plate BDM 0476. The vehicle has not yet been located.

Kull is described as a white male, 5' 9", weighs 180 lbs, has long blonde hair, and blue eyes.

Fitzgerald Chief of Police Robbie Evans warned the suspect was armed and should not be approached. Anyone who sees him should phone 911. Story is developing . . .

"Bastard killed one of our own in blue," said Rae. "That's him alright. That's him. I recognize his mug from the surveillance photos Marco took in Atlanta. Call him now. Shit! We've got to see if the meeting is still on for tomorrow in Charleston. It may be our only chance to nab him."

"My question is, why did he resurface back in Fitzgerald?" said Jake, closing out the news article to call D'Arata. "Can't be coincidence."

D'Arata picked up the call on the first ring. "Nathan Kull is the Phoenix," he stated, without saying hello.

"Marco, you're on speaker. Rae's here, too."

"How'd you make the connection? How'd you know?" she asked.

"Visual match at first, Rae," said D'Arata. "Saw a news alert on TV and his face jumped out at me, but then I saw Fitzgerald and—"

"That's what I thought, too," interrupted Jake. "What the fuck's he doing back in Fitzgerald? That's where he originally disappeared from."

"Right! Exactly," said the Army criminal investigator, talking quite fast. "No idea, Jake. No idea. But I called the Fitzgerald police chief to compare notes. Based on the dash cam video they have, he thought at first maybe this was one of those anti-cop hate groups who ambushed the officer. Then I told him our situation, that we might be looking for the same guy. They're still processing evidence from the scene, but they had already pulled a few finger prints. The Georgia Bureau of Investigation analysts also got involved early. Any way, long story short, we got those prints digitized and sent to our Army crime lab up at Fort Gillem and they made an immediate positive match on the latent prints found on this scene to the prints found in all those art thefts in the NGI database, including our West Point boy!"

"Yes!" said Jake.

"Fitzgerald PD also pulled DNA evidence, too," continued D'Arata. "But it'll be awhile for those results. Anyway, they traced his rental back to Hartsfield and the GBI found video of him there at the rental desk. He rented the car under his real name, Nathan Kull. They had a copy of his New York driver's license. That's his ID in the news. He flew down from New York City. We've got all the flight information. No return trip. The FBI is getting a search warrant for his address in New York City and taking over the manhunt since it involves the loss of a law enforcement officer."

"Man, so many questions," said Jake, now fully awake and trying to wrap his head around all the events. "What, um? What'd they see on the dash cam?"

"Yeah," said Rae. "Did they catch him in the act?"

"They did. I saw it. The fucker ambushed the officer from behind. Hit him in the back of the head with a big flashlight. Cop's head then hit the pavement hard. Blunt force trauma looks to be the cause of death."

"Jesus," said Rae.

"Good God," said Jake.

D'Arata sighed on the phone. "And the fucker then stole his piece and his radio. So we know he was listening in after he fled. And he's armed."

"Wait, you said he hit him with a flashlight?" asked Rae. "Weird."

"Yeah, I know," replied D'Arata. "That throws the chief's theory out the window because cop killers use guns and they ambush them while they're sitting in their patrol car. It's a cowardly act, not hand-to-hand assault. Flashlights aren't your close-in weapon of choice either. A knife is more like it. Plus, he was wearing all black clothing. Had a black backpack. Wore a black hat, black gloves, black boots."

"And was operating in the dark," added Jake.

"Obviously, he was pulling some kind of job," said D'Arata. "That makes the most sense, knowing who he is. Maybe he got caught in the act? Who knows? The thing is you can see his reaction in the video that he is shocked and upset he killed the cop. I don't think it was his intention. He checks the cop's pulse in two different areas then throws some F-bombs after he realizes he's dead. He clearly panics, stumbles to his rental car, and peels out in a frenzy. I think he knew he fucked up big time."

"Very interesting," said Rae.

"And a key piece of evidence was his gloves. He took them off to check the pulse of the officer, but left them behind in haste. Also forgot his hat. We've got great DNA evidence off both. But the gloves had red clay on them. Caked really hard on the fingertips like he was digging somewhere around there. There are all kinds of cops scouring the scene, but until daybreak we can't get the full picture. They've already searched the buildings he was parked next to, some theological seminary. Found no evidence of dirt inside. All of the doors were locked. No forced entry. No evidence of digging around there yet."

"But was he was digging something up?" asked Rae. "Or maybe moving something?"

"Or burying something?" said Jake. "You said he wore a backpack.

Could be for his tools or to transport whatever he had to retrieve or bury."

"Right," said D'Arata. "And in light of our military expert meeting in Charleston, maybe he was actually retrieving the two Nazi trophies?"

"Hmmm, very likely," said Rae. "Otherwise, why not fly down directly to Charleston? Why fly to Atlanta and rent a car and then head directly south instead of east to Charleston? So strange."

"Was there anyone else in that rental with him?" asked Jake. "Anyone else seen with him on video at the airport, too? Any travel companions he sat with on the flight down? Perhaps a woman? We know this Mona Lisa is setting everything up for tomorrow. She is the main contact with LaMar."

"And according to your eyewitness pilot, it was a woman who also picked up Phoenix when he landed in Fitzgerald and first disappeared over a year ago," added Rae.

"Yup, I'll recheck the videos, but I didn't see anyone else," said D'Arata. "He looked to be a lone wolf."

"What's your next step now?" asked Jake.

"I've got to make sure our proof of life meeting isn't canceled," answered D'Arata. "It's scheduled for 2 p.m. today at a hotel in Charleston. The other problem is Antoine LaMar, our boy who's going to be there with the military authenticator. He recognized Nathan Kull's face – this Phoenix – on the news, too. He's trying to fucking back out now, thinks he's going to get whacked if Phoenix finds out he's turned. He's literally freaking out. We've got agents with him to make sure he doesn't skip town."

"What do you want me to do at this point?" asked Rae.

"Sleep as much as you can. Stay on schedule to meet us tomorrow morning in Charleston at our rendezvous point. Going to be a long, complicated day with the manhunt going on. And Jake, I know we've kept you at arm's length on the investigation, that it's been an Army CID op, but things have changed now that Phoenix is a fucking murderer. I'd like for you to be there, too, brother. Give you the pleasure of seeing this go down."

"I *want* my husband to be there," added Rae, squeezing Jake's hand.

"Count on it, Marco. Talk soon, brother." Jake ended the call.

"You still got some of that Ambien left?" asked Rae, referring to his sleep aid for the occasional insomnia he experienced.

"I do."

"Good. That's they only way we are getting to sleep tonight," said Rae. "We're going to need the rest so we can think straight tomorrow."

"Or shoot straight."

11

U PON BREAKING THE NEWS LAST NIGHT THAT HE
was leaving the country, Phoenix and Mona drank like fish and had
sex for hours knowing they'd probably never see each other again. Their last
time spent together was an escape they both had craved, especially under the
stressful circumstances of his accidental killing of the cop and their plans
today to close the biggest deal of their corrupt lives.

While Phoenix had been passed out drunk and snoring, Mona did some
snooping. Terrified for her own life after learning he killed a cop, she needed
her own insurance in case she was implicated. She quietly rifled through his
clothes and found, within his riding jacket, her lover's wallet and passport.
She then secretly took a cell phone picture of both the passport and driver's
license within the wallet. Now she knew of Frank Alan Mason and where
he lived. All that aside, she still had a job to do.

She had been sweating the meeting, supposedly still on at 2 p.m. at the
Hilton Garden Inn Waterfront where she now sat at the bar in the hotel's
restaurant sipping a cocktail, although she still knew not in which room.
If the client's broker, Antoine LaMar, had recognized Phoenix on the news
it might already have blown the entire deal out of the water. She knew
those two had met twice in Atlanta: the first time when Phoenix delivered
the stolen Civil War general's hat to his client, and secondly, when LaMar

drove him to the airport to escape in the Cessna. But LaMar knew this was a rough business they were in and people get killed along the way. Surely, he could overlook the dirty parts in light of the payday they'd all be getting.

Phoenix, still disguised as Frank Mason, sat across the room at a table in front of a big screen television watching a sports game and having a beer himself, backpack with trophies at his feet. The rest of the bar was fairly packed with lunch time guests. His back was to Mona, but he could clearly see her through a reflection in the sunlit window facing the marina on the Ashley River.

He had arrived much earlier on his motorcycle and scouted out the hotel for any signs of law enforcement or a set-up. The only thing he saw was an ambulance rig parked in the lot with the two-man crew eating lunch in the front cab. Other than that, all was clear and now they simply were waiting on a go-to room for the meeting.

Mona hadn't heard from LaMar all morning as to which room that would be and now she'd risk a call to see if the meeting was still a go in fifteen minutes. She needed this deal and wanted nothing more than to dump the Nazi items. She'd even accept a few million less if they tried negotiating her down. Still, it would be her biggest score ever. Just thinking about the tens of millions of dollars made her also give serious pause as to getting out of "the life." It was proving all too deadly.

She was happy Phoenix was calling it quits, too. Having that known cop killer out of the picture actually gave her a sense of relief. Besides the Latino gang members in Atlanta that he'd confessed to killing during some late night pillow talk, she wasn't sure how many others he'd killed she didn't know about. What if he wanted to burn her bridge for good, too? Sure, he was a joy in bed and the most interesting and incredible man she'd ever worked or slept with – a true legend in both aspects – but who knows if she'd be next on his hit list.

LaMar picked up her call after a nerve-wracking ten rings. He actually seemed glad and relieved that she had called and still had interest in the meeting. He apologized for not calling her sooner because he was ensuring a safe location for his authenticator to do his work. He asked nothing about Phoenix, and, in fact, asked if she was coming alone. She replied, yes, and asked if he had the down payment with him. He assured her he did and told her she was to meet him and his authenticator in Suite 203. She said she'd be up shortly.

Popping up on the lobby elevator, she was at the door within minutes. She knocked despite the 'Do Not Disturb' sign on the doorknob. Someone inside came up to the door and paused. She assumed they were looking through the peephole.

The door unlatched and swung open. A bald, mocha-skinned man appeared and quickly scanned Mona from head to toe. He had beautiful light blue eyes and long eye lashes, wore diamond earrings in both ears, and had on an impeccable black suit and lots of bling on his wrists and fingers. A gold cross with a circular gemstone hung from a necklace. He was exactly as Phoenix had described him. In fact, Phoenix had nicknamed him Mocha.

"Mr. LaMar, I presume?" asked Mona.

He nodded and gave her a quick up and down. "A pleasure to finally meet you in person, Ms. Lisa." His voiced wavered ever so slightly. He shook her hand and motioned for her to enter the suite, then stepped out into the corridor and looked both ways to see if she'd been followed.

It was now time for LaMar to play the role scripted for him by Army CID special agent Sergeant Marco D'Arata. The agent, his armed team, and the Tununda couple were across the hall listening through a secret microphone and recording everything through a hidden camera in the suite. D'Arata told LaMar when the "room service" knocked, the take-down would occur, but only after the authenticator verified both items as legitimate.

Or if things seemed to go to shit.

Mona entered the suite through a long foyer with a bathroom off to the side. The main room had a king-sized bed and a lounge area with a sofa, chairs, coffee table, desk, and television. Sitting in one of the chairs was a stout, handsome, gray bearded man who looked in his mid-fifties. Dressed in a sharp blue suit with a red tie and white pocket square, the man stood up, smiled, and held out his hand.

"Erhardt Hoffmann. It certainly is a pleasure to meet you, my dear." His Charleston tidewater accent was soft and gentlemanly. It put her at ease.

"Mona Lisa," she said in a sultry voice. "Pleased to meet you, too."

"Love the name," Hoffman winked. "Please, do sit." He gestured toward the sofa.

"And I love the family background on your website," replied Mona, placing her purse on the sofa before sitting down. She wore a white button down blouse showing ample cleavage, and a high gray skirt with knee-high black boots to highlight her firm thighs. Crossing her legs ever so slowly, she leaned back on the sofa and pushed her chest forward. "Your parents certainly make the case for opposites attracting."

Hoffman smiled and sat back. His eyes couldn't help but wander over the attractive woman. "Oh, you should have heard the arguments around the dinner table. They refought the war just about every night. But they still do love each other very much, even in their ripe old age now."

"I can imagine. I'd love to be a fly on that wall. You'll have to tell me more about the Elvis Presley gigs your father booked before I leave," Mona said, knowing she made an instant connection. This was a good start.

"Oh, they are epic," Hoffman said.

"Can I get you anything to drink?" asked LaMar, holding open the mini refrigerator to show her a selection of beverages.

"I'd rather we get down to brass tacks," Mona said, taking control of the meeting. "First, show me the money, honey."

"First, stand up so I can check you for a wire, babe," LaMar retorted.

"What?" said Mona, taken aback.

"Not taking any chances," he replied, motioning for her to rise as he stepped in her space. "A lot of fucking cash exchanging hands today and millions more to come. You know the game." LaMar slipped into his role. It was coming naturally.

Mona actually liked that she was dealing with legit people who didn't take anything for granted. It gave her more confidence that she could close the deal. "Fine. Check me anywhere you want, love. I'm all yours."

LaMar checked her purse first, and then patted her down thoroughly. He looked down the front of her blouse and even raised the skirt up her thighs ever so slightly, noticing she wore a white thong. Mona didn't flinch a bit. She rather enjoyed it. She had nothing to hide.

Only millions to gain.

"You learn your moves with the TSA?" she asked seductively. "Maybe we can do it again sometime."

"Perhaps," LaMar smirked, face reddened, thrilled at feeling her up. He walked over to the armoire, opened a cabinet door, and pulled out a black briefcase. Placing it on the table in front of her, he flipped open the cover to expose stacks and stacks of one hundred dollar bills. "All there. Three hundred thou in Benjis. You can count it if you like."

Satisfied, Mona nodded. "No need. I trust you. Just give me a moment and you'll see the trophies shortly." She placed a call to Phoenix's burner and gave him confirmation. Grabbing the briefcase of cash, she rose to her feet. "Gentlemen, I will be slipping out to retrieve your items and then I'll call to tell you which room we'll be meeting in next. We have a change of venue if you want to see the trophies." She turned to leave.

LaMar and Hoffman looked at each other perplexed. "This wasn't part of the plan," said LaMar. "You're supposed to bring them here to *this* room. The cash stays here until we see them ourselves."

Expecting this reaction, Mona turned and hissed like a viper. "You *never* said that. The deal was we get this deposit hands-down. This money was only meant to secure the items from other bidders. We gave you exclusivity, and kept our bargain. *That* was the deal." She was pissed and slammed the briefcase to the floor.

"I don't like this," said LaMar.

"Listen, if you want proof of life, if you're serious about cutting this deal, then wait for my call and you will see them. Otherwise, I am leaving for good. Got it?"

Again, the two men looked at each other. Hoffman gave a quick glance to the gold cross necklace around LaMar's neck to remind him of what he wore. The gem stone in the cross was in actuality a secret microphone. LaMar gave a slight nod, then relented to Mona. He had no choice or he'd blow the sting altogether. Besides, he knew full well the cash was counterfeit anyway. Although leaving the room was a scenario D'Arata planned for when he gave LaMar the necklace microphone, it also posed an enormous risk having the two men out of camera range.

❖

Minutes later

Meeting Phoenix in the stairwell on the first floor, Mona took hold of the backpack with the trophies. She gave him the briefcase of cash. They had to be quick. He pointed to a side pocket on the backpack and unzipped it. Inside was the dead cop's stolen pistol and extra magazines. He told her she might need the pistol for protection, that there was a round in the chamber, and no safety. Just aim and squeeze the trigger.

"We had a good run together, babe," she said.

"We did, hon, we did," said Phoenix, setting the briefcase on the floor and hugging her. He then passionately kissed her.

"How will I know you made it safe to where ever it is you're going?"

"My Dark Web email account," he said, backing off and grabbing the briefcase again. "Send me a message after you wire my share. I want to hear all about how it went down. I'll respond, I promise."

"I will. I will."

"And perhaps one day, Miss Maya Levana, I'd like it if you could join me in my new life. I've never met anyone like you – and I don't want this to end – this crazy exciting thing we've got."

Mona stood silent in shock. He knew who she was all along.

He shrugged his shoulders in feigned innocence and winked. "I followed you one day in the city. You've got a really nice gallery."

Now it was Mona's turn for an embrace. She squeezed him tight and kissed him on his neck and lips. "I figured you knew," she said between kisses. "More importantly, yes, I'd love to join you one day and live that new life. I've certainly never had a man like you ever before either. We make one hell of a team. Don't we?" She sniffled and her eyes welled up.

"We sure do. Good luck up there. And I'll talk to you soon." They kissed one last time and Phoenix exited the building while Mona blotted her nose with the back of her hand. She then headed back inside to the new meeting room.

Within a minute of a phone call to LaMar, he and Hoffman were in a conference room on the first floor seated across from Mona. The backpack was in front of her. The door was locked and she had placed a 'Do Not Disturb' sign on the doorknob that she'd stolen from a guest room. A large plate glass window at the far side of the room revealed a beautiful view of the Ashley River with many sailing vessels plying the water.

She extracted a dirt-encrusted ammo can, then placed the backpack on the chair next to her to have access to the pistol. "Proof of life, gentlemen!"

Hoffman extracted a small notepad, pencil, and a magnifying glass from his coat pocket. Next, came a pair of bifocals he placed on his nose, and finally white cotton gloves that he slipped over his hands. He shimmied to the edge of his chair, elbows on the table, licking his lips, eyes wide. "This is going to be the highlight of my career."

"Mine, too," said LaMar. "We're all going to take a hefty commission from this deal."

"I might even have to retire," Mona replied in a sultry voice. She popped the lid off the metal ammo can and pulled out the baton, still wrapped in cloth. Next came the pistol box which she pushed across the table to Hoffman. He impatiently swung the top open. His lips parted.

"Hitler's famous golden gun," he whispered.

"I think I said the same exact thing when I first saw it, too," said Mona.

"Absolutely exquisite!" Hoffman picked up the gold-plated pistol and immediately ejected the magazine of six bullets. He then pulled back the slide to make sure there wasn't a bullet in the chamber either. "Safety first," he said, winking.

Holding up the small pistol, its gold plating shimmering brightly in the sunlight filtering through the window, he said, "A gorgeous artifact of dark history. It was said that Hilter had a specially sewn pocket in his pants to carry this gun in." Hoffman then went silent, inspecting it at many different angles with his magnifying glass. He glanced down at his written notes several times to cross reference the symbols and German phrases engraved on the gold plated surfaces.

"While he's doing that," LaMar started. "My client wanted me to ask you a question. Well, more of a request, if you will."

"Sure," said Mona, shifting to address LaMar.

"As I'm sure you're already aware, the provenance behind both these objects is incredible as it is," he said, waving a hand as he spoke. "Their unique stories give them their value. But when Phoenix, ah, *obtained* them from West Point, that opened up a whole new chapter of possession."

Mona arched her eyebrows and tipped her head in agreement.

"My client wishes to gain the *full* story of where the objects went between then and now. It's an essential part of the legend and it preserves their immortality in time. By the way, that last part is exactly what he told me to say." LaMar thought to himself that was exactly what Jake Tununda told him to say.

"Oh, I agree completely," said Mona. "The story is more important than the actual item sometimes. But I'm a bit reluctant to . . . "

"Indeed," Hoffman chimed in. "Take your name for instance: Mona Lisa. The painting stolen from the Louvre in 1911 by a thief named Vincenzo Peruggia. That da Vinci painting was certainly popular before it was stolen, but the frenzy of worldwide publicity and the mystery *after* the theft exploded its value. Now look at that painting. It is priceless. Simply priceless – *because* it was stolen. The same goes for this pistol." Hoffman nodded to the pistol in the palm of his hand. "Have you seen some of the stuff on TV in the last year? The documentaries, the history shows, the conspiracy theories all dedicated to the mystery surrounding this specific theft? It's insane, I say."

Mona sighed. Hoffman made complete sense, but she wasn't sure if she should give up the details that Phoenix had confided in her one night in bed about six months ago. Her iPhone suddenly started ringing in her purse. Maybe it was Phoenix reading her mind, she thought.

"One second, excuse me," she said, unzipping her purse to see who was calling her. She looked at the caller ID and ended the call. "Just my niece. Sorry about that." She placed her phone on the table in front of her.

"Mona, listen," said LaMar. "I'm going to play the only hand I've got and it should persuade you. My client is willing to pay your *full* asking price on both pieces. He wants them. Period. No negotiating. No bullshit. It's sentimental to him given his German heritage. And money is absolutely no object, understand? His family is filthy fucking rich." He paused. "And we can probably do lots more business together with him in the future. Understand?"

"I understand," said Mona, her heart racing at the fact that they were offering her full price. "May I ask, though, how did you find this client? All you've told me is he's from South America somewhere and is related to Göering."

LaMar waggled an index finger at her. "Ahhh, I have my secrets and you have yours on how we land our clients," he said, meeting her eyes. "After all, we're still competitors, are we not? Let's leave it at that."

"No. If I'm going to open up, you've gotta give me something, too," she said, still not giving in. "I'm just curious is all."

"Alright," LaMar acquiesced, following his script after she took the bait. "Basically, after I saw your postings on the Dark Web advertising these two pieces, I went fishing for known black market collectors to represent. It's the only way I get paid as a broker. And you know I have some big players in my repertoire. Well, one whisper led to another whisper who led to my client. It was a long, slow process, but I finally struck gold – pun intended."

Mona laughed.

"Ultimately, I had to be vetted myself in person and had to fly down to a tiny village in the Argentine province of Cordoba, which incidentally is mostly a German community full of fucking Nazi fanatics. In fact, it could easily be mistaken for a village in Bavaria itself. The legend around this place is that Hitler escaped Germany via a U-boat and resettled in this village and eventually died in 1972, that he never committed suicide in 1945 while in his bunker in Berlin." That clever Jake Tununda, LaMar thought again. He had pulled this story from a *Hunting Hitler* show on the History Channel.

"What's the name of this village?" asked Mona.

LaMar shook his head. "Sorry, not going to reveal it. It's where my client lives. That's all I'm giving you. Trust me. He's legit. My life and Hoffman's life depend on it. We're not fucking with you."

Hoffman piped up. "On this transaction alone I stand to make triple the amount of money I make in a year selling military relics from my collection.

It's a huge professional risk for me, but how in the hell could I pass this opportunity up? We're talking dealing with a descendant of Hermann Göering himself. This is history in the making!"

That answers my question about his participation, thought Mona.

LaMar cleared his throat to get Hoffman to stop talking. He snapped his fingers and told him to get back to work. "Anyway, his people strip-searched me before I was able to meet with him. Strip search. Crazy. That's where I emailed you from, asking if the two items were still available. And it's directly where I got the cash from, too."

"Incredible," said Mona. She decided to stall a little, noticing a voice mail was left on her iPhone on the table in front of her. She touched the screen to access the numerical keypad to enter her access passcode, then quickly tapped four times on the #3 key.

Hoffman caught the code out of the corner of his eye.

Mona tapped the voice mail app and listened to a quick message from her niece. All she wanted was to tell her aunt that she'd be back in the city in a week. "My niece. Coming back to town from college is all." She clicked the phone to lock-out mode again and set it back on the table.

"My client wants to move quick on this deal," LaMar persisted. "Like I said, full offering price. One phone call and everything gets wired to your account. Okay? Satisfied? Now, come on, *you* talk."

With a deep sigh, she relented. She couldn't refuse and had nothing to lose. Phoenix was clearly now out of the picture and would soon be out of the country. He'd have no idea she spilled the beans on him. "Okay, I'll rehash what Phoenix told me. What do you want to know?"

"Excellent," said LaMar, rubbing his hands together. "Now, when I took Phoenix to the PDK airport in Atlanta, I figured he had the pieces in his backpack, right? But, I never did see them. Off he flew and that was the last I ever heard of him. Poof! He's gone. My question is, how the fuck did some punk-ass Sureños-13 gangbangers in Atlanta get ahold of the treasures? They even had the mask Phoenix used at West Point. There were pictures in the news from the gangbanger's own phone showing him holding the stuff up. The FBI then kills the thug they thought was the real Phoenix."

Mona didn't hold back. "Phoenix told me his plan was to stash the Nazi trophies and the Union general's hat at a storage facility when he drove into Atlanta. Then he was going to get some sleep after the long drive from New York while you and I worked out where and when he would deliver the hat to your client."

"Right. I remember us trying to work that out," said LaMar.

"But he got carjacked by those thugs in the parking lot at the storage facility," she said, rather dramatically. "They knocked him out cold, stole his phone, and his rental car and everything in it. Never took his wallet, though. Guess they just wanted the car. Their mistake."

"Whaaaat? Holy shit," said LaMar. Even Hoffman looked up for a moment, too.

"What does he do?" continued Mona. "Couldn't call the cops obviously. Well, he already had the code to get into the storage facility. No employees were around that time of night so after he gets inside, he told me he then climbed up into the ceiling tiles and crawled through the rafters into the main office area like a damn monkey!"

"No way," LaMar laughed, egging her on.

"Yeah, I know," said Mona. "He then reviews the security camera tapes and sees what happens to him. That it's four punks. After that, he gets into the company computer system and tracks down the location of his iPhone using that GPS tracking app. Pinpoints the location of his phone at some apartment complex and the next morning, after renting another car and purchasing a laptop, he finds one of the thugs with his phone. Just a kid in his early teens. He kidnapped the kid and held him hostage, beat him, interrogated him as to who the other culprits were, and where his loot was. Of course the kid sung like a bird."

"You've gotta be kidding?" asked Hoffman, completely mesmerized at the story. "This is the stuff movies are made of!"

"Tell me about it," said Mona. "I should write the screenplay."

"So, what then? How'd he get the trophies back?" asked LaMar.

"Phoenix said he contacted the leader of the gang on the phone offering to make an exchange, but the guy didn't give a shit about the kid he was holding hostage. So, to make them take notice that he was serious, Phoenix learned from his hostage all about their drug operation. He then fucking firebombed one of their drug houses with a Molatov cocktail. But it was a meth lab and exploded. He killed a gang member inside."

"Jesus," LaMar said quietly, looking down.

"Yeah, he's no choir boy," said Mona, rather solemnly. "He threatened their drug business. Their main source of income. Well, they wanted to talk after that. Phoenix made them drop off a backpack with the two Nazi relics in it at a train station in Atlanta, but he paid some homeless guy to retrieve the backpack. Said he made a quick backpack switcheroo in the middle of a crowd and saw the homeless guy get caught by the gang who were lying in wait to ambush him."

"Wow!" said LaMar.

Mona was on a roll now. "Phoenix then sneaks away in a taxi and was dropped off near Le Maison Rouge for the delivery to your client. But before he got there he called 911 posing as one of the gang members, and said there was a civil war going on. He framed them for taking the boy hostage, the death of the meth lab guy, and, get this, even the theft of the West Point treasure, too! Told the cops where to find the gang leader and the cops took it from there. The FBI swatted the man's house and gunned him down. That's how Phoenix got away with it."

"He killed that boy, though, didn't he?" asked LaMar. "They found him in the trunk of a car severely beaten and stabbed to death."

"Jesus Christ, I didn't know that," said a visibly shocked Mona, shaking her head. "He never told me about that. I just assumed he made the exchange."

"And the next day, I get approached by my client's contact asking to help Phoenix escape to the local airport," said LaMar, filling in the pieces to the story. "So, he *did* have these two treasures with him then?"

"Yes, he had them both at that time," replied Mona. "I picked him up when he landed in Fitzgerald, Georgia."

"Fitzgerald?" asked LaMar, playing dumb. "Where the hell's that?"

"South Georgia. Middle of fucking nowhere. Farm country. You see, I flew into Savannah and rented a car to go meet him there at some tiny little runway. He told me later that he hijacked the pilot at gunpoint, forced him to land there. Hijacked him with Hitler's gun."

LaMar laughed out loud. "No fucking way! My client will love that. Man, Phoenix sure does have some big balls."

Mona smirked. "You've no idea," she said again in her sultry voice.

"Hmmm, so what happened next, after you picked him up?"

Mona was thrilled again to brag about her intricate role in the cover-up of the theft. She leaned back on her chair, crossed her legs and relaxed. "He had me drive him to some cemetery. I had to wait in the car, and then he hopped the fence and went in. Oh wait, let me back up. Before I arrived I actually had to buy a few things at an Army-Navy surplus store. This ammo can," she pointed to it on the table. "And that liner to protect the baton." She reached over and unwrapped it to reveal Göering's diamond encrusted ceremonial baton. "Also a trench shovel and a flashlight."

"Did *you* ever see these two items, though?" asked LaMar.

Mona nodded. "Yes, in the car. He showed them both to me. Couldn't believe it. He took everything into the cemetery with him and said he placed them in that ammo can and buried it."

"Where?" probed LaMar, knowing the story was getting recorded.

"No idea," she shrugged. "Said he could not get caught with them. Was part of his insurance if the Feds ever nailed him. Kinda like a bargaining chip given all the crimes he's wanted for."

"Yeah, I remember him telling me that when I asked him why he stole them in the first place. Said the same thing to me. Insurance. Guy's a fucking master chess player."

"Yup, best in the business," Mona sighed.

Hoffman returned the pistol to the box and snapped it shut. "If I may interrupt, so far so good. The pistol *is* totally legitimate. All the markings and engravings *are* accurate. It's the real thing."

"Excellent," said LaMar. "Proceed with the baton, Mr. Hoffman." He turned back to Mona. "Then what? What happened after he buried them?"

"That was pretty much it," answered Mona. "I mean, I drove him to Savannah. We spent the night at the Bohemian. I gave him my rental to take back to New York and I caught the next flight out in the morning."

"So these have been buried in the cemetery ever since?" asked Hoffman, reaching for the baton, bifocals sliding down his nose.

She nodded.

"Amazing story," LaMar said. "And when did *you* get them back? Once I contacted you or did you have other buyers first?"

Mona paused. She shifted nervously and recrossed her legs. She looked down. "Well, it was last night. They were delivered to my B&B room."

"By Phoenix?" asked LaMar, a little too forcefully.

"I guess so. I never did see him in person," she lied.

"You don't know where he is?" LaMar asked.

"Listen, enough fucking questions!" Mona spat. "End. Of. Story."

"Okay, okay, I'm sorry," LaMar said, holding up his hands in surrender. "We'll leave it at that. Helluva story as it is." He stood up and started pacing.

Mona snapped at Hoffman who was inspecting the baton with his magnifying glass. "Satisfied yet? It's fucking real, too."

"Almost," mumbled Hoffman, ignoring her bark. "It's looking good."

"Listen, Mona," said LaMar, turning around, a bit pissed-off and totally going off script. "I saw the fucking news this morning. Phoenix killed that cop. Well, Nathan Kull, I should say, did it. He's the same guy I helped escape Atlanta last year. I need to know where he is and if he's going to fuck up this deal in any way. I trust you, but I do not trust him."

Before she could respond there was a loud knock at the door. "Room service!" yelled a man's voice.

LaMar spun around. "You fucking kidding me? Hold on. I got this."

Room service? Mona thought strangely. "You guys order food?"

Hoffman feigned ignorance and merely shrugged his shoulders.

LaMar hustled over to the door a little too quickly.

Gotta be a mistake. She slid her hand to the side pocket on the backpack and grasped the pistol. *There's a 'Do Not Disturb' sign on the handle. Something's wrong.* "Hey! Don't open that door!"

He ignored her and fumbled with the dead bolt.

Mona stood up and quietly crept up behind him. She extended her arm, pistol in hand, finger twitching on the trigger, and pointed at the door.

Hoffman saw everything as if in slow motion. When Mona stood up armed with a pistol, he reached under his coat for his own firearm. As he stood up, he made a snap decision. He snatched Mona's iPhone off the table and pocketed it in his coat. He stood across the table, slightly behind her.

"I said, do not open that door!" Mona ordered.

LaMar didn't even look back. Instead, he twisted the lock and swung the door half open. Camouflaged soldiers wearing helmets with visors stood before them.

"Military Police!"

Seeing a fully-armed soldier barking at her, Mona flinched and depressed the pistol's trigger with an ear-piercing bang. Having never fired a gun before, she pulled her aim slightly to the right. The bullet's trajectory accidentally caught LaMar in the back of the head. The exit wound blew blood and skull fragments all over the soldier. LaMar ragdolled to the floor.

Mona's pistol report was so unexpectedly loud she screamed and involuntarily closed her eyes while unwittingly pulling the trigger again. Her next round hit the lead soldier in the upper leg.

An even louder bang now filled the room. This time Mona felt a burning sensation above her ear. Her vision instantly went black as Hoffman's .45-caliber hollow point bullet bore through her skull, and punched a fist-sized hole out the other side of her head, splattering blood and brains against the wall. Hoffman immediately backed far into a corner after he shot her and dropped his gun on the floor.

As Mona's body slid down the blood splattered wall, the door was kicked wide open and the bloody lead soldier opened up with his shotgun. The rapid reports were thunderous and eardrum-bursting as buckshot ripped Mona's body apart. Another soldier, armed with an AR-15 close quarters assault rifle, popped three more rounds into her head for good measure as her body lay crumpled on the floor. Shouting soldiers then barged into the room and spread out.

"Hold your fire!" screamed Hoffman from his corner sanctuary, ears ringing from all the gunfire. He was on his knees and had his hands thrust in the air so the soldiers would see he was unarmed. "Hold your fire!"

The lead soldier – helmet and visor covered in blood and bleeding from the leg – limped up to him pointing a smoking shotgun. Hoffman nearly shit his pants. He then recognized the chiseled jaw and Roman nose of

Sergeant Marco D'Arata and breathed a sigh of relief as the Army CID special agent lowered his weapon.

"Hoffman is okay!" shouted D'Arata. "I've got him."

Several more armed personnel poured into the suite behind him.

D'Arata grimaced and leaned against the wall, blood soaking his BDU pants and dripping onto the floor. A man and woman dressed in civilian clothes, who Hoffman recognized as Jake and Rae Tununda, entered the conference room, too. Their guns were drawn, but soon holstered at the sight of D'Arata.

Rae bent down and inspected D'Arata's leg. "Heavy bleeding. We might need to apply a tourniquet." She turned toward Hoffman. "Give me your belt just in case." Hoffman scrambled to help out.

Jake bellowed behind him at the soldiers. "D'Arata's hit. Get the paramedics in here NOW!"

"Jake, your knife," ordered Rae.

"Hang in there, brother," said Jake, addressing the fellow Freemason D'Arata with the fraternal term of endearment. He extracted a tactical knife clipped inside a cargo pant pocket and sprung the blade open.

"We're gonna take care of you, Marco," said Rae as Jake handed her the knife. "Let's get you down on the floor. I need to cut away this pant leg to find the wound."

Jake took his shotgun and helped D'Arata sit down against the wall. Rae positioned herself between his legs and immediately stuck the blade through his lower trouser leg and started slicing the blood-soaked material from his boot all the way up to his groin.

"Be careful, Rae," said D'Arata with a forced smile as he took off his helmet and wiped his face. "You slip up and my wife will kick your ass."

"Don't worry, hon," replied Rae, cutting the pant leg side-to-side to expose his upper thigh and underwear. "I'm good with my hands." She looked up into his pale face and winked.

Handing the blade back to Jake, Rae received a handkerchief from a shaking Hoffman and started wiping down D'Arata's bloody leg. On his inner thigh, she found the entry wound pumping out blood. An artery was severed. She immediately applied pressure.

"Belt!" she said to Hoffman, who instantly complied. "Good. Now keep pressure on the wound." While Hoffman kept the bloody handkerchief in place, she wrapped the belt around D'Arata's upper thigh and started to tighten it. Grunting, the Army agent reached for Jake and pulled him close.

"Brother," he whispered woozily, looking Jake in the eye. "I'm not ready to meet the Grand Architect," referring to the name that Freemasons gave God. "Not yet, man."

"Don't worry," Jake said softly, "I've got a trick or two up my sleeve to fool him."

From another one of his pockets, Jake took out his black whiskey flask. *"Elixir of Life.* Take three long gulps." He then pulled out a tiny personal first aid bag, unzipped it, and found a small green pouch labeled QuickClot® Combat Gauze. He tore it open.

D'Arata tipped the flask and chugged. When the moonshine hit his throat and belly he let out a satisfactory howl.

Unrolling the white gauze, Jake addressed Hoffman, another fellow Mason, who was pale and sweating profusely now. "I'm going to pack this into his wound. As soon as I finish, you need to apply pressure again. Don't stop for a good five minutes. Got it, brother?" A wide-eyed Hoffman nodded several times.

Rae tied the tourniquet belt in a knot and backed away. "Go, Jake."

"This is gonna hurt, Marco."

"Just fucking do it," said D'Arata, his head spinning with dizziness.

Rae clutched D'Arata's hand. Hoffman removed the handkerchief. Jake took a strip of the gauze and started stuffing the material into the bullet hole. He used his index finger and jammed the gauze deep into the wound. D'Arata threw his head back and yelled in excruciating pain.

Jake knew quite well that QuickClot was a proven life-saver on the battlefield and used in all branches of the military. It was also available for emergency services, law enforcement, and civilian use since the agent in the gauze created a hemo-concentration effect in the blood to promote clotting and coagulation right at the source of the bleeding.

He worked fast, packing the gauze tightly into the hole with his finger until just a small piece was left hanging out. D'Arata had just about passed out from the intense pain, coupled with loss of blood, and a heavy injection of moonshine. Hoffman was handed a fresh towel by another soldier and applied it over the wound with pressure as Jake had ordered.

Just then, the paramedics showed up. Rae explained to them the nature of the wound and the actions they just took to stabilize the victim. As they took over, Jake, Rae, and Hoffman backed away, all three in a daze.

12

RETURNING TO SAVANNAH FROM A VISIT AT THE Medical University of South Carolina Hospital, where CID Special Agent Marco D'Arata was recovering, Jake maneuvered his SUV in the narrow back alley behind his River Street building and parked in a darkly shadowed cobblestone-lined alcove inside the bluff. He rubbed his tired eyes from the four-hour roundtrip.

His cell phone rang. It was Rae. He stayed inside his running vehicle as he had a lot to tell her. She had been sleeping back at their home on Skidaway Island after taking a bedside shift herself with D'Arata's wife and kids last night.

"Hey hon, you get some sleep?" he asked.

"God, yes. I needed it. How's Marco doing?"

"Making steady progress," said Jake. "Expected to be released from the ICU within a week, but he'll be stuck in the hospital for a good while longer to monitor his recovery. Oh, and get this: the docs even joked when he was first admitted to the emergency room yesterday, that they'd never seen a gunshot patient so happily drunk. So much so, that he demanded more *Elixir of Life* moonshine and no other painkiller!"

Rae laughed and remarked that the moonshine was a life-saver.

"So I spoke with a CID officer who was there visiting Marco, too. Even though LaMar ate a bullet and Mona Lisa was turned into Swiss cheese, we scored a major victory for the Army by recovering the pistol and baton. On top of that, we got the full background story of the theft. It redeemed Marco's personal standing with CID brass. They're putting him in for a promotion and medal."

"Wow! So happy to hear that. He's a tenacious pit bull. It paid off."

Jake explained to his wife that since U.S. Army interests were satisfied in the recovery of the two Nazi items, the CID was forced off the case, even though there was still an active arrest warrant for the original theft by Kull. The most important crime to solve now – out of a slew of unsolved cases attributed to Kull – was the murder of the Georgia law enforcement officer, which put the FBI back in the driver's seat as the lead agency now calling all the shots.

"It's a huge embarrassment for the FBI," said Rae. "Hell, if they didn't mothball the damn case over the last year, that cop would still be alive."

"Listen to this," said Jake. "Mona Lisa's wallet in her purse? Found out her real identity: Maya Levana. She is – was – a well-known art gallery owner from New York City. The FBI already searched both her gallery and brownstone residence and guess what they found?"

"What?"

"They found six valuable paintings reported stolen from a fraudulent art gallery onboard an Alaskan cruise ship. That theft took place not five days ago. But through a passport check, they also found out our Nathan Kull was a passenger onboard when it happened. He boarded in Vancouver and departed in Anchorage. He's now their prime suspect in that case, too. Google it when you get a chance. The art gallery was fraudulently selling reproduction Giclée prints as originals instead of the real paintings. Kull set a fire onboard as a cover-up to steal the real ones."

"Jesus, no wonder they call him the Phoenix. Lights shit up and then disappears. How'd your meeting go with the FBI?"

"Not good, Rae. Not good. Highly fucking contentious."

"Uh-oh."

As a participant in the Army sting operation, Jake had been summoned to a post-raid informational meeting with FBI agents in Charleston.

Along with the FBI's new special agent in charge who arrived in town from Columbia, South Carolina, there was also an Army CID liaison from Hunter, and Erhardt Hoffman, who was recently released from the hospital. They wanted Jake's version of events in light of the loss of life of two individuals and the wounding of an Army special agent.

"I learned from Hoffman that the special agent in charge, Peter McNabb, had been demoted from a top management position in D.C. You remember the agency's big political corruption scandal with the fake Russian dossier and the purge of all those Hillary Clinton lovers that followed? Rumor has it that this asshole McNabb should be in prison, but he cut an immunity deal. Sold some other agents out. He's been in Columbia ever since."

"Great. Just great. They assign a tainted asshole to our case."

"Well, that fucker accused you and I of conspiring to steal Mona's missing iPhone. I almost punched him in the mouth. And then I advised him that any further contact with us would be through our attorney."

"Good!"

"Before I left, McNabb announced the case was under strict embargo. That they were keeping the names of the deceased from the public and their next of kin, and subsequently from Kull himself in hopes of catching him. They want him to think the sale of the Nazi relics to LaMar still took place. The only thing they're releasing to the public is that two individuals were deceased as a result of a drug deal gone bad since so many guests heard all that gunfire."

Finally, Jake told his wife he was now back at the 'Menagerie,' as he called his new business. "I'm going to swing some hammers and blow off some steam and then have a drink next door at *Books 'N Booze*."

"Okay, hon. Love you."

"Love you, too, babe."

Upon ending the call and stepping outside, Jake flinched as a distraught Sammie Greenhall emerged from the shadows.

Jake exhaled loudly. "Sammie? Jesus. You scared the crap out of me. What's going on? Everything okay?"

"No, Mr. Jake," said the frazzled teenager, his black eye looking better. "I, I, I need help. I dunno who to turn to. It's that son-of-a-bitch, Buzzut."

Jake placed a hand on Sammie's upper arm. "He hurt you again?"

Sammie shook his head and started talking quite fast. "I got my savings account back from him on my birthday on Sunday, but there was nothing there. I saved up $6,000 the last five years working my ass off and there ain't a penny left of it. All's I got is the cash you gave me from them rings." Sammie sighed deeply.

"And-and-and then a letter came in the mail yesterday, some kinda notification for Pappy because his land is being sold. Couldn't make any sense of it. So I met with Beulah Brown. She's our island's librarian and historian. Well, she almost had a heart attack when she saw what Buzzut did. But she said it all looked to be legal since he is the guardian. He did things by the book; gave the probate court notice of the land sale, and got their approval. He has complete authority, she said."

"Slow down," said Jake. "What'd he do exactly?"

Sammie threw his hands in the air. "Buzzut's selling our house. He's selling Pappy's boat. And he's selling all the land. All 33 acres. It's been in our family since 1871, Mr. Jake! The letter said him and the buyer are supposed to finish their deal in three days time at some lawyer's office over in Darien."

"What?!"

Sammie had tears in his eyes. He clenched his fists, veins bulging in his forearms, and he started pacing. "He took advantage of us, Mr. Jake. All this time he was supposed to be acting in our best interests. It's bullshit! Pappy and me didn't know nothing about this. He'd never agree to sell the land. He wants the bloodline of the descendants to stay on the land. I'm the one who's supposed to inherit it since everyone else is gone. We had a will before Buzzut got into our lives. It said the Greenhall's would never sell the land, that we'd put it into a land trust for residents of the island if we ever couldn't afford it. But that will disappeared. He stole it. Buzzut scammed us. We got nothing left. I'm gonna be 18-years-old and homeless!"

Jake pulled Sammie close. He slung an arm over his shoulder and reassured him by saying that everything would be okay; that it'd all work out, and no one was going to steal his land or Pappy's boat. Jake honestly had no idea know what to do, but at least his words calmed the teen somewhat.

"You don't understand, Mr. Jake," said Sammie, stepping back. "Beulah called up the real estate agent in Darien demanding to know what all was going on and they said I'm supposed to move out of our house the day of the sale. If I don't, then they're gonna get the sheriff with an eviction notice and make me move out by force. They're kicking me out! And then Buzzut's gonna move Pappy into a nursing home over on the mainland, too."

"Oh, God," said Jake.

The teen rambled on. "Pappy said he'd barricade himself in our house if the authorities ever tried to kick us off our land. That he'd make a final stand and go down shooting. And he *will*, Mr. Jake. He *will*. I know him best and he's got a mean streak."

"I would, too, Sammie," mumbled Jake, sweeping a nervous hand through his hair.

Sammie looked around and lowered his voice. "I drove the boat here so Buzzut wouldn't get it. It's down at the dock, but I need to hide it somewhere. Pappy ordered me to do it. Said don't let Buzzut ever find it because the boat alone is worth like half a million bucks."

Jake stood dumbfounded.

Sammie dug in his pocket. "Pappy told me to give these to you as payment for helping us. Says you keep 'em." He held his hand out displaying three SS *Totenkopf* rings.

Jake blinked several times. "What the–?"

"They're yours, Mr. Jake." Sammie dropped them in Jake's hand. "We need help. If that's not enough, Pappy says he's got hundreds more."

Jake stared at the rings in his hand. Off the top of his head they were worth close to $30,000. "More? Hundreds more?"

Sammie nodded. "That's what he said."

"Alright, alright," Jake sighed, looking up at the sky, his mind a crazy mess. *What a complete shafting Sammie and his great-grandfather were getting. So fucking unfair.* He'd read about elder abuse and guardian abuse before, but what Buzzut was doing was outright a dagger in the back. He pinched the bridge of his nose and squeezed his eyes shut for a moment wondering how he'd become so involved. It was these damn SS rings, he realized, opening his eyes and looking at them in his hand. He should have just heeded Rae's advice and never have looked for Sammie on Sapelo Island. This wasn't his responsibility or his predicament. But at the same time there was a wolf out there preying on the innocent and vulnerable. He couldn't just tell Sammie to work it out on his own. That wasn't in his DNA. Besides, he'd offered help and now the kid needed help. That was the Masonic thing to do.

Jake looked up to Sammie. He was in game mode. "Alright, here's what we're going to do. Listen closely."

✵

An hour later
Moon River Court
Skidaway Island

Jake stood on his private dock overlooking Moon River on the southwest shoreline of Skidaway Island. His beautiful Spanish villa-style home stood behind him, a good distance away, on their five acres of heavily wooded and landscaped property. Soon he heard a distinct rumble like an oncoming Harley Davidson hog as Sammie motored the vintage speedboat, *Doctor Blackbeard,* up the river towards him.

Jake waved, then guided Sammie right into his boat house where the two of them made short order in getting it lifted out of the water and away from prying eyes. Within less than a minute, the clever Sammie even rendered the Chris Craft engine inoperable by pulling the cable going from the coil to the distributor. By removing that critical component in the ignition system, the engine would never fire, no matter how many times the ignition key was turned over. Jake removed the black stern pirate flag and wrapped the cable in it before finding a hiding place. After covering the boat with a tarp, Jake locked the doors, then engaged the alarm system.

Next, he needed to get Sammie back home to Sapelo to retrieve all the paperwork they had. His plan was to get everything to his own high-powered Savannah lawyer the following morning for an immediate review hoping to find some loophole to stop the sale of the estate. Jake's secondary goal, if it presented itself, was to meet Duff Greenhall himself and ask him the story behind all of his skull rings.

Originally, he planned to drive to Sapelo, but it was already too late to catch the last ferry from the mainland over to the island. Instead, he and Sammie took *Lizzie*, Jake's ArrowCat power catamaran, for the 20 mile boat ride down the coast.

Having already told Rae of Sammie's problems with his ex-guardian LeShaun Greenhall, she never questioned that Jake had to go to Sapelo to help the kid out. She prepared a cooler of food and drinks and packed a travel bag for his overnight, while he changed into different clothes more fitting for a hike up a mountain. She now approached in their golf cart and parked at the dock where she unloaded next to some other gear Jake had already prepped there.

One of his most essential items was his Community Emergency Response Team (CERT) emergency go-to kit. It was a Modular Lightweight Load-carrying Equipment (MOLLE) backpack with the exterior Pouch Attachment Ladder System (PALS) webbing. His kit was chock full of essential life-saving gear needed for rescues, medical emergencies, and survival in extreme situations. As a volunteer member of the Skidaway Island CERT, a trained rescue specialist position through the Federal Emergency Management Agency (FEMA) and the local fire department, Jake was always prepared to assist those in dire need.

Whether it was a deadly hurricane, a house fire, a local car accident, or someone in need of medical treatment, CERT members were trained in first aid, search and rescue, fire suppression, and other skills to supplement local fire departments when they faced a manpower shortage. They were the support unit when natural or man-made disasters happened. With Skidaway Island as a barrier island to the mainland, major thunderstorms, hurricanes, and flooding were the primary threats to the gated community of some 7,000 residents. After the island evacuated during the massive Hurricane Irma strike in 2017, he was one of the few who stayed behind to help out the local firefighters and EMTs.

But Jake customized his backpack to hold gear more fitting of his days as a combat infantry officer with the Army's 10th Mountain Division, where he saw various deployments throughout the world. His additional gear allowed him to respond to any active shooter incident or perhaps start his own. He handed the backpack to Sammie, onboard his boat, and the kid almost fell over from its weight.

Also on the dock was a camouflaged gun case for what appeared to be a normal hunting rifle. Jake unlocked it and pulled out something Sammie didn't expect; a semi-automatic designated marksman rifle (DMR) in a burnt bronze finish. It was based off the army-issued M110, but Jake made some additional modifications to the already proven weapon system. The rifle was chambered in 7.62 mm with a ten-round mag, a 5-25x scope, retractable bipod, suppressor, and adjustable stock. Sammie's eyes widened.

"Damn, Mr. Jake," he said. "I bet that'd do a number on the wild hogs we got on Sapelo."

"Yeah," said Jake, grinning "I figured we might need a little more firepower than your old twenty-two. You know, in case you need to shoot at trespassers again." He opened the action and verified it was unloaded. He handed Sammie the rifle and told him to store it in the cabin.

Lastly, he handed Sammie the cooler and his overnight duffel bag. With that, Jake's boat was loaded up and ready to shove off.

"Fire us up, Captain!" He ordered Sammie. "I'll get the lines."

Rae came over to him as the catamaran bubbled to life. "You almost forgot this," she said, placing his khaki paddler's hat on his head. She was well aware of the unknown he was getting himself into – but also knowing it's what he lived for. "Listen, I'm going to pull some strings and do a background check on that fucker LeShaun. I'll text you what I find out."

"Thanks, babe."

She leaned up and gave him a long kiss. With an index finger in his face, she said, "you come home to me, Jake Tununda."

He kissed the tip of her finger and promised her he would.

In a matter of minutes, *Lizzie* motored around a bend in the river and disappeared.

13

J AKE LEANED OVER, INTRODUCED HIMSELF, AND
shook Duff Greenhall's veiny hand as the thin elderly man sat slouched
in his paint-chipped porch rocker. With a cigar protruding from his
thick lips, he revealed a wide gap between his front two teeth. A halo of
blue smoke swirled about cropped gray hair peeking out from under his
signature WWII veteran baseball cap. A German MP40 submachine gun
lay across his lap, box magazine fully loaded.

Jake placed his free hand over both their clutched hands to conceal
a quick motion he made with his thumb. A surprised Duff squinted at
Jake with faded light blue eyes through a smeared pair of glasses. As his
wrinkled, weathered face seemed to light up a little bit, he immediately
made the same secret motion with his own thumb.

Sammie, standing next to Jake, had seen that deliberate cupping of the
hands before when Duff met certain other men, but never knew what took
place under that concealment.

Jake and Duff though, shared an instant bond of trust, for they
knew it was a secret gesture that told one man to another of their mutual
membership in the oldest fraternity in the world: the Freemasons.

Duff groaned and stood up slowly. He was a slender-framed man of
no more than 5' 7" with a wide nose, deep sunken cheeks, droopy jowls,

and a thick, gray unkempt beard with one long braid that ended in a red ribbon wrapped around a tiny withered-up snake's head. He wore faded bib overalls and a white, button down, long-sleeved shirt rolled up to his elbows. An amulet with tiny blue stones hung from his neck. At the end of it dangled a two-inch long alligator tooth.

Setting his stogie aside in a nearby ashtray, and leaning his weapon against the covered porch wall, he spoke thick Gullah twang in a slow, sing-songy voice. "Oonuh travelin' mahn uh duh Craft. Ain many us left dese days. How old oonuh be, young brotha?"

At first Jake paused, not quite sure what he said, but then it clicked and he thought he'd try a bit of humor on the old timer. "Brother Greenhall, I'm well over the hill. I'm in my forties."

Duff guffawed and rolled his eyes. "O'er duh heel? O'er duh heel? Enty, boy? Hell, oonuh jus a yungin'. Uh dun been retired longa dan oonuh been alive. Uh da one o'er da heel, shee-it. Come on now. Sitcho ass down rite-chere. We krak teet." He snapped his fingers and pointed at a free rocking chair. Sammie sat in another chair next to Jake.

"Seegyaa'? Shyne?" asked Duff, plopping back down in his rocker.

Sammie leaned over to Jake. "Cigar and moonshine, he asked."

"Absolutely," nodded Jake, now slightly comprehending the different pronunciation of English words. "You know, Sammie gave me one of your famous *Elixir of Life* jars a few days ago when I came looking for him to buy that SS *Totenkopf* ring, and I've gotta tell you, it's now my new favorite liquor. Damned tasty and damned powerful. My wife said so, too."

Duff nodded his approval. "Uh-huh."

"I even gave him one with an alligator tooth in it, Pappy," said Sammy as he bounded down the front porch steps to a 5-gallon stainless steel pot atop a burning blue flame cooker supplied by a propane tank.

"Oooh, oonuh gots a rare jar, in-deed," said Duff, fingering the gator tooth on his necklace. "Uh dun cunjuh majik in dem jars, fo sho'. Yep, Sammie dun say 'bout oonuh comin' on out hee-uh an fine-in' us. Trespassing! Welp, oonuh dun cutta fine deal wit him fo dem seven G's. Lord know 'e need it."

"My pleasure," said Jake, not exactly sure what he'd just heard.

"Look, look," Duff continued, reaching for a nearby jar of moonshine with an *Elixir of Life* skull label on its frosty glass surface. As his hands shook, he unscrewed the lid. "Jus gots dis one outta da freezer. It best wen cold. Sip an pass it now. Dis here be history, brotha. History. Drink up tuh history now. Go on. Don'tchu be shy."

Jake took the jar, glanced at the label, and took a healthy sip. As the cold alcohol slipped across his tongue, his taste buds lit up like a sparkler. The white lightning then slid down his throat and instantly warmed his insides. He blinked several times, then said, "So good!"

Duff smacked him on his back and grinned.

"Hope you came with a big appetite, Mr. Jake," shouted Sammie from down on the grass. "We're having a Georgia low country boil freshly delivered from *Lula's Kitchen* down in the Hammock. Just heating it up." He lifted the pot's lid with an oven mitt and stirred the boiling water of colorful ingredients with a wire scoop. "We've got about 15 minutes more."

Duff smacked Jake on the thigh this time. "We's got in dere shrimp, crabs, red sausage, red potatoes, rutabagas, big ol' onions, carrots, turnips, an corn cobs. Wit a whole bunch 'o spices."

"Love it," said Jake. "Can't wait."

"Go on, boy. Oonuh take another swig uh my elixir."

"I think I will, sir," said Jake.

As he indulged in another sip of the cool potent moonshine, Duff pulled a cigar from a box and handed it to him, along with a cutter and a lighter. Jake trimmed the cap off his cigar then toasted the tip first before placing it between his lips and lighting up. Rolling the cigar while puffing, the end flamed high with every breath, causing a cloud of thick aromatic smoke to float around his head.

"Dat's it. Dat's I'ma talkin' 'bout," said Duff, seeing how Jake knew proper cigar lighting etiquette. "People dese days all terrified uh smokin'. Buncha bullshit, oonuh axe me. Been smokin' seegyaas all my life. Up tuh seven a day ain dun did me in yet. Ain a lick uh cancer. Secret is oonuh don't swallow da smoke. Don't suckitin an oonuh be jus fine. Dat's duh health-ee way tuh smoke. It be all 'bout duh taste an jus relaxin' anyway."

After replacing the lid on the boiling pot, Sammie took a seat next to

Jake back up on the porch. He sipped from the jar of moonshine then leaned over to Jake and whispered that Pappy liked him and was now deliberately easing off the Gullah language so Jake could understand him better. That he only used it on strangers or as a bit of show for the reporters. Jake winked at the teen.

Pulling out his iPhone, Jake asked Sammie to take a picture of him and Duff. Jake held up his cigar and the jar of moonshine, squatted down next to Duff, and smiled widely as Sammie captured the pair together. Sammie then showed Duff the picture and the old man smiled showing crooked yellow teeth.

"Sammie told me you're 93-years-old now," Jake said, making light conversation. "That right?"

"Uh-huh. It's been a long life fo' sho'." Duff shrugged his bony shoulders. "Don't know why I keep on livin'. Don't know what God has planned fo' me, so I just keep on gettin' on. I'm doin' alright, though. I still got all my wits 'bout me," he said tapping his temple. "I still got my memory. I can still walk, talk, hear, drive a truck, drink whiskey, smoke a seegyaa', and fire a gun."

"You're one lucky man," smiled Jake, already feeling the effects of the booze and cigar smoke. It was a hell of a happy buzz. "I hope I can do half that if I reach your age."

"Tell me, brotha. Where's your lodge at? You with them Georgia blue lodge boys?"

"No, not with any Georgia lodge." Jake said. "I visit a lot of lodges and make historical presentations, but I'm more of an independent Mason, if you will. I was deployed in Iraq when I became a Master Mason. Was in a military lodge called Land, Sea, and Air Lodge Number One of Iraq, but it's now belly up. Now I just pay my dues to the Grand Lodge of New York. What about you, Duff? Where were you raised a Mason?"

"I was raised a Prince Hall Mason right here on Sapelo back in '43 right before I joined the Army," replied the old man with a bit of pride in his voice. "Was down there in our Masonic lodge in Hog Hammock inside the old Farmer's Alliance Hall. But our chapter done died out many years ago. Never had enough officers to even open the lodge. I'm like you. I've had the

Masonic tools to live by all my life. It's not the lodge that makes the brotha. We know in our hearts we are men of good will who *act* to stop injustice. Most importantly, we help a worthy brotha in need no matter his skin color, his religion, or his dadgum politics."

"So mote it be," said Jake, taking an instant liking to Duff.

Both men took a moment and pulled on their cigars. The mood was reflective and peaceful. Jake took in the twilight landscape from the raised front porch vantage point. The house was gorgeously shrouded in darkness by kingly live oak trees, tall pines, and wide magnolia trees swaying in a strong breeze. The covered front porch was partially lit by several citronella candles to keep the bugs at bay, but the nice aroma of the low country boil kept the air sweet and tasty.

Jake glanced around the weed-infested yard where several old vehicles lay among cabbage and slash palms: a rusty Ford pickup truck with a big 'I Be Geechee' bumper sticker, a scratched-up, rusted-out Chevrolet El Camino, and a beat-up four-wheel All-Terrain-Vehicle. There was even an old graffiti-covered yellow school bus sitting in front of a boarded-up abandoned trailer home near the tree-lined bluff.

The long dock at Greenhall Landing ramped down the bluff with *Lizzie* floating lazily at the very end section among the swaying, seven-foot-tall cordgrass of the salt marsh. Beyond was glimmering Blackbeard Creek and a beautiful rust-colored evening sky painted over a dark forest silhouetting the mysterious Blackbeard Island.

Duff handed Jake the moonshine and urged him to 'sip it and pass it' again. Jake obliged and shuddered when the booze hit the back of his throat. His eyes even went slightly out of focus looking at the skull label before he handed the jar over to Sammie.

"That big double X mark on the skull's forehead on your label," Jake asked. "Is that a Masonic symbol?"

"I'll tell you what I tell everyone," mumbled Duff, cigar in mouth. "It's what you want it to be."

"A disguise?"

"Perhaps?"

"Hey, Pappy? Me and Mr. Jake got *Doctor Blackbeard* all hidden away," said Sammie, changing the subject. "It's up on the lift in his boat house on Skidaway Island. I even pulled the cable to the coil just like you told me."

Duff grunted his approval then looked at him with one eye open as cigar smoke pestered his other eye. "You give him them three rings as payment?"

"Sure did."

"Listen," said Jake. "I really don't–"

"Shush now," interrupted Duff, waving a hand. "Don't wanna hear it. You keep 'em, for helping us out. We're in a world of hurt right now and I ain't gonna let that motherfucker Buzzut get away with it. Ain't going down without a fight. Sammie done told me what y'all did to him up there at your River Street store. Told me you don't take nobody's shit."

"I couldn't believe he whipped Sammie right before my eyes. And then he flashed me his pistol and told me to back off," said Jake.

Duff stroked his bushy gray beard. "I read about what you and your wife did there in Savannah last year defending yourselves from that assassin, too. Buzzut almost made the same fatal mistake in pissing you off, huh?"

"Fatal is an understatement," chuckled Sammie. "He was about to eat a wall of lead from two women, too. Wish it happened. Our problems would be solved, Pappy."

Duff rocked in his chair, nodding his approval, and then touched the braid in his beard with the snake's head and ribbon. "You see, Jake. I knew about you from the newspapers, some of the things you were involved in, that British gold you discovered up in New York, how you got that Civil War general's hat back to the West Point Museum. Uh-huh. How much you love history and the military. I even remember seeing you at brotha Tommy Watie's funeral procession last year. And now you helping us out, no questions asked. Hm, hmm, well, giving you them rings was the least I could do for hiding my old boat."

Jake sucked on his cigar and exhaled a cloud of smoke. "I appreciate all that, but I do have questions about those rings, though."

"I know. I know." Duff waggled his head. "We'll get to that. I promise. Tonight I'm gonna make some big decisions. Big decisions involving Sammie, uh-huh."

"Sammie's a great kid," said Jake. The young man heard the compliment and smiled at Jake.

Over his eyeglasses, Duff looked directly at his great-grandson. "He's a strong young man. If not for him, I'd be long dead of a broken heart." Sammie looked down. "He's all I lived for during my mourning period when Buzzut exploited me and convinced a court that I done needed a permanent guardian." Then he raised his voice in anger. "I wasn't incapacitated then and I ain't now!" He lowered his voice then shook his head. "I was just depressed, that's all. Very, very sad and needed time to talk to the spirits of my deceased family."

Nobody said a word for awhile. Cigar smoke lazily filled the air under the porch eave, then whisked away as the wind picked it up.

Sammie bounded down the steps to check on their dinner again. A cat meowed and emerged from under the porch, attracted to the savory Southern fare. She immediately saw Sammie and skittered over to rub against his leg as he adjusted the heat on the cooking pot. Sammie leaned over and scratched her back. "Hi ya, Cleo." He flipped her a piece of shrimp that she gobbled up like a grizzly bear chomping on freshly-caught salmon.

Jake grabbed his phone and snapped a photo of Sammie and the cat, then showed it to him to garner a smile. Before he set the phone back down, he tapped an app called Voice Memo and started recording, unbeknownst to both Greenhalls. It was something he often did, given the chance. He had learned that much information usually got lost in a conversation, especially when booze was involved.

Jake cleared his throat. "If you don't mind, Duff, I can take that letter of notice and your copies of the contract on the sale of your estate to my lawyer in Savannah tomorrow. He's one of the best there is. He's the reason I was able to purchase that old warehouse down on River Street. Might be some kinda loophole to get that contract stopped or at least delayed."

"Nuh-uh. Waste of time," Duff replied, nixing Jake's suggestion. "Sammie, while you was gone, I drove down to Mikey Dixon's – that retired lawyer down in the Hammock. He confirmed what Beulah Brown said. What Buzzut did is all legal. I have *no* rights. *No* say in the matter. *No* way to stop him in three days when he closes the deal on the land. Simple as that. Mikey said the sheriff would definitely come out and evict us if we didn't leave."

Sammie pounded his leg in frustration, then double-stepped it back up the porch, and reached for the moonshine. "It's not fair, Pappy. They can't do this to us. They can't kick us off the island. I've taken Buzzut's abuse for five years – him whipping me, slapping me, punching me in my face and my stomach, and I'm *not* going to let him do this to us. I'll stand with you." He took a big gulp of 'shine and bucked his shoulders when it went down.

"Guys, listen, don't get emotional," lectured Jake, trying to ratchet things down. "Act rational. Don't do anything extreme or rash." As soon as the thought left his mouth, he knew he was a total hypocrite.

"Hmmm," said Duff. "Too late. I went to Buzzut's house and I told him straight to his face that I already had you hide my boat, Sammie, and if he touches you one more time I would shoot him." Duff grabbed his burp gun and placed it on his lap for effect. "And then I said if he sells my land, I would shoot him. And if he tries to force me into a nursing home, I would shoot him. And then after I riddle his body with bullets, I'd burn his ass to a crisp, stick him in a pluff mud hole, and feed him to the fiddler crabs where the tide ebbs and flows twice in 24 hours. Ain nothin' be lefta him."

"Oh no, no, no," said Jake, rolling his eyes. "You threatened his life?"

"I sure did! I stand to lose everything that matters in the world to me."

Sammie couldn't believe what he'd just heard. "You said all that to him, Pappy? Right to his face? What'd he do?"

Duff nodded. "Told me he hoped I had good aim and then slammed the door in my face."

The old man then took a long drink of moonshine and passed it to Sammie who also took another shot. No one said a word again. Soon the silence grew awkward.

"Umm, Pappy?"

"Yeah, boy?"

Sammie sat down and sighed heavily. "Umm, I've got a confession to make. I-I-I stole something from Buzzut's house. You talked about us getting leverage in hiding the boat, well, I thought if I stole something even more important to him, like what he was making his money off of, that maybe it would give us even more leverage to stop the land deal."

"Whatchu do, boy?" Duff grunted, one eye glaring at him.

Sammie swallowed hard. "Sunday night when I went to his house to get my savings account info . . . well, right before I left I heard his radio chirping in that code language I'd heard before, so I decided to spy on him."

"You did?" asked Duff, cigar back in mouth.

"Yaas'suh. I hid our truck, grabbed my rifle, and I followed his UTV hauling a storage trailer he kept in his woods. Followed him all the way out onto that old abandoned causeway over the marsh to Cabretta Island. He was in this little hiding spot in the woods on the southern tip of the island at Big Hole. Nobody ever goes there, not even the campers on the north part of Cabretta. Took me a long while to sneak up, but I watched him through my rifle scope and umm, well, I s-s-saw exactly how he makes his money."

"Well?" said and impatient Duff. "Go on. Spit it out."

"He smuggles drugs onto the island."

"Motherfucker," gasped Duff.

"By water?" asked Jake.

"No. By air. He uses a drone. Biggest I've ever seen."

"Son-of-a-bitch," Jake murmured, both surprised and impressed.

"Keeps it hidden in the storage trailer," said Sammie. "The sides fold down and it turns into a launching platform with lights. Attached to the drone was a big plastic bin." Sammie used his hands to show them the dimensions.

Jake smoked his cigar and listened.

"He stuffed stacks of cash into the bin. And then I spotted lights from a ship way out on the horizon. They flashed a few times and Buzzut flashed back with a big spotlight. And then his drone took off and flew over the ocean. Super fast. No lights. Never even heard it. I saw Buzzut was wearing like a headset covering his eyes, and he had a remote control, and he just sat there like a statue in the dark and flew the drone.

"Took about a half hour and it returned," he continued. "He checked the bin, cash was gone, and he pulled out all kinds of packages of drugs. Stuff I've seen before when he'd have me boat him around the coast. I even saw him snort some white stuff. Then he folded the trailer walls back up, and off he drove back over to his house. By the time I hiked back, he had all of his window blinds down and I couldn't see anything inside. I know he's got surveillance cameras, so I didn't dare go near his house. But last night I drove on down there and snuck back into the woods to spy again and saw the trailer just sitting there. It's kinda small and lightweight so I pulled it through the woods and all the way back down the road to where I had the truck hidden, hitched it up, and brought it home. I've got it hidden under a tarp over by the bluff, over there." He pointed past the dock further up the bluff to some bushy trees.

"You stole it?" asked Jake.

Eyes wide, Sammie nodded.

"You tell anyone else about this?" asked Duff.

"Nuh-uh."

"Keep it that way," said Duff. "Ooh, boy, he gonna be pissed! You done good, Sammie. I ain't mad at ya. That is gonna be some damned good leverage we got now."

"Phew!" sighed Sammie.

"That will be our ace-in-the-hole," said Duff. "We threaten to go to the authorities and turn his ass in if he don't nix the land deal."

"No," said Jake. "First you have to *prove* he is running drugs. You need hard evidence, like a video of him actually flying the drone and getting the drugs. It's Sammie's word against his as the guardian. He has the leverage. Besides, you've already threatened him with bodily harm, Duff. Who will the cops believe?"

"But we have evidence," said Sammie. "His drone."

Jake turned and wagged his cigar at him. "You are threatening his livelihood. He's probably working with a major drug cartel and you are expendable, Sammie. Both of you are. He'll have you taken out in a heartbeat by some cartel thugs."

The Greenhall's didn't say a word, knowing Jake was right.

"Now, listen to me. Here's what I think y'all can do, *first*. The safe route." Jake paused and gestured to Sammie to pass the jar of 'shine. He took a shot from the jar, gritted his teeth, and continued. "In order to close any real estate transaction, both parties have to be there in person, and sign off on all of the paperwork at the lawyer's office. If one of them is, ah, *temporarily* incapacitated, shall we say, then the deal doesn't go through. It gets postponed. This will buy you time, Duff, to figure out a better strategy rather than you putting a bullet in his head and living out the rest of your days in prison. Or worse, both of y'all getting killed in return."

"But what if Buzzut is *permanently* incapacitated instead, Mr. Jake?" asked Sammie, his words slurred. "And no one knew how it happened?"

Jake was left speechless. He pursed his lips. *Jesus, they're talking outright murder again.* Silence permeated the air once more. All that could be heard was the wind blowing through the tops of the trees and a loud purring cat. And then he heard Becky Holden's voice in his head warning him about getting involved with Doctor Blackbeard. Jake felt like he should just grab his shit and go. This whole episode was going down the rabbit hole.

Duff shifted in his rocker and broke the tension. "Then the sale is off forever and I am a free man once again. And Sammie and I can live in peace for the remaining time I'm here on this earth – on our land, in our home, making our own decisions."

"That's a strategy I like the best, too" said Sammie. "And then I can become Pappy's legal guardian and watch over him the right way."

"Whoa, there!" Jake blurted out. "I only meant incapacitating one of the parties to the point where they would back out of the deal. Have you spoken with the buyer? Maybe he or she will empathize with your situation and call it off."

Duff shook his head. "I found out who the buyer is from Lucy McEver, she's a real estate agent who lives here on the island. She'd already done some digging when word spread about the land sale. You see, she's opposed as hell about turning this island into a hotel and golf resort, too, so she took it personally. Found out everyone's worst fears come true. Buzzut sold the island out to a man named Harvey Westwood, one of the biggest private resort developers in the world. He owns a corporation based out of Atlanta called Dreamscape Hotels & Resorts. He's gonna turn this island upside-down."

"You have to immediately go to the media then," Jake implored. "Call all the reporters that interviewed you in the past. They'd love a David and Goliath story like this. If you get national publicity on this, Duff, then both parties will be under pressure to nix the deal. That's all I'm talking about. If that course of action doesn't work, then make Buzzut some kind of compromise offer he can't refuse. Use the hidden boat or the drone as your leverage in that sense. Don't go overboard, though, okay?"

"Overboard sounds good to me," said Duff in all seriousness. "I can whip up a root concoction to knock him out and we can wrap him up like a sack of potatoes and toss him overboard with an anchor. Make him fuckin' disappear for good. He's got it comin'. Hell, the sands of time for me are runnin' low as it is. You don't think I know that? I ain't got nothin' to lose. I'll take the fall. Sammie will get off scot-free."

"I didn't mean killing him, for fuck sake!" Jake blurted out. He stood up and nearly fell over from the effects of the corn whiskey. Cleo, the cat, scampered away, startled. Jake rudely stubbed out his cigar. "Listen, I offered to help Sammie, but this has escalated way too far. It's not my damn fight–"

"You ain't never broke the law, brotha?" Duff asked in a nasty tone, admonishing Jake. "Come on, man. You keep wanting to find the *legal* solution to this, instead of doing what's *right* to save lives."

Duff was spot on, Jake realized, which caught him in a moral quandary. He had no response whatsoever, having broken the law many times to do the right thing. And had taken down many a bad guy in the process. It's just that he wanted to keep his nose clean, live a normal life as a law-abiding citizen. Things were going so well for him now: new marriage, relocation to Savannah, a new business to focus on.

"What if I made *you* an offer you couldn't refuse?" Duff then asked, taking off his eyeglasses to look up at Jake straight in the eyes.

"Are you threatening *me* now? Are you out of your mind, old man?"

"Sit your ass down, boy!" shouted the old man, pointing to the chair. "I ain't threatening you. My offer is something that will go down in history as one of the greatest treasures ever discovered." He then pointed a finger at Jake. "You wanna know where I got all those goddamn skull rings from? Sammie doesn't even know. No one knows. How 'bout I show you *thousands* of them? How 'bout I show you a German U-boat commandeered by Americans and used to smuggle Nazi loot into the good ol' U.S. of A? It's a secret that's been buried for over 70 years. It can be yours if you help us get rid of Buzzut. How's that for an offer you can't refuse?"

Give me a U-boat? Jake's jaw dropped. *And thousands of skull rings? I must be drunk as fuck or this guy is casting a spell on me.*

Cleo poked its head out from under the porch and sauntered over to the low country boil looking for scraps on the ground.

"Now, sit down, shut up," Duff ordered. "And listen."

Jake plunked back down, grabbed the moonshine jar, and tipped it for another swig.

"Pappy? W-what, what you talkin' bout?" slurred Sammie.

"Sammie, our dinner's done," said Duff. "Even the dadgum cat thinks so. Let's eat first and then I'll tell y'all some stories I ain't never told nobody else. Now, pass that 'shine over here. Gonna be a long night. Got a lot to get off my chest."

14

WITH A FRESH CIGAR CLENCHED BETWEEN HIS teeth, Duff asked Jake, "You ever hear of *Operation Overcast* right at the end of WWII?"

"Overcast?" Jake pursed his lips. "Nope." Head spinning and belly bulging with tasty low country boil, he'd never felt better. But he also knew he needed to stop with the moonshine so he could pace himself while Duff spilled his guts about the past. He knew from experience to just let someone talk all they want, to be a good listener, and they would reveal some of their deepest secrets. Plus, he started his recorder app again to capture it all.

"How 'bout *Operation Paperclip*?"

"Now I have heard of Paperclip," said Jake, his words coming out slowly. "It was a secret government operation to smuggle Nazi weapons engineers, scientists, and intelligence officers into the United States. We stole their best human assets as spoils of war."

"All to fight the Red Scare," added Duff. "Because the Russians were doing the same. We gave some of the worst Nazis new identities and used them against the Commies. You're talkin' some of the dirtiest, nastiest war criminals in human history. Men who committed mass genocide."

"Yeah, I know. It's sickening. Was a huge secret our government kept under wraps for decades. If I'm not mistaken, *Operation Paperclip* only became known in the 1970s, but some files are still classified even today."

"Yup," said Duff.

Jake shook his head. "Man, if the public found out right after the war what our government was doing, giving these Nazis a free ride after so many of our boys died over there, heads would have rolled."

Duff shifted in his rocker. "Let me tell you how it started. *Operation Overcast* was the original name of the program in the summer of '45 right after V-E Day. But ya see, President Truman never knew about it. Nuh, uh. It was created behind his back by the heads of the intelligence agencies in each of the military branches. A year later the named changed to *Paperclip* and was only then officially authorized by Truman. *Paperclip* was said to be terminated in 1947, but they continued it in secret."

Duff coughed a little and placed his cigar in the ashtray. "What happened was the OSS, the Office–"

"Of Strategic Services, the predecessor to the CIA," added Jake.

"Uh-huh," grunted Duff. "Well, the way it came about was almost by accident. The OSS busted a highly-organized military black market network that was funneling loot from the American-occupied war zone back here to the States. You talkin' a supply chain through land, air, and sea. It started while our boys were still fightin' at the front getting their asses shot up, myself included.

"These rear-echelon motherfuckers were profiting big time in stolen treasures. I mean, sure, everyone stole stuff. Everyone got themselves a war trophy or a keepsake, myself included." Duff tapped his MP40. "Looting was rampant among the troops and you could ship stuff back in huge boxes and they hardly got inspected."

Jake nodded, knowing quite well how many war relics in his own collection made it back here to the States.

"But this particular theft ring was *the* most organized," Duff stressed. "They were doing it in bulk. It started with a rogue Army truck team that worked for the Monuments Men at their Wiesbaden collection point. The leader of this gang was a military police officer who called the shots."

"You've got to be kidding?" said Jake. "I've never heard about this."

"It's true," Duff said. "They were armed guards assigned from a regular

Army unit because the Monuments Men never had enough manpower. There were lots of truck teams and they were entrusted with collecting and securing all treasures found in the U.S. zone and bringing them back to the collection point where they were supposed to be registered. But this rogue team frequently diverted many of the treasures they were ordered to protect. They stole gold, silver, jewelry, artwork, rare books, even bags of gold teeth plucked from the mouths of dead Jews. Hell, anything of worth they could get their grubby little hands on. They was raping the same treasures that the Nazis raped all across Europe."

"Never knew this," said Jake.

"Yup," said Duff. "Stole shit right under the Monuments Men's noses."

"Sounds like the book I'm reading, *Nazi Gold*," said Sammie, as he was feeding Cleo food scraps from his plate.

"It does," said Duff. "But that book takes place a few years later when just about everyone got in on the act. What I'm talkin' about now is the spring and summer of '45 right when the war ended. The way this gang got busted was from the Art Looting Investigation Unit of the OSS. The ALIU. They were supposed to be finding out how the Nazis stole all the treasures and where their caches were, but instead they stumbled upon this Monuments Men truck team by accident.

"Under interrogation, they found out their transportation system involving an official Army Air Force courier flying their stolen stuff to Bermuda where the Navy part of their gang handled the last leg back to various ports in the States. But instead of this truck team getting court-martialed and sent to prison, the OSS ended up recruiting them sons-of-bitches. They wanted to now use their secret network to smuggle important Nazi fucks back to the States, too. Human smuggling."

"How'd you know all this, Duff?" asked Jake.

"Because I read the dadgum *Operation Overcast* mission orders about the very first Nazi who was smuggled in!" shouted Duff.

Jake was taken aback. "What?"

"He was onboard a captured German U-boat operated by a hand-picked American crew of Navy convicts from the Portsmouth Naval Prison in Maine. The OSS liked this particular Nazi because he commanded four concentration camps and developed state-of-the-art research into interrogation techniques, like truth serums. They done plucked a 'forbidden fruit' and were taking him stateside to use as their pawn."

"What the–?" Jake's lip curled. "I've read about rocket scientists like Wernher von Braun, but I never knew we were taking executioners, too."

Duff lifted his eyeglasses and rubbed his eyes. "September '45, I'd just gotten home from Europe that summer. I was young like you, Sammie. Wasn't but a twenty year-old combat vet. But even though the war was technically over in Europe, the authorities assigned me to Coast Guard patrol for this part of Sapelo Island. Just me, my .22 rifle, and my horse.

"Well, lemme tell you, that big ol' Homestead Hurricane hit at the same time and we're lucky we survived being up here on higher ground. Ya see, I saw some flares that night way out in the ocean, probably from a boat in distress. Thought I'd go out and see what I could find the next morning. You ain't seen nothing like it. Water was all the way up the bluff." Duff pointed toward Blackbeard Creek. "I could step right off into it. Dadgum storm surge flooded everything.

"I boated on over to Blackbeard Island and all's you could see was them big oaks up on the high north side of the island where all the dune ridges and troughs are." He pointed to the horizon then swept the air with his hand. "Everything else all around there was swamped."

Duff then paused. He closed his eyes, shook his head, and sighed deeply.

"Alligators were everywhere. The ones that survived were in a feeding frenzy. There were even dead ones being eaten by the live ones. Every animal you can think of was floating dead in the water. Especially birds." He paused again, his hands started shaking.

"I, I, I had to shoot them alligators to try and save . . ." The old man then shut down. Ten seconds later, he resumed his story. "Well, I found a conning tower sticking out of the mud – about twelve feet high. Didn't know it at the time, but it turned out to be the smallest, stealthiest U-boat in the *Kriegsmarine*, a type twenty-three class. Was wedged in one them real deep troughs way back in the woods there. Normally ain't nobody could ever get in there because them woods are so thick with underbrush, but with the water so high I floated right on in. I never told the Coast Guard or nobody that I knew that sub was there. Never told a soul.

"That is until now," Duff stated.

A U-boat wreck used by the U.S. for smuggling Nazis? Jake couldn't believe what he was hearing.

"Did you go inside? What happened to the crew?" Sammie asked, bouncing with excitement at Pappy's stunning revelation that a lost submarine was sitting over on Blackbeard. "How many were there?"

Duff coughed. He shook his head. "I've said too much. Said too much. The point I'm trying to make is I found those mission files onboard. I done got the name of the Nazi and of each crewman, and even the top government officials who authorized *Operation Overcast*. Identities on all of them. Hell, them files even show a list of all the military gang members in the entire smuggling ring and how they did it. From Germany to Bermuda, to Harris Neck, Georgia. I had the smokin' gun in my possession, boys!"

"That's dangerous information," murmured Jake.

"Indeed," Duff said, raising an index finger. "But powerful, too. And it paid off for me. Lemme tell you a story."

Jake's eyebrows arched. As if what he'd heard already wasn't enough.

"You see, when I got arrested by a McIntosh County sheriff's deputy two years later in '47 for running moonshine over to Shellman Bluff, I knew he was involved in the same military smuggling ring on the mainland because his name was on the list. He started interrogating me. Slapped me in the face something fierce wanting to know where I was making all my moonshine. Said he was gonna blow up my distillery.

"Well, I dropped the A-bomb on him instead. Said I knew he provided local protection for his pals at Harris Neck. I told him I knew what they was up to, smuggling Nazis in, bringin' all that war loot in."

"Holy shit," said Jake. "What he'd do?"

"That dadgum white devil pulled his revolver on me and put it against my forehead." Duff turned his hand into the shape of a gun and placed his index finger right between his eyes. "He threatened to do me right there in my cell. Didn't matter if I was a combat vet and took a bullet for the war. Nuh-uh."

Duff laughed derisively. "Now, I done killed my fair share of Nazi motherfuckers back in Italy – some of Germany's best infantry fighters they threw at us – so this racist deputy sheriff wasn't going to intimidate me. Nuh-uh. I stared him down. I threatened *him* now and demanded a phone call or his world would come crashing down. And you know what? He gave in. I done got ahold of the Master-at-arms captain who was stationed over at Harris Neck. He was the Navy's stateside head honcho for the OSS smuggling ring and my get-out-of-jail-free card. Or so I'd hoped.

"I told that Navy captain that if I didn't get out of jail, then my kinfolk have orders to deliver photographs of those original *Operation Overcast* orders to Ed Murrow so he could broadcast their illegal operation on the radio nationwide and blow their whole scheme out of the water, himself and the sheriff's department included. And all the way up the Pentagon's ranks.

"Damn," said Jake. "That was an A-bomb you dropped."

"I think the captain had a heart attack, I tell ya," Duff chuckled. "He got the deputy on the line and chewed his ass inside out. I got released immediately. They patched me up, even apologized to me! Next thing you know I'm getting orders for my moonshine not only from that deputy himself, but also the Navy captain, too, for his officer's club at the Livingston House on the Harris Neck base. His boys drank so much moonshine after that I could hardly keep up with production.

"But I think a lot of my 'shine was flown back to Europe where they sold it for a sizeable profit. The sheriff's department never ever messed with us Greenhall folk ever again. We had them by da *balls*, I tell you. By da *balls*. And they treated us nice."

"Hot damn," Sammie whistled.

"Ultimate power lies not with the man who holds the biggest gun," stated Jake, "but with the man who holds to most political leverage."

Duff snapped his fingers. "Ain't that the dadgum truth right there! Having possession of those secret documents saved our lives. We were swimming with the sharks and we survived. You wouldn't believe how some of them players in the smuggling ring became famous politicians and businessmen later on in life. Why's it okay for them to profit from it and not us little folk?"

Jake didn't have an answer. He knew Duff was right.

"Back in them days, blacks and whites were equally armed with guns and both sides knew it," explained Duff. "It was how we kept peace between the races here in the county. Blacks had pistols, rifles, and shotguns, and we carried them on our person, in our trucks, and in our homes. Mutually assured destruction was the deterrence when Jim Crow laws were still a way of life. The sight of a gun put people on their best behavior."

"It's like that famous quote," said Jake. "God may have created man, but Sam Colt made them all equal."

"Exactly!" said Duff. But he waggled a finger at Sammie. "But like Jake said, just having guns wasn't enough. It's the man who holds the most political leverage who holds all the cards. Having evidence of *Operation Overcast* and putting that threat out there to expose it gave us Greenhall's the political edge over the other blacks. It protected our kinfolk for many, many years after the war. I only used that threat that one time in jail and never again. It gave us, um, what's the word I'm looking for? It gave us—"

"Immunity," said Jake.

"Yaa'as, that's the word. Immunity. It's how I built our family fortune. It's how we played the dirty game. It's how us Greenhall's earned *respect*."

"Damn," said Sammie. "I never knew." Cleo jumped up and nestled on Sammie's lap. Her belly was full and she started purring when Sammie scratched her back.

"Lemme tell you something else, Sammie," said Duff, all jacked up and on one hell of a roll. "Back in them days boatloads of blacks in McIntosh County were rule breakers. Had to be. Life ain't fair, and if you toed the line and played by the white man's rules, you'd still be livin' on the plantation. But when ya start breakin' the rules and takin' risks and thinkin' for yourself and stop followin' the herd, well, ya just get ahead."

Jake nodded unwittingly.

Duff went on, looking directly at Jake now over the rims of his eyeglasses. "I learned that in the Army. I was in the 92nd Division, a black division segregated from the rest of the Army: the only Negro infantry unit to see combat in Europe during WWII. All of our enlisted and most junior officers were black, but the higher officers were white. I was with the 370th Regiment in a reconnaissance platoon.

Jake lived for this oral history. He placed his elbows on his knees, leaned forward, and absorbed every word that came out of Duff's mouth.

"Once you're in battle, you had to break the rules in order to survive, Sammie," said the old man, turning to his great-grandson. "Had to adapt, had to be creative, and be ruthless at the same time or you'd be dead. When we were advancing so high in the north Apennine Mountains of the German Gothic Line, we had to resort to pack mules and horses to transport our gear because vehicles were useless. I remember we even had two Italian blacksmiths helping us out hammering horseshoes from German barbed-wire pickets."

"Damn, Pappy, you never told me that story."

"Well, you're gonna learn a lot more tonight, Sammie. The time has come." Duff asked for the moonshine and took a big gulp.

Smacking his lips, he continued. "Hell, we'd even steal chickens from the Italian farmers and make fried chicken right up there in them snow-covered mountains. We'd barter with Italian refugees we'd come across in towns or along the roads: a few packs of cigarettes or chocolate bars could buy you crucial intelligence on the location of German defenses. But you know, when the fightin' started and we were side by side with our brother warriors – men from our 1st Armored, plus South African troops, Brazilian troops, and Italian partisan fighters – the color of your skin didn't matter one bit since we all were bleeding red. The Italians to this day treat us Buffalo Soldiers as heroes.

"But you know what? The German Army, which we were up against, well, they had orders to not take any prisoners from the 92nd Division because we were black. This was the official Nazi ideology because we were considered not fully human to their *master race.*"

Jake nodded, knowing the truth of how bad Nazism was.

"We were up in Sommocolonia, Italy when the worst day of the war came for me. My recon platoon from the 370th was attached to two platoons of the 366th. Them boys in the 366th was green as hell, though. Only action they faced was performing guard duty back at an Army Air Force base. Some hadn't even fired their rifles yet.

"Well, we led them up to that little mountain village. I was point man.

Right up front. It was unoccupied at the time and we hunkered down, but then that night we got surrounded by hundreds of Germans when they swept down from the mountain. We were trapped. It was just 70 of us black GIs and 25 Italian partisans against German infantrymen from an elite mountain battalion. We knew they wouldn't show us mercy and we fought like Hell Hounds for our lives that whole next day. It was brutal, lemme tell you. Brutal, the things I saw."

Duff took a deep breath. "We used everything you can think of. Hand-to-hand and house-to-house. When we ran out of ammo, we stole their weapons. Soon it was down to every man for himself. Some of them greens in the 366th even deserted us, they were so terrified. I was a savage, fighting for my own life. I shot dead two of them in the house I was hiding in, and used a garrote on another one. You strangle a grown man with a garrote, lemme tell you it is one of the worst ways to go.

"But Sammie, it didn't matter," blinked Duff. He took his glasses off and rubbed his eyes again. "He'd a done the same to me."

"Jesus," muttered Sammie.

"Some of our boys hid in the cellar of a nearby home, but them Nazis brought out the flamethrower and torched them alive. Shot 'em like dogs when they jumped out the windows on fire. I saw the whole thing. Heard their screams. My brothers in arms. Fuckin' horrible nightmare."

Duff shook his head back and forth as he spoke, the horrifying memories spilling from his mind as if he were back there that day once again. His eyes had already teared up and were bloodshot, but he wanted to let loose.

"If it wasn't for Lieutenant John Fox calling in that artillery strike right down on his own position, we'd of never made it out alive that night. Guess how many survived out of the 95 that were trapped? Eighteen of us. *Eighteen*. But Fox took out one hundred of them bastards alone when the shells hit on top of him. Got the Medal of Honor for sacrificing his life, but not until many years later.

"But you really wanna know how I survived that battle? How the hell I got out?" He pushed his eyeglasses back up his nose.

Sammie and Jake nodded simultaneously.

"I was wounded," Duff said, pointing to his knee. "Was shot in my knee cap. Could hardly walk. Was trying to escape. And this old German soldier captures me crawling out of a burning cellar. Sees my condition and is gonna off me right there. Puts me against the wall and aims his rifle at me. I put my hands up and pray. He doesn't shoot. He grabs my hand and looks at my ring? Recognized me as a Freemason from my ring and pats his chest to tell me he's one, too." Duff raised his hand and showed Jake and Sammie his scratched up gold Masonic ring with the square and compasses symbol.

"That old veteran soldier done looked around to make sure no one saw him, gave me a drink of water, put his finger to his lips, and then – I'll never forget it – tipped his head and whispered, *'schnell.'* It means 'go.' He let me go. He let me go and I made it back to our lines. I survived. All because of our fraternity. Doesn't matter our ideologies or our loyalties to an army, or the damn color of my skin. It was because of pure brotherly love of a man about to lose his life. That old soldier defied Nazi orders to not take any black prisoners, but he saved another man's life. Mine. Mercy. Praise be to God, he showed me mercy."

Duff sighed and gathered his breath.

"So true," said an astonished Jake. "There are many instances of enemy Masons helping each other out on the battlefield. Goes on all throughout military history. Sammie, bottom line is they broke the rules to do the right thing for someone's survival. Meeting another Mason on the battlefield is sheer divine providence. That's God giving us another chance in life."

Duff grunted his agreement. "Breaking the rules was the same thing when we came back here to McIntosh County, one of the most corrupt, poverty-stricken places in America. You got the double-whammy if you were a minority. But here's the rub: it ain't always easy to go back and start playin' by the rules again. You get a taste for gettin' away with things and it ain't easy to know when to stop breakin' them, you hear me?"

Isn't that the truth, Jake thought.

Sammie agreed. He'd heard many a story from Pappy, but nothing as detailed as that battle he was in and how he survived. He wouldn't be alive today if not for that German soldier. He could tell an angry fire had been lit inside of his great-grandfather after learning how Buzzut was abusing him. And he was spilling his guts because he was ready to face his maker if he didn't win this one last battle. It stunned Sammie to the core. And it also emboldened the young man to do what needed to be done.

"Look," said Duff. "The bottom line is you gotta be real careful what rules you break because, as the Good Book say, you reap what you sow, and the Lord might come back and bite you in the ass one day when you least expect it."

"That's called Karma," said Jake.

Duff turned to Jake with a bit of a smirk. "It seems, looking back on everything, that breaking the rules is the Greenhall way of life. You see, our family continuously made moonshine on this island from Reconstruction on up until the 1980s. It was the crop we produced, simple as that. Back when Prohibition came about, shit, my own grandpappy would say our moonshine demand 'went through the roof.' "

Duff moaned and shifted in his chair to readjust himself more comfortably. "All the black folk on the mainland were drinkin' it. All them rich white folk were drinkin' it, too. Grandpappy said they always had lookouts on the island in case the sheriff or them revenuers came over to bust our stills and arrest us. Busted some other folk and blew up their stills, but never found ol' Doctor Blackbeard's, though. Nuh-uh. We had our still and our barrels of 'shine hidden away real good, for sure. No one knows where it's at to this day but me and Sammie. Isn't that right, boy?"

"Yaas'suh, that's right, Pappy."

Duff played with his beard again. "I do have to say, though, that our direct protection right here on the island before and after the war was solely because of Dick Reynolds. He bought the island in 1934 when he was only 28-years old after he done got his family inheritance of some twenty-eight million buckaroonies."

Jake whistled.

"Was one of the richest men in America, a real playboy," said Duff. "Over thirty years he lived here. Loved this island. It was his oasis. He also really improved living conditions for us poor black folk. Employed just about everyone looking for work. He had a cattle and dairy farm and timbered the land. Constructed many of the buildings you see now down at the Marine Institute, too. Brought electricity to the island. Even built the largest airstrip in the country at the time for his private plane. That man renovated the South End House to what it is today. Was the first house on the coast that had plumbing and air conditioning. Unheard of in the 1930s!"

"That's the Reynolds Mansion down in Hog Hammock, right? Can't wait to see it," said Jake.

"Uh-huh. We all called it the South End House. Over the years, I became good friends, a loyal. Me, Banks, and Fred and Cracka Johnson, were the ones closest to Dick. Us four, me the youngest. Mmm, hmm. Sure was some fun times.

"And then I started breaking the rules again. Hell, I was a Greenhall," Duff snickered. "I started supplying Dick his medicine – *moonshine* – because he was also a raging alcoholic. He would just drink all day long. One time he stayed in his specially-built treehouse over on Cabretta Island for three weeks straight just drinkin' up there in his little escape from the world.

"You see, Cabretta's a two mile stretch of beach, dunes, and driftwood that he and his second wife Marianne would go to quite often. You know what's funny is Dick always believed that the pirate Blackbeard buried his treasure there instead of over on Blackbeard Island like everyone else thought." Duff pointed again to the silhouette of Blackbeard across the creek. "Blackbeard has it's own treasure, for sure, just not a pirate's treasure."

Jake raised an eyebrow. *The U-boat.*

"Any way, we done begged Dick to come down from his treehouse, but all's he said was, 'bring me more booze.' He loved our *Elixir of Life.* Couldn't get enough of it. So, that's what I did. I brought him more and more over the years. Never did charge him a penny.

"And then he done went off to war like I did, only he fought in the Pacific with the Seventh Fleet. Was a chief navigator onboard the *U.S.S. Makin Island.* Received the Bronze Star. His portrait in his Navy uniform still hangs down there in his mansion. Brings back a lot of memories whenever I see it. Our bond was even stronger as war vets."

"I bet," said Jake.

"Speaking of treasure," said Duff, slapping his knee when the memory popped into his head. "When Dick was married to his third wife Muriel – a strange, bitchy snob – they fought and fought so much that he accused her of trying to kill him. They done got separated in '59 and he was so afraid she'd come back to the island to kill him that he posted some of us servants as armed guards at the docks. I guarded Raccoon Bluff, of course. But when they was married he thought she was stealing from him, too, and so he started hiding his wealth."

Duff kept on talking. He was an unrelenting motor mouth. Sammie and Jake couldn't get a word in. "One time when she was off the island Dick ordered me and Bill Bosch to go down to his wine cellar at the big house to grab fifty- to one hundred-pound canvas bags stuffed with dollar-sized gold coins. We loaded dozens and dozens of these bags into his Jeep and drove around the island to bury them in secret places. Back then, one fifty-pound bag was worth ten thousand dollars! You do the math. He literally made a treasure map of the locations and how many bags were buried in each spot."

Duff looked to Sammie. "One of the places where we buried a bunch of them was over at Skeet Field in Shell Hammock down by Marsh Landing."

"You think there's some still there?" asked an excited Sammie, who then took another shot of moonshine. "We have to get a metal detector."

"Nah, nah, nah. It wasn't until Dick left the island for good that he had me and the boys dig all them bags up for good one night. Loaded them all up on his freighter and they were gone forever."

"Did you get any of them coins, Pappy?"

"Well, let's just say that a whole lot of them bags weighed a lot less when they came out of the ground. A lot less!" Duff's face was wreathed in smiles. "You bet yo' ass I did! How you think this big house here got built?"

Sammie smiled.

Duff winked. "But I spread the wealth, too. A lot of folks were near-destitute at the time. But like I said. Sometimes you gotta break a few rules."

Jake smirked and shook his head. It's exactly what he did with the British gold coins he unearthed in upstate New York: took a bunch for himself before turning them in. Finder's fee, he called it.

"But that Dick, he smoked like a chimney," Duff went on. "About ten packs a day. In the end he tried quitting. Promised his last wife Anne Marie he would – she was his nurse – but one of us loyal servants was slipping him cigarettes behind her back. She got wind of it and fired the entire household staff at the mansion. You talkin' folks who worked there twenty years.

"In the end, Dick got around in wheelchair, was bedridden, sickly, had a bedpan, and an oxygen tank. Rough shape. It was a pity to see him like that. Could hardly breath before he left the island for good in '63. Emphysema. Died a year later over in Switzerland at age 58. So damn young. Makes me feel so lucky at my age to have no problems. Kind of ironic, though, isn't it, since his family fortune was built on cigarettes?"

"Yeah, really," agreed Jake.

"So why do you think he gave me that speedboat of his, huh Jake?" asked Duff. "Because I was supplying him with moonshine for all them years he lived here. He never forgot me. That boat was his gift to me personally. Good man. Had his own demons like we all do, and pissed off some island folk here, but I loved him like a big brother." Duff drew a breath.

"Generous man," said Jake, taking advantage of the break. "Listen Duff, is there any way I can see that U-boat on Blackbeard tomorrow?"

Duff ignored him at first, looked him over, paused a long time, then asked, "You ever hear that famous sayin'? Not sure who said it, but it goes like this: 'We sleep safely in our beds because rough men stand ready in the night to visit violence on those who would harm us.' "

"I hear that a lot. I even say it a lot myself," Jake admitted.

"Are you that rough man ready in the night?" asked Duff. "Of your own free will and accord, are you willing to help me and Sammie out? Because if so, then I will reveal to you where that U-boat wreck is. I'll take you right to it, son. And we'll go inside."

Sammie pulled back, seemingly in shock. Cleo jumped from his lap and disappeared under the porch.

Jake stammered for a response, shocked as well. Finally, he spoke. "You said earlier this U-boat can be mine. But what does that mean actually? I can't just *take* a U-boat. I can't *claim* it as mine. The federal government will claim it since you said the Navy captured it in the first place. Plus, it's on federal land, too."

"You can claim the *discovery*, Jake Tununda," said Duff. "And I will give you all of those skull rings left inside of it as compensation for *incapacitating* Buzzut. Plus, anything else of value. There's still some treasure left in there that I didn't pilfer over the years."

"Sammie," said Duff. "Don't you worry. You'll be taken care of, too. Trust me. You're family. I'm giving you most everything left in my secret hiding spot back at my old house. Lots of hidden cash in there I've never shown you. But now's the time to get it all out before any sheriff comes to kick us out. Enough there for you to go to college if you want. Or to start that *legal* distillery you been dreamin' of."

A drunken Sammie sat stunned.

"Helluva generous offer you're making both of us," Jake said. "But I also want the *full* story of that U-boat and how you've kept it hidden all these years. All the details. Nothing left out. I want your story to go along with my discovery, should I choose to go public with it one day. Plus, I want proof first. I want to see the U-boat first and then we'll act. You have to put your trust in me, as well. It's a two-way street."

"I'll give you proof of them treasures I took from the wreck first," said Duff, taking off his eyeglasses. "I'll even show you the original *Operation Overcast* papers and you can keep 'em when our deed is done. But I ain't gonna show you where that U-boat is until we take care of Buzzut. That's my compromise. And your incentive. The wreck itself will be your ultimate prize. But I'm warning you, brotha, you're gonna be tapping into a world beyond the grave. That U-boat is sacred ground and you have to respect that. You just be very careful of who you open up that Pandora's box to."

Jake sat silent, thinking. He rubbed his eyes. His mind was a drunken whirlwind of thoughts. *What exactly do they mean by incapacitate? How far are we going to go?* He could hear his wife's voice inside his head now, admonishing him for taking another dangerous risk. But these two Greenhall's are all but helpless. They will lose everything in a matter of days. It will destroy them both if they lose their ancestral sacred land. It would also eventually destroy the island. He couldn't sit idly by and watch it all go down the drain and do absolutely nothing.

"Offer accepted," said Jake. "You're a damn good negotiator, Duff. Hit my weak spots. Terms are: you show me proof of those treasures you took from the wreck and those mission files first, then after the deed is done, I get to see the wreck itself, and claim discovery, and take ownership of everything inside of it. But I make the rules on how to *incapacitate* Buzzut," Jake demanded. "You play by my rules and don't break them. Understand? That goes for you, too, Sammie. This is for your future."

"Understood, suh." Sammie extended his hand to Jake to shake. "But we've only got until Thursday night to pull this off. Friday morning is when he's due in Darien to close the deal and he'll catch the morning ferry over. After that it'll be too late."

"We'll do it, Sammie," said Jake, accepting his handshake.

"Terms accepted," said Duff. "Stand up with me right now, look me in my face, and promise me on the five points of fellowship of a Freemason."

Jake lent a hand to Duff to help him rise. They closed together and embraced, making physical contact at certain points on the body that only Master Freemasons would know where. Jake then whispered in Duff's ear a single, ancient, secret word before finishing with the phrase, "You have my Word."

Duff whispered back the same word and phrase.

"So mote it be," they simultaneously said together.

15

Tuesday, night
Hoffman residence
Charleston, South Carolina

ERHARDT HOFFMAN POPPED ANOTHER ASPIRIN, fearing he was going to have a heart attack. He chased it with a swig of *Firefly Sweet Tea Vodka* from his cocktail glass – his fourth drink of the night. The racing heart and sharp pain in his chest weren't so much a result of him blowing Mona Lisa's head off at point blank range, rather it was because the debriefing earlier that day with Army CID and FBI agents had filled him with an endless sense of paranoia that they would discover he was the one who stole her much-coveted missing iPhone.

He placed his cocktail glass on the table and glanced at that very phone laying next to it. Pushing back on his living room recliner to elevate his feet, Hoffman picked up a tiny USB flash drive next to the phone. His thoughts then drifted back to the last two days.

The thing was, he'd completely forgotten he even stolen the damn phone since he was so shaken up on scene after killing the arrogant broad. Having a shotgun pointed in his face, and then helping the Tunundas with D'Arata's bloody leg wound, he ended up going into shock. Another paramedic crew was called and they had to triage and transport him to the hospital. It was only when he stripped his clothes off in the emergency room that he found her phone in his pocket. And that's when the paranoia first kicked in.

He still wasn't exactly sure why he took the phone in that split second decision. Perhaps it was because he saw her passcode and would give it to D'Arata to gain access to it when they took her into custody? He never bargained for actually taking a life. That weighed on him hard. She was a means to an end to get to Phoenix. It all just happened so fast and he had to react to protect the good guys coming in through the door.

He thought for sure that with Mona's phone in his possession that Phoenix would track him down knowing how ruthless he was. Hoffman did, however, have the foresight at the time to enter Mona's passcode and immediately turn off the Find My iPhone app so the device could not be GPS tracked to his location.

On Monday morning, though, when he had been released from the hospital to go home and relax on sedatives, all he could think about was digging into her life to find some kind of communication with the master thief. He just wanted to see what he could dig up. It's what thrilled him deep down and why he took on cases like this: to bag the bad guys – and gals, for that matter.

While inspecting her phone, he discovered Mona's real name was Maya Levana. She was an art and antiques expert and gallery owner in New York City. He even listened to several voice messages, including one from her niece – the same call that came in during the meeting. But what he had discovered in her Photos app sent him reeling.

He found a picture of a passport for a Frank Alan Mason from Saint Lucia. The headshot bore a striking resemblance to Nathan Kull, albeit with short hair and a goatee. He also found a picture of a Saint Lucia driver's license with the same headshot. The driver's license listed an address of 5 Coconut Way, Vieux Fort, Saint Lucia. What was quite interesting, he noticed, was the timestamp on the photos. It showed they were taken early Monday morning around 4 a.m., well before the hotel meeting that day.

After comparing that passport photo with the photo of Kull's New York State driver's license plastered all over the news, he made an immediate connection that any investigator worth their salt could detect. He instantly did an AirDrop of those same photos over to his computer, and then copied them onto a tiny USB flash drive.

He had found Phoenix's new alias identity. He knew where the killer thief could already have gone. Opening up Google Maps, he typed in the address and it pinpointed to a road not a quarter mile from the beach on the east side of Vieux Fort in the Coconut Bay area. Clicking on satellite view, he saw the residence was just one of several spread out on a road overlooking the ocean. There was ample tree cover and plenty of privacy between each home. Other nearby lots looked to be under construction. Zooming in from the top-down view, Mason's home looked to be modest in size with a long driveway and a private pool.

Apparently no one else knew where Phoenix lived except the now-dead Mona Lisa. And himself.

But what would he to do with this crucial evidence?

His choice was black and white. It was the stereotypical angel on one shoulder and the devil on the other, apropos of how he grew up in a household with a Nazi mother and an American patriot father. He was a 5th generation Freemason and he could never soil the family name, he knew that much. The key was to not get himself arrested – or killed – for the evidence he now possessed. As a Freemason, he lived a life of trying to do the right thing, keeping his passions in due bounds, maintaining his integrity. Highly respected in his field, and working with the FBI on several past art crime cases, he never ever risked ruining that reputation by engaging in untoward activities.

Until he was called into the debriefing meeting earlier today.

Present was Jake Tununda, an Army CID liaison officer, several FBI field agents, and Peter McNabb, the FBI special agent in charge assigned to take over the Phoenix case. McNabb turned out to be the biggest, most condescending prick he had ever encountered. The man had been demoted from a top management position at FBI headquarters in Washington and was out for blood to redeem himself, no matter who he ran over in the process. A true political shark if there ever was one.

After reviewing the audio and video of the hotel meeting, the FBI investigators were all clueless as to where Mona's phone went after she moved the meeting to another room and out of visual monitoring. That phone was crucial to their case to hunt down Phoenix, McNabb had explained, admonishing the Army guys for their sloppiness.

One FBI agent speculated that when Mona was on the phone listening to her voice mail that it was really Phoenix tipping her off she was being trapped in a sting operation. The only one left alive to actually witness Mona speaking on the phone, Hoffman told investigators she said she was merely listening to her niece's voice message about coming home from college. They drilled him as to how he knew that. He lied and said he overheard a young woman's voice on the phone at the time and he simply took Mona's word for it.

Also unable to locate the whereabouts of the case of counterfeit cash, McNabb theorized that Phoenix was there all along watching Mona Lisa himself, got the cash when she left the room, then slipped in later disguised as an EMT after the shooting. That he was the one who had a hand in her phone's disappearance.

Hoffman kept his mouth shut.

When the Army agent pushed back against this theory, saying agent D'Arata hand-picked and vetted the EMTs, McNabb then accused members of the Army team of stealing Mona's phone. Jake Tununda came to the Army's defense and knocked over a chair, he was so irate. The meeting was halted so everyone could compose themselves, albeit this peace was only short-lived.

Thoroughly pissing everyone off at that point, McNabb then directly accused the Tununda couple of the phone theft and that private citizens should have never been interfering or contracting with an Army case. That wild accusation almost earned him a busted jaw by Jake. He got in McNabb's face, told him to eat shit, and walked out saying they should contact his attorney when they found evidence against him.

It was a crazy scene, but Hoffman knew he was the reason for it. Hearing again Mona's recorded story of how Phoenix kidnapped a boy, tortured him, and stabbed him to death, and then blew up a gang member in a meth lab, Hoffman became more livid at the FBI for blowing off CID agent D'Arata's claims last year that they had gotten the wrong man. It's why he had agreed to work with D'Arata and the Tanundas in the first place. He wanted to throw it back in the FBI's face when they captured Phoenix.

Only Phoenix had struck again by taking the life of that innocent cop in Fitzgerald. This angered him even more at the FBI's initial incompetence. That, and lingering questions why this high-profile case would be handed to some political D.C. prick with a credibility issue."

Why give McNabb evidence of Phoenix's new identity and his whereabouts? Already demoted for wrongdoing, he couldn't be trusted. Why give him the credit for taking down Phoenix? It was D'Arata's case all along. He wanted those trophies back, appreciating their true value, not the FBI. D'Arata was the one now proven right. And what'd he get? Almost losing his life with a bullet to the leg by that cunt Mona.

Besides, Hoffman wasn't even sure the FBI could even legally nab Phoenix in Saint Lucia, let alone the many months it would take to extradite him or even stand trial. Hell, Phoenix would hire the best lawyers, drag out the case for a year or two, and in the end probably negotiate a plea bargain for a lesser sentence. He had all kinds of wealth and stolen goods socked away in his many storage lockers, according to Mona's story. If he confessed to all of the other crimes he committed, gave up all that loot he had in storage, or ratted out key players in the black market, the FBI would surely reduce his charges.

Hoffman had seen this movie before. In the end, he knew that Phoenix would never be executed for the lives he took, nor serve a life sentence. Instead, he would probably disappear into the witness protection program and rise somewhere new, yet again, in due time.

The darker thought of personally stopping that from happening appealed to him more. Ultimately this was why, when asked point blank by McNabb if he knew the whereabouts of Mona's phone, he flat out lied.

Hoffman exhaled loudly back to the present. This paranoid internal mental tug-of-war exhausted him. Combined with the effects from the four glasses of vodka, his eyes grew heavy and his mind finally threw the off-switch. Still clutching the flash drive, his chin touched his chest, and his breathing slowed. Soon, all that could be heard throughout his house was deep snoring, like an idling chainsaw.

16

S HOTGUN CRADLED IN HIS ARMS, SAMMIE SLOWLY
walked point down a narrow game trail leading to his great-grandpa's
old abandoned house in heart of the Greenhall estate. Sharp palmetto palm
fronds brushed his shoulders and scratched his face. A headlamp attached
to his straw hat lit the way through the encroaching black forest and dense
underbrush smothered in kudzu.

The trail was familiar to Sammie as Pappy had dispatched him several
times in the past to go on moonshine runs from a secret stash. The path
grew tighter over the years, though, and would have been taken over with
flora if not for the fauna that kept it matted down.

The trail was all that remained of what was once a single lane, crude
dirt drive that started at East Perimeter Road. It went from the main house
they currently lived in, and then bent south paralleling the bluff to the old
homestead they were now headed to. The last time a vehicle used it was back
in the 1980s when Pappy's wife died and he moved out. Over the last thirty
years, Mother Nature had since woven her thick green impenetrable web
and all but reclaimed the road back into her lush domain.

Several times Sammie had to shoulder his shotgun and use his machete
to slice through a branch or a patch of kudzu blocking the path. MP40
slung over his shoulder, flashlight in one hand, and a hiking staff with

a serpent's head in the other hand, Pappy was right behind him, albeit walking at a snail's pace given his advanced age. Jake brought up the rear, his powerful semi-automatic rifle at the ready with an attached LED rail flashlight illuminating his path. His CERT kit was strapped to his back and his head was covered with his paddler's hat, neck and ear flaps down. All three men wore long sleeve shirts, gloves, pants, boots, and even gaiters to protect their lower extremities from snake bites. They were heavily doused in bug repellent to ward off the gnats and mosquitoes that followed them every step of the way.

"What we've got to watch out for the most are the hogs," said Sammie, addressing Jake at the back of the line. "If you hear a rustling or something snorting, stop in your tracks and get ready to shoot them sons-of-bitches."

"They travel in big packs and will run your ass right over," Duff added. "They're killers. Open up on them and don't stop shooting."

"And keep an eye out for wild bulls and cows, too," added Sammie. "There's a two-thousand-pound Brahma bull that likes to graze on our land. Nuts the size of pineapples. Don't go pissing him off."

Jake couldn't help but chuckle.

"Oh, and there's also a freshwater pond where the old house is at, too, brotha Jake," warned Duff, pointing inland to his right. "It's fed by an artesian well and it's loaded with alligators because birds like to nest there. Little gatuhs, though, no more than four or five feet. Sammie has kept the big ones managed over the last few years. They're not really aggressive, but if one happens to come at you, just shoot 'em in the head."

"10-4," said Jake, a grin plastered across his face. He couldn't believe what he'd gotten himself into: snakes, feral pigs, wild bulls, alligators, and a supposed hidden treasure somewhere. He was loving every minute of it.

Among the many dancing shadows of the night were dozens of bats feasting on the bugs. They quietly zipped all around the men, visible only in their flashlight beams against the encroaching cloud cover of the nighttime sky. Jake also heard some louder, stranger buzzing sounds, almost like swarms of bees, but then again it could have just been the wind gusts whistling through the tree tops. Looking up several times he thought he saw a large black bird of some sort swooping overhead beyond the tall pine tree canopies. Buzzards, perhaps, he thought. Even with all the mysterious sounds emanating around him, still he was happy to be outdoors and living life to its core.

But he also had a nagging feeling someone or something was watching them, perhaps even trailing them. Several times he held back and scanned the trail behind him with his scope, but never saw anything before hurrying back up to Duff to make sure the old man wouldn't topple over.

The dense underbrush of golden broom sedge, dense wax myrtle, and sharp palmetto prolonged the hike to almost 30 minutes before Sammie could cut his way through to their destination. Luckily, the hogs decided to leave them alone, although plenty of fresh scat marked their presence.

Off to Jake's left was the bluff, dotted with cabbage palms and waist-high panic grass now blowing in an even stronger wind. A drizzle of rain marked an incoming storm that had developed over the ocean. About thirty feet to his right, surrounded by cedar and magnolia trees, was the freshwater alligator pond. When he panned his flashlight over its surface, red glowing eyes of alligators reflected back at him.

Sammie soon announced they were coming up on the old place. Large mounds of kudzu started appearing on each side of the trail. When Jake turned his flashlight on them he saw they were old rusted cars and trucks, the vegetation having grown directly on top of hoods or even through exposed engine blocks. Other mounds of weeds and tall grass were strewn across the ragged landscape, covering gutted household appliances and a variety of other yard junk.

A probe of his flashlight ahead revealed another massive mound of kudzu. Silhouetted against a cloudy sky flashing with distant lightning, he could make out a one-story cottage with a gable style tin roof and a moss-covered brick chimney.

Walking closer, he observed a collapsed covered front porch through the weeds. He also noticed rotted wood siding and boarded up windows. The dilapidated vernacular-style house looked to be three or four bedrooms sitting high atop a crumbling foundation. It reminded him of a scene from a horror flick, that no one would dare enter, but always did. While Sammie and Duff cut their way through the brush to the rear of the house, Jake lingered and panned his flashlight around to the other side.

Underneath a large live oak tree with thick spidery branches and the ghostly drapery of Spanish moss, a four-foot high crumbling wall topped with shards of blue colored glass caught his eye. Curiosity got the better of him. He walked up to the wall through tall grass, stopping at a closed, spiked-topped, iron gate entrance.

Beyond the gate were narrow headstones jutting up from the weeds, some made of thick stone, others of rotted wooden planks, but all were covered in green-brown moss. As Jake drew closer, he saw that the taller wooden planks were painted in vibrant, yet faded colors, their tops shaped like heads and faces painted in black. Small leather pouches hung around each of the heads and they all had hand-carved epitaphs running down their lengths. One old stone marker had a date as far back as 1879.

At the far end of the cemetery, Jake's light panned across a grave slab partially raised off the ground. A triangular-armed, metal cross pattée was stuck in the weeds in front of it. It looked like the Southern Cross grave marker for Confederate soldiers in the Civil War and it struck him as very odd that it would be in a cemetery with slave ancestors. Then again there were rare instances where black slaves did fight with the Rebels.

Not lingering on the thought, he swept his flashlight beam again and caught a stand-alone, but larger gravesite off to his left near the gate entrance. It seemed the biggest in the cemetery.

This one was made up of a raised stone vault topped with a thick horizontal memorial slab. A vertical headstone stood at the head of the vault. A large alligator skull hung from the top of the headstone, with a thick white candle melted onto the top of the skull, its hardened wax rivulets having run down its snout. On the headstone were large engraved letters marking the interred remains of 'Doctor Blackbeard, the Founder. Birth unknown. Death 1898.'

On top of the slab, and most of the other stone grave markers, were stacks of tiny mementos: pebbles, coins, matchbox cars, tiny toys, and other sundry items. He knew from visiting plenty of other cemeteries that placing a small stone or favorite personal items of the deceased on top of a grave was a way of marking your visit to someone you loved.

Behind the large vault sat four newer headstones. They shone the brightest in the cemetery, free of moss. He could easily read their Greenhall names and saw that the two males had Masonic emblems carved on their stones and the two women Eastern Stars. But all four shared something in common – the date of their deaths – the same day five years ago. Sammie's parents and grandparents lay here side by side.

More objects now appeared between the grass at the base of the grave markers. Not only were there artificial flowers and glass candles, which was expected, but he also noticed, ceramic pots, handmade grass-woven baskets, a moss-covered doll of a black baby, a rotted cuckoo clock, a bottle of still-corked wine, a porcelain cat, and even a stuffed bunny rabbit. He knew these personal objects gave the spirits something to enjoy or play with in the afterlife. But he also saw something that sent a shiver down his spine.

Snakes.

Long black snakes slithered through the grass and around the personal mementos. He must have seen a half dozen of them, one even climbing up a gravestone.

As his flashlight-mounted rifle panned around the rest of the cemetery, an array of colored antique glass bottles lit up like a rainbow. They were hanging upside down on nails around the thick circumference of the oak tree. There were close to fifty bottles all around the trunk, he figured, admiring the spectrum of shimmering light.

Just beyond the tree over the perimeter wall, Jake suddenly saw two glowing orbs in the woods further back. He blinked, not sure if his eyes were playing tricks on him because of the colored bottle reflections. The orbs then blinked, too, he heard a low growl, and his old battle arm wound tingled. He realized some type of animal was watching him. The eyes went dark and a black hulk shifted in the shadows.

A tap on Jake's shoulder and he flinched.

"Come on, follow me," whispered Sammie.

"Wait, Sammie," said Jake, aiming his light back on the tree. "Tell me about this tree with all the bottles on it. What does it mean? I've never seen anything like it in a cemetery."

"That's the tree of remembrance," said Sammie. "Each one of those bottles represents the individuality of each soul who passed on and whose body is buried here in this family cemetery. Pappy says it best, though. He says: 'a family without a knowledge of their history is like a tree without roots, that the soil that grew your tree must always remain sacred.' "

Jake agreed. "It's up to the living to keep in touch with the spirits of the dead. Otherwise, they'll be forgotten. And why the broken blue glass on top of this wall, too?" he asked. "Is there some kinda meaning to it other than to keep interlopers out?"

"Sure is," said Sammie. "Blue glass is meant to ward off evil spirits so the good ones here can rest in peace. The haunts don't like the color blue because it symbolizes water and they hate crossing water, so it is said."

Sammie then led Jake to the rear of the house where Duff had already lit up one of his cigars and was puffing away nonchalantly creating thick clouds of blue smoke which helped scatter the swarms of bugs. Sammie stepped up on the rear porch and used his machete to decapitate a bush that was growing through the floorboards in front of the back door.

Knowing he'd locked up the house on his last visit, Sammie panned his headlamp on the porch floor until it centered on an overturned terra cotta pot. He reached in and pulled out a black bullfrog lawn ornament. Lifting the back off the bullfrog, a hidden key was revealed. With a twist of the key in the deadbolt, he unlocked the door, replaced the key and bullfrog, and allowed Duff to enter his old home first. He motioned Jake to hold back a moment.

The old man crossed the threshold and stopped. He blew more cigar smoke all around him in more of a systemic manner and then started mumbling strange words in Gullah. "Ooman, ooman, duh sweetness of my life. Hear me now, ooman, oonuh hubban be a knockin'."

"He hasn't been here in a long time," Sammie whispered in Jake's ear. "He's praying to the spirit of Nana, asking her permission to enter, to watch over and protect us. Telling her he misses her and will see her soon."

As Duff continued his prayer, a halo of mosquitoes buzzed around Jake and Sammie. They fruitlessly tried to wave the unbearable critters away.

After another minute a speaking in Gullah tongues, Duff tapped his hiking staff three times on the floor. "She says we can enter, but we must not stay long, for something is amiss." Sammie and Jake piled in and slammed the door shut, locking it behind them, relieved to be free of the bugs.

They were in what was once the kitchen, but it was piled high with every imaginable item Duff's wife – a hoarder addict – could get her hands on. Except most of it was now covered in black filth, mold, and rodent excrement. She had ultimately died from her addiction when the unsanitary conditions led to her catching a deadly bacterial infection. No amount of Hoodoo root magic from Duff or modern medicine from a licensed doctor could save her. When he moved out after her death, he left everything as it was to appease her spirit if she ever wished to visit in the afterlife.

The three men could hardly move there was so much shit piled about. Jake tried turning but his backpack caught a stack of cardboard boxes and sent them tumbling over. Several squealing mice jumped out of one of the boxes then disappeared deep into the pile of trash.

There was only one means of travel: a tight gap leading down the main hallway to the bedrooms and front living room. They slung their weapons over their shoulders and Duff led the way, pushing back several cartons filled with moldy old books. He didn't go very far when he told Jake and Sammie to hold up, that he had to get something from his old bedroom, and disappeared around the corner.

The pair stood and faced a wall covered in yellowed newsprint. Two glass picture frames hung askew in front of them.

"That's me when I was Master of the lodge," said Duff upon his return. He pointed to a black and white photograph showing a group of smiling black men, and curiously, one white man with an obvious chipped tooth. The men were posed in front of a wooden structure with a square and compasses mounted above the front entrance. Live oaks framed the outer edges of the photo. "That's our old lodge down in Hog Hammock."

Jake nodded, admiring the picture. It was a typical group photo of Masons he had seen many a time. They were dressed in black suits, bow ties, and Masonic regalia, including white gloves, officer's jewels, and aprons. As Master of the lodge Duff, looking to be in his late twenties with a thick black beard, stood in the middle of the group and was the only one wearing a top hat.

Duff looked thrilled to see the old photo once more. "Brings back so many memories." He pointed out each black member by name. "There's ol' Maxwell, little Jackson, the talker Walker, Grovner, Evans, Gardner, and Hall." He skipped the white man, though.

"What's his name?" asked Jake, pointing to the white man.

Duff coughed in his hand. "Ahh, well. That brotha was, ah, umm, he lived here on the island and worked for me a number of years. Artistic fellow. Helped me design my *Elixir of Life* label."

"You don't remember his name?"

"Bill Bosch," said Duff, blinking rapidly.

Jake thought it strange that Duff deliberately tried to avoid the man's name. After all, he had named him when he spoke about burying Dick Reynold's gold. "I thought Prince Hall lodges only admitted black men. What year was this picture taken?"

"The picture? Oh, '53, I think. But Prince Hall lodges here in Georgia have admitted white men going back to 1866. We accept men of all races and color. It's some of them dadgum good ol' boy crackas here in Georgia that have a problem admitting black men into their lodges," replied Duff, rather heatedly. He looked up at the other frame. Inside the glass was a decorative white leather apron chock full of hand-painted Masonic symbols. He tapped on the glass with his finger. "Now, this here's my old apron."

On the triangular flap of the apron, between two Greek columns, Jake saw one universal symbol that stood out the most. It was the skull and crossbones. Above it was a Latin phrase. Jake spoke it out loud: "Memento Mori – remember, we all die."

"Memento Mori," Duff mumbled, shaking his head, closing his eyes.

"You paint all that yourself?" asked Jake. "It's incredible work."

Duff abruptly coughed again. "Bill painted it for me." The reminiscing was over. Rather impatiently, he turned to Sammie and knocked on the wall three times. "For the love of God, Sammie, get this unlocked."

Sammie bent down and pulled out a little skeleton key, this time stashed in a hole at the bottom of the wall's baseboard. He lifted the Masonic apron frame and exposed underneath it a highly recognizable, five-pronged, petal-like pattern of a Keyhole Urchin, the cousin of the sand dollar. It was carved into the face of the wall. In a barely noticeable notch within the carving, he inserted the key. Turning it clockwise, they all heard a click that unlocked a mechanism inside. Pushing against the wall, Sammie opened a hidden door to reveal a set of crude wooden steps leading down into a dark basement. Crisp cool air wafted up. It smelled pungent and sweet.

Sammie lent Duff a helping hand to get down since there was no railing. He told Jake to hold up so there was no extra weight on the old steps. Once they made it down, Jake descended the narrow staircase himself. Running his hand along the bumpy, shiny surface of the wall to support himself, he knew the foundation must have been very old. Rough and granular, it was made of different materials besides typical cement. He saw many crushed sea shells embedded within.

"These foundation walls are made with tabby," said Duff, watching him. "A mixture of sea shells, sand, ash, water and lime, and then usually a stucco finish put on top. One heck of an invention that lasts hundreds of years. What you're touching right now was originally built in the early 1600s by the Spaniards. Most of the stucco has come off and we had to make some repairs over the years, but it's pretty much stood the test of time being underground."

"Simply amazing," said Jake, making his way to the basement level stepping onto a sturdy wood planked floor. The cool air felt great. He took his hat off, wiped sweat from his face, and stowed the hat in his backpack. They were in a wide foyer-like area with another door opposite the bottom of the stairwell. A wooden bench sat flush against one wall and Duff had already taken a seat for a much needed rest.

Sammie reached up and grabbed a hurricane lamp hanging from a hook. "There's no electricity any more down here so we have to light one of these up. Saves on our flashlight batteries." He shook the lamp and heard liquid fuel sloshing around inside.

Jake noticed that the ceiling was made up of thick wooden cross beams supported by wood columns. He felt as if he were in an old underground barn room.

Duff slipped his hand inside Jake's elbow and tugged him to sit down on the bench next to him for a break. "All these big pieces of timber came from

Sapelo live oaks – most indestructible hardwood in the world. I remember my daddy telling me that our kinfolk who bought the land constructed all this in secret for years. Then they covered the top of the foundation surface with dirt and in no time all the underbrush completely covered it up, camouflaging the whole thing. You could walk on top of it and never know what's down here where we are."

Duff then stomped a foot on the thinner wooden floor planks. "But this here floor, though, was put in last. It was made from wood that floated across Blackbeard Creek the day after a tidal wave hit during the worst hurricane that ever struck the island."

"The Homestead Hurricane you mentioned in 1945?" asked Jake.

"On no. We're talkin' 1898," said Duff. "Much worse. Destroyed the quarantine station's big hospital just across the creek on the south end of Blackbeard Island. Flattened the place. Killed a lot of folk across the island, even some in our family. Wiped out crops and livestock just about everywhere, too."

"Damn," said Jake, fishing in his backpack for a water bottle.

"All this wood came floating across the creek and once they got permission everyone just rowed out and grabbed as much as they could, so the story goes. They built Raccoon Bluff's old First African Baptist Church over there on East Perimeter Road with that wood. People said it was divine providence," Duff snickered. "I say, it was just grabbing opportunity when it comes a knockin'."

Pointing up, Jake asked, "But obviously, your house above us wasn't the first structure here, right?"

"Right, right," said Duff. "The history told by many griots was that at this exact location stood a Spanish garrison and tower that overlooked Blackbeard Creek. It was for protection of a mission of priests called San Joseph de Sapala, trying to convert the Guale Indians to Christianity. Was the very first time that African slaves were brought to the island, too – damn, evil Spaniards," he sighed. "But wait until you see how big it really is down here. Like a labyrinth. Come on, Sammie. Light that damn thing up for heaven's sake."

While Sammie struggled to light the lamp, and Jake chugged some water, Duff continued talking about the history of the underground structure they were in.

"Them Spaniards ruled here for almost 100 years. We were told the original wooden garrison on top of this was burnt down when they fled the island. When the Scottish and English landowners took over, they done replaced the fort with new buildings and expanded on this here foundation. And then some French noblemen lived here for a short while in the late 1790s, too. I guess they was outcasts from the French Revolution and thought they'd come on over here and start a plantation. One of 'em ended up shooting his own nephew dead over a land dispute. I think that was the first recorded murder on the island."

Jake was fascinated by the history, listening intently at Duff's amazing memory. He passed his water bottle to the elder man who took a long swig.

Wiping his mouth with a sleeve, Duff didn't miss a beat. "According to what our slave ancestors said, even those buildings collapsed and the land again took over, hiding this foundation for many, many years. Was like wilderness back then. It was only *after* the Civil War that freedman Amos Greenhall bought his 33 acres in 1871 and started clearing the land, that he discovered this ol' underground fort."

A warm glow illuminated inside the hurricane lamp's globe. Sammie adjusted the flame's intensity and lit up the foyer. He shut off his battery-powered headlamp.

"So, ever since our family owned this land, the old fort has been in private hands," Duff explained as he leaned on his walking staff to stand up. "No one ever knew about it except us kinfolk. It's why we built right on top of it – to literally hide it in plain sight – and so we'd have a place to refrigerate food, store our wares, and eventually distill moonshine in secret where no revenuer could ever find us."

"Ahh, I see," said Jake, also rising from the bench "And y'all have kept this a secret ever since?"

"Yup," nodded Duff. "There were legends floatin' around on the island about a secret Spanish fort, but not even the big millionaire land owners knew the exact location of this place. Not Howard Coffin in the early 1900s, not Dick Reynolds up until the 1960s, not even all them scientists and archeologists from the University of Georgia or the DNR. Why?" he asked, turning to Sammie.

"Because we never gave them access to our land."

"Damn right. For us, this is sacred ground." Duff slammed the tip of his staff on the floor to make his point. "Plus, we was armed, too. Unless he had permission, ain't no man would step foot on our property without getting shot at. We took potshots at trespassers, poachers, and even some of them know-it-all college professors. It's how our reputation of not messin' with a Greenhall became well-known."

"Oh, I believe you," chuckled Jake. "Trust me. You taught Sammie here quite well."

"But come on, follow me inside," said Duff, turning to the wide oak door in front of him. Carved into the face of the door was a second Keyhole Urchin pattern. He used his hiking staff and rapped three times on the carving. "Through here I'm gonna show you our moonshine operation. How it all fits together room-by-room. And then at the very end, I'll show you the treasure room." He unlatched the door and it squeaked open.

In the next room, all sorts of canned goods were in storage on wooden shelves that lined the walls. It looked to be a large pantry cellar. There was a work table with tools and a chair. On the floor sat canvas sacks of rotted corn meal and ripped open bags of yeast. A tall, covered wooden barrel, mounted on wheels, stood nearby.

"Hey Duff, I've got a question. Who originally taught your Greenhall kinfolk how to make moonshine?" Jake asked.

"Sammie, can answer that for ya," said Duff, slapping Sammie on the back. "Time for you to give Jake the history of moonshining and a tour of our production facility down here." He took the lamp from his great grandson and placed it on the table. "Tell him everything I've educated you on in the last few years. When you open up your own distillery, this here underground facility is going to be a must-visit part of your tour. And don't forget, Sammie, you need to charge an admission fee for it, too. People love history and will pay to hear our story – especially if it's in a dadgum old Spanish fort! So now's the time to show off everything you know, boy." Duff pulled out the chair from the work table and plunked down to be part of his audience.

"Go for it, Sammie," urged Jake.

"Mr. Jake," Sammie started. "The Greenhall slave ancestors learned the original distillation process from Thomas Spalding, who owned the island back in the 1800s. He was descended from Scotland. As everyone knows, the Scots have been making whiskey for ages. It's ingrained in their culture. Blacks on the island learned how to distill corn into whiskey from him. It became quite common among us folk. Everyone was doing it since everyone grew corn on the island. But us Greenhall's perfected it over the years."

Jake nodded, eyes glued on Sammie as a comforting glow from the lamp cast across his dark face.

"It became part of our Gullah-Geechee culture," continued the young man, now gesticulating with his hands as he spoke. "Problem was a lot of blacks made shit for 'shine. Was like poison because they used bad equipment, like kettles with lead seams that leached out when heated up, or fuel tanks or radiators from old trucks. Or they took shortcuts and added extra ingredients because they had no respect for the process."

Duff interrupted and smacked Jake on the arm. "They called that shitty 'shine 'popskull' because the next morning your eyes would pop out of your skull from such a bad hangover."

"But the Greenhall's only used high quality metal, like copper," said Sammie. "It made a huge difference in taste and purity. We also kept everything very sanitary down here."

"I didn't even allow my wife to come down here," scoffed Duff. "You saw how she lived like a pig upstairs, God rest her soul. This was my workplace, and my father's, and his father before him. Like a fraternity. No women allowed because they have loose lips that sink ships."

"By the early 1900s, the Greenhall moonshine became the best on the island," lectured Sammie. "To the original makers, it was an art form that we took pride in. It was thick in our blood, like gold fever."

"God, I know that feeling," said Jake.

Sammie kept on. "The process was handed down through the root doctors in our family: the Hoodoo practitioners known as Doctor Blackbeard. Would take the process seriously like a ritual, acquiring the ingredients from the sacred land, adhering to the spell they cast to make the right, potent elixir. If it didn't come out high quality, then the Doctor would pour it all away. But when the batch was good, people would say, 'that's just what the *doctor* ordered.'"

"Ahhh," said Jake.

"You see, blacks on the island are very superstitious, very religious, and they respected the reputation of a root doctor. You'd never ever cross one. And that's how the legend of Doctor Blackbeard was born, more or less. My Pappy here, Mr. Duff Greenhall, is the last in a long line of Doctor Blackbeards since the passing of his own son and grandson – my father. I'm hoping to carry on our family legacy one day. To never let it die out."

"Brilliant, Sammie," said Duff, slapping his knee. "Spot on, just like I taught you. Beautiful words you use."

"Yeah, you are not going to have a problem raising capital funds, trust me," said Jake. "You are a natural salesman. I'm already getting thirsty for some more *Elixir of Life*!"

Sammie smiled a thanks. "There's still some more I want to say before we get into the distilling process itself. It's how that name came to be."

"Go on. By all means," urged Jake, leaning against a shelf, arms folded across his chest.

Sammie smiled, enjoying this part of the story the best, placing himself back in a history he never experienced. "Black folk from all over the island loved our 'shine and so did the Scots-Irish white folk. A lot of white timber workers and fishermen – hard, tough men, real drinkers – well, they'd visit our old drinking barn near the entrance to the property at East Perimeter Road, and my great grandmother would charge money for a shot of 'shine. Even on Sundays there would be men stopping by for shots before church! The thing is, everyone got along harmoniously. And that's the key to life, isn't it? To live harmoniously. Well, people kept on coming back for more, so the story goes, and our moonshine really earned its own name of the *Elixir of Life* from all the folks that drank it. Why?

"You could say our pure corn whiskey is disguised like clear spring water – the essence of life, but man, ours packs a punch you weren't expecting. Kinda like how life is – you don't know what to expect. Well, our moonshine was a mood-enhancer and it turned people into the happiest human beings alive, forgetting all their troubles in life. And us Greenhall's loved making it because we were making people in our small community happy."

Whiskey-making, a noble cause, Jake thought to himself. He'd never thought of it that way.

"I remember my wife even used to cook fried chicken in the corn liquor and sell it to the folks at the barn," said Duff, licking his lips. "One of my favorite meals, for sure. That put a smile on people's faces, too."

"Moonshining became a farming cash-crop for the Greenhall family," said Sammie. "But because it was *illegal*, we had to keep an eye out for the revenuer. It's why the founding Doctor Blackbeard took the operation underground. Literally. Especially during the Prohibition era when the millionaire Detroit auto executive Howard Coffin owned most of the island. He was dead set against any alcohol and allowed the revenuers to come on the island looking for stills. They found some and blew them up with dynamite. Arrested people, too. But never a Doctor Blackbeard. Ever."

"Lemme tell you something, Jake," Duff interrupted. "Wanna know *why* we made moonshine the illegal way instead of registering with the Feds and them confiscating our profits?"

Jake didn't even get a chance to respond.

"I'll tell you why. To make our moonshine product, we already paid the government taxes on the corn, taxes on the yeast, taxes on the fuel, taxes on the equipment. Taxes upon taxes upon taxes. And then, as a result of the fruits of our hard work and ingenuity, we are told that magically another tax appears if you try and *sell* that moonshine to anybody. If you don't pay *that* tax, then you're stealing from the federal revenue and they'll throw you in prison for a felony and destroy everything you built over your lifetime. Does that make any goddamn sense to you? Does that sound like justice or fair play? Nuh-uh. So, all of us moonshiners do it as a way to flick our middle finger to The Man."

"Love it. But how'd you really get away with it?" asked Jake. "How'd you keep it so secret for so many years? I mean, never getting caught."

Sammie spoke up. "For one, we only distilled at night so no one could see the steel blue-colored smoke that would rise from our secret underground chimney in the next room. The other thing was a strict code of secrecy among us blacks. No one informed the revenuers on each other. And in the rare instance it did happen they would have a hex placed on them from Doctor Blackbeard."

"Yup, they were treated as a Judas figure in the community," said Duff. "Their farms would burn down or some would just disappear altogether. It's why people learned right quick you don't mess with Doctor Blackbeard."

Jake arched an eyebrow. That was quite obvious, he had learned.

"Okay, so, let's get into how exactly we made the moonshine," segued Sammie as part of his spiel. "It's a five-stage process."

Jake tried to mask his impatience. All he wanted to see was the treasure room at this point. But he wasn't going to be rude to his hosts. Sammie was doing a test run presentation on Jake as his audience and he wanted to stay attentive. This was their way of life and he respected that.

"Well, in this here room," started Sammie, "was the first stage: it's where all the cornmeal, sugar, and yeast was stored. That'd all be mixed together with water in this barrel here into what is called corn mash. Water was the most important ingredient, though. The purer the better to sterilize out all the germs when the mash gets heated up later. We're fortunate on our property to have an artesian well with the softest, finest-tasting water on Sapelo Island."

Jake nodded, listening closely.

Sammie went on. "And then in stage two, this mash had to be periodically stirred to start the fermentation process. It took many days." He pointed to the end of the pantry at another closed wooden door. "Come on, grab your gear and follow me. We're going into the distillery room next."

At the door, Jake noticed a five-armed starfish carving. Duff rapped three times on the carving, again with his staff. Sammie opened the old rusty hinged door and Duff entered first with the hurricane lamp. Lit up by the lamp, the next room looked about twelve feet square. There were more tabby walls, more support beams and columns, benches, and even a cot in the corner with a nearby skillet and coffee pot sitting on a table. Everything was covered in spider webs and dust.

The room was also full of various sized alligator skulls painted with strange symbols. They hung from the walls and support posts. On top of each skull was a burnt-down, waxed-encased white candle. Jake figured it had to do with more of the family's Hoodoo magic.

But the most impressive item was a well-used, copper, brass and wood still in the middle of the room sitting atop and surrounded by a brick kiln. A long chimney pipe jutted up from the top of the kiln and went right up through the wood ceiling to the ground level above. A stack of rotted split hardwood was scattered nearby. Next to the kiln were two metal-banded oak barrels. The still was attached to the middle barrel with a copper arm. The middle barrel was attached to the end barrel with a copper pipe that turned into a coil inside that barrel.

While Duff unslung his burp gun and plunked down on the bed, Sammie continued his presentation. "Stage three – the actual distillation process. This is how it's done in a nutshell: once the corn mash has been fermented and the sugars have turned to alcohol, we pour it into this big 150 gallon copper still. You put the cap on top, and start to heat it up with firewood underneath. Seven gallons of mash makes about one gallon of moonshine. The kiln keeps the heat trapped and disperses it around the still but allows the smoke to rise through the chimney pipe here and up through the ceiling there and into the light of the moon. Hence, moonshine."

Jake was genuinely taking a keen interest in what Sammie was explaining now. The distillation process was really a world unknown to him. What he had in front of him was where the time immemorial magic of whiskey-making took place.

Sammie gestured again with his hands to explain the process. "As the mash boils, the resulting vapor, or the alcoholic essence of the spirit, rises up through this arm, and travels down into this middle barrel here, what's called a thumper keg. This is where it is double-distilled. That's what the two disguised X's on the forehead of the label mean."

Sammie looked over to Pappy to see if he was explaining correctly. Duff nodded his approval.

"It's called a thumper keg because you hear a thumping sound when the vapors enter. It acts as a secondary boiler. Those double-distilled vapors are then brought into this end barrel filled with cool water. It is a condenser

barrel. The vapors travel through this here copper coil called a 'worm'."
He twirled his finger in a spiral. "At this point is when it's reconverted as a
purified liquid in the form of ethanol."

Sammie stood next to the end barrel and pointed down to a tiny open
pipe protruding from the bottom. At the very end of this pipe was a thin
curved bone about three inches long. Positioned underneath the bone was
an empty glass Mason jar. Sammie pulled the bone from the pipe.

"Now, this is kinda funny actually, but this little bone here is actually
a raccoon's penis bone," said Sammie with a grin. "We use it to control the
flow of 'shine that comes out of this pipe so it doesn't splash all over the
place. It's a tradition for 'shiners."

"What?" blurted Jake with a wide smile.

"All true!" said Duff. "And here in Raccoon Bluff we've got lots of little
dick bones all around us."

All three men burst out laughing.

Gathering their wits, Sammie spoke again. "The final liquid that comes
out of this pipe is collected in glass jars or jugs. That's your moonshine and
you can start drinking it right away."

Duff stood up from the cot using his staff and walked over to Sammie
and Jake. He slapped Sammie on the back. "A fine job so far, Sammie.
You're explaining it in simple terms that's easy to understand." He turned to
Jake and squeezed his arm.

"But wait, there's a little bit more," said Duff. "Sammie, don't forget
'heads and hearts,' he urged.

"Ah, yes," said Sammie, remembering the key part of the distillation
process. "Jake, the real art form in this process, and a closely guarded secret
to each moonshiner, is knowing when to shut off the flow of purified liquid
that you're collectin'."

Like a stagehand, Duff pointed down to the condenser barrel pipe with
the tip of his staff.

"Ya see," continued Sammie, "the first drops that come out are called
'heads' – they contain methanol which can kill you or lead to blindness.
At the very least it will give you a severe headache. The 'hearts' are the
middle of the run that contain the best tasting alcohol. The saying goes,

'you always get rid of your heads and keep your hearts.' When you double distill through a thumper keg, like Pappy used to, you know you have the best alcohol at around 120 proof and the best tasting. That is the highly potent moonshine that gives you no hangover in the morning. That is the white lightning that we called the *Elixir of Life*."

Sammie smiled, raised his hands, and spread his arms in a gesture that the lecture was over.

Jake clapped, thoroughly impressed with what he had just learned from the tag-team of the Greenhalls.

"Come on now, let's show Jake the inventory room," Duff said, leading them to yet another wood door in the corner of the distilling room. This door also had the carving of the starfish on it. Duff tapped the carving three times again with his staff. It was a ritual he never forgot – like knocking on wood to scatter any bad spirits within. "And if you've been paying attention to these carvings on each door, you'll start to make sense of the skull label on the jars. This is the fourth stage in the process."

Duff pulled the door open with a groan. He entered a wide room the size of a two-car garage, supported by even more wood columns and beams. Two more hurricane lamps hung from columns. The room was full of wooden shelves stacked from floor-to-ceiling against opposite walls. Jutting through the ceiling and cutting into one of the crumbling tabby walls was a thick root of a tree from above.

The shelves were filled with dozens of one-gallon glass jugs and several hundred glass Mason jars of clear moonshine. On each jar was the *Elixir of Life* label. Duff placed his hurricane lamp and his MP40 on a work table sitting atop an old faded oriental rug in the middle of the room. A stack of the wrinkled yellowed paper labels were scattered across the table's surface next to a stiff brush and an open container of long-hardened glue.

Jake picked up one of the labels. He recognized the two Keyhole Urchins plus the two starfish on the circular border and how they matched the carvings on the doors. At the top of the circular border was a five-pointed star. He was sure he hadn't seen that yet. It had to be the fifth stage in the moonshine making process, he surmised.

On the table was also a large box made out of alligator leather. Jake looked inside and it contained dozens of alligator teeth.

"This is the last room in the fort," said Duff. "Closest to Blackbeard Creek. It's where the *Elixir of Life* is prepared for distribution," he said. "What's left of it anyhow. I haven't distilled a drop since my wife died. This is the stage where we'd glue these labels onto the jars, pop in a gator tooth every now and again, then pack 'em in boxes disguised as motor oil."

Jake's eyes wandered back to the skull label. "I see the two Keyhole Urchins and the two starfish, but not the star on top. So what's the fifth stage? Is there something I'm missing?

"There is," said Duff glancing up at the ceiling. "We'll get to it."

"Okay," Jake nodded. "But let me ask you something about this label. These swirling eyes? Any meaning to them?"

"Oh sure," said Duff. "Those eyes be a buzzin,' is all. Effects from 'shine. But if you notice, they're also raccoon eyes disguised for Raccoon Bluff."

"Ah. I see it. Very clever, Duff. Very clever," said Jake.

"Inside the eyes are little five-petal flowers. Those are Cherokee Roses. They grow all over this property. And did you notice the two sharp teeth?" asked Duff. "Those are actually gator teeth."

"And what about the big symbol on the forehead itself?" Jake asked.

"Well, not only are they double X's, meaning you're getting a better liquor than most," Duff explained, "but that full symbol is called a 'vèvè.'

It's an ancient Hoodoo spirit symbol that promotes success and provides protection in commerce or the marketplace you're doing business in."

"Ah, so that's what that is. Makes sense in your line of business. But is there another meaning to it, though?" pressed Jake. "I mean a Masonic meaning. That symbol is very similar to our fraternity's Masonic square and compasses. Not exact, but I think it's more than a coincidence, am I right?"

"You're right, brotha" answered Duff, eyes wide, staring at Jake. "There is a special hidden meaning that is personal to me . . . and well, to someone else who was once a very close friend of mine. The placement on the forehead is definitely a disguise for us Masons, too. Specifically, the third degree during our initiation with the murder of Hiram Abiff after being confronted by the last of the three ruffians."

Jake cocked his head. "The final ruffian's death blow to the head with a mallet because Hiram Abiff wouldn't reveal his secret?"

"Precisely," said Duff, snapping his fingers. "It's about keeping a promise. You will learn more about its Masonic link to the U-boat, trust me. Until then no more questions about this skull. Understand?"

"Yes, sir," said Jake, his head instantly filling with more questions.

Sammie cleared his throat. He had gotten the other two hurricane lamps all lit up, casting a bright orange glow in the large room. "Ahh, to change the subject, ahh, once the labels were in place, then we'd haul 'em out to the dock for pick-up by the bootleggers."

"How'd you get it all out of here, though?" asked Jake. "I don't see an exit from this room."

"Look up," said Duff.

Jake looked up at the wood planked ceiling while Duff pointed to a rope with an ominous looking grass-made Hoodoo doll hanging from it.

"Trap door, folding ladder in the ceiling. Go ahead. Pull on the rope."

Jake snatched the rope and pulled it gingerly. Out of the ceiling popped a hinged wood frame with a folded ladder. He pulled all the way down until the frame stopped, then grabbed the ladder, unfolded it, and let the lower extension rest on the floor to create a natural staircase.

Sammie walked over with a hurricane lamp to give Jake a light source. Jake looked up to where the ground opening would have been and saw the inside of a rectangular stone box covered with a smooth stone slab and an iron ring hanging down. Engraved into the stone slab's underface Jake recognized a multi-faceted five-pointed star as a match to the one on the skull label.

"What's that up there?" he pointed with furrowed brows.

Duff cackled with delight. "That's the fifth and final stage – the nautical star symbolizing distribution of the moonshine by water. That stone up there is the underside of Doctor Blackbeard's tombstone inside the family cemetery." When Duff said the name Doctor Blackbeard, he held up air quotes. "No one is buried in it, of course," he winked. "It's the only other way out of here besides going back up through the house."

"But symbolically," Sammie said. "It is delivering our elixir back to the surface to those mortals who want to drink it. It is the resurrection of the spirit rising through the grave. From there, they used to load it right on boats at the old dock. But that's all torn down now."

"This is really incredible what you've done," said Jake, highly impressed with the organization of their moonshine making process and how it all symbolically ties into the label with real meaning and many hidden disguises. He could see the true uniqueness of the *Elixir of Life* as a marketing brand and why Sammie was so determined to make it all legal into a real business for the general public to enjoy.

"But Jake," warned Duff, placing a hand on his elbow to steady himself while looking up the ladder. "If you exit this way, for real, you better beware of two things: one that the cemetery is a snake's nest."

"I know. I saw them all over the graves."

"Now you know why the border on my skull label is ringed with snakes," said Duff. "Including the hidden snake within the black beard."

"What's the second thing?"

Duff's eyebrows arched. "That'd be the legendary Hell Hound that guards the cemetery. He was Doctor Blackbeard's first pet they say. It's why no one ever trespasses in there, except a Greenhall, because we know how to tame him."

"What in the hell is a Hell Hound?" asked Jake.

"Well, it appears somewhat different to those who have seen it," said the old man. "Some say it's like a cross between a massive feral hog and a huge, furry black dog. Stands about four feet high and has nasty tusks with razor sharp yellow teeth, and glowing red eyes. Has a really foul odor like brimstone."

"Are you shitting me?" asked Jake, incredulously. "Come on. It's just a ploy to keep people away from this secret trapdoor, isn't it?

Duff shook his head. "He's real for sure, and yes, the story does serve a purpose, but this hound has been around for generations. He appears to people all over the island, mostly around old cemeteries, but he'll then vanish in thin air. Kids have seen it, old folks have seen it. I've seen it."

"I have, too," said Sammie, looking up. "Right in that cemetery after we buried my parents and grandma and grandpa."

"Legend has it that it's a guardian to the 'other side,' Duff said, "Done conjured up from one of the first root doctors in our family. That if you enter a cemetery, you first have to ask 'for leave' of the spirits so they don't mess with you. If you don't, then the Hell Hound will run you off to Hell. This demon dog has kept unwanted visitors from disturbing our dead for many generations. Just sayin'."

"Duly noted," said Jake, not sure if those red orbs he saw earlier in the cemetery were the actual Hell Hound's or not now. "Are we headed up that way to get out?"

"No, I just wanted to show you how we used to get all this 'shine outta here is all," said Duff. "You have to move that heavy slab and it's a real pain in the ass. Haven't done it in some thirty years I'd imagine."

Jake sighed, refolded, and returned the trap door back up into its ceiling hideaway. "Okay, so I've gotten the history, I've gotten a distillery tour, now how about you show me this so-called treasure room with Nazi loot. We're running out of time if I'm going to help y'all."

"Indeed," said Duff, guiding them with the lamp back into the center of the room. He leaned on the table with the labels, then paused and turned to Sammie. "You don't even know where it is down here, do ya? The entrance is right here in this room."

"No suh, Pappy," said Sammie. "Must be hidden real good because I've been here many times and never even knew it existed."

"Right in front of your eyes," said Duff, stroking his beard.

"What?" said Sammie, looking all around.

"Go on and move this table and pull up that rug. There's a secret passage underneath going down into the fort's dungeon."

17

ANOTHER RIFLE REPORT SPLIT THE AIR AND JOLTED *Kapitänleutnant* Werner Witte back to his senses. The gunfire was followed by the distant sounds of splashing water and the muffled, yet horrifying guttural screams of a man in his final death throes.

Witte's eyes went wild fearing what lurked outside U-2370. Both the bridge and conning tower hatches were obviously open, hence the light spilling in and lingering smoke wafting out. *But opened by whom?* Survivors of the American skeleton crew? People who may have found his wrecked sub? His fight still wasn't over. He had to act.

Pumping with adrenaline and a renewed sense of urgency, he managed to sit up despite severe pain that shot down his side. He took an inventory of his injuries: cracked ribs, a swollen knot on the back of his head with congealed blood, a chipped tooth, and general bodily bruising from the horrendous lashing the hurricane had given him the night before.

Standing upright and clutching his side, he stumbled over a canvas bag that had expelled its contents of a German silver dining set. Wet currency was stuck everywhere as he stepped through the bulkhead door guided only by the sunlight above. Once inside the miniscule control room, he looked up some twelve feet through the two open hatches and saw a tree branch with green leaves. Blue skies and white clouds were beyond. It was like heaven calling. He gripped the ladder to ascend up to the bridge – to supposedly escape his tomb. Or, he thought, *will this only lead to my death?*

Out of the corner of his eye, something caught his attention.

The bulkhead hatch to the engine room and stern was wide open. Someone had indeed gotten out. He realized he needed to sweep the boat for any more survivors first. And to arm himself from the potential threat that lurked above.

Searching frantically for a flashlight, he found one still secured to a wall clamp. In the beam of his light, he located the chief engineer's body crumpled in the corner of the control room. He didn't even resemble a human anymore. It was just a bag of bones.

Debris lay scattered about the body: crumbled charts, writing utensils, nautical tools. He also noticed a belt holster that still held the engineer's pistol. Unsnapping the holster, he drew the firearm. It was a .32-caliber Colt Model 1903. The magazine was full so he chambered a round. Witte stepped over the body and entered the engine room to conduct his search.

Water from broken pipes hissed loudly and valves dripped incessantly. "Hello? Anybody in here?" he asked in English. His light searched for survivors, though there weren't very many available hiding places.

The large diesel engine block dominated the center corridor. Busted crates, open suitcases, collapsed boxes, and even an Army officer's footlocker lay on its side. One box had broken open revealing glass jars of gleaming gold coins with Nazi eagles. Spoils of war. It didn't surprise him in the least.

Looking about the deck, he saw one open crate that was filled with stolen paintings and drawings. That crate, and several others, had a stenciled label denoting it had originated with the U.S. Army's Monuments, Fine Arts and Archives (MFAA) special collections point Wiesbaden, Germany. He had no idea what that unit did.

Still another container held solid gold statuettes, reliquaries, and jewelry. He ignored all of the treasure and continued aft as best he could, crawling over damaged equipment that had detached from the walls.

Witte found no one else alive. He did find the two other corpses from the air attack that had been moved back near the toilet: the radar operator and OSS agent Baker. Knowing now that the mechanic, the helmsman, and the VIP passenger Bosch were the only ones missing and presumed to have escaped, he reversed course back to the control room.

Catching his breath and rubbing his temples, he rested an arm on the ladder up to the bridge. Another glance up and he felt a warm breeze beckoning him to ascend. Off with his life vest and rain gear, he was now down to a sweat and grease stained light blue shirt, and bell-bottom dungarees, looking like any other USN crew member.

A moan suddenly bellowed fore of the galley from the torpedo room.

A survivor!

"Hello, anybody there? Help me, please," groaned a man.

Witte's face contorted. "*Was zur Hölle? (What the Hell?)*" He knew that voice. It was the so-called 'passenger' they were bringing to the American coast: Mr. Bosch.

But his thoughts immediately raced back to when he took command and stabilized the sub after the air attack. It was when he shockingly learned who Bosch really was and what *Operation Overcast* was really all about.

While catching a breather in his old captain quarters after repairs, Witte surprisingly had spotted his personal aluminum briefcase – issued to all German U-boat captains – hidden under his cot. He knew it had been confiscated upon surrender of his sub, and during his prison interrogation he was forced to reveal the number lock to allow access to his mission files. After that, he thought the briefcase had surely been looted along with just about everything else on his sub. It was quite a souvenir item with its high specification engineering, waterproof seals, anti-corrosion material, and even an imperial Nazi eagle engraved into the lid.

Remarkably cocky on the American's part, though, it had been returned to the boat and apparently was being used by Mr. Baker for his own secret mission files. He could reason why, since the aluminum briefcase was virtually indestructible and perfect for sealing sensitive documents. Witte tried the combination lock, and voilà, it popped open.

What he learned in that treasure trove of documents turned his stomach.

While not five feet away, as the chief engineer slept from sheer exhaustion, Witte had thumbed through the paperwork. After all, he had justified, he was again in command and it was his original U-boat. He figured he had every right to know what his cargo was, human or loot.

He had read that his commandeered U-2370 was a key transportation component from Bermuda to Harris Neck, Georgia in a covert mission named *Operation Overcast*, the name he'd overhead before when two of the crew had gotten drunk. The operation was authorized by the Joint Intelligence Objectives Agency (JIOA), a subcommittee of the Pentagon's Joint Chiefs of Staff.

It was *"a secret recruitment program run by high-ranking representatives of army, air, and naval intelligence to smuggle top scientists, doctors, engineers, industrialists and other assets from the Third Reich."* Men apparently like one William Bosch, *"who were valued for their knowledge and expertise."* Theirs was the very first attempt with Mr. Bosch. More would be coming.

He also learned that the dead OSS agent, Mr. Baker, was supposed to hand over the German to other agents at Harris Neck, who would then transport him to an Army-Navy interrogation center in Virginia called P.O. Box 1142.

And William Bosch, of course, was just his alias. His real identity revealed someone altogether more sinister.

William Bosch was in reality *Sturmbannführer (Major)* Franz Heidel, an officer of the Nazi SS (*Schutzstaffel or Protection Squadron)*, the armed wing of the National Socialist Party. His file summarized how Heidel had been assigned to the *SS-Totenkopfverbände*, a branch who ran the concentration camps. He rose up the ranks and became lead interrogator at the Dachau concentration camp serving under the notoriously brutal Theodor Eicke before he took over as its *Kommandant*. He then went on to command three other concentration camps: Auschwitz, Buchenwald, and Niederhagen. In all four camps he commanded, he'd personally executed scores of inmates with his own Luger.

Witte read that later in the war he was transferred to the *SS-Einsatzgruppen* death squads. He knew those units had gone into the eastern European territories conquered by the Nazis and participated in the mass exterminations of undesirable persons, mostly Jews. Turns out Heidel was even awarded the Knight's Cross of the Iron Cross with Oak Leaves for his so-called distinguished service to The Party.

Later in the war, as the tide turned against Germany, his file said that Himmler assigned Heidel to the demolition crew at the SS headquarters of Castle Wewelsburg. He then fled to Austria and was subsequently captured by the Americans.

But to Captain Werner Witte, this Nazi was someone he was all too aware of. Franz Heidel was the known executioner of his own father, Otto, for crimes against the state.

His father's crime? Being a Freemason.

Otto Witte was just one of the estimated 80,000 Freemasons that the SS murdered in concentration camps and in mass executions throughout the war, according to stories he'd heard from Germans citizens and other military men who despised the Nazis as much as he did. Millions more men, women, and children, particularly of Jewish ancestry, were also being exterminated, he found out as the war progressed. But the Nazis didn't stop with just Jews and Freemasons. He knew of the murder of political opponents, resistance fighters, gay people, the physically and mentally handicapped, priests, gypsies, Communists, Roma, Serbs, Polish intelligentsia, and even Jehovah's Witnesses.

After reading Heidel's file and before he could confront him with the damning information, the violent hurricane had slammed into their boat, requiring his presence up top to navigate.

But now, after narrowly surviving himself, he was filled with renewed rage that this ardent Nazi bastard – of all people – was still alive, too.

William Bosch called out again, begging for help. The captain momentarily lifted his eyes to the sky, then glanced up the dark main corridor toward the torpedo room. His eyebrows grew together.

The decision was instant.

Snapping into action, he made his way back through the forward bulkhead hatch. "I'm coming," he announced, as he plowed through the remains of the galley cabinet, weaving his way past currency spilling from broken suitcases.

"Hello? *Kapitän* Witte? Is that you?" Bosch yelled.

"*Ja*, Herr Bosch," replied Witte, as he lifted a suitcase of cash and set it aside. He pulled back the torpedo room curtain and panned his flashlight at the two tubes.

The port torpedo hatch was shut tight. The starboard tube door was wide open. A fetid, shit-colored, gooey muck was packed inside and had also oozed out onto the floor in a large pile. The flow of mud was filled with shiny silver objects – by the hundreds it seemed.

At the bottom of the pile, in a pool of water and oil, he found Bosch's exposed head, his wavy blonde hair floating in a black fluid. His forehead had a gash across it and his face was bruised and smeared with muck, blood, and grease. The rest of his body was buried underneath the heavy wet mound, unable to move. Bosch emitted a deep sigh of relief upon seeing the captain.

Witte tried to discern what had happened, but Bosch beat him to it.

Bosch chuckled. "Would you believe that I was able to fit inside the torpedo tube? That's one good thing about being a small man. It saved me from that horrific storm. All this um, stuff, the Americans were smuggling was jammed in here, too." He spoke calmly as if engaged in light dinner conversation.

"And when the sub struck whatever it was that stopped us, the impact must have collapsed the outer tube door and filled this tube with all this mud, which instantly sent me flying out like a backfiring torpedo. Guess that's when I was knocked out. I'm just glad I'm alive and this water hasn't risen any further. That would be a horrible way to go."

While Bosch chattered on, Witte bent down, gritted his teeth from the pain of cracked ribs, and picked up one of the shiny objects.

They had spilled out of an open cylindrical German Army mortar ammunition container partially buried next to another container – sealed tight. Both had been expelled from the mud-filled torpedo tube Bosch had been shot from, too. Witte remembered this cargo back in Bermuda. There were four containers total. The mechanic even said the empty torpedo tubes would make an excellent storage space. Little did he know a man would fit in there as well.

"Help me out from this mess," Bosch said. "I can't move. I can barely wiggle my fingers. My head hurts, my back hurts, but my legs, I can't feel them at all. I'm trapped. Oh, thank God you found me, *Kapitän!*"

Witte ignored him, staring at the object in his hand: a silver ring. He instantly knew its identity. They were quite popular in Germany among Party fanatics. His pulse beat faster with rising anger.

"*Kapitän?* Can you dig me out, please?" pleaded Bosch again.

Witte tossed the ring in Bosch's face. It bounced off his cheek. The trapped man grew silent and confused. He stared at Witte in surprise.

Witte then pulled open the other torpedo tube door and aimed his flashlight inside. He saw two more mortar ammo containers. *If these are both full of rings, too, there must be thousands of them,* he thought. Setting down the flashlight and pistol and pulling out the nearest container, he unlatched the cap. Sure enough, it was filled to the top with the same rings. Again, he became utterly disgusted.

The rings were the infamous SS *Totenkopf* Honor Rings or Death's Head. Some called them Skull Rings because of the symbol of a *totenkopf* (skull) and crossbones – an icon perverted by the SS to mean absolute obedience until death – obedience to the Party and their godlike *Führer*, Adolf Hitler. They had been given to all ranking officers in good standing as a personal gift from the head of Hitler's paramilitary organization, *Reichsführer*-SS Heinrich Himmler, for their achievements, loyalty, and commitment. Through this allegiance, they were bound to one cult-like figure – Hitler – not to the country or citizens of Germany.

SS men would automatically and without remorse carry out the most heinous acts imaginable that the regular military would never touch, unless forced to do so. The torture, maiming, and death squad massacres they inflicted on the enemy's army and the people of other countries that stood in their way were infamous throughout the war. It's why the SS were so feared and so detested over the *Heer (Army)*, the *Kriegsmarine (Navy)*, and the *Luftwaffe (Air Force)*.

Witte had heard that upon an SS officer being killed in action or retired, his ring was to be retrieved and returned to SS headquarters at Castle Wewelsburg where they were supposedly kept in a secret shrine to honor those who served. What made each ring unique and highly coveted was the inscription inside the band testifying to which officer the ring was actually awarded and the official date of the award. Each ring had Himmler's signature and was cast and hand-finished by specially commissioned jewelers. The rest of the ring's band was wreathed in oak leaves deeply embossed with a number of symbolic Armanen runes.

"*Kapitän* Witte? Are you okay? Why so upset? Can you please dig me out? I cannot feel my legs."

Witte stood frozen, lost in thought.

Ironically, the Freemasons used the same symbol of a skull and crossbones to remind themselves of the famous Latin phrase *Memento Mori*, meaning "remember, you too, will die." That we all are mortal no matter our lot in life, the titles we hold, the pride we take in ourselves, or the riches we've accumulated. Death is the equalizer and comes to us all. Therefore, we should live our lives to the fullest, being just and moral for the greater good of our country, and of our fellow man. That we should not judge a man based on his race, ethnicity, class, religious beliefs, or his political persuasions, but instead by his character, his merits, his word, and his actions. It was the essence of Freemason ideology. And it's why the Nazi Party banned it as a political threat to National Socialism right after Hitler came to power in the mid-1930s.

Captain Witte knew this ideology by heart because he was a Freemason himself – in secret. His membership had deliberately been kept off his Masonic lodge's register so the Gestapo could never learn of his association to the fraternity. It was done at the behest of his father, Otto.

He finally spoke. Distinct disgust laced his hardened voice. "So you want me to help you escape, is that correct, *Sturmbannführer?*"

Bosch blinked several times then raised his eyes toward Witte.

"*Ja, ja, ja*, it is *Sturmbannführer* Franz Heidel of the SS, I presume?" asked Witte with stinging sarcasm. "Head interrogator at the Dachau concentration camp? And will you be taking all of these *Totenkopf* rings with you as you carry on your elaborate new disguise?"

Bosch stammered in shock. His chin quivered.

Witte switched from English and now spoke solely in German. "You're so happy to be alive? A new beginning using all of these rings as your ticket to a new identity?" Toying with Bosch, he squatted down and grabbed a handful of mud and rings then dropped it onto the trapped man's face. "Using your comrades' deaths so you can buy your own freedom? So pathetic a rat you are."

Bosch spit out mud.

Witte stood up abruptly, grabbed the flashlight, and panned it around looking for something. He found an object that would do. It was a heavy wrench with a long handle.

"No, no, *Kapitän*, you have me mistaken with someone else," Bosch said desperately. "I can assure you I am William Bosch, not this SS major you speak of. I hate the SS! I am merely an administrator from Frankfurt—"

Witte bent down again, eye-to-eye with Bosch. *"Kuhscheiße (bullshit)!"* He then placed the flashlight on a box and aimed the beam onto Bosch's buried torso. "But let's see for sure, shall we?" He started digging at Bosch's left shoulder using the wrench more or less as a shovel. In no time, he had the shoulder and upper arm exposed from the mud and immediately started tearing away at the man's shirt.

"What are you doing?"

"Ruhe! (silence)," snarled Witte. He ripped the shirt open down to the elbow, then started digging the rest of his left arm out. Once the arm was free, he grasped it at the wrist and yanked it over the trapped man's head. On the inside of Bosch's bicep, just below his armpit, he found what he was looking for: a small tattoo of the letters 'AB' in a Gothic typeface.

Witte twisted Bosch's arm backwards, and stomped his boot onto the elbow joint, breaking it instantly. Bosch wailed in excruciating pain. His arm flapped limp, splashing uselessly in the muddy water.

Bosch thrashed his head from side to side. "Why? Why?"

"Last night I read the mission orders held by the OSS agent in charge. And I read your personal file. I know who you really are. You are Franz Heidel. It's all there. Your matching photo and even a picture of this same blood group tattoo of AB. All SS are required to get these tattoos. You, *Sturmbannführer,* are a fucking liar!"

Franz Heidel's eyes went wide. He knew the game was up.

"Franz, Franz, Franz," Witte mocked, shaking his head. "In your file, I read of your capture in Austria by the Americans. They said you were just another selfish rat on a sinking ship, shedding your SS uniform and wearing civilian clothes, scampering about for your own survival. That you have no family to worry about and only yourself to look after. But one of your own men betrayed your real identity. Ha! Ha! Ha! So ironic, *ja*? The Americans said you stood out as one of the smarter rats for the things you engaged in at Dachau – specifically your interrogation techniques. They said after the tide turned against Germany, when it was clear that we'd lose the war and the Russians were coming, that you put your exit plan into action. That you, in a very trusted and privileged position, admitted moving treasures and artwork to secret locations as a means for your future financial survival. You even said in your own words, these were the "bargaining chips" that saved your life. And the motherlode was all these *Totenkopf* Honor Rings. But you're a trapped rat again, Franz. Only now you're at *my* mercy."

Heidel had no response. He was mortified.

Witte wasn't finished. "And I saw your new American identity papers: a passport, Social Security card, birth certificate. Even a Georgia driver's license. All the things you need to start a new life in disguise under the name of William 'Bill' Bosch. You're supposed to be a traveling salesman for a furniture company out of Atlanta. How clever."

"I, I, I–"

"But you've nowhere to go now," shrugged Witte. "Why these Americans were letting you into their country is beyond the pale knowing full well you were *Totenkopfverbände* and *Einsatzgruppen*. Doesn't matter now if you're from Frankfurt or Atlanta. You're all mine, you *verdammte (damned)* SS!"

Witte stretched and picked up the wrench. Pain tore at his side. He didn't care. He stood tall again and smacked the head of the wrench repeatedly into the palm of his other hand.

"What are you going to do? No, no . . ." Heidel swallowed hard.

"Tell me the truth and I *may* spare your life by not bashing in your *fucking* skull."

"Okay, okay, I will. I will."

"Were you at the Dachau concentration camp?"

"I don't know," said Heidel, tears forming in his eyes.

"You don't know?" Witte laughed derisively. He raised the wrench over his prey as if to strike. "I mean, how can you forget the thousands of German citizens you interrogated, tortured, and used as slave laborers? You worked them to death there. All those undesirables, all your political opponents. And the ones that didn't comply? They got a bullet to the head — from *you!* Is that what you want now, a bullet to the head?" He glanced over at the Colt pistol and pointed to it with the wrench. "The easy way out? Wouldn't that be so nice? Now tell me the truth, Franz. Were. You. At. Dachau?"

"Yes. Okay? Yes, I was there. I am *Sturmbannführer* Franz Heidel, okay?" the SS officer finally admitted. "Please. Please. I'm sorry I lied. Please, I beg you, show me mercy. I was only following orders from Himmler. But now I denounce him. I denounce the *Schutzstaffel!*"

"*Lügner! (liar),*" yelled Witte. "*Schweinehund (pigdog)* to Hitler."

Witte heard something behind him back in the galley area. A crunch of some sort. He snatched up the pistol and spun around. A quick glance back through the dim light revealed nothing but water dripping from broken pipes and rising steam.

He then rolled up the right sleeve of his own shirt until his bicep was exposed. It revealed a intricate tattoo. With the flashlight, he illuminated his arm so Heidel could see.

"After I surrendered this U-boat to the Americans and they took me prisoner, one of the first things I did in prison was I had one of my crewmen tattoo me with these symbols. Why? Because I was finally free from The Party. No longer was I forced to be loyal to a political party I never believed in. Surrendering this boat was my rebirth. And so tell me, what does this symbol brand me a member of?"

Witte's tattoo was the tool of geometric compasses intersected by the tool of a measuring square. Below that was an hourglass atop a scythe. The Latin phrase *Memento Mori* was scrolled below both marks.

Heidel didn't say a word, but his curled lip gave him away.

"Come on, Franz! I've secretly been a member of this *dangerous* organization since before the war even started," goaded Witte. "When the Party banned our institution and sent our members to Dachau is when

I joined. Yet, I still served the Fatherland. I didn't serve out of loyalty to the damned *Führer*. He labeled us as *undesirables*. We were deplorable and irredeemable in the eyes of all you Nazi fanatics. Now I ask you again, *what am I?*" He touched the square and compasses mark on his arm. "*What* is this a symbol of?"

Heidel closed his eyes. "You are a Freemason."

"*Ja*, I am! And you were responsible for the death of thousands of my brothers at Dachau, were you not?"

No reply.

Witte repeated it, screaming. "Were! You! Not?"

Heidel's eyes popped open. His lips trembled. "The war is over. Let's work this out. The Americans want me to help them fight Communists. To find Russian agents, extract information, and turn them. They are interested in how I interrogated prisoners with what is called a truth serum. I am not lying. We conducted electro-shock, hypnosis, and psycho-surgery. These things are valuable to the Americans. Communism is our new enemy."

Witte spit on the SS man.

Heidel began to weep. "I, I, I regret what I did. I am no longer SS. I pledged my loyalty to the Americans. And you can start over with a fresh identity, too. Come on, you were working for them anyway."

"I was forced to. I had no choice. You went willingly through bribery."

Heidel sniffled. "Yes, I did. It saved me from being hanged. These *Totenkopf* rings are like trophies for the Americans. I took 4,000 of them from Castle Wewelsburg. They're yours to negotiate with now, too. Just please let me live and I will forever be indebted to you. Please, I will serve you the rest of my life as your indentured servant. Please, I beg you, *Kapitän*."

Witte snickered, completely ignoring Heidel's pleas and bribes. "I read smuggled letters about you from a Mason of my banned lodge. He was imprisoned at Dachau and your name was at the top of the list as the one most responsible for atrocities there. I only knew you by name on paper, though. But they physically described you as having classic Aryan breeding, but remarkably short in height. No wonder you fit inside this torpedo tube. And to think you were in front of me this whole time, a passenger in my own boat."

Terrified, Heidel blabbered desperately to convince Witte not to hurt him. He had one last card to play. "There's thousands more of these rings buried at Castle Wewelsburg. I know the exact location. I'm the *only* one. I never told the Americans this, but Himmler personally ordered me to hide all of them in a secret chamber while *Sturmbannführer* Heinz Macher was supposed to destroy the rest of the castle with dynamite. That chamber is loaded with thousands of precious paintings, jewels, relics, gold, and more. Let me prove it to you. *Please.* Find the Van Gogh painting. It's in one of these containers. There's a drawing on the back of it that leads you right to the secret chamber within the castle. I can show you–"

"*Halt die Klappe, du Metzger!* (*Shut up, you butcher*)," hissed Witte, aiming the pistol at Heidel's head. "You think I'm going back to Germany like some damn Heinrich Schliemann seeking the lost treasure of Troy? You want to bargain with *me* now, is that it? The same way you bribed your way out of the hangman's noose to join with these corrupt Americans. No, you will receive the same fate as my father."

"Your father? What?"

"Otto Witte of the Free City of Danzig," Witte said proudly. "Recipient of the Iron Cross for bravery in World War I, as a submariner. My father was a Freemason at Dachau in 1940 and you were witnessed putting a bullet in the back of his head as he kneeled in front of you. And now you will die at the hands of a Freemason, as you so justly deserve."

"No, no. *Please!*"

With that, Witte lowered the pistol but raised the wrench high. He screamed, "*Memento Mori,*" then slammed the wrench down as hard as he could onto Heidel's forehead. The crushing blow cracked the SS man's skull. Blood spewed from the wound.

Heidel's eyes bulged, then blinked three times. His mouth fell open.

"*Memento Mori!*" A second heavy strike smashed his forehead again. A spray of brain matter peppered the captain's face. Uttering the same phrase, the third and final death blow shattered the skull like a broken plate. He left the wrench embedded halfway inside Heidel's disfigured head.

As a token of Masonic vengeance.

A whisper behind him: *"Memento Mori."*

Witte spun around. A young dark-skinned man angrily stared back at him. Before Witte could raise his pistol to shoot, a rifle stock crunched into his nose. The German captain's eyes rolled in the back of his head, and his body ragdolled like a heavy rock dropped into the ocean.

Deep down he sank.

Back into his iron coffin.

18

AFTER MOVING THE TABLE, ROLLING UP THE RUG, and prying up several loose floorboards, Sammie and Jake unveiled a crude flight of crumbling tabby steps leading down into a narrow black passageway.

The trio left their weapons topside, each grabbing a lamp, and slowly descended into the hole. The air was cold and dry. The stairs ended and they stepped onto a sandy soil filled with rough fragments of broken shells. Straight ahead was a short tight tunnel encased in crude tabby. It soon opened into a doorless chamber no bigger than a tool shed.

Sammie entered first, cussing aloud in excitement. Jake entered next, his hair brushing against the low ceiling. He placed his lamp on the floor and took out a spare flashlight from his cargo pant pocket.

Duff hung his lamp on a hook just outside the entrance before shuffling in himself. "All this plunder was taken from the U-boat wreck," he said. "This is the stolen loot they were smuggling back to the U.S. from Europe. Here's your proof, brotha."

Awestruck, Jake panned around taking in the small chamber's tightly packed treasures stacked on old wooden shelves. He saw old suitcases bulging with paper currency: reichsmarks, francs, pounds, and dollars. Next to them was a crate filled with large glass jars. Each jar contained different denominations of gold, silver, and bronze coins from various countries. Unscrewing one jar, he scooped up a handful of gold coins relief-embossed with eagles and swastikas. He couldn't help but shout an excited obscenity himself now. *Talk about one helluva 'wow' moment,* he thought.

The crate of jars was stenciled with the wording: U.S. Army Monuments, Fine Arts and Archives (MFAA) Special Collections Point, Wiesbaden, Germany. The Monuments Men.

Jake knew they were the special Allied force of 345 men – museum directors, curators and conservators – who risked their lives to find and keep the world's masterpieces from being destroyed by the Nazis. But he also knew that well over 150,000 pieces were still missing to this day – a tiny fraction of which he was now staring at. These items were apparently looted by the rogue Army truck crew Duff told him about.

Sammie stood in front of a shelf that displayed an array of relics in crates labeled MFAA, as well. He shook his head in amazement. One crate held a gold statuette of a woman, several small marble sculptures, and an ornate porcelain Chinese vase. Another crate held a box and, when Sammie opened it, he pulled out a beautiful, hand-sized, gold hourglass. Next came a glimmering necklace with precious stones, and finally a diamond-encrusted pocket watch with a Nazi symbol on it. Another shelf held finely-crafted silver bowls, even an exquisite silver and ivory tea set sitting on a large silver serving tray. Sammie picked up a 10-inch high tea pot, took off the lid, and looked inside for the hell of it.

Jake hit another rack that contained an Army officer's three-foot wide footlocker. He slid the olive drab box off the shelf and unlatched the lid. Inside was a partially burnt Nazi flag. Pulling the flag away revealed a treasure trove of Nazi-related pilferage. He found a German officer's ceremonial sword, a dagger, a combat bayonet, and a fighting knife. There were badges, patches, medals, ribbons, a Nazi armband, a polished black SS helmet, gorget, and even a full SS officer's dress uniform neatly folded up, along with a pair of black leather officer's boots.

Jake grabbed a boot and flipped it over to look on the sole. Near the heel he found a stamp with an SS rune. He remembered when he was browsing Erhardt Hoffman's militaria online shopping site a similar pair going for

$6,000. If Hoffman saw all these original items in this room, Jake thought with a wide grin, he'd have a wet dream,

Returning the boot and looking up, he reeled back in surprise. A man's angry eyes stared back at him. Pressed against the wall in the back of the shelf, a miniature face sat. Jake hit it with his flashlight and instantly recognized the most infamous mustache in all of history. The head was a three-quarter life size bronze bust of Adolf Hitler. Jake almost wanted to punch the damned bust, but knew it had immense value, both historically and monetarily.

Underneath the bust, he noticed a pair of books with red covers. Sliding them out, he discovered they were a two volume set of *Mein Kampf (My Struggle)*, Hitler's famous autobiography and political manifesto. The would-be dictator wrote it while incarcerated in the early 1920s during a failed coup attempt in Germany. Jake flipped open a few pages in the first volume and saw that it was an original from 1925. He also saw Hitler's famous signature. This rare set of books he knew was worth well over $80,000 alone.

Sammie pulled a box from a shelf and started thumbing through old paintings, drawings, and prints. He hadn't a clue how valuable some of them were and mistakenly ripped the corner of one watercolor painting. Duff gasped and told him to watch what he was doing. Sammie backed off, hands in the air in surrender.

Duff moseyed over to an aluminum briefcase in the corner. An imperial Nazi eagle was engraved on its lid. Dialing 0732 into the number lock, he popped the lid and extracted a waterproof rubber pouch containing a stack of file folders. "Come on over here," he urged Jake, as he unsealed the pouch.

Duff handed him the files. "What's this?" Jake asked.

"Proof of everything I told you about the U-boat and *Operation Overcast*."

Jake flipped open a folder and started thumbing through aged yellow papers. The cover sheet had a Top Secret stamp on it, a subject headline of *Operation Overcast*, and an address of P.O. Box 1142 in Virginia.

"Unbelievable," said Jake to Duff. "P.O. Box 1142 was a secret military intelligence unit who interrogated prisoners at Fort Hunt. It only became public knowledge just a few years ago. This is incredible."

"It's a treasure trove for historians like you, Jake." The old man then wandered back to Sammie, giving Jake some time to whet his appetite.

Five minutes later, Duff loudly rapped his staff to snap Jake out of his trance. Jake raised his head from the file folder and blinked. Duff motioned for him to join him across the room. Shoving the mission files back in its pouch, and returning it to the briefcase, he stood next to the old man.

Again with his staff, Duff tapped the top of a cylindrical wooden container with a rusted steel lid and base. The lid was hinged and tightly clasped shut. "Here's one of four containers I found on the U-boat. It's chock full of them skull rings. I took two of them off the sub, but emptied one of them already. Sat down here one time countin' how many rings were inside, then I melted most of them down and sold silver bars afterward. Another ring container had busted open on the sub, but there's still one more full one sitting inside the U-boat's torpedo tube where they was originally hidden."

Jake inspected the cylinder at the old man's feet. The wooden container looked well over 20 inches tall and 9 inches in diameter. Stenciled in faded white letters in the German language, he could make out that it said 'mortar ammunition' for the *Wehrmacht*. He grabbed the handle on the lid and lifted it. It felt like 25-30 lbs. Taking a knee, he struggled to unclasp the rusted cap.

"Now, before you go openin' that, brotha," said Duff, placing a hand on Jake's shoulder to stop him. "How about whatever's inside this here container I'll let you *keep* as an advance payment for you helping us out with Buzzut. That okay?"

Jake's eyes went wide, like a kid about to open a gift on Christmas day. His heart pounded. "Sure. Totally okay. I accept."

He flipped open the lid. Inside were silver *Totenkopf* rings filled right to the top. The little skull and crossbones were like a nest of silver spiders with black eyes coming alive. "Holy f–!"

"Told ya, didn't I?" said Duff with a shit-eating grin. "Ain't no bullshitter."

"Good Lord!" said Sammie, standing over Jake.

Jake shoved a hand inside and came out with a half dozen rings in his palm. "Un-believable." He looked up at Duff and stuttered. "You, you, you realize how much this, this – all these rings are worth?"

"Uh-huh," said Duff with a wink, enjoying Jake's excitement. "The one I counted held almost a thousand of them."

"If each ring is worth seven grand on average . . . holy shit," Jake mumbled under his breath.

"Like I said, I'ma gonna give you this here container of rings, Jake. But everything else in this room goes to Sammie. Sorry."

"Jesus, Duff. No need to apologize."

"Really, Pappy?" said Sammie. "Really? Oh my God."

"Yup," Duff nodded with watery eyes. "All yours, Sammie. You pursue your dreams. You open up a legal moonshine distillery and you make it into a successful business and employ the residents on the island and you will save our lands for another 100 years to come. You do it for me, Sammie. Keep the legacy of Doctor Blackbeard alive. I love you, young man. I've always loved you. I'm so sorry you had to bear the pain of your parents and grandparents passing away all at once like you did at such a young age. And then all of that abuse you've taken from LeShaun, it hurts me deep down inside."

Sammie stood up and gave Pappy a bear hug. Pappy started bawling. Jake's eyes welled up, too.

"Go on and grab some of them American dollars," Duff said to Sammie. "Get as much as you can. Get some of them gold coins, too, and a necklace, and that pocket watch. Don't be shy. Go on now, fill up your trousers, boy. We can come back later on and get all the rest. But I want you to get yourself a safe deposit box at a bank and put it all away as a little nest egg for now. That way no one can break into our home and steal it."

Sammie started filling his pockets. "Yaas'suh, Pappy! Yaas'suh."

"Hmm, what's this?" said Jake, staring into his ring container. He pointed to a piece of old cloth. Sammie kneeled down next to him.

Jake told him to hold the cylinder steady and he reached inside to grasp the corner of the material. Pushing away a bunch of rings, he got a firm hold, but realized the cloth was wrapped around some type of piping. Jake stood up and with both hands, managed to pull the cloth and pipe straight up and out. The pipe slipped out of his hands and clanged on the ground, leaving him still holding the tube of rolled-up cloth.

Brows furrowed, he let the cloth drop to reveal a canvas that had also been wrapped around the pipe.

He unfurled it.

What he discovered was an oil painting that had been removed from its stretchers. The subject was a man in a straw hat with a backpack and walking stick, apparently taking a stroll down a country road. The oil brush strokes were thick and cracked in places.

The painting wasn't at all spectacular to him in the least. *Kind of ugly,* he thought, underwhelmed. Certainly not something he'd hang in his house. Then again, he was far from being an art connoisseur. It was the question of *why* this painting was stashed inside the cylinder that perplexed him the most. It was being smuggled, of course, so it meant something to someone somewhere. Obviously, it held immense value.

"Hell's that doing in there?" asked Duff.

"No idea," said Jake, laying the painting down.

"Looks like a kid painted that dadgum thing. They call that art? Pfft!" Losing interest, he and Sammie walked back to a shelf to continue pilfering.

Jake flattened the painting down, whipped out his cell phone, and took a few pictures. He looked for an artist's signature, but couldn't find one.

He then flipped the canvas over out of curiosity hoping to get some kind of identification. Instead, what he found on the backside was a crude ink drawing of geometric shapes and arrows pointing to a circle, a spiral, and a little skull and crossbones. He had no idea what in the world this drawing meant, other than there was certainly some type of connection because of the

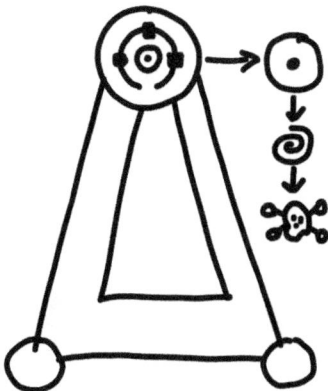

clear *Totenkopf* symbol. *Must have something to do with the SS,* he thought.

Jake looked up to say something to Duff and Sammie, but then shut his mouth. Perhaps this discovery was something he should just keep to himself, he figured. Snapping a picture of the drawing, he then re-wrapped the painting around the pipe again, covered it with the cloth, and inside his backpack it went. Clamping shut the ammo container of rings, he lifted it up, grabbed a hurricane lamp, and exited the room. Excited beyond belief, he slowly took the tabby steps back up to the basement level.

And immediately smelled smoke.

19

Duff Greenhall's old home
Greenhall Landing
Sapelo Island, Georgia

LESHAUN HOVERED HIS 'DRAGON EGG' DRONE twenty feet above the old Greenhall shack, observing Duff, Sammie, and the unknown man enter it after tracking them through the woods. It was a risky maneuver to drop so low given the potential tree branches catching the blades and causing a catastrophic failure. But his pay-off justified the risk.

Nobody threatened him. Not even his grandfather.

Yesterday morning, when Duff and that lawyer Dixon confronted him, and the old man threatened to shoot him and burn his body to a crisp, it sent LeShaun into a fit of uncontrollable rage. The fact that Duff bragged that Sammie hid *Doctor Blackbeard* away, sealed the teen's fate, too.

Knowing someday his stolen firefighting drone would come in handy, he started implementing his plan that same day, giving it several short test flights, and reading the manual for a refresher on how to deliver the Dragon Egg. It was all rather simple. He even caught part of his yard on fire when he test-dropped an egg. After disabling the lights on the drone, he just had to wait for the cover of night to commit his deadly crime.

When it grew dark enough, he remotely flew the small, blacked-out firefighting drone from his Hog Hammock home overlooking Cabretta Island by simply following the long white sand beach north up to Blackbeard

Creek. He sat comfortably on a deck chair inside his screened-in porch, wearing a FPV (First Person View) video goggle headset and viewed the flight path through the drone's HD camera. It was as if he were a miniature pilot inside the aircraft. A short distance up the creek and he easily spotted the long dock at Greenhall Landing. He was surprised to see an unknown pleasure boat docked at the floating end section near Sammie's Zodiac.

Overhead spying then began with thermal imaging. Maintaining a safe altitude and fighting increasing winds driving a light rain, he zoomed in the heat-sensing camera on the home and clearly observed Duff, Sammie, and the unknown man leave the house. They skirted the abandoned trailer homes and junk cars of deceased family members, and headed south into the woods. LeShaun almost panicked because he wanted to firebomb the main house when they slept, but now his prey was well awake and headed elsewhere. Plus, his fuel and battery life were already depleted by a quarter.

The trio proved easy to track, though, given their flashlight and body heat signatures on thermal camera. They appeared as white ghosts against a black background. It took some time hacking through the dense ground cover before they reached an old cottage in an overgrown field not too far from the bluff.

LeShaun knew this location to be Duff's abandoned home, a place he had avoided as a kid, considering it haunted – especially since his grandparents practiced their Hoodoo magic shit there. His grandmother died there, too, after living a disgusting hoarder's life. He'd almost forgotten about the place because it was virtually impossible to get to anyway. From high above, he watched as the unknown man paused near the old family cemetery panning a flashlight around. Sammie joined him. Soon they both walked to the rear of the house where Duff was and all three disappeared inside.

Now was the time for LeShaun to act. He didn't care who the stranger was at all – merely collateral damage in his mind. His targets were Sammie and Duff. The old house would be their grave.

LeShaun pressed a button on his flight unit, holding his breath, wondering if the rain would have any effect on what would happen next. The button triggered a mechanism to start the chemical reaction of the first of six Dragon Eggs. Each orb was filled with potassium permanganate powder. After the first egg dropped through a small on-board tube, it was then injected by an industrial syringe filled with liquid glycol. It was at this point he had a mere ten seconds to release the egg before the ignition process started.

He dropped the first egg onto the back porch of the house where his intended victims had entered, hoping to hinder any chance of escape. Within seconds, a small blow torch-like flame erupted from the side of the ball. It immediately caught fire to the dry wood and surrounding vegetation. As the ball melted, the plastic added additional fuel to spread the flames. He smiled with relief. The light rain didn't hinder the fire at all.

He repeated the procedure for the next five eggs, dropping them around the perimeter of the home, and even managing to land one inside the house through a hole in the collapsed front porch roof. Little did he know, out of the six deployed eggs, one failed to ignite. The dud lay nestled in weeds on top of the hood of an abandoned pick-up truck sitting close to the house.

Within minutes, the house was ablaze. With vegetation surrounding it, a dry wood frame structure, and the overloaded combustible materials stacked inside, soon a fire of incredible proportions erupted. The fire doubled in size every minute as the home became fully involved with flames reaching twenty feet in height. LeShaun was sure nobody inside would survive. His deed was done.

He watched the destruction from his hovering drone as it spread into the surrounding ground cover eating everything up in its path. It took all of his flying skills to keep the drone from crashing due to a fast approaching thunderstorm off the coast. Finally, after ten minutes, he had to bug out from low fuel and heavy rain. The rain, he realized, was now a blessing in disguise. Since the house was already destroyed, the three occupants dead, hopefully the rain would put the fire out, increasing the chance that no one would notice what had happened for days to come.

He was also banking on the fire going undetected because of the isolated location on the island, many miles from the main community down at Hog Hammock. Plus, Duff's old home was surrounded by large live oaks to mask the bright glow. The only way anyone could even see the structure fire would be from the air or directly on Blackbeard Creek at Raccoon Bluff.

Flying the drone back into his compound and securing it in his garage, he then monitored his police and fire scanner the rest of the early morning hours for any emergency calls. The only dispatch he heard was a fire department response for a lightning strike setting a tree ablaze over on the mainland near Meridian.

A lightning strike: that piqued his interest as a nice alibi. In the days ahead, when the fire would eventually be discovered and the bodies found, he could merely play dumb and speculate that the house had been hit with lightning on this stormy night.

Once the storm passed, the scanner went silent the rest of the night.

LeShaun celebrated by snorting a line of cocaine through each nostril, followed by a drop of Liquid O heroin inhaled through his nose, too. After two glasses of wine, he fell into a deep, narco-induced hallucinatory slumber.

He slept soundly, until Yahoodi, the Sapelo Island boo hag, paid him a disturbing early morning visit.

And then his nightmare began.

20

Duff Greenhall's old home
Greenhall Landing
Sapelo Island, Georgia

A S THE STRUCTURE FIRE RAGED ABOVE GROUND, below in the tabby basement, the immediate danger was toxic black smoke drifting down from the low ceiling. Jake had no idea what was causing it, but knew they would all succumb if they didn't escape.

He frantically screamed down into the dungeon for Sammie and Duff to get the hell out, that smoke was filling the basement.

Jake ditched the hurricane lamp and the ammo can of rings. He slung his rifle over his shoulder and turned on his LED rail light. As Sammie and Duff stumbled up the stairs, Jake aimed the flashlight beam onto the thick stream of smoke accumulating above. Following the trail, he saw it pouring in from the previous chamber.

Dashing through the open door and into the distillery room, he followed the smoke trail again as it grew thicker and lower. Still he couldn't find the source.

Around the corner and through the next open door, he entered the pantry room where he now started to feel heat.

Here, the smoke covered the top half of the room, forcing him to bend low for fresher air. Through the open door leading to the foyer with the tabby staircase up to the main level – their primary means of escape – he saw the glow of flames and felt the brunt of the heat. Reduced to crawling, he made his way to the base of the stairway, only to find it was filled with flaming debris collapsed from the house level above.

Sitting in front of him on fire was the secret wall panel door from the top of the steps. It was the first piece of compromised structure to have fallen down the stairs. Duff's old lodge photo had already burnt away, and his framed Masonic white leather apron had slipped loose and lay shattered on the floor at arm's length.

Jake used his rifle, braved the heat and smoke, and caught the frame with the end of the suppressed barrel. He pulled it in and tried to grab the old apron only to burn his hand on hot glass.

Dragging the frame away from the heat, he backed into the pantry room on his knees and finally managed to snatch the apron from within. Hastily folding it up, he shoved it in a cargo pant pocket, then slammed the pantry door shut. Jake knew that shutting the door was just a temporary hold before it too would eventually be consumed.

Just then another portion of the house collapsed and tumbled down the stairway smashing against the pantry door. Smoke poured in from the gaps at the top and bottom of the door.

He backed out and entered the distillery room, slamming that door shut, too, creating yet another fire wall. There, he met a terrified Sammie.

"The house is on fire above us," Jake shouted. "Where's Duff?"

"B-b-back in the inventory room," said Sammie with wild eyes. "He took in some smoke and is coughing real bad."

"Okay, here's what we're gonna do," implored Jake, taking off his backpack. "We need rags, clothes, anything we can stuff into the cracks of this door to stop the smoke coming in. That's what's going to kill us first. We have to stop the smoke." He rummaged through his backpack, pulled out a t-shirt and started stuffing it into the crack on the top of the door.

Sammie pulled off his own shirt and started packing it on the bottom of the door. Together they managed to pack enough material into the gaps to bring the flow of black death to a mere trickle.

A coughing Sammie ran over to the old still's chimney pipe and pulled the flue open. The smoke in the room immediately started clearing and rising to the surface.

"Good thinking, Sammie!"

Bolting out of that room and shutting its door, they reentered the inventory room. Duff was up on the trap door ladder fiercely coughing while trying to slide open the grave slab to the cemetery above – now their only means of escape.

"Duff, get down from there!" shouted Jake. "Stay out of the smoke!"

The old man stopped pulling on the iron ring and started to back down.

"Sammie, stuff this door, too," said Jake, turning his back on Duff for just a moment. He pulled out a rescue blanket from his pack and handed Sammie his tactical knife. "Cut it in strips and pack it tight, top and bottom. This is our last line of defense. If we don't get this room sealed, we're fucked. If any fire catches that moonshine, we're gonna blow sky high. I've gotta open that grave slab and get us outta here."

Just as he turned back to Duff on the far side of the room, he watched as the old man lost a step on the ladder and tumbled backward, losing his grip. He fell hard from about three feet up and landed squarely on his knee with a loud grunt. Duff immediately curled up into the fetal position, clutched his injured knee, and writhed in pain.

"Oh God, no!" Jake rushed over. Sammie was at his side as they both consoled the elderly man and assessed his injury. Jake knew that at Duff's advanced age a simple fall could do way more damage than the obvious knee injury. He was proven right when Duff couldn't even sit upright, complaining of a severe back and hip pain, too.

"Sammie, keep an eye on him. I'm going for the slab." Jake scampered up the trap door ladder, grabbed the iron ring and pulled backward on the grave slab. It refused to budge.

"Jesus Christ," he muttered under his breath, sucking in black smoke. Coughing it back out, he took another step up the ladder and now used his shoulder as leverage. "It's not working!"

Refusing to give up, he gave it another go.

Duff recovered enough from the initial fall and managed to sit up with Sammie's help. He looked up and watched Jake's futile efforts.

"I don't think you're gonna move it, Jake," Duff said with a rasp, followed by several coughs. "Must be sealed shut with salt and what not. It's been too long since it's been moved." He coughed heavily again. "I got an idea, though. That thing is made of cement. It's old and brittle. Go on and get down from there."

Jake gave one last straining grunt and failed again to slide the slab. He jumped down off the ladder nearly out of breath and started hacking.

"Sammie, get my MP40," ordered Duff. Sammie complied. "Now, y'all stand back." From an angle while seated on the floor, he aimed at the slab near the top of the ladder.

"Whoa!" said Jake. "Watch out for ricochets–"

Duff let loose with a burst. The distinctive burp of the gun was impossibly loud in the enclosed chamber. Sammie plugged his ears. Jake ducked by instinct and turned his head. Chunks of old cement fell from the slab. Another burst and Duff laughed and coughed out loud. It was working. He was punching holes in the slab like a jackhammer.

Dust formed at the top of the ladder as rock fragments flew all around the room. As Duff continued to chisel away with his submachine gun, Jake joined in with his high powered rifle. He fired in the same spot, blasting even bigger chunks from the slab.

"Sammie, get your shotgun going," shouted Duff. "You got deer slugs loaded up, right? Don't just stand there, boy. Get in the action!"

Sammie snatched up his shotgun, kneeled down, aimed, and joined in with the thundering blasts of the other two weapons.

Duff's MP40 clicked, his 32-round box magazine spent. Jake's rifle ammo was depleted, too, but he ejected his magazine and slammed home another. Lastly, Sammie went through all six rounds of deer slugs and started reloading more.

A large piece of cement holding the iron ring fell to floor with a clang.

"Okay, cease fire, y'all. Cease fire," screamed Duff, still in his seated position and covered in dust and cement fragments. "Let's see what we got," he said loudly. "Go on up there, Jake."

"What!?" shouted Jake, ears ringing from all the gunfire.

"Get up there and see if we busted through!" repeated Duff, at the top of his voice.

Jake nodded and handed his rifle to Sammie. He took out his hand flashlight and shined the beam up the ladder noticing dust and smoke being sucked out of a large hole to the outside. It was big enough that they could definitely escape. There was flickering light through the hole and he even felt wetness on his face. After bounding up the ladder, he slowly raised his head and shoulders through the slab to cautiously peer outside.

Even though a light rain shower peppered his face, he felt intense heat as the cemetery was ablaze all around him. Beyond the steaming iron spikes of the cemetery gate, not 20 feet away, was the immense fireball of what used to be Duff's old home.

Jake flinched as the roof gave way and the walls collapsed inward. Flames licked even higher. The house was now reduced to a large mound of burning wood and tin, lighting up everything around it, including the droplets of rain falling through a haze of black smoke.

Flames danced all around him as he panned with his flashlight on dozens of soot-covered headstones inside the walled-in cemetery. He saw black snakes slithering away and others fried to a crisp. Several trees were also fully ablaze just beyond the wall. They swayed with the wind and showered the ground with bright orange sparks.

Once he got his bearings, it looked as though the line of fire that was currently frying the cemetery was now headed north – the same direction as the main Greenhall home and dock. With a healthy wind pushing it, the fire would eventually destroy even that piece of property, too, if it wasn't stopped in time.

Jake dropped his head back in the hole and looked down at the Greenhall men. Duff was trying to bend his knee, which was a good sign. "Your house is totally destroyed," Jake shouted. "Collapsed in on itself. It's still on fire. A ground fire is everywhere and sweeping through the cemetery. Trees on fire all around–"

An animalistic shriek filled the air. It was a horrifying sound. Jake's eyes grew big and he popped his head back outside. With his flashlight, he turned all around seeking the source of the sound.

Through the cemetery gate he spotted a humongous black hairy beast, its back on fire, running in circles and snorting loudly. Jake exhaled in abject terror. The beast turned toward him, its eyes burning red hot. It had a long muzzle and two long tusks. When it opened its jaws, sharp yellow teeth were revealed.

The Hell Hound.

It was as wide and tall as a cow. Duff was right. It looked like the offspring of a massive hairy pig and a Great Dane on steroids.

As if on cue from a horror movie, a flash of lightning silhouetted the flaming beast as it reared up on its hind legs and reached a height of almost eight feet. A wicked loud crack of thunder followed. As flames licked its thrashing head, the beast let out another shriek of fury before slamming its front paws on the ground with a deep thud. It then charged directly at Jake.

The thing smashed into the iron gate, sending it flying off its hinges. Jake ducked back down the hole.

"Sammie, your shotgun!" he screamed. "It's the fucking Hell Hound!" Sammie tossed his shotgun up to Jake who immediately thrust his body back through the hole and aimed for a shot.

But the beast had disappeared.

Just then he heard frantic squealing all around him as a pack of wild boar, their backs on fire, breached the gate gap and poured into the cemetery.

In rapid pumping action, Jake let loose with the shotgun, dropping three of the feral hogs in their tracks. In seconds, he had spent all the deer slugs. Leaping over a grave marker, a crazed boar came right at him. Jake slid down the ladder just as the pig dove through the hole.

Midway down, it hit him in the shoulder with its hard head, knocking him off the ladder, and hard onto his ass. The pig slammed against the floor and tumbled over in grunting rage. Before it could get up, Sammie, having previously reloaded Duff's MP40, opened up on the pig.

The boar squealed as Sammie riddled it with bullets. Finally, its bloody, burning, smoking body twitched its last signs of life.

"I love the smell of bacon in the morning," deadpanned Duff.

Jake blinked several times. He just sat there out of breath, pain in his shoulder, ass bruised, and not believing what he had just heard come out of Duff's mouth. And then he laughed heartily.

Sammie aimed up the ladder with the MP40, ready to shoot any more pigs that fell from the hole. "I guess pigs really can fly," the teenager snickered.

Jake couldn't help but cough again with laughter.

Relief permeated the air as the three men breathed a sigh of relief that the onslaught of beasts seemed over.

"Brotha, this ain't no Hell Hound!" said Duff, poking the dead boar with his foot. "That there's just a big ol' feral hog."

"No, no, no," countered an incredulous Jake, standing up with a painful moan. He angrily pointed up to the hole. "I saw a beast up there a good eight feet tall when he stood up on his hind legs. Had red eyes, tusks. It was a big, black fugly thing, its hair on fire, and it charged right at me. It knocked the damn gate down and disappeared, and then that pack of pig fuckers came at me. I know what I saw, Duff. I know what I fucking saw."

"Okay," said Duff, raising his hands. "Okay, I believe you."

"Me, too," added Sammie.

"If he charged you and then took off," said Duff, with a cough, "that means we're safe to go up into the cemetery. We have his permission."

"Safe?" said Jake, shaking his head in disbelief. "Safe? Ahh, so he opened the gate for us. So nice of him. What the fuck? We can't go up there. It's like a napalm strike. And there's crazed animals on fire running all around."

Before he could finish his bitching, a downpour of rain came in through the hole as if a faucet had been turned on. Jake looked up and let the water stream down his face. He closed his eyes and prayed.

God, please stop that fire.

When he opened his eyes, something long and black fell from the opening above. It landed right on his head and shoulders.

A snake.

A three foot long black snake then fell to the floor at his feet. Jake screamed and jumped back like he had stepped on a landmine. He tripped over his own feet and fell hard on his ass again, crawling backward as the snake slithered toward him.

Sammie nonchalantly bent over and grabbed the creature, securing its head in a strong grip. "No need to worry, Mr. Jake," he said smiling. "This here is a kingsnake. They're non-venomous."

Jake breathed a sigh of relief and then lay flat on his back out of breath.

"Kingsnakes are the good ones that hunt and kill rattlesnakes, cottonmouths, and copperheads – them poisonous ones," said Sammie.

"Cemetery is loaded with them," said Duff. "But most people don't know they're harmless to humans. They serve their purpose to keep *cowens* and *eavesdroppers* out."

Jake nodded, catching Duff's use of Masonic terminology to describe intruders and trespassers.

Sammie scrambled up the ladder with the snake and pushed his torso through the hole. After tossing the snake, he scanned the scene of destruction all around him. Suddenly, a bright bolt of lightning and an ear-piercing crack of thunder ripped the air. Sammie scrambled back down the ladder, scared shitless at almost being struck.

The storm was directly on top of them now. All they had to do was wait it out since the cellar was almost cleared of smoke. Jake and Sammie went back into the other rooms and inspected the integrity of the doors. They made it all the way back to the pantry door leading up to the ground level, and even that was still intact and not hot anymore. Twenty minutes later, the thunderstorm passed.

Jake went up the ladder first to make sure it was safe. The deluge had reduced the house fire to a smoldering ruin. All that remained were several patches of flames still flickering in the depths of the pile. The ground cover and woods around the house had turned into a smoking, hissing swamp. Dead hogs lay around the hole and there was no sign of the Hell Hound. The worst of the black smoke had since drifted away and stars started to appear from the clearing skies.

Jake gave the all clear and helped Duff out of the hole. Sammie was last, making sure Duff didn't fall and injure himself again. Jake then scampered back down and retrieved the cylindrical ammo container of skull rings. He wasn't about to leave that behind after everything he'd gone through.

21

A T JAKE'S INSISTENCE, DUFF AGREED TO MEDICAL attention. At Duff's insistence, Jake agreed to keep the fire secret. He did not want word getting out that his old house had burned down for fear the authorities would come onto his property and discover his underground stash of illegal moonshine and dungeon of Nazi loot. There was nothing of value in the house anyway, he explained. The underground was what mattered the most.

Upon escaping the garrison, they soon realized that no one on the south end of the island – not even the volunteer firefighters – knew the house had burned to the ground and was subsequently extinguished by the rain. Jake decided that getting Duff to a hospital was the first priority, since the old man was complaining of throbbing pain in his knee, back, and hip. Trying to find out how the house suspiciously caught fire would have to wait until daylight approached.

The problem was he couldn't call 911 since he had no phone service, let alone arrange an ambulance to pick Duff up, since one didn't even exist on the island. The best field triage Jake could muster was splinting his leg and giving the old man some over-the-counter pain pills from a first-aid pouch in his CERT pack.

After he and Sammie scrounged around for debris to camouflage the busted escape slab in the cemetery – now the only access to the underground garrison – the trio slowly made their way back to the main house. Jake carried his ammo can of rings in one hand and helped prop Duff up with his other. With Sammie's assistance, they helped him limp down the scorched game trail. Duff was clearly exhausted and in intense pain by the time they reached the main house.

At the dock, they loaded the elderly man onto Jake's power catamaran, *Lizzie,* and fired her up. Sammie made his great grandfather as comfortable as possible with pillows and blankets. Completely spent, Duff barked out where he wanted to be taken, then immediately dozed off.

Their destination was ten nautical miles way at Shellman Bluff, the nearest fishing village on the mainland from the north end of Sapelo. Duff had told them there was a youth summer camp and private dock there on the peninsula just before reaching the bluff. The camp was owned by the Masonic Home of Georgia, located up in Macon, a non-profit residential child care facility funded by the Masons to provide for children in need. The kids spent their summers at the camp, but this time of year it was all closed up – a perfect rendezvous point for a Mason in need.

Sammie took the helm to get them out of the Greenhall Landing tributary and up the winding Blackbeard Creek to Sapelo Sound. He had the best navigational knowledge and knew where to avoid oyster shoals, mud flats, and sand bars – especially at night. Once they reached the choppy waters of the sound, Jake took over and cautiously drove the boat the rest of the way through the darkness. Motoring by spotlight and keeping his speed down so as not to rattle Duff, the normal half-hour ride lasted an hour.

Halfway across the sound, Jake's iPhone gained cell service again. A slew of texts poured in along with one long voice mail from Rae. She'd been trying to reach him since early evening concerning her background check of LeShaun Greenhall. He listened immediately to what she had to say.

"Jake, my contact with the GBI came through on LeShaun Greenhall. Luckily, his juvie records weren't even sealed. He was a real piece of work when he was a kid. Apparently, like a terror on Sapelo Island. Hated by everyone.

When he was twelve, he assaulted an 80-year-old woman three different times – punching her in the face, whipping her back with a branch, and setting her hair on fire. When he was fourteen, he broke into a man's house, defecated, and placed the pile of feces in the freezer. When he was sixteen, he broke into another house, stole a shotgun, shot a neighbor's dog, and then cut its head off.

The parents even sent him away to a school for troubled youth, but he ran away. Finally, at eighteen he left Georgia and moved to Miami where he developed a nice rap sheet of armed robbery, assault, drug possession, and drug dealing. Did a few stints in Florida State Prison. The guy's a career criminal. How in the hell the court appointed him guardian of a teenage boy and an elderly man is a fucking abomination.

Oh, and get this – as if it's a surprise. He's a classic deadbeat dad, too. Skipped out on his three baby mamas and nine kids in Florida, leaving them all to live on welfare.

But wait, there's more! Most recently, about a year ago, he was the main person of interest in the theft of a prototype firefighting drone for the DNR, used for starting controlled burns. It was stolen at Lumber Landing on Sapelo Island, the police report said. Case went cold. But I Googled his name, along with drones, and lo and behold, LeShaun is quite the avid drone hobbyist. Belongs to a local RC flying club. He even won some drone races.

Basically, the guy's a fucking cancer wherever he goes. Stay far away from him. I know you, Jake. You have good intentions, but you've got to let these domestic problems work themselves out on their own time. Domestics are a dead-end. And I don't want you taking that road. Come home. I love you."

LeShaun involved in the theft of a firefighting drone that deliberately started brush fires? *Well now,* Jake thought. *Isn't that convenient?*

Jake had Sammie take the helm, then dialed Rae and woke her up, rehashing everything that had happened at the house fire, their escape, and Duff's injuries. He asked her to wake up Becky Holden, a registered nurse, have her grab an oxygen tank and a medical kit, and for both of them to drive down to the Masonic Home Camp at Shellman Bluff where he'd meet them so Becky could assess the extent of Duff's injuries. Discretion was key, he stressed. They didn't want to attract any police or ambulance presence at this point. With that, he ended the call and turned to Sammie.

With a whisper, he asked, "did you know about LeShaun being involved in the theft of a firefighting drone last year on Sapelo?"

Sammie said he heard about it, but never knew LeShaun was even involved or questioned about it. "I didn't even know he owned a drone until Sunday night, Mr. Jake."

Jake had an idea: he started to Google the drone theft incident. Sure enough, he found an article a year ago from *The Darien News* explaining details of the theft that coincided with Rae's report. There was a video link to the prototype drone and a demonstration of how it worked with orbs, called 'Dragon Eggs.'

As Sammie watched the video over Jake's shoulder, he started cussing. He then reached in his pocket and pulled out an exact replica of one of the Dragon Eggs in the video. It was blackened with soot and partially melted.

"Look what I found at Pappy's house," said Sammie, curling his lip.

"What the–?" cursed Jake, glaring at the teen. "Where the–?"

"When we were looking for stuff to cover the grave slab with, I found this sitting on his old truck parked next to the house." He handed Jake the dud orb. "Looked like it didn't belong, so I pocketed it. I had no idea what it was."

"What you found is evidence, the truth that–," said Jake, placing his hands on the dash and bowing his head to control his growing anger, "that your fucking uncle tried to murder us with that drone he stole." Jake looked at Sammie sternly. "I remember buzzing sounds in the wind when we were walking there and saw something dark flying overhead. Thought it was a bird or bat or something and now realize it was his drone tracking us. He waited until we got inside the house then lit it up. We weren't in there very long, ya know?"

"Right," said Sammie, with clenched fist, "and then it catches on fire immediately. This changes everything for me, too, Mr. Jake. It's not about the land anymore. When we get Pappy to a safe place, I want to go back. Eye for an eye. I'm going to burn Versailles to the ground."

"We're going to end this once and for all," Jake hissed, staring ahead at the dark waters.

"You know," said Sammie. "I bet he thinks we're dead and never escaped that burning house. No one even knows it burned, let alone anyone being inside of it."

Jake nodded. "We can use that to our advantage. But does he know about the basement and the moonshine operation?"

Duff piped up, coughing, having stirred from his slumber. "We never allowed LeShaun near our house when he was a kid, never told him about the basement. My son, LeShaun's dad, never even told him either. They had so many problems with him when he was young they couldn't trust him. That boy was the black sheep of the family and the best thing that ever happened was him leaving the island. No one missed him."

"This actually will help us then," said Jake. "If he thinks his biggest threat has disappeared and is dead, then he'll have his guard down when we hit him."

"Good," said Sammie.

Now perusing his texts, Jake saw one from Erhardt Hoffman that sounded somewhat urgent. The collector wanted to meet him in person regarding what happened in Charleston. Jake texted back that he was involved in a delicate situation requiring a few days before he could be freed up.

But on a whim, knowing that Hoffman was an expert in German militaria, he sent him an additional text with a photo attachment of the painting he found in the ammo can. He asked Hoffman if he could identify it, the artist, and any story behind it. Told him it was Nazi loot being smuggled back to the States from Germany and that he had just discovered it and it could be worth a lot of money. He also included a picture of the geometric drawing on the back, asking if he could make any sense of it.

By the time they arrived at the private river dock of the Masonic Home Camp and tied up, the first rays of light started to appear behind them on the eastern horizon. The cluster of cabins at the camp were all shuttered and a nearby pool was covered for the season. No other cottages were within view because of the heavy tree cover. A half hour went by and headlights finally approached up the long private driveway.

The ladies had arrived.

Becky immediately ran to the dock and hopped onboard the boat. She introduced herself and went to work attending Duff. In no time, she had determined that indeed he needed to get to an emergency room. Not only did his coughing concern her, but his knee had stiffened up to where he needed Jake to carry him to Rae's SUV.

Breathing through an oxygen mask from the bottle that Becky brought, Duff refused to be taken to a public hospital. He explained that he could not afford his name getting out that he'd been injured. Too many questions would follow, word would get back to Hog Hammock, the news media, and people would start showing up in droves.

Becky offered to take him to her Cherokee Rose Manor elderly care home in Savannah's historic district where she could have a doctor make a house call and where his privacy was guaranteed. It would be the ideal place where he could rest safe and secure, she said. Duff agreed, but he insisted that Sammie remain with Jake, that their mission on Sapelo was more important.

Propping the old man up in the back of the SUV, and strapping his seatbelt in, Jake slipped him a memento from his past. He handed him his folded up, hand-painted Masonic apron he had rescued from the fire. Tears flowed from Duff's eyes.

Rushing to get back onboard *Lizzie,* Jake asked Rae to follow him. She unsuccessfully tried to glean from him what the mission was that Duff had referred to. All she got in return was Jake unlatching a German ammo can showing her hundreds upon hundreds of SS skull rings. She was floored.

He then gave her a rolled-up cloth with an old painting in it telling her he had discovered it hidden inside the ring container. The smuggled painting was unknown to him, he explained, and most likely very valuable, and that she should immediately put it in their home safe along with the container of rings.

As he lugged the ring can to the SUV and stowed it in the back, he told his wife that he needed a couple more days on the island to finish his mission. That if all went well he'd be making a bombshell discovery. Rae thought about asking for details, but she knew better. They all said their goodbyes and the SUV took off back up to Savannah.

✪

30 minutes later

During the boat ride back to Sapelo, Jake brainstormed his next moves. They needed to take advantage of the dark while everyone was still asleep on the island. They decided to recon Versailles first and try to observe and track Buzzut. They'd have to develop a hasty plan based on their findings, then neutralize the target, transport the body, and make it disappear. How that would be accomplished, he wasn't quite sure at the moment. Running on no sleep at all, he had to go by instinct, for on Thursday Buzzut would cut the Greenhall land deal down in Darien.

Jake asked Sammie to tell him everything he knew of their intended target. Sammie revealed Buzzut's house layout, the exterior surveillance camera locations, access routes to his secluded property, known weaponry, his patterns and habits, how often he got food delivered and at what times, and even the days that his maid showed up on the morning ferry.

After consulting a map of Sapelo Island, Sammie and Jake determined that avoiding the residents in Hog Hammock altogether, plus any road traffic, was paramount. They simply could not be seen. Period. They'd have to avoid people at all costs and travel through wooded or dense underbrush areas to get to Versailles unseen.

The only way in was by water.

Sammie knew the island best and picked an ideal place to launch their land operation: a narrow stretch of waterway only accessible at high tide. It was a marsh tributary that emptied into the ocean, splitting Nannygoat Beach and Cabretta Beach at a place called Big Hole. This was the same place where Sammie saw Buzzut stage his night drone flight. It would give them a feet-dry access point and the same means of travel along the old causeway to hit Versailles from the ocean side instead of the populated Hog Hammock side. They'd inspect Buzzut's launch site for clues, then proceed up Cabretta Island across the marsh.

But they couldn't take *Lizzie* up the tributary because it was too shallow, even at high tide, which peaked around noon.

On their way back to Sapelo, they docked Jake's boat at Greenhall Landing. While Sammie checked the fuel in his much smaller Zodiac and transferred their gear and weapons from *Lizzie*, Jake ran into the house to grab something from his night bag left on his guest bed: NoDoz® caffeine pills. He and Sammie downed two each. Soon they were in the Atlantic en route south to their destination.

In no time, Sammie piloted the rubber craft up the shallow tidal creek, switched from the outboard to the quieter trolling motor, and stealthily reached Big Hole. They pulled the craft into the woods, then camouflaged it with vegetation.

22

AFTER INSPECTING BUZZUT'S DRONE LAUNCH SITE and finding nothing of interest, Jake and Sammie moved through the woods of Cabretta Island and onto the open causeway just as sunlight broke over the ocean behind them. Jake showed the youngster how to tactically move down an open corridor using an overwatch and leapfrog technique so as to not be seen.

With one man always using his rifle scope to scan ahead and giving a hand signal that the route was clear, the other moved up 30 yards at a time passing his teammate. That man then provided overwatch while the other man bypassed him, repeatedly leapfrogging each other across the causeway until they entered the safety of the dark woods on Sapelo Island.

Crossing the dead-end road, avoiding the driveway into Versailles, and entering the treeline, Sammie guided Jake to a safe spot a good distance away from the home.

The house wasn't really big compared to his own place on Skidaway, Jake thought, but for the residents of Hog Hammock who lived in one-story vernacular cottages or trailer homes most of their lives, it would be considered a mansion.

Versailles was simply a raised, two-story, low-country style home with a second level main living area and open front porch overlooking the salt marsh and Cabretta Island. Floor-to-ceiling windows ringed the front half of the house, allowing people to see clear through the open interior layout. It was dark for the most part with several interior lights casting a low glow. There were no exterior lights on, but through binoculars they saw motion detector security lighting illuminate when two feral cats crossed its path.

The house looked to be three bedrooms with the living space no larger than 1,500 square feet, although the lower level between the support columns provided walled-in storage space. There was also a windowless, closed one-car garage presumably where Buzzut kept his UTV. Ample mowed yardage surrounded the house, while sculpted bushes and palm trees dotted the landscaping.

Jake and Sammie's first priority was to pinpoint each of the surveillance cameras and the angles they covered. A blind spot was needed to access the property undetected. If they were caught on video breaking in and entering, just relying on disabling or stealing the video recordings out of Buzzut's surveillance mainframe wasn't enough to mask their presence. Jake feared that Buzzut's videos were automatically uploaded to a cloud archive on the internet. If the pair were ever investigated, that cloud would provide irrefutable evidence of their culpability.

They noticed the first camera under the front roof eave, covering the front stairway up to a deck. Another camera was spotted on the near side of the house covering the driveway and yard. At the rear was a set of stairs leading up to a rear door entrance. A third camera was found above the stairs, but it was angled out to cover the entire backyard and treeline. They could clearly see it wasn't aimed down at the staircase. This was the blindspot they could exploit to get in.

Sammie took point and they slowly crept through the dark woods to check the far side of the house. They found no cameras because a row of palm trees obscured any view. Sammie pointed out that Buzzut's master bedroom was also on this side. Through the leafy palms, they could see that his window blinds were up, and half the window left open.

If they needed to enter the home, Jake realized this side offered the only way into the property. They would have to break cover from the woods, run the short distance across the side yard, hide under the palms, inch along the side of the house, get under the rear porch, and make their way up the rear entrance stairs. They could only hope the back door would be unlocked. If not, they'd have to jimmy the lock or force their way in. Jake didn't like any of this. It made him extremely nervous, especially if Buzzut had superior firepower inside.

From their low angle, though, they couldn't see clear into Buzzut's bedroom to know if he was even home sleeping. That was soon solved when Sammie scampered up a live oak and perched himself hidden in the Spanish moss about ten feet up. Jake joined him and took a camouflaged spot to start their recon. Not 100 feet from the rear corner with the driveway still in their sights, they started observation through their scopes, penetrating into Buzzut's room.

There, in his bed he slept, his chest slowly rising up and down. Covers off, he wore only boxer briefs, an obvious morning erection protruding from the top of his underwear. Through their powerful scopes they could even see drool running down his cheek from an open mouth.

For the next half hour as the sun came up, they took turns looking through their scopes while the other rested his eyes. Nothing stirred inside the house, no one else was there. Buzzut never moved an inch.

An approaching vehicle perked both men up. Headlights could be seen through the far treeline coming their way along the road in. It turned into Buzzut's driveway, parked near the rear of the house, and cut its lights. Sammie and Jake swung their rifles to see who was driving. The vehicle – a large black SUV – Sammie recognized as Buzzut's Lincoln Navigator. A small female with long black hair got out then went to the rear hatch.

"That's his maid, Keisha Tyler," whispered Sammie. "Comes twice a month. I guess I got my days wrong. Sorry. She blew it for us."

Jake remained silent, watching the thin, somewhat attractive black woman as she gathered a large bag of supplies from the truck and flung it over her shoulder. She then proceeded up the rear stairs and onto the raised back deck where she rang the doorbell. Buzzut didn't move, the pair noticed. She rang again. The man remained still. A loud knock on the glass door and still Buzzut remained sprawled out in the bed like a corpse.

Keisha tried the door knob and it was locked. Frustrated, she reached up and ran her fingers across the top of the door frame and found a hidden key. Unlocking the door, she replaced the key and went in, shutting the door behind her.

"Bingo!" whispered Jake. "You see that, Sammie? That's our way in."

"Yup, so stupid to leave a key there. Everyone does that."

They heard through the open window as she loudly announced her arrival and shouted LeShaun's name a few times. Watching through their scopes, no reaction came from him in bed.

She entered his room and saw him lying there. A 'wow' expression formed on her lips when she saw his long hard penis halfway out of his boxers. Dropping her bag of supplies on a chair, she crossed her arms in thought while staring at his cock. A wicked grin spread across her face and she kicked off her shoes, then dropped her jeans around her ankles. Off with her shirt and bra next, and lastly her panties. She stood up buck naked, her gorgeous body slowly crawling onto the bed.

"You're uncle is about to get one helluva wake up call," said Jake.

"Daa-umn," whispered Sammie. "He-he-he's one lucky dude."

Keisha slowly pulled LeShaun's boxers down his legs and slipped them off with a toss to the floor. She grasped his member and started licking and sucking while anticipating his surprise when he awoke. Still, there was no reaction from the man.

With a confused look, Keisha spoke his name loudly. Again, no reaction. She shrugged her shoulders, then proceeded to squat over him. Grasping his erection, she guided it into her vagina. Within seconds, she threw her head back in sexual ecstasy and rode him up and down. Her black hair swung every which way, her mouth wide open, eyes rolling in the back of her head.

LeShaun's mouth closed, he swallowed, his eyes fluttered, and his head turned back and forth. He was coming awake.

✦

Inside Versailles

It started with an erotic dream of LeShaun having sex on the beach with a panting Keisha riding on top of him, their naked bodies bathed in sunlight with ocean waves crashing about them. Keisha's brown eyes flashed with delight and a beautiful smile filled his lover's face. She threw her head back and flung her long hair all about. But when his face met hers again, there was nothing there but a translucent black veil. Keisha's face was gone.

LeShaun's throat dried up, he swallowed hard. He squeezed his eyes shut and shook his head to try and make the veil disappear. He became angry and selfish – the veil ruining the intense pleasure he felt in his loins.

When he opened his eyes, the black veil was still there. He blinked, confused, but knew he was now fully awake from the dream. The veil then slowly lifted away. What he saw next terrified him to the bone.

Keisha's fine black skin had morphed into a bright red, wrinkly leather. Her white teeth turned yellow and rotten, eyes black as coal, hair in dreadlocks. Keisha was the Boo Hag, Yahoodi. His worst nightmare was riding the life out of him.

LeShaun screamed in horror and raised his arms to fight back. He clutched both hands around Yahoodi's neck and squeezed hard. She frantically tore at his arms and face with her long nails, deeply scratching him until he bled and let go. Screaming obscenities, she retaliated and went for his eyes, trying to gauge them out. He swung a fist and connected with her cheek, sending her tumbling off the bed and onto the hardwood floor.

LeShaun sprang up as she crawled under his bed to hide. Enraged, he picked up the entire bed and flipped the box spring and mattress over at once. From the inside of the box spring, thick rolls of rubber-banded cash dumped all over the floor. A picture fell off the wall. An end table and lamp overturned.

Yahoodi wailed in fear at the wrath of the large man. She grabbed the broken lamp and threw it at him, screaming for him to leave her alone. LeShaun ducked. The lamp shattered a wall mirror, sending shards of glass all over the floor like ice from a spilled drink.

Pouncing on her body and pinning the tiny witch down with his legs,

LeShaun started pummeling her face. He beat her with fists and elbows until she screamed no more. But that wasn't enough. He then took her head in his hands and repeatedly bashed the back of her skull against the floor. Still in wild frenzy, he stood up and stomped her head with his bare feet.

Yahoodi's face was a crushed, bloody mess.

LeShaun backed off, out of breath. Blood poured from the scratches on his face and arms. "You're dead, Boo Hag!" he yelled, bent over at the waist, hands on knees trying to gain his breath.

Feeling victorious in defeating the evil witch, he couldn't stop staring at the dead woman between breaths. Suddenly, he cocked his head as her face seemed to transform before his eyes. Only now he recognized Keisha's distinct features, especially her wide open, glazed-over brown eyes. The red leathery skin of the witch had morphed into her black skin again, her hair also now black and silky as it was before.

Realizing he had a drug-induced hallucination and mistakenly murdered his maid thinking she was the Boo Hag, LeShaun started sobbing, his body shaking all over.

But the witch was real – she wanted to take my life. She attacked me. I only acted in self-defense.

He rose to his full stature, wrapped his arms over his head, and bawled loudly while spinning in circles of outright despair.

Sammie did this. He put the hex on me. Duff taught him. Those burnt bastards have come back from the dead to haunt me.

Confused, crying, and pacing around the bedroom, slicing the balls of his feet on shards of glass, he stumbled into the bathroom. There was only one thing now that would ease his mental anguish: Liquid O. He needed it to shut his mind off – like a light switch – or he felt he'd go absolutely insane with grief.

The small eyedropper vial of the potent drug was stashed in his medicine cabinet along with other drugs for his personal use. Filling the eyedropper to its capacity, he bent his head back and released several drops of the heroin into his nostrils to inhale – way more than he needed. Usually, one drop did the trick. The drug worked instantly as he snorted it into his system. He swayed on his feet and dropped to the floor in a heap, vial still in one hand, eyedropper in the other, head flung back against the bathroom cabinet.

As his vision blurred and he drifted out of consciousness, the last thing LeShaun Greenhall saw was an Indian staring down at him, pistol pointed in his face. Strangely enough, this bold act and the stranger's face seemed all too familiar, like he was having déjà vu.

"Bye, bye, Buzzut," whispered the man.

The guy from the shop in Savannah! LeShaun closed his eyes and promptly passed out, his body slumping on its side.

❂

Outside Versailles

Jake and Sammie watched through their rifle scopes as the naked pair engaged in sex, then unexpectedly turned on each other and fought like wild screaming fiends. At first they didn't know what to do, the fight happened so fast.

Jake said he'd snipe LeShaun after he punched Keisha, but when the bed flipped over, it covered the window they were looking into. Now they were the ones in a blindspot, their long-range firepower all but useless. There was nothing he could do to save the woman from their perch in the tree. He had to go inside to confront her attacker.

"Take this," said Jake, handing Sammie his semi-automatic designated marksman rifle. "Stay here and cover me. If you have a clean shot on Buzzut, take it, but do not go into that house unless I say so. It's going to get ugly. Wait here until I give you the all-clear. Do you understand?"

"Yaas'suh."

Jake jumped down from the tree and unholstered his 1911 pistol, a much better weapon in close quarters over a bolt-action sniper rifle. Sticking to the side yard blindspot, he sprinted across the lawn and hugged the wall of the house underneath the palm trees. Around the corner, he double-stepped up the back stairs. The rear door was still unlocked and he quietly stepped across the threshold.

Inside he heard LeShaun wailing out loud from the master bedroom. Jake stealthily moved in the direction of his voice down the back hall, pistol at the ready. A sneak peek around the corner and he saw the box frame of the bed leaning up against the window. Rolls of cash and loose currency were strewn across the hardwood floor. Glass was everywhere. Keisha's naked battered body lay in a pool of blood, her face bashed-in, eyes wide open, clearly dead.

He could hear LeShaun rustling around in the bathroom mumbling to himself and sobbing some more. Slowly, Jake made his way into the room glancing down to make sure he didn't crunch any glass under his boots.

Through a reflection in the bathroom mirror, he saw a naked and bloody LeShaun snorting a liquid from a small eyedropper. The man then crumbled to the floor. Jake entered and pointed his pistol in LeShaun's face, ready to pop a .45 ACP round through his head.

"Bye, bye, Buzzut," he whispered.

But Buzzut passed out before his eyes.

Jake kicked him in the gut to wake him up. No response. Zombie mode again. Something to do with the medicine he just took. Jake bent down and looked at the vial in the unconscious man's hand. The label read: 'Liquid O.' He now knew what Buzzut had inhaled. This shit was black tar heroin in liquid form. He had read about its lethality to drug users. One or two drops was all it took for a high. Any more could kill you.

Looks like he neutralized himself, Jake hoped, backing out of the bathroom and making his way to the bedroom window. He looked over the box spring and mattress and waved his hand out the window, then gave a thumbs-up. Peering down inside the box spring, he saw a ripped corner and dozens upon dozens of stacks and rolled-up wads of cash stashed inside.

Sammie, a rifle in each hand, soon met Jake at the rear door. Jake told him to leave the guns outside. "Don't touch a thing," he said, turning his back. "Inside my backpack, lowest pouch with the red cross on it. There's some latex gloves inside. Put them on right now and get me a pair."

Sammie did as he was told and both men were now secure from leaving fingerprints. He then ordered Sammie to go into a different pouch of his

CERT pack and pulled out a knit cap and a balaclava he used in cold weather. They put them over their heads.

"We can't leave any trace evidence, not a single hair from our heads," explained Jake. "And wipe the sweat from your forehead, too."

Jake motioned Sammy inside, stopping outside the bedroom. "We don't have much time," he said. "I don't want you in there. It's a bad scene. Keisha's dead. Your uncle fucking murdered her."

"What about *him*, though?" asked a nervous Sammie, glancing over Jake's shoulder and into the bedroom. He saw Keisha's naked bloody body on the floor. "Where's he at?"

"In the bathroom passed out from drugs. He's still alive, but mark my words, Sammie, I'll finish him off. Trust me. I just need to evaluate the crime scene to make it look like an accident."

"Okay. I understand."

"Listen, what I want you to do now is find his surveillance system and see if you can replay the time when we approached the house in case he has any hidden cameras we don't know about. Okay?"

Sammie nodded.

"I also want you to keep watch on the road. Shout if you see anyone coming. If so, we bolt out the rear door and back to our hiding spot. Okay?"

"Got it."

"Good. You wouldn't happen to know where Buzzut keeps his backpacks or luggage or a duffle bag, would you?"

"No," said a perplexed Sammie. "Why?"

"Because there's is a shitload of cash all over his bedroom. Looks like he was storing his drug money in his box spring and it dumped out when he flipped it over. I think we just found the capital for your new business venture, don't you agree?" Jake winked.

"Yaas'suh! Here, take my backpack for starters."

"Okay, now get to work. And keep your eyes peeled."

Jake checked on LeShaun, reviewed the evidence, and retrieved the vial of Liquid O from the man's hand. It was still half full.

This shit is like death in a bottle, Jake thought. *Time for insurance.*

Opening LeShaun's mouth, he poured the rest down his throat, and placed the vial back in his hand. Buzzut was already a zombie from the drug anyway. Jake was merely ensuring he'd never come back to life again.

Perusing the open medicine cabinet, he found a stash of various other drugs in ziplock baggies with the labels of Flakka, Fire, and Devil's Breath. He knew the latter was some serious shit, almost like a truth serum.

"Hmmm," he pondered, *this will come in handy if I ever need to interrogate someone.* In his pocket the baggy of Devil's Breath went. He also found two more vials of Liquid O. He opened one, then poured it down Buzzut's chute, the empty bottle being tossed onto the bathroom floor.

Added insurance won't hurt, he thought.

In several minutes, he'd check back to see if Buzzut's heart stopped beating. Police would think suicide by massive overdose after they saw the two depleted vials. It'd be confirmed once the medical examiner ran a toxicology report. Given the naked state of the two bodies, Jake hoped investigators would plainly see a domestic murder-suicide over sex, money, and drugs.

After taking care of Buzzut, Jake found a duffle bag in the closet and started filling it with the drug money still inside the box spring. While Sammie confirmed from the living room that he was able to replay the video at the time of their approach and that they weren't in it, Jake had already pulled half of the cash from the stash and zipped up the duffel bag. He staged it at the rear door, then filled up his and Sammie's backpacks next. Deliberately leaving behind a dozen rolls of cash inside the box spring and some scattered on the floor, he wanted it known to investigators that's where the money had spilled out from, and a possible motive for murder.

A final check on Buzzut confirmed he was indeed dead. He had foamed at the mouth with vomit, his breathing stopped, he shit and pissed himself, and there was, of course, no pulse. Jake snapped a few iPhone pictures of the dead man and a few more in the bedroom of dead Keisha for personal security purposes if the crime scene got manipulated when the grisly discovery was made. Plus, they'd be proof to show Duff that he had fulfilled his promise.

"Sammie!" hissed Jake. The young man appeared at the bedroom door. Jake handed him his cash-full backpack "The jig is up. Your uncle is stone cold dead. I gave him a taste of his own medicine. Now let's get the fuck outta here."

"Guess what I found?" said Sammie, holding up some old papers.

Jake shook his head.

"I found our family will and the original deed to our land from 1871!"

Jake slapped the teen on his back. "Excellent! Now let's go."

At the back door, Jake slung the bulging cash duffle bag over his already-full backpack and grabbed his rifle. They regrouped back to their blindspot in the woods, popped another NoDoz, avoided the security cameras once again, then exfiltrated off the property.

Again leapfrogging their positions across the causeway, they made it back to the Zodiac undetected, albeit completely exhausted and soaked with sweat. Stowing their loot and gear, they pushed the boat out into the rising tide, scanned ahead for any early morning beachgoers or boaters, found the coast clear, and motored into the ocean for the short ride back to the safe haven of Greenhall Landing. There, they never set foot on ground. Instead, they transferred everything to *Lizzie* and took her out of Blackbeard Creek back into the ocean for the return journey back to Skidaway Island.

Alternating who took the helm and who caught some sleep, they made it back to Jake's house by the early afternoon. Immediately they went up to Cherokee Rose Manor, saw Duff, and started weaving a cover story so no one would be implicated in LeShaun's death.

23

Friday
Cherokee Rose Manor
Savannah, Georgia

RAE READ THE *DARIEN NEWS* ONLINE ARTICLE out loud from her iPad so Jake, Sammie, and Duff could hear what had been released to the public about the discovery of the bodies on Sapelo Island two days ago.

New details have been made public in the alleged murder-suicide of a Sapelo Island man and his housekeeper. The McIntosh County Coroner's Office has revealed that 46-year-old LeShaun Greenhall died of cardiac arrest most likely due to a drug overdose after he killed his housekeeper, 33-year-old Keisha Tyler, by beating her to death.

The two were found dead in Greenhall's Hog Hammock home late Wednesday afternoon by Stephanie Johnson, an employee of Lula's Kitchen, *who stopped by the residence to pick up some restaurant items from a previous delivery. Johnson told investigators, "Saw his door was wide open and I noticed a bunch of those darned feral cats walking in and out of the house. I called for LeShaun, but he didn't answer, so I went in. And that's when I found them in the bedroom."*

A toxicology report should confirm that a lethal dose of heroin was in Greenhall's system at the time of his death. Investigators say that open vials of Liquid O were discovered on his person in the bathroom where he was found dead. *Liquid O is the street name for black tar heroin in water-based form. Greenhall also had scratches on his arms, chest, and face suggesting that Tyler fought back before he killed her.*

Greenhall appears to have had a long history of criminal behavior according to his record in Florida, which shows convictions for drug possession, drug dealing, armed robbery, and assault, resulting in years of prison time. Tyler was charged in 2016 for prostitution and heroin possession in Atlanta. She became his housekeeper a year ago. It appears, though, that given both bodies were naked at the time of their discovery in Greenhall's bedroom, a sexual assault was not being ruled out.

Tyler died of blunt-force trauma to the head, according to the coroner's office. Her body was found next to an overturned bed that held $275,000 in newly minted bills. Investigators believe Greenhall was engaged in maritime drug smuggling operations given the variety and amount of drugs found in his home. They included: Liquid O, Fentanyl, Flakka, crack cocaine, powdered cocaine, and marijuana. Officials estimate the street value at over $3 million.

Also recovered at the residence was a firefighting drone stolen a year ago on the island. Greenhall was a suspect in that theft before the case went cold.

The gruesome discovery of the bodies sent shock waves throughout the peaceful, close-knit community of 35 residents. No one could even remember the last time such a violent crime had occurred on the island. Crime is virtually non-existent, so much so that no police force is needed. People simply don't lock their doors – with the exception of LeShaun Greenhall, locals say.

In a news conference on Thursday, McIntosh County Sheriff Jimmy Jenkins said that Greenhall fatally beat his housekeeper sometime before 11 a.m. He said there had been no history of violence at the address and that Greenhall had moved there five years ago upon becoming the legal guardian of his nephew and grandfather, well-known WWII veteran Duff Greenhall, following a tragic accident that took the lives of four family members.

Beulah Brown, a long-time resident, told Darien News that Greenhall kept to himself and was not well-liked in the small community since moving back to the island. Brown said Greenhall was the scourge of the island during his youth, having committed many juvenile offenses before running away and moving to Florida to carry on his criminal career. She said, "it was just a matter of time before he did something really bad. Everyone knew the Devil was in that boy." Although Brown said she was shocked about the tragic incident, she was, "not surprised it involved LeShaun. Not one bit." Brown walked off from our reporter with these final words: "Good riddance. Sapelo Island is a better place without him. I just feel sorry for the poor girl."

"Sapelo island *is* a better place now," Duff Greenhall stressed, sitting up in his third floor king-sized bed at Cherokee Rose Manor. The owner, registered nurse Becky Holden, was downstairs in her office leaving Jake, Rae, and Sammie to visit the bedridden man.

Duff had sustained a severely bruised hip and an anterior cruciate ligament tear to the knee from his fall off the ladder, the same knee he took a bullet in during WWII. His leg was now elevated and knee wrapped with a bandage and ice pack. All he could do was rest, according to a visiting private doctor that Becky had arranged when he first arrived.

After spending the last four days within the confines of the two-story, brick Italianate style manor overlooking Monterey Square, he was becoming rather quite comfortable in the environs. The four-post bed, the high ceilings, beautiful decor, paintings, tall windows providing views down onto the square, and the hustle and bustle of city life – he found rather entertaining, compared to how he lived his secluded life on Sapelo Island. Not to mention the attention Becky and her staff were showering him with, especially the scrumptious delivered meals from the famous *Mrs. Wilkes Dining Room*, not two blocks away.

After Sammie and Jake returned to Savannah Wednesday afternoon and showed Duff pictures of LeShaun's death, they had to produce a consistent cover story when the bodies were discovered and investigators would eventually notify the old man of his grandson's death and might ask of their whereabouts.

Duff got word back to Beulah Brown in Hog Hammock that same Wednesday afternoon that he'd fallen down on the dock early Tuesday night when his feet got tangled up in Cleo, their feral cat, as they were headed out for a boating trip up to Savannah.

Their story was, that he and Sammie were going up to the city for a business meeting with Jake Tununda, owner of *Tununda's Military Menagerie*. They had planned on selling him some WWII German rings for the man's collection. He said that Sammie took him on *Doctor Blackbeard* directly to Tunundas house on Skidaway Island, but that his injury had gotten worse and he needed medical attention. He was then transported by vehicle and checked into Cherokee Rose Manor because the Tunundas knew the owner. He said he didn't want all of the hullabaloo if reporters found out he'd been hospitalized.

The story indeed provided a solid alibi when a McIntosh County investigator arrived Thursday morning at Cherokee Rose Manor to inform Duff of the death of his grandson LeShaun and the housekeeper.

Everyone was in on the partially-true story, including Becky, when she confirmed with the investigator that Duff was, in fact, her patient and had checked in Tuesday night after he was driven there. He didn't go to a hospital, she explained to back up the story, because he demanded privacy from all the media attention that would surely follow if his name got out.

The investigator then drove out to Skidaway and found Sammie at the Tunundas. Under questioning, he confirmed he was the lone person who boated Duff all the way up to Savannah that early Tuesday evening. Sammie even showed the investigator three *Totenkopf* rings that they had planned on selling.

The Tunundas played along with the ruse, too, Rae even offering up that she was the one who drove them to the manor and how Sammie had since been a guest at their home so he could be closer to his great grandfather in Savannah. They even showed the investigator the antique speedboat *Doctor Blackbeard* sitting in their boathouse.

The investigator completely bought into their story and told them they would be ruling the case a murder-suicide.

But the best news of all came when the McIntosh County probate court contacted Duff to inform him that the real estate transaction that was supposed to have happened had of course been canceled and rendered null and void. And that the buyer even wished to extend his sympathies, too, for the tragic loss of another Greenhall family member.

Duff played on those sympathies and demanded that the court make

Sammie his new guardian and conservator in order to get all Greenhall assets in his great-grandson's name. That it was Sammie who had been taking care of him all these years while LeShaun was running drugs and mentally and physically abusing them both. He threatened a lawsuit of negligence against the court for LeShaun's abuse if they didn't comply with his wishes. The court scheduled Sammie's first appearance later in the week in Darien to expedite the new guardianship arrangement.

Jake's conscience was clear and he was ecstatic that everything had worked out the way it did – especially getting Sammie on track to be the new guardian and rightful heir to the Greenhall land. Although luck played a huge part in LeShaun's demise, in his mind's eye he merely assisted the piece of shit with a speedier suicide, thus fulfilling his promise to Duff and Sammie in neutralizing their immediate threat. He, of course, didn't tell his wife Rae that, nor would Sammie ever let on. That was a secret they shared. Jake only admitted to Rae that he had witnessed LeShaun taking the self-inflicted overdose after he'd murdered the woman.

Rae didn't question Jake. She knew she was already an accomplice in the ordeal when her husband appeared up at Shellman Bluff early Wednesday morning with an injured Duff Greenhall, a container of Nazi skull rings, and a stolen painting.

And then when he showed up with a duffle bag and backpack of cold hard cash Wednesday afternoon back at Skidaway Island, she knew he'd done something highly questionable. After hearing how LeShaun had beat the poor woman to death, she actually took deep satisfaction in helping them count all the cash. It came to some $3.25 million. Given LeShaun's criminal career and her law enforcement background, she felt absolutely no remorse that a literal piece of human garbage had offed himself.

While spending the last two days with the Tunundas, Jake and Rae acted as surrogate parents to Sammie. It was quite clear the battered teen needed some special attention after all he had gone through. He absorbed their love like a sponge, having no parental figures in the last several years.

Jake helped him open a new bank account in Savannah and even educated him on how to limit his deposits to $9,000 in cash so as not to arouse any IRS red flags at the $10,000 mark, which would trigger an investigation.

He also helped the teen secure a large safe deposit box at the bank for any secret holdings. Although LeShaun's drug money still sat in Jake's massive home safe for the time being, once the dust settled Sammie could start secretly transferring it to his new bank box.

Duff cleared his throat. He had an announcement to make. "And now the prize for all your efforts, brotha Jake," he said. "I've got a treasure map for you of Blackbeard Island." He handed Jake a folded piece of paper. "I done snatched it from the bedroom of my old house before we went down into the garrison. Damn lucky I did or else it would have gone up in flames."

"What's the prize?" Rae asked facetiously, glancing up from her iPad. "Pirate's treasure?"

"Well, you might say that, young lady," replied Duff with a bit of a smirk. "The prize is a World War II German U-boat pirated by a secret American skeleton crew. It got wrecked on the island during the 1945 Homestead Hurricane and *yours truly* was the one who found it! Been a secret ever since. And now your husband here is gonna claim discovery of it and everything he finds inside. Ain't that right, Jake?"

"What?! Oh my God," said Rae, dropping her iPad. "Is this for real?" she asked her husband.

A shit-eating grin and a humble nod gave her the answer. She stood up and sat next to her husband to view the treasure map.

"Told you I was up to no-good," Jake smiled. "Sorry, I couldn't tell you earlier. Everything happened so fast."

"I need a drink," chuckled Rae to Duff. "Got any of that moonshine?"

"Oh, y'all be gettin' plenty," Sammie chimed in with a grin as he too sat close to Jake and stared at the map.

"I am coming with you this time, hon," Rae whispered to Jake, looking down at the crude pencil drawing.

Jake saw that the map showed the outline of the north end of Blackbeard Island and its trail system. The same symbols found on the *Elixir of Life* label and the doors in the basement garrison were also drawn on the map along a wavy line leading to a Nazi symbol. Each symbol also had some letters and numbers next to them.

"Jake, you're not keeping me in the dark on this one. I want to be there."

Jake squeezed Rae's hand in agreement, but he warned her of the risks in a rather clever phrase. "Remember, if you eat fire, expect to crap sparks."

"I know," she said. "I'm ready."

"Now Sammie," said Duff. "I'm gonna need you to be the scout and take them back deep in them woods there on the north end of Blackbeard. See that Nazi symbol on the map? That's where the U-boat is. First, use your Zodiac to come ashore at The Boneyard. Okay?"

"I'm listening, Pappy."

"Get there after the sun goes down. Make sure there's no boaters or hikers or rangers about. Everyone should be off the island by then. Then y'all just need to get off the beach and take the East Trail for about a mile south. That's the easy part. What you want to do is look for the big alligator skull chained to a live oak tree. It'll be on your left – the ocean side. It's pretty high up in the tree and no one's ever taken it down."

"Got it," said Sammie. "I was hiking there last year with a high school friend and it was still there. Never knew who put there in the first place. Funny, it was you all along, Pappy."

"Yup, I used a chain from the sub to do it. Once you see it, that's where you go into the forest and start your trailblazing. Head due east toward the ocean. You're gonna have to machete your way up and down them deep troughs and high ridges there. But you should find those wayfinding clues I drew on the map and y'all be fine. I even added grid coordinates to each location if y'all have one of those handheld GPS thingamabobbers."

Duff continued to address Sammie. "When I was making my forays over on Blackbeard during my mourning period, Sammie, I wasn't lost like everyone thought. I was back there in them woods with a compass and a map writing down grid coordinates like I was back in WWII. Them dadgum rangers looking for me almost got wind of where the U-boat was."

"Ahh," said Sammie. "So that's what you were doing."

"Them coordinates will take you right to each symbol. You'll see two Keyhole Urchins, two starfish, and lastly, a large nautical star. They'll all be carved into the oaks about head high."

Jake nodded, too, listening closely to his directions.

"When you get to the star you'll see a big ol' mound of brush in the middle of a deep trough filled with muddy marsh water. That's the conning tower. The wreck is sitting deep in the pluff mud in that pond there. Me and Bill laid a log across it to the conning tower. That's the only way in. But I'm telling y'all, be careful because I dunno if it's rotted through or not."

Jake, and Rae were completely silent. It sounded like something from an Indiana Jones movie. Right up their alley.

"Be sure to bring some dadgum bug nets to wear around your head or you'll be eaten alive. Wear gloves and long shirts or the Spanish bayonet will slice ya. Make sure you're wearing gaiters around your legs or them snakes will kill ya. And speaking of gators, there's some big motherfuckers in that pond around the wreck there. You better be locked and loaded when y'all cross the log."

"Still want to go?" Jake asked Rae.

"Heck yeah, I do," smiled Rae, punching him in the arm.

"It was them gators that killed two of the American crew members who survived the wreck, ya know," Duff suddenly revealed.

"What?" asked Sammie, as he, Jake, and Rae all stared at Duff.

Duff's eyes gazed down, his voice became softer. "Yep, that's the part I never done told nobody about. Two poor souls. They was wearing their life jackets and saw me in my row boat. I was out early that morning after the hurricane hit and flooded the islands. It was September 17, 1945 when this happened. Will never forget that day.

"Figured I'd do my Coast Guard patrol and have a look at all the damage it caused and see if I could find out what those flares were I saw from the night before. Figured there had to be a shipwreck. I rowed all the way over to Blackbeard, up to the northeast point."

Sammie moved over to Duff's bed and sat next to him.

Jake already had his iPhone in hand and started recording the conversation. He wanted this piece of history on record.

"Well, I done seen these two men in my binoculars from a distance and they was waving and shouting. They were American sailors dressed in blue shirts and dungarees, and when I rowed up they jumped from some metal platform and into the water and started swimming towards me. They were so desperate to be rescued, so scared. I done screamed at them to get the hell outta the dadgum water because I'd seen gator heads pop up. But they didn't listen. Was too late and they got swarmed like piranhas. I started shooting them gators with my .22, but there was too many of them. The most horrible deaths I'd ever witnessed, two men getting torn to shreds, howling in torture, and pulled underwater to be eaten alive. All they wanted was to be rescued."

Rae placed a hand over her mouth.

"I couldn't do nothing for 'em," said Duff. "So I rowed up to the platform. Didn't know what the hell kind of Navy ship it was at first since it was all shot up and bent and twisted and rusted and all the paint just about peeled off. But I got up on top of it and looked down an open hatch all the way down in and knew it was a sub that got wrecked and washed up into the middle of the island. Ain't never seen a sub before other than pictures. But all's that was visible on the surface was that conning tower. The rest of it got sucked down some twenty feet in that pluff mud quicksand in one of them deep troughs. There was even a live oak tree toppled over on top of it.

"I done figured there'd have to be more submariners inside so I started to go down the ladder wondering if I'd find a bunch of dead bodies. Smoke was coming out of it and I wasn't so sure what the hell I was getting myself into. Was shaking like a leaf going down into that black hole of death. To me it felt like I was entering a coffin. Sure enough, I found another dead crewman in the control room. The place was a mess, damaged beyond all reckoning. Steam spraying out of pipes, wires sparking, water dripping everywhere, shit all busted up."

"Jesus," Jake whispered.

"I figured it was gonna catch on fire, and I'd best get on out of there and report it, but then I heard two men talking."

Duff paused and swallowed.

"And?" urged Sammie, placing a hand on his Pappy's leg.

Duff reached over and took a sip from a glass of water, then started telling his remarkable story again. "They were speaking German."

"What the hell?" said Jake, looking at Rae, then back to Duff again.

"Arguing. Screaming. Very angry. I snuck up on them in the dark.

They were up in the torpedo room at the bow of the boat and I could see a flashlight. Went through the bulkhead hatch and had to watch where I was stepping cause there was so much debris everywhere. But I snuck up on them like a bobcat and just listened. Sounded like one man was interrogating the other, who was trapped on the floor. Kept hearing one word over and over again that I recognized, though." Duff swallowed again.

"What was that?" asked Rae.

"Freemason," the old man replied, looking at her, then to Jake. "And then the man hit the trapped man with a wrench and busted his skull in. Hit him three times. Each time he hit him he said, *Memento Mori.*"

"Remember, we all die," Jake translated with a whisper.

"I knocked that motherfucker out with the butt of my rifle," said Duff, excitedly. "Broke his nose. Tried to stop him, but was too late – again. And then I noticed all them dadgum skull head rings scattered all over the place.

"Y'all, that's where I first found them," Duff emphasized, looking at Sammie. "They were stashed in them cylinders inside the torpedo tubes and they'd done spilled out. The dead man on the floor was covered in a pile of mud from the trough that pushed into the torpedo tube door at the bow when the boat got wrecked."

"And the man you knocked out?" asked Sammie.

"Turned out to be the sole survivor," Duff solemnly replied, tears in his eyes, voice shaking. "Wasn't an American at all. Turned out to be the *original* German captain of that U-boat, but he was a POW. Turned out to be a fellow Freemason. Turned out to be one of my closest friends in life."

"Was he the white man in your lodge photograph?" asked Jake.

Duff nodded and sniffled. He lay his head back on his pillow and closed his eyes. Sammie held his hand. "Everyone knew him on the island as Bill Bosch. But that was just his alias. I'm the only one who knew his real name. *Kapitänleutnant* Werner Witte to be exact. Commander of U-2370, a type twenty-three – the smallest U-boat class in the German Navy."

Duff sat up. "Werner told me he surrendered his sub to the U.S. Navy in May '45 and then was taken to Portsmouth Prison in Maine. Was beat up pretty bad in that prison. But some months later, he was forced to captain his own sub again with a rogue American crew of Navy submariners recruited from that same prison. This was the start of *Operation Overcast* that I was telling you about."

"And the man he murdered on the sub? Who was he?" said Jake.

"*That* was Bill Bosch."

"Huh?" asked Sammie, with a puzzled look.

Jake and Rae looked at each other, too, also quite confused.

"I don't get it." Rae said.

"Bill Bosch was the alias given to the Nazi son-of-a-bitch the Americans were smuggling back into the States," said Duff. "His real name was Franz Heidel, an SS major and executioner at the Dachau concentration camp. He murdered thousands of Freemasons, including Werner Witte's father. When Werner found out who he was and that he survived the wreck, too, he said he acted in pure rage and revenge and beat Heidel to death right then and there on that sub. Wasn't going to let him get out alive."

"Holy crap," said Rae.

"I had Werner hog tied up. He was injured and in distress and thought I was going to kill him for what he'd done. Thought I was the dadgum black Devil. Confessed everything after he came to. He spoke excellent English. Spilled his guts, just him and me in that sub."

Duff suddenly paused.

"And?" Jake asked impatiently.

"He said I'd find two more bodies in the stern and that the captain and first officer had been killed up on the bridge during a night air attack by one of our own bomber patrol planes some 20 to 30 miles off the coast of Sapelo. That American plane strafed the boat and dropped depth bombs on top of them, damaging the sub so bad it couldn't even submerge.

"Said the remaining survivors all worked together and patched the boat up. But then to make matters worse, they got caught in the Homestead Hurricane. The sea took the bodies of the captain and first officer during the storm. They barely made it to Sapelo Sound is what he told me. Saw the lighthouse beam. That's when he popped off them flares. The sub was completely disabled and adrift in the waves at that point, he said. Was like a bottle floating in a stormy sea, he said. He gave up and found a hiding spot and prayed to God he'd make it out alive."

Duff coughed several times, then cleared his throat. He drank some water from a nearby glass on his end table. While Sammie and Rae waited patiently for his story to continue, Jake started typing a phone text message to Alex Vann's wife, Marissa, who he knew was still up in D.C. doing research at the National Archives building.

It read: *Marissa, if you're still at the National Archives, please do me a favor. Check WWII coastal patrol records for a bomber attack on German U-boat around September 17, 1945 off coast of Georgia.* He hit the send button.

Duff smacked his lips and wiped them with the back of his hand. "I saw a Masonic tattoo on Werner's arm and I examined him as only a Freemason could and determined his story was true to his word. I assured him that I was obligated to save his life now and to provide protection and shelter."

"For a worthy man, it's what we do," said Jake. "Even for our enemy."

Duff nodded. "I told him how I owed my own life to that German Freemason soldier that let me live in Italy so I was bound by duty to save his life in return. He even showed me that metal briefcase I showed you, Jake. He gave me the code to unlock it, and that's where I first read the *Operation Overcast* mission orders from the OSS and how that Nazi fuck Heidel had this new identity of Bill Bosch given to him by our own government."

Jake nodded vigorously, having read just a few pages himself from that top secret OSS file down in Duff's dungeon. He knew he had to get back there to retrieve that briefcase. It was like a pot of golden history for him.

Duff clasped his hands tightly. "But we decided on that day, down in that sub, that what Werner did would remain in that sub. A justifiable killing on moral grounds. Vengeance for Freemasons the world over."

Jake nodded again. It's probably what he would have done given the same circumstances.

Duff rubbed his eyes. "We left Heidel's body and all them sailors in there to rot away once I found out who those Navy men really were and the heinous crimes they committed to land in prison. Rape, murder, torture. There's four corpses in that sub. That's what I was warning you about. It ain't a pretty sight. It literally is an iron coffin with a true skeleton crew inside. Worst of all, their angry spirits are still trapped down there, too. They haven't been released, so be very careful. They like to mess with you."

"Damn," mumbled Sammie. "It's haunted."

"Oh my God," said Rae.

"I convinced Werner to steal the identity of Bill Bosch since we had all of his official papers. Told him he had to stay on Sapelo Island in my house or else he'd be assassinated on the spot if we reported the sub and the OSS found out he was still alive. It's why we had to keep that wreck a secret."

"Ahh," said Sammie, finally grasping the various name changes. "So, this SS officer Heidel, who was supposed to be Bill Bosch, was killed by Werner Witte, who then took Bill Bosch as his own alias name?"

"Exactly," said Duff.

"What a move," said Rae.

Duff coughed, pausing his story again to catch his breath. Everyone listened intently, wanting to know what was coming next.

"I nursed him back to health and gave him a place to stay on our land. Taught him how to speak like a Southerner – even some Gullah-Geechee. He just blended in with the other white laborers on the island. Was very skilled and a hard worker. Got a job on a lumber crew and stayed on the island for many years after the war working hard labor for Dick Reynolds. I didn't even tell my own family who he really was. Only that I trusted him with my life. No one knew his real story, other than he was a laid-off furniture salesman from Atlanta fallen on hard times and seeking work on the coast. With me vouching for him as a fellow brotha Mason, no one asked questions."

"He survived in plain sight under your protection," stated Jake.

"Was family to me. Like an older brother," said Duff with a wide smile showing off the gap in his teeth. "Learned the ways of our people. We even did lots of gator hunting at night together in the freshwater ponds and creeks. Man oh man, them were the days. Being out at night under a flambeaux, shooting, and hauling them gators into our boat. Those gator hides provided damn good money. Plus, the meat was good eatin', too. We'd split it with the other families."

Duff grew silent in thought. He then abruptly started speaking again. "Yeah, I trusted him so much I eventually showed him our moonshining operation. He provided security, especially when the bootleggers loaded up at the docks. He done loved my burp gun. One time he let loose with it in the water and they respected him mightily fine after that."

"That's funny," said Jake. "Would have loved to have seen that."

"Later on he taught me about advertising, that I needed a visual presence in the marketplace for our 'shine to prove it was safe after the big poisoning back in '51 up in the Atlanta slums. A big, fat ass white bootlegger named Fats Hardy spiked his moonshine batch with methanol meant for racing cars. He poisoned some 350 poor blacks. Killed forty of them. They dropped like flies. Hardy got a life sentence for that. And you know why they didn't give him the death penalty for killing those forty souls?"

Jake and Rae shook their heads.

"Because the State of Georgia didn't have an electric chair big enough for his 360-pound fat ass!" Duff stated.

Astonished by the tale, Jake and Rae stared at him.

"Nobody ever labeled their moonshine jars before them deaths. So that's when Bill and I designed the famous *Elixir of Life* logo together. He was very creative and talented with a pen. We started putting printed labels on our jars and we certainly stood out from all the rest. Demand went through the roof once again. People loved that label. They liked being part of a mystery."

"Wow," said Rae. "This is one incredible story."

"Wait, wait a second, Duff," said Jake. "I've got to ask you something about that label. You said before when we were down in your garrison that the Hoodoo protection vèvè on the forehead was also Masonic in nature given its location – the whole Hiram Abiff legend – but that it even had a more personal hidden meaning to you and a close friend of yours. Did you mean Werner Witte?"

Duff agreed with a nod.

"Does it, um, is it placed there on the forehead because that's where Witte struck and killed Heidel? Kind of like a mark of vengeance?"

"You're exactly right, Jake." Duff pointed an index finger at him. "We branded that Nazi motherfucker with the mark of the Masons to honor the tens of thousands of Freemasons who were murdered during the war. But for me personally, it was a way to remember that German soldier who saved my life in Italy. And for Witte, he said he wanted a special way to remember his act inside that sub to honor his father's death, while also acknowledging me for what I did for him in return. And just the fact it was placed on a skull of death, well, for us, it also meant resurrection. The start of a new life." Duff extended both hands, palms up, a gesture Jake took as receiving a most important secret revelation.

Jake was flabbergasted. The skull label itself had so many hidden disguises, but as a Mason, the forehead vèvè and the many meanings behind it clearly was the most powerful symbol of all. *What an ingenious cryptic mark they came up with,* he thought.

Duff continued his tale. "Bill and I made several secret trips back to the U-boat and pillaged some of them treasures. We had to be careful with the batteries, though, leaking chlorine gas. That's when I got me those two skull ring containers. Should be one more in there still intact. The other one spilled out all over the place. But Bill wanted nothing to do with any of the loot. Considered it all cursed. Hated the Nazi party to his core as did most in the *Kriegsmarine*, but he did love his German heritage. We kept all that loot down in the dungeon, which you saw, Jake. Sold some of it off over the years to keep us afloat."

Jake nodded vigorously. "So you kept it under wraps and used it as you needed, right? And what about the sub, though? No one's ever found it after all these years? No one ever came close?"

Duff shook his head. "No siree, son. At first we camouflaged the small conning tower so no one could see it. The rest of the sub is buried in the muck deep down in that trough in pitch black water you couldn't even see if you were flying over it. Eventually, the brush and weeds overtook everything and made it damn near impossible to get to, let alone be seen. Looks like a little bitty island out in the middle of the pond now. We made some carvings on the trees to mark the only way in – same symbols used on our moonshine label."

Just then Jake received a text message back from Marissa Vann. *No problem. Still at archives. Thrilled to.*

"But, Pappy, what ever happened to this Bill Bosch, err Captain Werner Witte?" asked Sammie. "Is he even still alive?"

"Well," sighed Duff. "He left Sapelo for good in '56. He had to. Ya see, Dick Reynolds employed a lot of Germans on his staff. Picked them up as cheap labor back in the 1930s when he visited Germany on his luxury yacht. One man, a Karl Weiss, was even his personal chef up until the end. Another man was his personal steward, while other ex-German sailors worked on his various boats. His first mate on his yacht was even a German U-boat captain from World War I who claimed to have fired the torpedo that sunk the *Lusitania*. Well, all these Germans were too close for comfort for Werner. One wrong word slippin' out while he was drunk and he was worried they would find out who he was, so he had to go. I took him over to Shellman Bluff and I never saw him *alive* again after that."

"Where'd he go?" asked Sammie.

"Said he wanted to travel the States. Told me he wanted to find his old U-boat captain's hat taken by a Marine guard when he was a POW at the Alcatraz of the East. The same Marine that murdered another U-boat captain in that prison. Well, he certainly found that Marine alright and his stolen hat. It was in Philly. Sent me a newspaper clipping where I read the Marine was beaten to a bloody pulp. Lost all of his teeth and was paralyzed from the waist down. The Marine told police a German U-boat captain named Werner Witte, a POW in 1945 from the Portsmouth Prison, attacked him, but they checked with the military who stated that Witte couldn't have been the suspect since their records indicated he fell overboard from a Navy ship and was lost at sea during transport to Bermuda in September 1945.

"Jesus," gasped Jake. "They officially killed him off after the U-boat went into operation for the OSS. He became a ghost."

Rae exhaled loudly. She was stunned by this entire story.

"And so he went on with life," continued Duff. "I got many letters from him. In the 1960s, he resettled in a big German-American community up in Minnesota. A place called New Ulm. He officially changed his last name back to Witte thinking it was safe since enough years had passed. Explained he loved his German heritage too much to be living under an alias, especially one meant for an SS officer. William Werner Witte was his new name, but people still called him Bill. Go figure."

The listeners chuckled a bit.

"Got a job at the local brewery and rose up the ranks to become plant manager. Married. Had three sons, many grandkids. Owned a nice yacht. Said he became master of the Masonic lodge there and so did his sons over the years. Was so happy for him. Done shipped him many jars of moonshine. But then the letters stopped abruptly some twenty years ago."

Duff sighed deeply and sniffled a bit. The room went silent. He wiped his nose with a tissue and continued.

"And-and-and . . . then his son contacted me. His eldest. Guess what his name was? Werner Greenhall Witte, middle name in honor of me. Said his father passed away in his sleep." Duff's voice cracked. "And in his last will and testament stated he wanted to be buried in the Greenhall family cemetery on Sapelo Island, Georgia. Because that's where he had spent some of the best years of his life, his son told me."

Jake inhaled sharply, a tear fell from his eye. And then he remembered the cross pattée with triangular arms in the Greenhall cemetery. He thought it odd at the time thinking it was the Southern Cross grave marker for Confederate soldiers in the Civil War and certainly wouldn't be in a cemetery of black slave ancestors. He never made the connection until now that the same style cross was used for German soldiers and sailors in WWII.

"And that's where he's laid to rest," said Duff, regaining his composure. "His whole family came down from Minnesota. They stayed at the Reynolds Mansion and we had a beautiful ceremony under the bottle tree. I hung a special blue bottle in the tree for his soul since I considered him family. And then his eldest son gave me his U-boat captain's hat. Said it was also in his father's will that it should go to me as a gift. The family said all they knew about it was that his father got it as a collector's item after the war and that he was a U-boat fanatic. Loved the history and read many books on the subject. Well, after the family left, I removed his grave slab and opened up his coffin and placed that hat on his head. And that's how he's buried."

"What a beautiful touch, sir," Rae said. "You gave him his true history back so his soul could rest in peace. I'm so sorry for your loss. I can tell you were very close."

"Thank you, young lady," said Duff. "I don't want to dwell on it. Werner lived a full life. I gave him a second chance and he made the most of it."

Duff paused again and sniffled some more. "Okay now. Nuff of that. Let me ask you then, when are y'all fixin' to get on over to Blackbeard to find my dadgum sub?"

Rae touched Jake's arm. "I've got a major meeting with a client tomorrow. Doing the reveal on an investigation, but then I'm free on Monday."

Jake turned to Sammie. "Treasure hunting on Monday, Sammie? We can take tomorrow to plan things out and get any supplies we need. Plus, I want to research this particular type of U-boat online so we know what we're getting into."

"Count me in, Mr. Jake!"

"Excellent," said Jake. "Monday it is then, Duff. I figure Sammie can return *Doctor Blackbeard* then, too, and we'll be his wingman with my boat back down to your place. Sound good?"

"Absolutely," replied Duff. "Wish I could come with y'all, but I'm living like a king up here. And hell, can't hardly even walk."

"Yeah, you're staying put, old man!" Jake winked. "I do think we need one more person to join us before we go in, though." Jake swiveled to Rae to get her attention. "Someone trusted and experienced to round out our team. We're gonna need additional muscle, another pilot who can handle *Lizzie* or Sammie's Zodiac. I want to take all precautions just in case."

Rae nodded her agreement knowing who Jake was going to suggest as he refocused his gaze on Sammie.

"We've gotta make this a stealthy mission that no one sees or hears about, especially any DNC Rangers or nosy boaters. You remember my buddy, Alex Vann? When we first met you on Sapelo?"

Sammie nodded. "Yaas'suh."

"I'd like to ask him to come onboard, if that meets your approval," Jake said, showing deference to Sammie. "It'll be just the four us."

"I'm good with Mr. Alex. I trust him."

Jake pulled out his cell phone. "Great. He and his wife Marissa are still up in D.C., but let's see if he's game for a good adventure."

24

AT HOME ON SKIDAWAY ISLAND, JAKE AND RAE sat across their dining room table from Erhardt Hoffman, the lost painting from the ammo can spread out in front of them. Hoffman's white cotton gloved hands were clasped together patiently.

"Please begin, Mr. Hoffman," said Rae.

"My pleasure, Mr. and Mrs. Tununda. The title of this painting is called *The Painter on the Road to Tarascon*," said Hoffman, reading slowly from a notepad with his deep Charleston dialect. "It's an oil on canvas painted in 1888 by none other than Vincent van Gogh."

"Holy–," Rae cussed.

"You're shitting?" said Jake.

Hoffman looked up smiling, sharing their excitement. "In fact, it is believed to be a self-portrait of the artist since there is a hint of red hair under his hat and he holds all of the tools of his trade." Hoffman pointed to these items in the painting with the eraser end of a pencil. "This is a *rare* self-portrait of his full body on the move. You see, most of his self-portraits were of him seated from the waist up."

Jake and Rae nodded with glazed eyes, not really grasping the importance of whether van Gogh was seated or standing.

Hoffman caught this and cleared his throat. "Let me cut to the chase.

Y'all have discovered one of the most important paintings missing since the Second World War. In fact, the Monuments Men Foundation has it on its 'Most Wanted Works of Art' list."

Jake's lips parted. Words failed him, he was in so much shock.

"Sadly however, it is listed as the property of the Bode Museum in Berlin, formerly the Kaiser-Friedrich Museum."

Jake pressed his lips tightly. Someone else rightfully owned it.

"Let me give the background of how it was lost and its last provenance," Hoffman continued. "There's two theories. The first: during the Allied bombing of Berlin in 1945, hundreds of pieces of artwork from some of the most valuable collections in all of Europe were moved from the museum and placed in Luftwaffe anti-aircraft towers for safekeeping. Those were called *Flaktürme* stations.

"It is believed that this van Gogh was sent, along with 417 others, to the Friedrichshain flak station in Berlin. When Allied bombing became so bad, some of the flak stations were emptied of their contents and transported via convoy to the Staßfurt salt mines art repository west of Berlin near Magdeburg. This was in early April 1945. Was this van Gogh in that convoy and did it make it to the salt mine, is the key question? Or, did it remain in the Friedrichshain flak station?

"The second theory is that on May 6, 1945, when the Russian Army entered Berlin, that same Friedrichshain flak tower suffered a devastating fire that demolished three floors of valuable paintings, sculptures, and relics. They were incinerated. And then, as the German guards deserted the station, the rest of the tower was looted by local Germans, as well as Russian soldiers. Thus, countless pieces of surviving artwork fell into the hands of unknown players. A lot of it was taken back to Russia as spoils of war. Some of which was repatriated many years later."

Hoffman looked up from his notes. "Essentially, the painting here made it through both scenarios and survived, of course, but we don't know where, when, and how this painting ended up wherever it is you found it."

"Really is a mystery," said Jake.

"Okay, so now onto the backside . . ."

"Yeah, this drawing was quite weird," said Jake. "But I think it has something to do with the SS because of that small *Totenkopf* symbol."

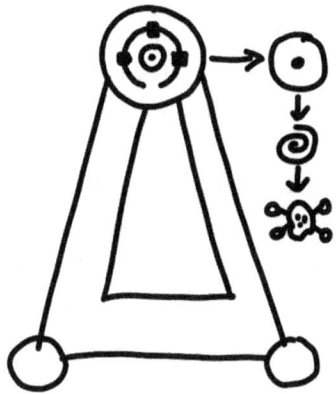

"I'm in agreement, Jake." Hoffman said, pointing to the geometric drawing on the back of the canvas. It wasn't but 3" high. "Would you believe, that this a floor plan of a very famous castle?"

"Get outta here," said Rae.

"In fact, I've visited it three times now in Germany," said Hoffman with a smile. "Instantly recognized it as Castle Wewelsburg, the SS headquarters during the war. It's the only castle of this triangular configuration with a tower on each of the three points. The larger North-Tower is obviously the focus of the three symbols to the right. Within that tower – underground – is the *Gruft* or crypt."

"Ahhh," said Jake.

"If you'd allow me to give a little background on this castle, it will all tie in with what I think those three symbols mean."

"Sure," said Rae.

"Absolutely," added jake.

"*Reichsführer-SS* Heinrich Himmler signed a 100-year lease on the castle in 1933 when he made it his headquarters and training facility. But it was in bad shape and needed reconstruction. It was an incredible amount of work. So what did the bastard do? He set up his own private concentration camp, called Niederhagen. It was made up of criminals,

POWs, and Roma people. He used them as slave laborers. Some 4,000 people. Half died over the course of the war.

"Now, that North-Tower in particular. Well, the SS renovated the sub-level room into a stone crypt for their cult. Originally it was the main cistern of the castle, but they turned it into some kind of shrine to commemorate the dead." Hoffman pulled out some printouts of the room found online.

"So look here," he said. "The original floor was lowered some 15 feet, and the foundation of the tower was reinforced with concrete. Twelve pedestals line the perimeter against the wall, each with a niche above it. Some believe this room was reserved for the remains of the famous SS generals, that their ashes would be placed in urns within the niches. Who knows? The room was unfinished." Hoffman shrugged his shoulders.

"But during construction they laid a gas pipe under the floor leading to the center of the room within this raised circle. See how there is only one entrance into the inner circle and how there are these three blocks or seating areas around it? The drawing matches the photo."

"Oh, yeah. I see that," said Rae.

"Now within that circle – the dot – is where that gas pipe ends. Historians think an eternal flame was planned for that hole there. The ceiling of the room is dome-shaped, all in stone, too. At its zenith is a decorative swastika. You have to remember, the swastika was an ancient symbol that appeared in different cultures. For Germans, it was an emblem of their race and meant 'the symbol of the creating, acting life.' Again, all very cult-like in this castle."

Jake shook his head, but kept on listening to Hoffman's background research, waiting patiently for his interpretation of the symbols on the back of the painting.

Hoffman pulled out some notes and read from them. "Here's where it gets interesting. On March 30, 1945 the U.S. 3rd Armored Division started mopping up the area. The *Burghauptmann* (commander), SS General Siegfried Taubert, abandoned the castle. Through seized records after the war, we have evidence that Himmler got word of this abandonment. So he ordered SS Major Heinz Macher, Himmler's personal bodyguard, SS

Major Franz Heidel, and some 15 specialists to destroy the castle with dynamite. They did this the next day."

"Heidel was there?" asked Jake.

"Oh yeah. Macher was in charge of demolitions. But Heidel was in charge of – get this – hiding all of the SS *Totenkopf* rings so they wouldn't be seized by the Americans!"

"Holy crap, that's the connection!" said Jake. "The legend of the lost SS rings. We read about this when we did our GoToMeeting on Sammie's ring, remember? They were supposed to be buried in some blast-sealed chamber, right?"

"Right," nodded Hoffman. "Estimates range between 9,000 to 18,000 rings were hidden away. Some say they're worth over $95 million. The treasure has never been found to this day. At least that we know of."

Rae shot Jake a glance. They locked eyes for a moment.

"But Macher ran out of explosives," Hoffman continued to read, not catching their look. "Instead, he put tank mines in the southeast tower, a guard-building, and the barracks, completely destroying those sections of the castle. They then set the castle on fire and told the local fire brigade to let it burn."

"Damn," said Jake.

"But the North-Tower remained relatively untouched, especially that sub-level crypt room," continued Hoffman. "And what I think is, that circle with the dot where the flame was supposed to go, is actually a hidden spiral staircase underneath, leading down into a chamber where the *Totenkopf* rings treasure is hidden. I think they filled that staircase with rocks and cement and sealed it shut."

"And we've got the clues to lead us right to it!" Rae exclaimed. "I think a trip to Germany is in order."

"Whoa, whoa, whoa, wait one second, Rae," Jake jabbed, holding up his hands with a shit-eating grin. "What for? Why do you need to go off *exploring*? It's way too risky and dangerous."

"Oh, you son-of-a . . . Alright, you got me. Touché, my love."

"Three days later," read Hoffman from his notes, finishing his story, "the 83rd Armored Reconnaissance Battalion seized the castle grounds and the Niederhagen concentration camp after locals reported that, quote, 'SS men had set fire to their barracks in the castle, changed into civilian clothes and fled.' Turns out Major Macher linked up with Himmler and they fled in disguise, Himmler as a police officer, Macher as an army private. They were trying to escape from the northern coast of Germany but were caught by some former Russian POWs at a checkpoint. Not knowing who he was, Himmler was handed over to the British, who interrogated him. He then admitted his true identity. But after a doctor tried to examine him, he chomped down on a hidden cyanide pill and killed himself. Macher was arrested and spent time in POW camps, then was released some years later. He survived the war and died in 2001 at age 82. Meanwhile, Major Franz Heidel fled south to Austria and was never heard from again."

"Man, that is a helluva story," said Jake.

"So, listen," said Hoffman. "What I'd really like to know is, where did you discover this painting?"

Jake coughed. "I cannot tell you at this point, brother. I'm very sorry. I hope you understand. However, I will be obtaining some documents – if you will – that will probably tell us the true story of how it ended up where it did. And once I assess all of that information, I *will* share everything with you. You have my word."

Hoffman shook his head dejectedly. "What are you going to do with this now?" A gloved finger tapped the painting. "Can I at least ask that?"

"How much is it worth?" asked Rae.

"It is inestimable," said Hoffman, flipping the painting back over so Van Gogh could be seen again. "But, similar lost paintings on the 'Most Wanted Works of Art' have values ranging from $80 million to $135 million."

Jake almost gagged. "It's immediately going back into my safe for starters," he replied. "After that, I honestly don't know what to do with it, Erhardt. What would you do? I mean, wasn't this protected as a treasure of Hitler's Nazi Germany? Why give it back no questions asked as if rewarding their atrocities? Is this still not a spoil of war for our side?"

"But it's not Nazi Germany anymore," Hoffman sharply countered.

"It's a matter of morals, right? Returning something that was never owned by you in the first place." Hoffman then sighed abruptly and looked down, lost in a moment of thought after realizing he was an outright hypocrite.

"Morals. Yes, indeed," said Jake, a little heatedly. "I understand. But this painting would have never seen the light of day if I and others hadn't taken some huge risks. I'm talking life and death risks that I cannot divulge yet, Erhardt. Surely us getting compensated for these efforts would also be the right thing to do, huh?"

Hoffman rubbed his bearded chin, not giving an answer. His eyes shifted from Jake to Rae and back again.

"Look," said Rae, trying to avoid any escalation between the two men. "What if we hired you on commission to broker a deal with the Bode Museum? We *do* want to return this painting, but we also want a share of its wealth – a finder's fee. Not just for us, but for a couple other people responsible for its discovery."

Hoffman sighed deeply again. He took his reading glasses off and rubbed the bridge of his nose.

Jake took his lack of a response the wrong way. "Come on, Erhardt. That's not asking a lot. It's done all the time. Both parties can negotiate a deal. You've done this many times. You have the business reputation and respect. And I'd wager to say this would be the biggest commission of your lifetime. Am I right?"

Hoffman's raised eyebrows answered for him.

Jake leaned forward and lowered his voice in seriousness. "Listen, brother-to-brother, when I found this painting the first person I thought of was you. You put your life on the line for Marco D'Arata, you took down Mona Lisa, and I know you still want to nail Phoenix's balls to the wall. I trust you. That's why you're here today. And I hope we've earned your trust, too. You're part of our team, man."

Hoffman nodded, but his eyes said something else.

"Furthermore," Jake relented, "Rae and I know nothing of the international art market and all the legalities surrounding it like you do. We need to learn how to broker these international deals on behalf of our respective businesses because I can assure you, there are more relics to come. I've seen them with my own eyes. This painting is just the tip of the iceberg. And you're gonna be very, very interested in being a part of this, believe me. Now, come on. Whaddya say?"

"You're right," Hoffman said, realizing the truthfulness of Jake's candor. Jake was a trusted fellow Masonic brother of exceptional character and bravery, and even somewhat of a rogue like himself. He and Rae were allies who shared the same desire to nail Phoenix as he did. "Forgive me. I agree with you. I would love to act as your art representative and mentor in this regard, brother. I do accept. But . . ." Hoffman looked down again.

"What's wrong?" asked an impatient Rae, holding out the palms of her hands.

"Okay, listen," interrupted Jake. "You may have broken the code to the *Totenkopf* ring treasure at the castle. I want you in on it when we go to Germany to seek it out. You speak German, you've been to the castle before. We're gonna need to negotiate and convince authorities that there's something under there. You in?"

"Of course I'm in. Absolutely, Jake. But—"

"But what?" snapped Rae, rolling her eyes.

"Morals," stated Hoffman. "I've got a moral dilemma myself and I don't know what to do. Perhaps y'all can help *me* out if I take on your commission and the exploration of the castle?"

Rae cocked her head. "Help you out in regards to this painting?"

"Well, no. It's, it's, well, it's what I wanted to talk to you about a couple of days ago when I sent you that text, Jake. You remember Mona Lisa's missing iPhone that the FBI is trying to find? Umm . . . I, I, I stole it in that hotel room right before I shot her."

Hoffman reached into the breast pocket of his suit coat and pulled the smartphone out.

Rae gasped.

"Oh shit." Now it was Jake's turn to squeeze the bridge of his nose. After a moment, he looked up. "Is that thing still on?"

"Yeah, why?"

"Give it to me." Jake snatched the phone from Hoffman's hand, touched the home button, and the screen lit up asking for a passcode.

"Goddamnit, Erhardt!" said an irate Rae, reprimanding Hoffman. "As long as this thing is on the FBI can issue a search warrant on this number and ping its whereabouts to find out its exact GPS location. And where's that? Right here on Skidaway Island!" She banged her fist on the table.

Jake pressed and held a side button and powered down the phone, taking it offline.

"I didn't know! I thought all I had to do was turn off the Find My iPhone app and I'd be safe. Oh God, I'm so sorry for getting you into the this. It's all my fault."

"We're totally screwed if they pinged this thing already," said Rae. She stood up and began pacing, then turned to Hoffman. "You better hope to hell she had this phone in another name they can't trace. What were you thinking?"

Hoffman stammered. He couldn't get any words out.

"Rae, what about the SIM card?" asked Jake. "Should we take that out? I think we need to."

"No need," she said. "On an iPhone the SIM only stores the customer's phone number and billing information related to the phone carrier. All other data, like music, videos, photos – that's in the iPhone's main storage. But we need to take the battery out of it, just to be on the safe side."

"Alright," said Jake. "I've done that before using a YouTube video. Takes some time and a lot of tools." He started doing a search for the how-to video using his own phone.

With a deep audible sigh, Hoffman reached into his coat again. This time he produced a USB flash drive. He laid it on the table. "I did an AirDrop and copied some photos from her phone onto this drive. There is a passport and a driver's license for a Frank Alan Mason from Saint Lucia – down in the Caribbean. Frank Alan Mason is an alias for Nathan Kull, aka the Phoenix."

"What? Why didn't you give this to the FBI?" asked Rae.

Hoffman shot out of his chair. "I ended up killing a person because of their incompetence in the case!" he said in a raised voice. "If the damned FBI had listened to D'Arata in the first place, people would still be alive today. I blew a woman's head off, and he almost died right in front of my eyes. You think that's easy to deal with, Rae?"

"Listen," said Rae, purposefully lowering her voice to calm the man down. "I personally know how emotionally traumatizing it is to take someone's life, but we have to go to the FBI with this information."

"And what about the cop in Fitzgerald, huh?" asked Hoffman, eyes afire. He snapped his fingers. "Dead! Just like that. You think that cop's family will get any justice? They had to start a damned GoFundMe campaign just to cover his funeral expenses. Nobody gives a shit about some rural Georgia cop."

"It's the FBI's case now," Rae pressed. "They're still the best investigative agency in the world."

"What's the dead cop's name?" asked Hoffman. "Do you even know? Jake, do you even remember his name?"

Rae looked down. Jake shook his head.

"See? He's already forgotten. His name was Everett Jenkins. No one ever remembers the victim, but they sure as hell know some celebrity master thief with a catchy nickname like Phoenix, don't they?"

Rae sighed. "You have to put your trust back in the FBI."

"Who did they assign to the case?" asked Hoffman, rolling his eyes. "Some political hack. He got demoted from management and sent down to a field office to save his fucking pension. Hell, he wanted to arrest you both just out of spite. Yeah, I am so trusting of the FBI. Pfft!" Hoffman spat in a sarcastic tone.

"They'll get Phoenix, especially since you found this information on him," replied Rae. "But who knows where he is right now? He could be in Saint Lucia or he could be in Somalia for all we know."

"Listen, I'm done fartin' rainbows on the FBI. I do *not* want Phoenix behind bars," Hoffman said sternly. "I do *not* want the FBI to find him. I want *us* to. I demand retribution! Pure and simple. And *that* is my moral dilemma."

"The FBI has the worldwide resources to hunt him down," said Rae. "We don't. Besides, Jake and I are not hitmen."

Jake's eyelids fluttered. He looked away.

"Well, give me the opportunity and I'll be the hitman," said Hoffman.

Jake abruptly pulled the painting from the table and rolled up the canvas. He then placed it inside a protective metal tube and rose up, addressing Hoffman. "I've got to put this back in the safe. Brother, how about you join me for a glass of bourbon and a cigar in my office? And your attentive ear?"

Hoffman nodded.

"Grab Mona's phone," Jake said. "We need to take the battery out of it. I found the video. Rae, if you would excuse us?"

"Most certainly."

25

PLYING THE CALM OCEAN WATERS DURING their morning trip from Skidaway Island, with Jake and Rae on *Lizzie* and Sammie piloting *Doctor Blackbeard*, the two boats arrived back at Sammie's house around noon.

While Sammie motored Duff's Chris Craft Continental into the boathouse, Rae tied off their power catamaran at the end floating section beside the Zodiac and started unloading gear onto the dock.

The last of their group, Alex Vann, wasn't due to arrive on Sapelo until later that afternoon on the four o'clock ferry. He was currently making the five-hour road trip down from Atlanta after flying in from D.C. and grabbing his gear back at his home in Dahlonega. He was expecting to be greeted at Marsh Landing by Sammie and Jake, who'd be providing transportation back up to Greenhall Landing.

Jake had already gotten word back from Alex's wife, Marissa, in D.C. She confirmed an air attack in the early morning hours of September 17, 1945 just as he'd requested and sent him an email that he printed out and skimmed over. And now, still standing at the helm inside the cabin of his docked boat, he unfolded it again to read it once more. Giving her just general information to go on, he was still astounded at the thoroughness of what she had found, and the cover-up involved. The email read:

Hey Jake, had to do some major digging and cross reference searches. Got down and dirty in some back room cabinets in the archives building. But you know me. I love this stuff. Well, I found something that fits your description. Below is my summary of an Office of Strategic Services report I found filed under Operation Overcast/Paperclip by an agent based out of Savannah, GA in late September 1945. It's worth noting this material was only declassified just a few years ago. Crazy, right?

The report involves a U.S. Navy Martin PBM-5S2 Mariner (Bureau Number 68225) "Flying Boat" from Squadron VPB-217 based out of Naval Air Station Banana River (now Patrick Air Force Base) on the east coast of Florida. This particular Mariner model was an improved submarine hunter with upgraded radar.

There was a crew of 12 trying to return to base with engine trouble after a long-distance patrol, but a hurricane (later named the Homestead Hurricane) was coming north up the Florida Atlantic coastline. (I even looked up the storm track and confirmed it). They had to divert their flight further north seeking an auxiliary landing strip.

The report said at 02:11 they obtained a radar contact for a surface vessel. Closing on the vessel, they turned on their high powered spot lights and immediately identified a Type XXIII German U-boat. These electroboats, as they were called, were considered "miracle works" of German high technology.

The PBM-5S2 Mariner's pilot, Lieutenant Commander Adam Davidson, ordered his nose turret gunner to open fire with his two, .50-caliber machine guns. They scored direct hits on the conning tower. Then they dropped two, 500-pound depth bombs set for a depth of 30-feet. One was a dud, the other detonated. They could not make another pass due to severe fuel loss, but they radioed the position of the attack at 31°22'N 80°52'W near the present day Grey's Reef National Marine Sanctuary. No other flights or ships were able to follow-up due to the approaching storm. They made an emergency landing at Harris Neck Outlying Landing Field, a small auxiliary anti-submarine air patrol base on the Georgia coast.

Now what's really interesting, Jake, is I also found the "official" public version that's been out there for years before the declassification. The version found on the squadron's history web page and other public sources out there.

The report was almost completely the same, except instead of a German U-boat being attacked by the Mariner bomber, it said they had mistakenly strafed and bombed a large whale. WTF?

Any way, hope this helps unravel your mystery. Alex told me you're onto something big involving Operation Paperclip, *but wouldn't let on as to what. Wants to surprise me. Good luck to y'all. Stay safe. Best, Marissa*

"Hey, what are you doing in there?" Rae asked in an impatient tone, smacking her hands together. "Chop, chop, sailor. We've got work to do."

Jake folded up the letter and re-pocketed it.

While the Tunundas transferred gear from their boat to the Zodiac for tonight's mission, Sammie had already made his way up to the main house. As he walked the gangway to the bluff, he caught a glimpse of his late uncle's UTV parked in the driveway. Approaching closer and turning the corner at the house, he saw the UTV had a trailer attached to it: Buzzut's drone storage unit.

Sammie instantly knew something was amiss. Before he could shout for Jake, three armed men pounced on him. They covered his mouth, lifted the struggling youngster off his feet, and dragged him away.

Several minutes later, Jake and Rae also made their way up the dock ramp and to the house, chitchatting and joking, both in a good mood. Jake was explaining to her how he and Sammie were going to take her to the Greenhall graveyard and down into the underground garrison and dungeon. That he needed to retrieve the U-boat captain's original briefcase from the dungeon which held the secret mission papers of *Operation Overcast/Paperclip*. Getting closer to the house, they too noticed the UTV with the trailer, and then upon turning the corner saw Sammie sitting on the front porch steps.

He was surrounded by three heavily built men armed with pistols. Two Latinos and a black man. They were dressed in jeans and t-shirts and had tattoos running up their arms, on their necks, and across their faces. The black man, a no-neck, bullheaded freak with a wide chest, pointed his firearm at Sammie's head.

Jake and Rae froze.

"Get over here, now!" barked the black thug, in a thick Spanish accent. The other two men drew on the couple.

Jake and Rae had no choice. If they turned and ran they'd surely be shot in the back at such close range. If they drew their concealed pistols, they'd be shot square in the chest. More importantly, Sammie would most likely be killed either way. Bottom line, they had been taken by surprise and they couldn't abandon him.

And no one being killed already meant these men wanted information as opposed to a straight hit.

Another Latino man, donning a beige suit coat, white dress shirt open at the collar, and a wide brimmed straw hat, then came bounding down off a front porch rocking chair. He smiled and held his arms wide, motioning for the couple to approach.

"Hello, my friends," he said, also with a Spanish accent. He looked middle-aged, wore a salt and pepper goatee, and had a killer's air of cocky confidence about him – clearly the leader of the four-man team. "Don't be shy. We aren't going to hurt anyone. We only came to recover our property is all."

"Then why are you pointing a pistol at Sammie?" barked Jake.

"Because he is part of our property," the leader calmly replied.

Jake looked at Sammie. The boy was in utter fear. His leg nervously twitched up and down. "This is private property. You're trespassing."

"What are you going to do, call the cops?" the bull-headed Afro-Mexican laughed.

The leader snapped his fingers and the man was silenced. "Excuse my manners for not introducing myself. I am, erm, Pancho Villa, regional vice president of a distribution company. And these are my associates, the Three Amigos." He swept his hand to the men surrounding Sammie. They all started laughing. Two of them then flanked Jake and Rae.

"We are here on business, nothing more," continued Pancho. "Unless, of course, you want to make it more."

"What's the nature of your business?" asked Rae, hands on hips.

"Well, beautiful, have we met before? You look awfully familiar. In fact, you both look very familiar. I see rings on your fingers. Married.

Hmmm. So what is your name, señora?"

Rae kept silent.

"Ahh, cat's got your tongue? No name, señora? Well, maybe your tough guy husband here can give me his name, eh?"

"Yeah, if you're Pancho Villa," Jake guffawed. "Then I'm the 'Bandito,' George S. Patton."

Pancho laughed out loud, catching Jake's historical reference to 2nd Lieutenant George Patton's actions during the Mexican Revolution in the early 1900s.

The U.S. military had been in pursuit of the famous revolutionary leader Pancho Villa for a cross border massacre in New Mexico. Patton had cornered the head of Villa's personal bodyguards while conducting America's first motorized assault, leading eight men in three Dodge touring cars. The young lieutenant single-handedly stood his ground as three Mexicans on horses rode directly at him shooting at close range. Patton responded with his Colt .45 'Peacemaker' revolver killing all three. He then strapped the bullet-riddled bodies to the hood of the cars and drove them back to General Pershing's expedition headquarters. Pershing was so impressed, he nicknamed him the 'Bandito.' Patton carved three notches into the ivory handle of his revolver and a legend was born.

"Bandito," said Pancho. "I like that. You know your military history. I think I know who you are now. It's on the tip of my tongue." Closing his eyes, he tilted his head back and stroked his goatee in a deliberate thinker's pose. He held that position for an awkwardly quiet twenty seconds.

"Ah, yes. Now I know," he finally said, snapping his fingers. "The Tunundas. Jake and Rae. From the American Heroes Channel. I used to love your show before they took you off the air. Finding all of that lost treasure – so exciting, living a life of danger and adventure. Reminded me of the *National Treasure* movies. You guys are famous," he said derisively. "Or I should say, *were* famous."

"Get to the point, asshole," said Jake.

"Ah, Sammie's big brawny bodyguard using an insult, no?" Pancho pointed to the UTV and trailer. "We are merely recovering our drone inside that trailer. We tracked it here with GPS. How it got here we do not know. Perhaps it was stolen after our employee Mr. LeShaun Greenhall tragically ended his life while indulging in our product, or so we read on the news. But who knows? All I know is that drone was on loan to him. It was an investment our, um, *company* made in his very successful franchise. It made Mr. Greenhall a very rich man."

Jake and Rae knew precisely what he was talking about. These were Mexican Sinaloa Cartel members coming to retrieve their narco-drone.

And their reputation preceded them.

Rae swallowed hard.

"Suh," said Sammie to the cartel VP. "I took it from my uncle. He was threatening to sell our land and to put my great granddaddy in a nursing home. I only did it to make him stop is all. I'm very sorry. I didn't know it was your property."

"You've got what you came for," said Jake, in a calmer demeanor now. "Now, please let the boy go. He speaks the truth and is sorry for his actions."

Pancho motioned for his henchman to lower the pistol pointed at Sammie. "Apology accepted, young Sammie. We know all about you and the role you played in your uncle's franchise. You, as boat captain on that old speedboat, are highly valued yourself. Especially knowing these waters up and down the coast. Don't worry, though, we've got our drone back now. But, of course, for your own actions you *will* have to be disciplined."

Pancho then swiftly backhanded Sammie across the face, knocking him off the step and onto the grass.

Jake and Rae lunged forward screaming.

They were met with pistols in their faces, stopping them cold in their tracks. "Hands in the air. Turn the fuck around," barked the black thug.

The couple complied. The two other Mexicans lifted the couple's shirts, pulled out their concealed pistols, then casually patted them down for other weapons.

From Jake they extracted a spring-loaded pocket knife. Rae's cell phone was confiscated while Jake had left his on *Lizzie*. Their other weapons were already down in the Zodiac apparently unbeknownst to Pancho and his amigos.

"Now turn back around and get on your knees. Hands on your head."

Again, the couple did as they were ordered. They sat on their knees. Pistols were now aimed directly at their foreheads. They both knew one wrong move and they were dead – their bodies would be chopped up and never seen again.

Pancho reached out to Sammie with an extended hand. "Come on. Come on. Get up. Your punishment is over. Come on. Up. Up."

Sammie pushed his hand away and got to his feet on his own. His cheek was red and already swelling. Fury flamed in his reddened eyes. He was tired of being beaten, but he could do nothing in retaliation against these armed brutes.

"Like I said, that's the extent of your discipline," said Pancho, hands behind his back, pacing in front of him. "However, due to your skills in making your uncle's franchise such a success, we are going to require you to resume your employment with the company. Our new base of operations will now be here at this secluded private property. The dock access is perfect. We'll probably have to install security cameras and take measures to patrol for intruders. After all, we don't want any trespassers, right Mr. Tununda?" He gave Jake a wink.

"My captain here, Señor Guerrero," Pancho said, motioning to the Afro-Mexican. "He will be your new boss. Why? Because he looks like the locals here, no? Will fit in quite nicely. We can't have any of us beaner outsiders on the island now, can we?" Pancho laughed at his own joke.

"Speaking of which," he continued. "You can address your new boss as 'Mr. G.' Other, less fortunates, know him as 'Chopper' because he likes to use garden shears to chop off the fingers of those who do not comply with our demands."

Sammie glanced over to Jake with pleading eyes.

Pancho cleared his throat. "Mr. G will live here with you and any other personnel he sees fits in order to bolster the compound's security and operations. As boat captain, you will be paid a handsome salary. Of course all tax free!" He winked at Sammie. "You'll become rich beyond your wildest dreams, young man."

"But, but–"

"Sshh!" hissed Pancho. "Mr. G will be the new drone operator, as well, and will train you on how to fly so that you, too, can operate this franchise on your own with your own recruits. We're looking at you taking over operations after three months of probationary service. Understood?"

Sammie looked at the Mexican boss with blank eyes.

The VP raised his hand to strike. He yelled in Sammie's face. "Understood?!"

Sammie flinched, then vigorously nodded his head in submission.

"Good. Now what do we do with the Tunundas?" Pancho asked out loud, pacing again, fingers to his chin in thought. Annoyingly snapping his fingers again, he said, "Ah, a boating accident. Yes, that's it!"

Looking at Jake and Rae with feigned remorse, he shook his head, snickering. "Unfortunately, your nice boat at the dock will have engine trouble and will somehow catch fire out in the ocean on a little pleasure cruise you had planned for tonight. With both of you onboard, of course. So sorry for your loss."

Rae dropped her head.

"Wait, wait, wait a minute," interrupted Jake. "Let's talk business."

"Ah, but there is no business to discuss, my friend. You are expendable. Especially since you now know our plans here for Greenhall Landing. And Sammie needs to be taught a lesson of what will happen to him and his great grandpa Duff if he ever so much as utters one word. Sorry, that's how the ball bounces. Wrong place at the wrong time. Gentlemen, let's get them duct-taped. I don't want to hear his voice any more."

"I want to buy Sammie's freedom," Jake blurted, as one of the Mexican men approached him, taking out a roll of duct tape from a pocket.

Pancho held a hand up for his man to stop. "Really? Kind of like buying a slave's freedom, right? Indulge me."

"Listen," Jake started. "Not only will my offer buy his freedom, but it will cover the production of more of your drones, the purchase of more boats for distribution, and a new base of operations. You don't want to do business here in this secluded location any ways. There is no cell phone service, no amenities, the air conditioning is broken, plus the bugs will eat you alive. And the DNR rangers routinely patrol the island. On top of that, the U.S. Fish and Wildlife Service headquarters is not a mile away across the creek on Blackbeard Island. They have armed Federal rangers literally at your doorstep. It's not a good place to do what you'll be doing. You'll get busted sooner rather than later."

Pancho stared at Jake, knowing full well he was right. Jake could see it in his body language. He even noticed Mr. G raise his eyebrows in agreement to his two associates.

Jake took advantage of their hesitation. "You'll be able to purchase a brand new luxury mansion with more acreage, a dock, and coastal access wherever you want along the coast of Georgia. There is so much real estate available for the taking. Most importantly, you'll still be in the shipping lanes just as you'd be right here."

"Okay Mr. Tununda," said Pancho. "You have my ear. I am very intrigued now." He motioned for Jake and Rae to stand up and relax. His men lowered their weapons. "But you're talking tens of millions of dollars to pull this off. What exactly are you offering? Blackbeard's lost treasure?" All four Mexicans laughed out loud.

"You might say that," said Jake, smirking back.

"Well? Spit it out."

"Ever hear of the painter Vincent Van Gogh?"

Pancho's eyes lit up.

"I have in my possession one of his rare lost paintings from 1888. It is called *The Painter on the Road to Tarascon*. I recently discovered it. It has been missing since World War II and it is estimated to be worth over one hundred and thirty five million dollars at auction. Think that will be enough to buy Sammie's freedom?"

Pancho rounded his lips as if ready to whistle. Mr. G beat him to it.

"I give you this painting, you take your drone back, and never set foot on this island again, nor ever bother Sammie again. Rae and I will pretend this meeting never happened. Hell, I don't even know your real name, but I respect your company and am quite aware of the force you can bring down on us at any time. We know our lives are in the palm of your hand right now. But be rest assured, you will gain our lifelong silence. Now, sir. Have we got a deal?"

"Where did you get this painting? Who originally owned it?"

"It was being smuggled back to the States at the end of war by the U.S. Navy. This is war loot stolen from the Nazis. I believe a museum in Germany will lay claim to it if you ever went public, but you're not in the business of going public, are you?"

"No, we are not."

"On the black market you can still sell this for tens of millions. I'd say you could get seventy mil for this. Some hot-shot billionaire will buy a Van Gogh in a fucking heartbeat. The Saudis and Japanese are big collectors in art, too. Seventy, eighty mil is nothing to them. You can set yourself up for the rest of your life. You can use it as collateral on loans for more product. Your options are endless with this priceless artwork. I know how your business works. This painting will be the new *Mona Lisa* once word gets out in your circles. Its value will skyrocket. It can be all yours if you let Sammie go."

"Mr. Tununda," said Pancho, arms across his chest. "You are quite the negotiator. In fact, you'd make an excellent consultant for me. I accept your offer." He extended a hand, palm up. "But under one condition."

He then pointed to Rae, and in a gentlemanly tone marked with pure arrogance, said, "Your lovely wife will be collateral as my guest."

"Lay a fucking finger on her, and I'll . . ."

"I know. I know. Or you're going to kill me. Blah, blah, blah," chided Pancho, brushing off Jake's threat. "Same for you, too, Tununda. You fucking bring anyone else into this deal I will have Chopper here cut off your wife's fingers and toes. After we gang rape her, of course." He then smiled for added effect.

Jake gritted his teeth in anger, but held back a response.

"We are staying down at the Reynolds Mansion. Stayed there before when we set up LeShaun with the franchise. We got lucky because a wedding this week just got canceled, and obviously I'd never stay at this shithole here."

"Do we have a deal?"

"How soon can you get us this painting?"

Jake checked his watch: 2:30 p.m. "The painting is at a bank in downtown Savannah. They close at five. The island ferry doesn't come here until four, so I've gotta take my boat if I'm going to make it up there in time. Listen, I'll bring the painting right to your doorstep at the Reynolds Mansion. Give me six hours total. Then there's a morning ferry you can catch and you can be on your way–"

"Oh no, I'm not spending another minute on this island. We're leaving tonight on my yacht." Pancho then asked Chopper, "What time do the staff leave the mansion at night?"

"They serve us dinner at five. Gone by six-thirty, the manager said. Then the entire place is ours. We'll have complete privacy."

Pancho checked his watch, then told Jake, "You've got *five* hours. Bring the painting straight to the mansion by 7:30 and your wife and the kid go free. Simple as that. I promise." He held out his hand.

Jake gripped it hard. They stared at each other for several seconds, then Pancho broke grip, twirled a finger in the air to his associates, and announced they were leaving.

Jake turned to Sammie, told him not to worry, turned to Rae, said he loved her, and watched as they were dragged to the UTV. He bolted to the dock for his boat, looking over his shoulder one last time as the UTV and trailer disappeared into the woods.

26

JAKE GUIDED *LIZZIE* INTO HIS PRIVATE DOCK, TIED off, and then dashed off to his house. The light of the day was fading, the shadows of palms, oaks, and magnolias getting longer over his lushly landscaped property.

Punching in his security code on the back deck entrance, he noticed the green all clear light blinked several times, then went blank. Something wasn't right, but he didn't give a shit at the malfunction. He was on a life-and-death mission to retrieve that painting and get back to Sapelo. But first he needed some firepower and his SUV to drive up to Savannah before his bank closed. Unlocking the back door, he ran into the house and made a direct line to his office where his large safe sat. Flicking on the lights, he entered.

Someone was sitting in his desk chair.

With a gun pointed at Jake's chest.

Jake froze. This was getting old. He raised his hands and shouted in annoyance, "Well now, who the fuck are you?"

The man was clean cut, wore amber-tinted eye glasses, had a handsome muscular face with a brown goatee, a deep bronze skin tone – obviously a sun worshipper – and was dressed sharply all in black.

He didn't recognize the intruder at first. And then it clicked. He'd seen this guy before. The passport picture from Mona's phone. His heart rate jacked up. It was Frank Alan Mason of Saint Lucia.

Or more appropriately: Nathan Kull, aka Phoenix.

The master thief stood up and moved out from behind the desk. He pointed to Jake's stand-up safe. "Open this safe. Now."

Jake lowered his arms and folded them across his chest in defiance. "You look very familiar. I know you."

Kull's eyes went wide.

Jake read bewilderment on his face. Then anger at being recognized.

"You are Phoenix, perhaps?" Jake goaded.

Kull's pistol wavered. He blinked several times.

"Nah, I'll just call you by your real name. Nathan Kull. Fugitive at large. Cop killer."

"Open the fucking safe or you're dead!" shouted a flustered Kull.

"Only I know the code, Nathan. If I'm dead, then how the hell can I open the safe?" Jake asked sarcastically.

"Shut the fuck up! Just shut up." Kull shook his head in frustration.

"What exactly do you want? I'm in no fucking mood."

"I want the Van Gogh in your safe."

"How the fuck do you know about that?"

"Mona Lisa's phone. A little app I wrote to access the microphone and track the phone's location. Installed it while she slept the night before the Charleston meeting," he bragged.

Jake shook his head, knowing he had been played.

"Never could trust her," said Kull. "Listened in on your botched sting at the hotel. That cunt spilled the beans on me. Glad she went down. I then located the phone on Erhardt Hoffman, of all people. Tracked him down, and have been listening and watching his movements all week long."

Jake sighed, his shoulders sagged.

"The guy's pretty fucked up after killing Mona. Screams a lot in his sleep. But hey, he saved me the trouble of doing Mona." He shrugged his shoulders smugly.

"You didn't hurt him, did you?" asked Jake.

"Nah, not yet at least. Thanks to him, I listened in on your meeting right here in this house. Got the GPS coordinates. And boom!"

"Fuck, man," Jake sighed, hands on hips.

"I heard you were the one that discovered the painting, how much it's worth, and that in your safe it went," Kull bragged, making Jake feel even worse. "Also heard about a secret drawing on back of it leading to some huge treasure of rings hidden in a castle in Germany. But then I lost the signal when you smartly dismantled the phone. Good move, Tununda. But too damned late."

Jake realized that Kull hadn't heard their conversation with Hoffman *after* the phone was shut down. That he saw the Frank Alan Mason passport and driver's license from Saint Lucia. That he knew where to find him. He had to keep that information secret.

"How'd you get past security on the island here?"

"Diversion," Kull spat. "Said I was looking at real estate. Does it really matter? I want payback from you. I want that painting. Your little sting only netted me a briefcase full of counterfeit bills. I'm owed millions for those Nazi trophies. Fucking millions that I *earned!*"

"First of all, you aren't owed shit," said Jake, jabbing an index finger in the air at Kull. "Secondly, Mona wasn't murdered in cold blood. We didn't execute her like the damn Gestapo. Antoine LaMar was our canary. He was working for us. So was Hoffman. We went in to arrest her and she put a bullet clean through LaMar's head, then she shot an Army investigator who almost bled to death. If Hoffman didn't act in self-defense, she would have killed him, too. We wanted to force her to turn on you! You've been our target all along. And now that the U.S. Army got our trophies back, well, guess what? We're officially *off* the fucking case. It's now an FBI case. They've been on a manhunt for *you* after you killed that cop in Fitzgerald."

"Stop talking."

"His name was Everett Jenkins. Married with three kids."

"It was an accident."

"It looked like an accident to me, too. That you just wanted to immobilize him and make your getaway. He surprised you. I get it. But you're still responsible for his death."

"And you're about to die, too, if you don't shut the fuck up and open your safe. I'm losing my patience, man."

"Listen, I believe you, okay?" Jake raised his hands in surrender. "I heard the entire story of how West Point went down, how the gangbangers in Atlanta carjacked you, how you got the trophies back, took out the kid, took out their meth lab – and the dude inside – how you set up their leader to get zapped by the FBI. Three gang deaths right there. Hey man, good riddance in my book. You had to do what you had to do."

Kull blinked several times. "The kid I regret. He knew too much."

"And how you ultimately got away? Hijacked a plane with Hitler's own pistol. Met Mona in Fitzgerald, buried the goods in a cemetery, and then went underground."

Still dominating the conversation, Jake thought he'd try flattery. "Honestly, how you adapted was very impressive. Ruthless, but impressive. You're a fucking legend, dude. A movie's going to made about you one day. Deep down you're not a cold hearted killer, I can tell. People just get in your way. Fuck up your plans. I understand that. So listen, I can pay you three million in cash right now for your loss, but there's no way you're getting my painting. I can't give it you."

"Why not?"

"Because, as we speak, my wife and a kid are being held hostage by the Mexican Sinaloa drug cartel and I'm buying their freedom with that painting. That's why I'm here. If I don't deliver, they get a bullet in the brain, their fucking heads chopped off, their bodies dismembered, and then fed to the fucking alligators. *That's* the reason why. No painting, I have no chance to save them."

"Not my problem."

Jake's face turned deep red. A vein popped in his neck. He didn't have time for more negotiation. "Listen, how the hell are you going to cash in that painting? You can't take it to Christies in London. The damn thing is stolen! A German museum will claim ownership. It'll be tied up in lawsuits. You know the game. In the end, you'll be lucky to get a couple mil any way."

"Shut up!"

"Hear me out, Kull," Jake said in desperation, pointing at the safe. "Three million in cash! Your payback. I need to save two lives. Please help me out. Don't let their blood be on your hands, too. Just take my money and run. Please. I'm begging you, man."

"Fine," sighed Kull, seemingly giving in. "Give me the goddamn cash. I won't take your precious painting. Now open the fucking safe."

Jake wasted no time. He keyed in the code to his safe and cracked it open. Bending at the knees, he snatched the duffle bag of drug money, unzipped it so Kull could see the cash, and placed it on the floor behind him. While Kull stared at the cash, Jake reached for one of his pistols inside the safe: a compact .380 sitting on top of the German ammo can full of skull rings.

Something hard slammed into his right ear. His vision went black for a split second and he saw sparks in his eyes. His head spun and his body gave out.

Collapsed on the floor, his eyes blinked open, vision blurred. He fought to stay alert and awake, but the pain in his head was unbearable.

Kull zipped up the duffle bag and reached into the safe for a leather tube. Opening it, he saw a rolled-up canvas and stole a peek at it. Smiling, he returned it to its case, grabbed the bag of cash, and made his exit.

In and out of consciousness, Jake heard the back door open then shut, and soon after, a motorcycle engine rev up.

Darkness then enveloped his vision and swallowed him whole.

Ten minutes later

Jake awoke in a flutter of pain. He managed to sit up against the safe and drew several deep breaths. Checking the side of his head, he found a big bump but no blood.

He checked his watch. Bank closes in fifteen minutes. *I'll never make it,* he thought, wobbling to his feet and supporting himself on the desk. Grabbing the .380 from the safe, he tucked it under his belt and staggered to the bathroom to down some Advil. Pocketing the entire bottle of pills, he made for his SUV parked in the garage.

Guiding his SUV down the driveway and accelerating through his neighborhood, he placed an immediate call to the bank. After speaking to the manager, he convinced him to keep the bank open, that he was on his way.

A second call went to Erhardt Hoffman. He told him to get the hell out of Charleston and to a safe place, that Phoenix had been tracking and listening to him on Mona Lisa's cell phone. That he knew he'd killed Mona and might be after him for revenge. Jake advised Hoffman to ditch her phone immediately, to not take anything digital with him that could be tracked, including his own cell phone in case Phoenix already had compromised it. He told him he needed to buy a burner phone in cash, and to call him when he was in safe location off the grid.

The next call he made was to Duff Greenhall telling him of Sammie and Rae's situation. By the time he ended that call he was racing across the Diamond Causeway toward Savannah.

A text from Rae chimed on his cell.

He knew the cartel was in possession of her phone.

A click on the text revealed a video. He pressed play.

Screaming from Rae as the camera panned from her face and then backed away. While two cartel thugs held her tightly on a chair, pressing one of her arms across a table, Chopper appeared in the video, ahold of her wrist. The video zoomed in and showed him wielding a set of pruning shears. Rae's pinky finger was inside the cutters, ready to be chopped off. He then heard Pancho's voice: *"You involve anyone else in our transaction or show up one minute late, off goes her pinky. And then her fucking head. Adios, Bandito!"*

✦

Thirty minutes later
Savannah Executive Airport

The time for Phoenix to fly the coop had arrived. Having placed an earlier call that morning to Dean Kennedy, his shady, yet trusted charter pilot for many years, his escape flight back to his adopted country was already prepping for departure at the new Savannah Executive Airport, a mere half hour drive from Skidaway Island.

After parking his stolen motorcycle, Phoenix entered the main lobby with a swagger in his step, like he owned the place. A locked duffel bag containing the cash from Tununda's safe was slung over his shoulder. The leather case holding the Van Gogh was also inside. He had taken both and left Jake with nothing but a bump on his head from being pistol-whipped.

Ruthless, but impressive, was how Tununda described me, he thought. *A fucking legend. I like that.*

An attractive female employee at check-in immediately jumped to his service. Phoenix presented his Saint Lucia passport as Frank Mason. He even charmed her with his fake British accent.

The woman merely glanced at his passport and proceeded to quickly key-in some information into her computer. She didn't even compare his face to the passport photo or ask him to remove his tinted glasses. After all, discretion was a key part of the airport's reputation for their luxury clientele.

After paying his service fees with a credit card linked to his shell-corporation, Mason was escorted out on the tarmac to his waiting jet. There were no security checks, no facial recognition system scan, no baggage check, not even a TSA presence at the little airport. At the plane, he greeted Kennedy and gave him a friendly hug.

It was that easy.

Within minutes, the jet soared from the runway and climbed out over the Atlantic Ocean heading due south. Mason made himself a stiff cocktail and kicked back in his leather seat.

He exhaled with delight, just a four hour flight to freedom.

And some $3 million in cash richer. And with a priceless Van Gogh unfurled in his hands. *Life doesn't get any better than this.*

Tununda didn't know what he was talking about. On the Dark Web there was peer-to-peer networking software to easily set up a Tor-randomized pop-up auction and have anonymous members on the black market bid for the painting. Using bitcoin as the digital currency to complete the transaction, all he had to do was deliver it and he'd make millions in pure profit.

He flipped the canvas over to look at the secret drawing leading to the castle treasure.

The canvas was completely blank.

Kull cocked his head and flipped the painting back over. He looked again at the artwork. Now something didn't seem right. The canvas was too new, too stiff. Where the brush strokes ended on the margin was a clean straight line instead of hand-painted strokes that randomly bled off the edge. Whipping out a cell phone, he clicked on a magnification app, and zoomed in on the artwork.

It was a fucking reproduction. A Giclée print.

Tununda burned me at my own game, he thought, with rising anger.

He then couldn't help but chuckle.

Ruthless.

But impressive.

27

TEARING AROUND THE SOUTHERN TIP OF SAPELO Island at full throttle, and entering Doboy Sound, Jake gained a full view of the Sapelo Island Lighthouse. Patterned with six alternate red-and-white horizontal stripes, the 1820 conical structure, restored in 1998, stood at 80-feet tall and was the nation's second-oldest brick lighthouse. Although the last rays of sunlight glinted atop its lantern room, its revolving navigational light still hadn't illuminated for nighttime operations. A glance down at his island map and he knew he had to make a sharp right turn before reaching the lighthouse. It would take him up Dean Creek, a tributary paralleling the lighthouse causeway.

Almost missing the mouth of the creek, he cranked the wheel hard right and his boat banked sharply, sending a wave of water over the cordgrass lining the narrow channel, while spooking a large white egret. A speedy jaunt up the creek and he throttled all the way down when he caught sight of the road and a pick-up truck. A man emerged from the cab. He was dressed in a black t-shirt with a white skull logo and wore his long black hair in a braided ponytail.

Jake glided *Lizzie* in up against the bank, reversed throttle, and tossed the anchor. After cutting the engine he snatched a metal tube containing the original Van Gogh painting – the one he'd retrieved at his bank in downtown Savannah – and jumped off the boat onto the soft marsh grass. He met his buddy, former Delta Force operative, Alex Vann, up on the road and they bumped fists.

Jake checked his watch. "Ten minutes to make the exchange."

Not for one second did Jake put his trust in the cartel VP to keep his word that no one would be harmed upon delivery of his painting. The cartel didn't operate like that. They were brutal sons-of-bitches who took immense pleasure in kidnapping, torture, death, and dismemberment.

By simply going online anyone could find their sadistic videos executing victims exactly like the Nazi Death Squads did. However, the Mexican cartel soldiers went even further. After death, they would saw off the heads of their victims and sometimes deliver them to their enemies as a warning. Most of the time, they would chop up their victim's limbs with axes or chainsaws and then toss the body parts into drums filled with acid to dissolve into oblivion.

Statistics compiled by the Mexican government linked more than 180,000 murders to the Sinaloa Cartel itself since 2006, and yet the world could give a rat's ass. Jake had lucked out, though. The Sinaloa officer on Sapelo was driven by pure selfish greed. Jake baited the hook and Pancho bit down hard. The Mexican thought he had Jake by the balls in taking his wife hostage, but he fucked up by letting him loose.

As soon as he had left Sapelo on the trip up to Savannah, Jake's very first phone call had been to his close friend Alex Vann. All along, in sporadic cell phone conversations during the trip up to Savannah and back, they had planned their next moves.

Alex never did catch the 4:00 p.m. ferry over to the island as originally planned. Instead, Jake directed him to charter a half-hour, one-way water taxi from the Shellman Bluff fish camp over to the Greenhall Landing. There, he retrieved Jake's DMR and a special spyware gadget from Jake's CERT pack left in Sammie's Zodiac. Alex then borrowed the family's old Ford pick-up truck for the 8-mile drive down to the south end of the island and made a couple of drive-bys past the Reynolds Mansion where he spotted two of the Mexicans deep in shadows of the recessed front porch.

Not the only vehicle to use the public roads around the mansion, he didn't arouse any suspicion, especially being in a rusty beat-up truck, which was quite the common sight. Along with several staffers, he observed a couple of bikers, and even some tourists walking around the mansion grounds taking pictures.

Parking the truck at the Nature Trail lot off Nannygoat Road, he was able to walk around the extensive estate grounds to get a better lay of the land. Staying out of visual range of the mansion itself, he meandered through the heavily shaded woods and bushes while using a small but powerful monoscope to recon the mansion exterior looking for signs of Rae and Sammie. When Jake's ETA drew closer, he returned to his truck and parked on the lighthouse access road for the rendezvous.

Jake asked, "You find the spy comm unit in my CERT pack?"

"I've got it," said Alex, opening the door to the truck. He snagged a small pouch, carefully reached inside, and pulled out two magnetic earpieces no bigger than pencil erasers. He handed one to Jake and they each inserted one deep inside their ear canals making them all but invisible. They then helped each other clip tiny microphones hidden on the inside collars of their shirts.

Alex then extracted a small Bluetooth module and turned it on.

"You good?" He asked Jake, testing the communications gear.

"I'm good. What kind of fire power did you bring?" asked Jake.

"I brought your long range DMR down from the Zodiac, but I'm glad I packed something smaller with me. Best close-quarters weapon around. I brought my MP5K with a suppressor and an extended mag."

"You're always prepared. Yeah, leave the DMR in the truck. Come on. We gotta go." Jake hopped in the truck.

Alex pocketed the module, got behind the wheel and cranked the engine. "What are you carrying?"

"Compact .380," said Jake, patting his crotch. "Let's hope my big balls can keep it in place. Okay, what's the sitrep?"

Alex grinned, stepped on the gas and peeled out on the shell packed road. "I was able to recon the mansion this afternoon. Got a good feel for my approach where they won't see me. I watched all the staff leave for the night. It's dark and quiet there now."

"Did you see Duff's man do his business?"

"The last staffer to leave was an older black man. I'm assuming that was him. Saw him come out from the service alleyway on the far side of the house. Let's hope he did what Duff asked him to."

"Don't worry. He's a Mason," said Jake. "Duff vouched for him."

"10-4. One of these days, I'll have to join your brotherhood."

"And what about the yacht at Marsh Landing? Any more cartel guys?"

"Negative," replied Alex. "Yacht's only a 45-footer. Registered in Miami. They've already got the drone loaded up hidden under a tarp. They're ready to leave."

"Okay, so we've got four targets to take down and two assets to rescue," Jake said thinking out loud, jaw clenched, game face on. He had detaching himself emotionally from who he was rescuing in order to maintain focus on his upcoming mission. He grabbed the bottle of Advil in another pocket, popped the cap, and downed a handful of pills, discarding the bottle on the dash.

"I'll let you out just ahead on the main road," said Alex. "Just follow it straight up to the mansion. Two punks were on the front porch near the empty pool. They're sitting in the shadows under the columns. But I haven't seen Rae or Sammie, Jake. I'm assuming they've been hidden inside somewhere the whole time until the DNR staff left for the night. God only knows where they are. That house is huge."

Alex motored up to Nannygoat Road and hung a left. A little ways down, he made a quick right onto a dirt road bisecting a grassy field. He then hit the brakes.

Jake opened the door and jumped out with the protective tube holding the Van Gogh. He adjusted his compact pistol wedged in his tight underwear against his package, and then walked at a brisk pace toward the mansion. The white mansion was barely visible down the road under the dark canopy of the many trees that dotted the estate grounds.

Alex continued up the dirt road to an abandoned greenhouse hidden near a treeline. He parked, grabbed his MP5K, and entered the woods.

"Jake, you copy?"

"I got you. I see the mansion up ahead."

"Let's use one cough for yes, two for no."

Jake coughed once.

"I've got your back. Moving in."

Jake coughed once again.

Through a Spanish-moss-filtered canopy of live oaks, magnolias, and palms, Reynolds Mansion, the luxury plantation home, appeared in all of its twilight glory. Beyond the four thick Ionic columns guarding the hundred-foot wide front piazza, and through a glass-walled front entrance, Jake could see the main drawing room cast in a warm glow of light.

Several steps down from the piazza was a five-foot-deep reflecting pool in the shape of a four-leaf clover. The turquoise-painted pool stood empty except for a white Carrara marble statue raised on a pedestal in the very middle. It depicted a kneeling woman, wearing nothing but jewels in her hair. Her hands were playfully tossed in the air, back arched exposing perky breasts, and seemingly longing for a lost era of carefree luxury.

That era had started in the early 1920s when millionaire industrialist Howard Coffin, owner of nearby Sea Island and its luxury Cloister Hotel, purchased Sapelo Island. He built his mansion on the 1810 tabby foundations of the original antebellum home of the previous island's owner, Thomas Spalding, who had named it South End House.

Coffin fully rebuilt that mansion which had fallen in disrepair after the Civil War. He added the second floor, full basement, and many of the palatial designs and stylistic themes present. With some 13 bedrooms and 11 bathrooms, it was one of the most luxurious homes on the coast of Georgia at the time, attracting many famous dignitaries, including aviator Charles Lindbergh, and U.S. Presidents Calvin Coolidge and Herbert Hoover.

The next owner of Sapelo was tobacco heir R. J. Reynolds Jr., who took over in 1934. He modernized the house over the next thirty years before moving away to Europe and selling the mansion to the State of Georgia. The DNR had managed the mansion ever since as a corporate retreat, conference center, and events venue for large groups.

Jake stepped off the beach road and walked across the manicured lawn, bypassing the reflecting pool. He saw both of the cartel guards stand up and draw their pistols, one entering the mansion.

Reynolds Mansion
South of Hog Hammock

"Well, what do you know? Here he comes," said Juan, one of the Mexicans sitting at a cast iron antique table outside the front entrance. "I'll be damned. Right on time." He stood up and poked his head inside a glass door inlaid with a pattern of Moravian stars. "Boss, he's here. Came out of nowhere."

"All alone?" asked the cartel captain, sitting on a sofa in the Great Room, admiring a painting hanging over the large fireplace of R. J. Reynolds Jr. dressed in his Navy blues.

"Yes, sir," said Juan. "Alone. And he's carrying some sort of tube."

"Good sign," said Pancho, standing up and pulling a pistol from his coat pocket. He screwed a silencer on the end of the barrel. "Everyone attach your silencers. Let him in when he gets here. Frisk him, too. Hey Jose," he said addressing the other guard, "you go relieve Chopper downstairs. I want him up here with us. You watch the hostages. We'll be down shortly."

"10-4, boss." Jose made for the right front corner of the room and disappeared down an open set of narrow winding cellar stairs in the floor.

Soon Chopper double-stepped up from the same staircase, screwing a silencer on his pistol, as well.

With just minutes to spare on his five-hour deadline, boating from Sapelo to Skidaway and back, Jake was escorted through the glass doors into the main room. Flanked by Chopper and Juan, he handed off the metal tube and caught his breath.

Chopper gave the tube to Pancho.

"Frisk him, Juan," ordered the boss.

While Chopper had Jake stand upright at gunpoint, the other Mexican told Jake to raise his arms while he frisked him up and down. He thoroughly ran his hands down Jake's legs, lifted the cuffs of his pants for any ankle-holstered weapons, checked his shirt, pants waistline, and pockets. But he wouldn't dare touch the other man's crotch, thus missing Jake's hidden firepower.

"He's good, boss," said Juan. "No weapons, but I found this." He held a small glass in the palm of his hand. "Don't know what he plans on doing with it."

"It's a jeweler's loupe," said Jake. "To magnify the painting up close. To prove I'm not fucking you guys over."

"Step into my library, Tununda," ordered a smiling Pancho, taking the loupe from his cohort and placing his pistol back inside his coat. "Chopper, you're with me. Juan, lock the doors and monitor the outside in case he brought company."

"I'm alone. Where's my wife and Sammie?"

"No worries, my friend. No digits lost, either. They're fine. Downstairs in the game room and bar. Probably having a drink and playing pool." Pancho winked at Jake to calm him down. "Let's inspect the painting first, shall we?"

A few seconds later, Jake let out a cough.

Pancho led him off to the left wing, past a white-painted grand piano, and through a set of intricately-carved mahogany doors into the library.

Book-filled wooden cases, wood paneling, floor-to-ceiling windows, and watercolor paintings of native birds lined the walls. A curve formed in the wall at the far end. Leather sofas and chairs around a coffee table on an oriental carpet marked the interior of the library.

A floor standing globe stood nearby, which Pancho nonchalantly spun as he led Jake to a long table with two tall lamps. He clicked both lamps on and unscrewed the cap of the metal tube. Emptying a rolled-up frayed canvas onto the table, his eyebrows arched. Unfurling it, he placed a lamp on each edge to weigh it down flat.

"Would you look at that?" Pancho said, leaning in for a closer look, obviously impressed. "*The Painter on the Road to Tarascon* by Vincent Van Gogh. The only fucking cell service is at the main dock. It's where I did a

Google search. This painting is a match. You were right, Tununda. It's one valuable painting. It's even on the Monument's Men most wanted list."

"You can tell it's gone through quite a beating, too," said Jake playing along, finally catching his breath. "But the condition actually adds to its value. Do not try to get it repaired or anything like that. It's the real deal and collectors like the wear and tear as-is. Makes a great story. I had it appraised by a well-known art expert and he assured me this is the 1888 original by the famous Impressionist painter. Fits his style. Look through the loupe at the brush strokes. This is no forgery or print reproduction with a dot pattern."

Pancho nodded and bent over with the magnification glass to inspect the painting. He wasn't even sure what he was looking for, but he made the motions any way, acting as if he were knowledgeable in the subject matter.

The cartel boss then asked where the artist's signature was.

"I asked the same question," said Jake. "My appraiser said he only signed the work that he thought would sell or if he was going exchange with other artists. He has tons of work that he never signed. But be rest assured, this artwork is priceless because of its provenance."

"I see," remarked Pancho, not even knowing the definition of the word 'provenance.'

Jake then coughed twice, placing a cupped hand up to his mouth.

"What's your problem?" Chopper asked behind him, pistol at the ready.

"Sucked in a gnat earlier," said Jake looking back at him, his eyes darting to the gun.

"Fucking bugs on this island are horrible," said Pancho as he flipped the painting over and examined the reverse side. He noticed a small pencil sketch. There was even a little skull and crossbones.

"What the hell's this?"

"No clue."

Pancho shrugged his shoulders and rolled up the painting, placing it back into its protective tube.

"Alright, let's go downstairs to the bar to celebrate our deal. And then you can get your wife and the boy back." He held out his hand and Jake shook it. "Like I said, I'm a man of honor. Plus, I knew you'd deliver. I was so confident I even had my guys pack their bags so we can get the fuck off this island tonight."

Jake merely coughed again.

Pancho led the way back into the Great Room, tube with painting in hand. Chopper strolled behind Jake, pistol at his back.

"Juan?" shouted Pancho, not sure where he was. "Juan?"

"Yeah?" the lookout shouted back from deep in the kitchen wing.

"Everything's cool. Come on downstairs and join us for a drink."

"You got it, boss," Juan shouted back. "Be there in a sec. Taking a piss."

Reynolds Mansion
Service entrance

Like a ghost gliding from tree to tree, Alex Vann had easily snuck up to the rear of Reynolds Mansion without spooking the four Mexicans inside. Luckily, there was only one chump on the first floor peering out of the front entrance windows. A real amateur. Alex easily kept an eye on him through a monocular he cupped in his hand.

With crucial information regarding the layout of the mansion gained from Duff, the former Delta Force operator slithered in the shadows and found a narrow back service alley that ramped down underground to a basement entrance.

"Heard that Rae and Sammie are in the game room with one target," he whispered.

Jake coughed back once in his ear.

Alex checked the door knob. Locked. Holding his breath, he ran his hand along the top ledge of the door frame. An access key. Just as Duff had promised – a little inside help left by one of his Prince Hall Mason brothers who worked at the mansion. Unlocking the door and entering quietly, Alex swung his MP5K compact submachine gun in front of him. By now he knew Jake was above him in the library, inspecting the painting.

"How many targets are with you?"

Jake coughed twice.

"I'm in the basement," Alex whispered into his microphone.

Winding his way through several zigzags of eerily quiet and dimly-lit basement corridors, the ceilings filled with pipes, ducts, and electrical conduits, Alex came to a dead-end at a wood-paneled door. From what Duff had told him, this was supposed to be the secret entrance into the Gun Room where Dick Reynolds had stored all of his hunting rifles, ammo, and gear. Going through here would allow him access into the entertainment areas of the expansive basement.

He pressed his ear against the door for a few seconds, then turned the knob slowly. Slipping inside and closing the door behind him, the room was like a black hole. He touched the flashlight on the rail of his gun and shot a quick burst of light to get a feel for the room.

Low ceiling, tiled floor, empty wood racks and shelves, about eight foot square. Door on the far end with some light shining through the bottom. He heard an ever so faint thwack and then a thump as if something had dropped on the floor outside the door.

Quietly stepping up to the door, he listened again, heard nothing, and then cracked it open just a hair to peek out. The next room was dimly lit by a single lamp in the far corner. He stepped through the Gun Room door, panned his gun about, and advanced.

He was in the Grill Room, a festive and colorful area with a long table, its face inlaid with tiles in a Spanish bullfighting motif. There were iron chairs, a corner booth with large throw pillows, and a large, three-hearth fireplace. The mosaic-decorated fireplace had grills across two of its hearths while the center was kept open for the main fire. When he noticed a narrow winding staircase leading above in the corner, he realized he was now directly under the Great Room.

On the opposite side of this room was another door with a small window revealing the brightly-lit adult game room and bar area beyond. The door was partially cracked open.

Sammie and Rae were supposedly being held in there from the

conversation he was listening to through Jake's open mic, but he saw no movement through the window.

He heard Pancho yell out above for one of his colleagues to join him in the basement bar for a drink. Alex pointed his weapon toward the steps, then back at the game room door.

"Are you coming down?" he whispered. "The other two targets are not located yet."

He heard a one cough response.

Alex's eyes went wild. His heart was pounding hard. He knew he needed to find and secure Rae and Sammie first and to take out anyone guarding them. He crept to the game room door, glanced through the window again, but still saw nothing.

With no time to waste, he pushed the door open and entered the room in short quiet steps, panning about with his MP5K. What was strange was he was stepping on a large sheet of plastic that covered the hard-tiled floor. He noticed a roll of duct tape nearby, too.

Was a contractor doing some remodeling?

Straight ahead was a leather sofa, card table, and chairs. Large square support columns ran the middle of the wide room. There were floor-to-ceiling paintings of pirates, and even a one-lane bowling alley. To his left, an old popcorn machine, a billiards table, and a ping pong table. To his right, a big screen TV against a wall, the rest of the room just around the corner.

Creeping further in, he kept his aim to his right along the wall and turned the corner. His eyes widened. At the foot of a boat-shaped wooden bar, face-up on another sheet of plastic, was one of the Mexican guards. Some type of silver serving utensil was pushed into his eye socket all the way up to the handle. A stream of blood had spilled from his eye and ran down his cheek onto the plastic underneath his body. A white billiards cue ball lay nearby, also on the plastic.

"One target down in the game room. No sign of assets. Get ready to send lead as soon as you hit the game room. I'm in position."

He heard one cough from Jake in his ear, and the men clopping down the stairs, entering the Grill Room.

Reynolds Mansion
Game Room

Jake listened to Alex's latest sitrep as he descended the tight cellar steps. He coughed once in acknowledgement, his adrenaline jacked up. This was it.

Only one man at a time could fit going down the steps, as it was barely shoulder-width. Pancho went first and turned the corner as the stairs jogged to the left. Jake was right behind him and Chopper gave him a poke in the back with his pistol.

As their heels clicked down the steps, Jake slipped a hand to his crotch, unzipped his barn door, reached in his underwear and extracted his hidden pistol. While he turned the corner, he used his body positioning to hide the gun under his left armpit as he crossed both arms over his chest.

Pancho never even looked back. He cockily made his way directly across the Grill Room and towards the open Game Room door. Bright light filtered out. Chopper was right on Jake's heels, poking him again.

"Wait until you see this bar. It's right around the corner here," said Pancho with a sinister laugh.

"Where's my wife?" Jake asked loudly.

Chopper pushed Jake through the door. The bar came into view on his right and all hell broke loose. Jake used the forward motion of the lunge to turn his body ninety degrees toward his enemy, and lifted his left arm to expose the barrel of his compact.

He pulled the trigger twice. It sounded like two firecrackers had gone off. Both rounds caught Chopper in the midsection. The air cracked near Jake's head. Three suppressed reports followed not a fraction of a second later. Right before Jake's eyes, Chopper took three more hits in the chest.

Chopper blinked at Jake, confused. As the bull-headed thug's knees gave out and his pistol fell from his hand, Jake spun to face Pancho.

The Mexican boss was already in the process of leveling his own pistol at Jake's head.

Jake heard a thwack, thwack, thwack – suppressed reports from a different firearm – and saw Pancho's head snap and twist with three neat little red holes on the side of his face. He looked at Jake, his eyes registering shock, before rolling in the back of his head. The dead man falling was able to get one wild shot off before he crumpled to the floor.

Pancho's bullet zipped by Jake's face and plunked into something behind him. Jake flinched. He then heard Rae snickering. He turned and saw her standing behind the bar, a smoking suppressed pistol raised in the shooter's position.

She winked, and whispered to him that his zipper was down.

Jake's jaw dropped, but he looked down and zipped up.

Alex appeared from behind one of the large support columns, smoke wisping from the suppressor barrel of his submachine gun. He quietly nodded to Jake with a finger to his lips.

"Pendejos!" yelled Juan tromping down the stairs into the Grill Room. "Why couldn't you wait! I wanted to snuff one them gringos!"

Jake shimmied to the side of the open door. Alex concealed himself behind the column again, and Rae stood her ground as bartender, ready to serve up another fountain of red.

Juan approached, but suddenly paused at the open door upon seeing Chopper's body just inside. "What the–?" A squishing sound stopped him mid sentence.

Juan's body fell face first like a domino. He landed right on top of Chopper's corpse, an ice pick sticking out from the back of his neck at the base of his skull. The thug's pistol cluttered away and his body twitched its last death throes.

Sammie entered the Game Room, fists clenched, veins bulging from arms, chest heaving. He spit on Juan's corpse. "I'm a slave to no man!"

Jake backed away from the doorway, now stacked with two bodies. He looked at Sammie. "It's all over, son. It's done. You got the last of them. You're free now. Come over here."

Overcome with emotion, Sammie staggered over to Jake who placed an arm over his shoulder. Alex and Rae moved in to cover them. The young man openly started weeping, then buried his face into Jake's shoulder. Rae joined them and hugged Sammie.

Alex glided past them into the Grill Room, saying he was going to cover the stairs just in case any more cartel thugs were in the house.

While Sammie shook with grief, Jake looked up. There on the wall, frowning back at him with hands on his hips, was a life-sized painting of the famous Blackbeard the Pirate. Dressed in a black and red outfit and a wide black hat, his signature long black braids hung from his beard to below his waist, red ribbons tied to their ends.

Jake looked into his Blackbeard's eyes, one was bright blue, the other a nice new bullet hole through it from Pancho's wayward shot.

Aye aye, Captain.

✺

Reynolds Mansion
Game Room

The trio unlocked and Jake asked what had happened in the room.

"They were going to execute us," said Rae. "That's what all this plastic is for. To roll our dead bodies in so there'd be no blood evidence. Pancho brought you down here, not for a celebration drink, but to put a bullet in your head. He never meant to keep his word. They even bragged they were going to put our bodies on their yacht, and feed us to the sharks tonight when they left."

"Fucker planned it all along," mumbled Jake, picking up the tube with his painting and placing it on the bar. "I knew it."

"Regardless if you showed up with the painting or not," said Rae. "He wasn't going to give you one minute past the five hour deadline. It's why they were all packed up and ready to go."

Sammie sniffled. "B-but, we got the jump on them, didn't we, Rae? She cut through her duct tape with her belt buckle and got her hands free. Snuck the cue ball off the pool table. When Chopper switched out with the other dude, Rae clocked the new guy in the head. Knocked his ass out cold. And then she grabbed a butter knife from the bar, and, and, and–"

"And I took care of him," finished Rae, grasping Sammie's hand. "Got his pistol, freed Sammie, and we hid behind the bar. When the door opened we thought it was another one of them bastards coming to finish us off. But Sammie knew of a secret escape passage under the bar. Isn't that right?"

"Yaas'ma'am. Come over here, Jake. I'll show ya." Sammie went around to the far side of the bar and entered through a swinging half door. He pointed to a wooden antique ship's wheel with a brass hub. It was about 16 inches in diameter and was attached to the wood paneling about waist high at the back of the bar. It looked like a simple nautical ornament to go along with the motif of the bar design. "Check this out."

Sammie grasped the wheel's top handle and cranked it to the right. It unlocked double cabinet doors about three feet high from the floor. He swung the doors open, got on his knees, crawled in, and disappeared.

"What the hell?" said Jake. He walked around the bar and entered, too. Getting on his knees, he crawled halfway inside and noticed a small dark chamber that he could stand up in. He called for Sammie.

"Jake, turn around," said Rae.

Jake backed out and stood up. Sammie turned the corner from the entrance into the room and stood in front of him at the bar. He wore a big grin on his face.

"You son-of-a gun," said Jake, smiling. "So that's how you got the jump on him from behind?"

"Uh-huh. There's another door inside that room that opens from the wall of the Grill Room. My Daddy showed this secret passage to me when I was like ten years old. He said Dick Reynolds made it for his own children to hide in because he was so afraid they were going to be kidnapped just like the Charles Lindbergh's baby was."

"I thought Sammie was still hiding in there," said Rae. "But then I heard Alex's voice saying 'target down' and 'get ready to send lead' and that's when you walked in with Pancho. Jesus Christ, that was close. I wasn't going down without a fight, though. No way, honey. No way in hell."

They heard a moan behind them. Turning, they saw Chopper move his arm across the floor reaching for his gun.

Rae aimed her silenced pistol and nonchalantly put a bullet in his head.

Sammie couldn't believe how matter-of-fact she did it, but knew that the Mexican executioner would have done the same thing to all of them. He blinked several times as blood pooled on the plastic around the thug's head.

"Hey Alex?" shouted Rae.

Alex stepped back in the Game Room. "What's up?"

"We need to get rid of this trash," she said, retrieving her confiscated cell phone from Chopper's pocket. "And fast. It was nice of them to lay out the plastic for us, though, huh? Will come in handy."

"I'll do a quick clear of the house and then I'll bring the pick-up around," said Alex. "We'll haul the bodies through the basement where I came in, then transport them in the bed of the truck over to your boat, Jake."

"Perfect," said Jake. "Then you and Sammie get their yacht at Marsh Landing and follow us out to sea and we'll dump the bodies and scuttle the motherfucker just like they were going to do to us."

"Damn right," said Alex. "We're still live on comms so I'll give you sit reps. You do the same." He left the Game Room and was soon bounding up the stairs to clear the rest of the house.

"Alright guys, let's check their phones first," ordered Jake. "See if they tried calling anyone or texted anything specifically revealing our names. Use their thumbs to gain access if you need to."

"Can I chop them off?" Rae mumbled cold-heartedly.

"We got some blood splatter that needs cleaning up on the wall and ceiling there, too," said Jake, pointing around.

"I know where they keep cleaning supplies down here," said Sammie.

"Cool, let's get to work everyone," Jake said. He then rubbed the side of his head. "Oh, and Rae? Guess who paid me a visit back at our house? It's why I almost didn't make it back here in time."

"Who?"

"You'd be surprised."

28

ABSORBING THE LAST RAYS OF DAYLIGHT, the salt-stunted skeletal remains of Blackbeard Island's once-mighty live oak trees illuminated the northeast shoreline like beacons in a graveyard. Their silver, bone-like spidery branches seemed to beckon Sammie's speeding Zodiac right up the beach to rest among them.

Not seventy years ago, these fallen warriors once stood shoulder to shoulder as an impenetrable wall against the destruction of their maritime forest enclave. But having been cut down one-by-one from the constant erosion of storms, high winds, and tidal shifts, this narrow stretch of beach now looked like the remnants of an ancient battlefield. The piles of rock hard dead trees that now littered the shoreline was known to locals as 'The Boneyard.'

Under the camouflage the skeleton trees provided, Jake, Rae, Alex, and Sammie wasted no time in dragging their boat up the beach. Soon it was hidden among the lush forest away from prying eyes.

The quartet of explorers immediately hit the East Perimeter Trail to begin their search for the wreck of U-2370. They were still armed to the teeth, but less on-edge after turning the tables on their would-be cartel killers the night before.

That night, they had cleaned up the mansion basement of any trace evidence, transferred the four bodies into the cartel yacht, and scuttled the boat some ten miles out at sea as planned. No one in the cartel would ever know what truly happened to them, leaving the team with the peace of mind they could live their lives without fear of retaliation.

The next morning Jake received a call from an unknown number. It turned out to be Erhardt Hoffman on his burner phone. Much to Jake's relief, Hoffman reported that he was secure in a safe new location and would stay there indefinitely until Phoenix was tracked down.

The team had then taken the full day for recuperation and further planning on their cross-island journey to the U-boat's supposed location. Alex and Rae even took turns spying on the U.S. Fish and Wildlife dock across Blackbeard Creek to see if a ranger was on duty and when the last of the employees left for the day. They had nothing to fear as the island was deserted of federal employees this time of year.

Sammie and Jake, in turn, disappeared for a couple of hours back to Duff Greenhall's burnt-out cottage home where they had re-entered the garrison through the graveyard. Down in the dungeon, Jake retrieved Captain Werner Witte's original aluminum briefcase used by the OSS agent in charge of the rogue sub. Having unlocked it with the secret number code from Duff, he reviewed the *Operation Overcast* documents contained within. Jake was now well-armed with the historical background of U-2370 from its surrender on May 11, 1945 to its final demise in the early morning hours of September 17, 1945.

He even knew the names of the American skeleton crew who had been recruited from the Alcatraz of the East.

And whose likely bodies still remained onboard.

Jake also reviewed *Kapitänleutnant* Werner Witte's own wartime record stuffed in the files from his interrogation sessions. Jake read that Witte was born in the Baltic Sea port of the Free City of Danzig in 1920. At the age of seventeen he spent eight months living in England studying art history at Exeter College, where he learned to speak English fluently. He followed in his father's footsteps and began his naval career with the *Kriegsmarine* in 1941 and underwent officer and U-boat training as a watch officer.

In 1942, he served on U-156 under commander Hartenstein and was involved in the sinking of the troopship RMS *Laconia*. U-156 and several other U-boats then attempted to rescue some 2,700 survivors, including 1,800 Italian prisoners of war. This humanitarian act had infuriated Adolf Hitler so much that he gave direct orders to abort the rescue. Hitler then forced Admiral Dönitz to issue what was known as the 'Laconia Order' forbidding rescue of any survivors of sunken Allied ships.

After U-boat commander training, Witte was given his first command of a large workhorse Type VIIC with a crew of 50 in the summer of 1944 while just 23 years-old. He went on four successful patrols along the U.S. eastern seaboard sinking eighteen ships while damaging five others.

He was then entrusted to oversee construction of the new Type XXIII *Elektroboote*, one of the most modern and technically-advanced submarines in the world at the time. Witte launched U-2370 out of Norway in early 1945 to patrol the British Isles, sinking five ships.

Late in the war, his U-boat was attached to *Gruppe Seewolf* and made the perilous journey all the way across the North Atlantic in one of the last desperate wolfpacks of the war. He scored a hit, and with the help of a sister U-boat, sunk a U.S. destroyer. Soon after, he surrendered his sub to an American destroyer that escorted his boat to the Portsmouth Naval Shipyard where it was put in dry docks for research.

The last notes of Witte's file stated he was a POW at the Portsmouth Naval Prison in Maine, but while being transported to Bermuda he fell overboard and was lost at sea.

My own government killed him off, Jake thought.

But now it was time to find *Kapitänleutnant* Werner Witte's ghost sub and to resurrect this fellow warrior's name in the spirit of Freemasonry.

In a joking mood, Sammie took point on East Perimeter Trail and quickly guided the others a mile due south. He keenly spotted the first of Duff's way markers in his headlamp beam, right where he said it would be – the large alligator head chained to a tree. Wasting no time, he chose a spot in the impenetrable wall of Spanish bayonet, bay, holly, and palmetto and started hacking away with his machete to carve a path.

Jake was several feet behind, giving the young man ample swinging room. Anything Sammie missed, Jake cut through with his own machete.

As their paced slowed to a crawl, swarms of mosquitoes and sand flies attacked the team. Wearing boonie hats with headlamps and long sleeve shirts and gloves, not a single inch of their skin was exposed except for their faces. Luckily, they heeded Duff's advice and donned their head nets along with dousing themselves in copious amounts of bug repellent.

The night air grew cooler and the wind picked up, whistling a constant low drone through the grand live oak trees while whipping their wizard beards of Spanish moss in a wave-like rhythm. With Alex providing navigation from a hand-held GPS wayfinding unit using Duff's map coordinates, Sammie guided the group to the first carved symbol on a live oak tree. It took several sweeps with their headlamps to find since it was rather faded, but for someone really looking hard, the Keyhole Urchin stood out well enough.

Already thoroughly drenched in sweat and breathing hard, Sammie was gladly relieved of his machete duties by Alex.

The going was slow and it proved incredibly tough to penetrate the underbrush of the maritime forest. All four had been nicked or scraped repeatedly from either dagger-like Spanish Bayonet prongs or sharp palmetto leaves. Blood from their cuts only added to the misery, attracting even more annoying gnats.

If sharp plants and swarms of insects weren't enough, they also dealt with the ups and downs of an uneven terrain the closer they approached the ocean. The leaf-covered forest floor they were now bisecting was made up of narrow, north-to-south, maritime dune ridges. It proved a nighttime rollercoaster ride of constant elevation changes causing them to trip, stumble, and twist ankles. They went from 25 feet on the top of the dune ridges down to water-filled, mucky 20-40 foot-wide troughs well below sea level. At some of the lowest points, the black quicksand-like matter nearly sucked the boots right off them. Several times they had to divert their path to skirt around much deeper ponds within the troughs, for greeting them was the occasional glow of red eyes marking an alligator.

After many water breaks, switching of duties, and respraying themselves with repellent, the group soldiered on.

Any amateur hiker would have long since turned back to the main path rather than spend another minute trailblazing up and down through the nearly impenetrable maritime forest.

Each member took their turn hacking away with a machete. At times, though, they were able to walk unimpeded among vast swaths of resurrection fern or around fetterbush shrubs that carpeted the floor under the big oaks. They listened to wildlife, from chirping bullfrogs, to hooting owls, to the snorts of flushed out feral hogs. They saw poisonous snakes on the ground and curious raccoons in the trees. And insects the size of their hands.

As dusk turned to night, a full moon eerily lit up the woods all around them. Shadows started to dance as trees swayed with the ocean breeze. But by then they had found three of the symbols and were looking for a fourth – another starfish. It was just over another dune ridge according to the GPS unit. Sure enough, after another ten minutes of exhaustive trailblazing, they stood at the tree with the carving.

Now all that remained was to find the star symbol farther east in the middle of the forest up and down another dune ridge and through another wall of underbrush. At that point they had to be on the lookout for a massive mound of flora twelve feet high – the supposed camouflaged conning tower of U-2370.

Utterly exhausted, but at the same time exhilarated with the discovery just ahead of them, the team trudged on over another narrow ridge. A cacophony of bullfrog calls rose as they made their way down into the next trough. Hacking through a tall thick wall of panic grass, a loud growl and splash of water startled them. Something big had just gotten spooked and took refuge in the water beyond. The bullfrog calls ceased altogether and several white egrets took off from the tree tops.

Sammie made it through the grass first and spotted an alligator tail before it disappeared under the surface.

As the rest of the group stepped close to the shoreline of the pond, their headlamp beams trailed the wake created by the creature. Emerging before them was the deepest-looking pond they had yet encountered. It had filled the trough almost entirely on each of its bordering sides. From left to right, along a dense shoreline of tall grass, the black water extended for hundreds of feet.

As the group inspected the water, the colony of bullfrogs went at it again with a deafening roar of chirping, grinding, and rasping sounds.

Lit by bright moonlight, the pond surface was pockmarked not only with small floating islands of thick plant life, but with many drowned skeleton-like trees. Some were still standing upright, while others had collapsed into a heap of white bony branches along the shoreline.

Another boneyard, Jake thought. *And this is just what's above the surface.*

Reflecting on the surface were rippled patterns of white. They panned their lights up into the trees and saw hundreds of white egrets hunkered down for the night.

But neatly blending in on the dark surface of the water were log-like shapes holding pairs of glowing red eyes giving them away as alligators. Most of them disappeared underwater, but some, with a much wider distance between the eyes, stayed stubbornly rigid on the surface. Those larger alligators were not afraid of humans stumbling into their well-hidden feeding hole.

About twenty feet away looking east, directly ahead in the middle of the pond, was the expected tall mound of underbrush. It looked to be about 12-feet high and was filled with vines, ferns, small bushes, and even several palm saplings. There was no indication a conning tower was even there, let alone an entire submarine hidden below the surface of the pond.

"This is it," said Jake. "But does anyone see the star symbol on any of the trees? According to the map coordinates, we're at the final location."

"And how the hell are we going to get over to that island?" asked Alex. "There's no freakin' bridge."

"Duff said there's supposed to be a log out to the conning tower, but wasn't sure if it still remained or not," replied Jake. "Keep an eye out for it, alright? Maybe it's on the other side. I don't know."

For several minutes, they searched with their headlamps, splitting into pairs up and down the shoreline. More alligators splashed into the pond as the intruders stepped into their territory.

"I think I found the bridge log!" said Rae, shining her light beam on a long, thick white tree trunk that started in the mud on shore and extending toward the conning tower mound. Halfway in the middle of the pond, though, it declined sharply and disappeared under the water. "It's submerged, damnit. No go."

"Shit," mumbled Jake.

"Over here!" shouted Sammie. He and Alex were at the far south end of the pond near a large dead oak tree, its many branches having already fallen into the water. "We found the star."

Sammie illuminated a section of the tree trunk. Facing them was the star carving just as it was in the *Elixir of Life* label. Several bright white alligator skulls laid at its base within the tall grass.

"Nice work, kiddo," said Jake, cracking him on the arm.

"Oh my God, what the hell's that!?" whispered Rae in a shaky voice.

She tore off her bug net and looked beyond the tree trunk toward the middle of pond, her powerful headlamp beam lighting up the water.

The symphony of sounds created from the bullfrogs instantly stopped. Silence permeated the air as if time stood still. Not even the wind howled.

There, standing just before the conning tower mound, knee deep in the water, were two Caucasian men dressed in light blue shirts and dungarees. They were instantly recognizable as U.S. Navy sailors from WWII. They even wore yellow life vests. Yet all of their clothing was shredded to pieces. Their skin was ravaged with deep gaping wounds that exposed bone and guts. Half of one sailor's face was even ripped off, showing his skull and hollow eye socket.

Lifeless and motionless they stood, staring at the visitors.

"Ghosts of the dead," whispered Sammie, peering out from the bug net he had lifted over his hat. "They're warning us."

The two ghosts suddenly started to move – towards the team. They slowly raised their arms pleading for help. Trudging through the water, they even creating wakes on the surface. It was all too real.

And completely terrifying.

Sammie backpedaled and hid behind Jake and Alex.

The ghost sailors walked in a perfectly straight line, one behind the other, getting closer. The team all backed off now. Rae tripped and fell on her behind, crab-crawling backward.

Abruptly, the ghosts turned ninety degrees toward the west, raised their hands over their heads as if signalling someone, and simply stepped off into the pond – as if stepping off a ledge. With a ripple, they immediately disappeared into the black void. A massive alligator tail then cracked the surface and the water bubbled and boiled in turmoil.

A sailor's hand and head broke the frothy surface – the man with the torn face. He issued a guttural howl that ripped through the air. His ghostly voice buckled the knees of each team member in absolute horror. The ghost was then pulled under in another splash of black soupy muck – the tail of the alligator again smacking the surface.

While howling death throes of the sailor creepily echoed away in the distance, they suddenly merged with the deep slow hooting of a nearby night owl perched high in a tree. It was all too surreal and freaked the group out as a whole.

Soon the water calmed, the bullfrogs began thrumming again, and the air whistled with the wind. The ghost men never resurfaced.

The shocked group stayed silent for a minute. Finally, Jake drew a deep breath and stuttered to say something, but couldn't form the words.

"Guys," said Rae nervously, climbing to her feet. "I don't think we should go out there. It's death replaying itself all over again. That was like a scene in a horror movie saying stay the hell away."

"I agree," said Sammie. "Pappy said this sub was like an iron coffin and we just saw those two men he tried to rescue over 70 years ago. The gators ate 'em just like he said. Never found one piece of their bodies."

"There's no way out there," declared Alex. "It's all water. Them gators will eat us alive, too. I don't know about this, bro."

"Everyone just calm down, okay?" said Jake. "Alex, man, you and I took down a damn Raven Mocker – and that thing was alive as hell. Just relax. What we just saw was a paranormal recording in time. Those ghosts can't harm us. They seemed like they were caught in a repeating loop, like a video that keeps playing over and over again. It's common in the spiritual world with a traumatic experience."

Jake saw reassured nodding heads.

"Now, listen to me," he continued. "I don't know if you caught it, but they gave us a clue on how to get to that conning tower."

"Huh?" said Rae.

"Just hear me out," Jake pleaded. "We've come too far to turn back now." He took off his gloves and fished out his smartphone. Tapping the screen a few times he pulled up a picture of a scale model of the U-boat, complete with officers in the conning tower and a crewman on the narrow deck. He had the others gather around to look.

"It's a Type XXIII U-boat sitting out there," he continued. "The smallest in the German fleet. I researched it online, found tons of photos from all different angles, and even looked at some scale models with crewmen to get a sense of how big it is. Like this. See here? It's only one-hundred and fourteen feet in total length."

Jake then gestured with his hands toward the pond as the others brushed bugs away from their faces. "It can only sit in one direction within this trough. North-to-south. I'm guessing it was pulled in with the storm surge of the hurricane and was probably swept right down one of these troughs all the way from the ocean until it embedded itself in this pond. Plus, another thing I noticed. That conning tower mound has a bit of an extension on the far side of it near the surface of the pond. See here in the picture? I think that extension is the muffler for the exhaust from the diesel engine. It was used while the boat was on the surface or even snorkeling. If that's true, it means we are standing near the bow."

Quite animated, Jake kept switching from the photo to looking with his headlamp out on the water. "The conning tower sits in the middle of the structure, right here, bisecting the deck. So you're talking about fifty feet of submerged deck to get to that mound in the middle. But the deck can only hold one person. It is very narrow. See how this crewman stands on it. Only about shoulder width. By my calculation that conning tower looks to be about ten-twelve feet above the surface, which means that deck is hidden just below the waterline. You saw how those ghosts were knee deep and walking in a straight line, right?"

"Yes," said Alex. Sammie and Rae nodded in agreement.

"That's our bridge in," said Jake. "We walk the underwater deck."

"Walk the plank is more like it," grimaced Rae.

"We get locked and loaded," said Jake. "I go first. You guys shine your headlamps in the water and cover me. I'll tap ahead with a stick or something to make sure I have a solid surface. We'll tie off rope on this tree and I'll trail a line. When I make it, I'll tie us off a guideline. We can do this! I'm not giving up."

"If Pappy could walk on that log to get out there, shee-it, then I can walk the deck I suppose," said Sammie with renewed bravery.

"I'm in," Alex flatly stated.

All heads turned to Rae. Jake gave her his best puppy dog eyes.

She smiled, ignored him, and turned to Sammie for a life lesson. "Do you know why women live longer than men, Sammie?"

The teen shook his head.

"Because we think there's a better way than walking blindly across an underwater bridge in the dead of night surrounded by hungry alligators."

Jake and Alex both chuckled at the way she framed it.

"Listen guys," Rae ventured. "I'm not willing to give up either, but I think Duff's original way is the only way. We must stay *out* of the water. Period. Walking *in* the water and creating any wake will actually attract alligators. And then as soon as one of you brave lads actually shoots one, the blood will attract even more, creating a feeding frenzy. Do you want to be the person stuck in the middle of a pack of feeding alligators knee deep in the middle of a swamp with only an invisible shoulder-width deck to walk on? No."

"No ma'am, when you put it like that," muttered Sammie.

She spun around and lit up one of the tall straight skeleton trees that lined the shoreline. "What we must do is walk on *top* of the water, on a nice wide log. A *new* log that we chop down and angle to reach the conning tower island. Just like Duff did. We must be patient, choose the right path, instead of walking out blindly. We have all the time in the world, okay? Agreed, my big brawny lumberjacks?"

"Agreed," instantly said Sammie.

Alex sighed heavily and nodded in tacit acquiescence.

Jake remained silent.

Now it was Rae's turn to put on the sad eyes. She touched his arm. "Please, Paul Bunyan?"

○

Late evening
U-boat pond
Blackbeard Island, Georgia

The tree they chose proved quite solid. It was a good two and a half feet in diameter at its base, narrowing down significantly toward the top but still wide enough to accommodate a walking path. Without an axe, it took over a half-hour of hacking away with just the two machetes and a hatchet that Jake had in his backpack. Both machete blades were bent by the time they finished, one even snapped in half, but the last chop had finally been made and they watched the dead tree fall toward its intended target. Holding their collective breaths, their aim was spot-on. The tree trunk crashed directly on top of the mound.

The top section shattered like shrapnel, split off, and tumbled into the water disturbing many nearby nesting birds who shot up in the air squawking. A good amount of the mound's vegetation was pulled away, exposing the front of the conning tower. The rest of the log rolled down the side and settled onto the U-boat's submerged deck, laying partially in the water. They couldn't have asked for a better outcome; they now had a direct elevated passage of some forty feet from the shoreline.

The team cheered, then collapsed in renewed exhaustion. Covered in dripping sweat, Jake passed a flask of moonshine around and they indulged in a little celebratory swig.

After a long rest, Jake took the lead to make the walk across the log. He held his 1911 pistol with a mounted flashlight at the ready for the first alligator head he saw coming his way. His other hand held the standing end from a coil of rope slung over his shoulder. The working end was firmly attached to another tree on the shoreline as an anchor point.

Alex positioned himself on the shoreline slightly off center of Jake. In the beam of his headlamp, he aimed his MP5K ahead on the log. Rae and Sammie stood on each side of him, headlamps ablaze. She had her Glock 42 while Sammie clutched his .22 scoped rifle.

And off Jake went.

He took slow soft steps and balanced himself rather easily on the wide log, never taking his eyes off the log itself. It wasn't until he got halfway that Alex shouted an alligator was approaching at his two o'clock position. Jake paused in mid-stride and looked over at the water. As soon as his eyes left the log, he lost his balance. He flailed his arms side to side like a bird trying to take off. Eyes immediately back on his narrow walkway and he regained his balance.

"Gator has stopped," shouted Alex. "He's just watching you. He thinks you're a bird, I think."

"Asshole!" Jake bellowed back, breathing hard, head still down, eyes targeted a few feet ahead of him. "Don't take your eyes off the damned log. I almost lost it." *And I almost pissed myself, too,* he thought.

"That's right!" said Rae. "We've got you covered, hon. Just maintain focus on your balance and moving forward. You're halfway there."

As Jake traveled ten more feet, this time Sammie let out a warning. "Jake, you have a gator at your nine o'clock now. I have a bead on him."

"I've got him, too, in my scope," added Alex. "Just ignore him."

Jake raised his pistol hand to acknowledge their message and kept on walking. Within moments, he made it to the mound of vegetation and grabbed ahold of a sapling to steady himself. He spun around to his nine o'clock, aimed his pistol at the water, and saw a medium-sized alligator swim toward him. He aimed at its head, but didn't fire. The gator stopped swimming, raised his head at Jake, opened his mouth exposing sharp white teeth, then flipped over in the black water and disappeared.

"Okay, made it!" he shouted across the pond. "All good." *Now I just need to clean my underwear,* he thought. "I'm going to find a place to tie off. Give me a minute."

"We've got you covered," said Alex.

Kneeling down on the log, he reholstered his pistol, then unstrapped his backpack to gain access. Unclipping his bent machete, he used it to probe a weedy, two-foot gap between the log and conning tower. The long bent blade submerged up to its handle before he felt a solid surface – the deck of the U-boat. He felt they could easily straddle that gap, but was reassured to know there was only a foot of water down to the deck if anyone happened to slip in.

Jumping over to the conning tower, he had good footing on a thick layer of decayed vegetation. He started hacking away at the plant life at the narrow end of the conning tower facing him. Pulling away vines and tossing sharp leaves into the water, after a few minutes the metal shield of the conning tower became exposed.

A rush entered his body. The moment of discovery.

It was, of course, rusted beyond recognition due to the salt-filled atmosphere for the last seventy-plus years, but nonetheless exciting all the same. Next he found five horizontal iron ladder steps that led up to the bridge, exactly where expected. This was the only access to get up and into the conning tower, down the main hatches, and into the interior of the boat itself.

He found the ladder rungs still to be quite solid and immovable despite the rust that had formed on their surface. Weaving his guideline rope through a rung, he pulled it as tight as it would go, then tied off several knots to secure it. Looking back down the log, the rope followed its length, providing another visual aid and back-up safety measure for the others to follow in case they lost their balance.

Jake donned his backpack again then climbed up the iron rungs and flung one leg over the lip of the bridge to gain access to the upper deck.

A massive creature squawked and jumped upward in a burst of beating air and feathers. It bumped into him and almost knocked him off the platform.

It was a huge blue heron. Jake nearly had a heart attack. Everyone's headlamps followed the bird's path as it rose into the air with its wide wingspan and flew off into the forest.

"You good up there!?" yelled Alex.

Jake's heart was beating so fast he started laughing in apprehension. "I'm good. But I think it's the second time I shit myself." He heard a smattering of laughter from the shoreline.

Stepping over the lip, he lowered himself into the bridge confines and removed his backpack once again. This time he took out several chemlight glowsticks, cracked them in half, and shook them up to give a fair amount of neon green chemical illumination in the tightly cramped space. He also hung another glowstick on the top rung of the ladder for a reference point.

The bridge lit up. It was big enough to comfortably hold four crewmen. He immediately noticed large holes and shredded metal all around him. *Had to be from the air attack that took the lives of the American captain and his first officer,* he thought.

With some clean-up of branches, leaf debris, and Spanish moss bird nesting material, he uncovered the bridge hatch. This rusted hatch, the size of a manhole cover, was the only way down into the conning tower and lower deck of the sub.

Duff had assured him that the hatch was not locked and that he'd specifically sprayed the hinges with heavy duty rust inhibitor over the years, but didn't know its current state. Jake wasted no time in grabbing ahold of a handle and pulling with all his strength. The heavy hatch groaned and immediately gave way, creaking fully open as several pieces of rust fell from the edges. A surge of hot putrid gases shot out of the hole and Jake turned away in disgust. The smell was overwhelming. He instantly vomited over the side of the bridge.

Wiping his mouth and then donning a surgical face mask from the first-aid pouch of his pack, he cracked another glow stick and dropped it down the bridge hole. It fell through the open conning tower hatch, bounced off the ladder in the control room and splashed on the floor far below. Through a thin layer of brown-streaked standing water, he could see the floor was made up of crisscrossed metal deck plates. He also observed that the conning tower hatch, just six feet below him, was secured open with a large latch. *Better do the same with this bridge hatch*, he thought.

Detaching two oversized carabiners from the PALS webbing of his backpack, he created a chain link latching one onto the hatch locking wheel and the other to the side of the bridge itself. This way no one or no thing – animal or human spirit – could close up the hatch and trap anyone inside.

Jake leaned over the bridge shield and aimed his headlamp toward the others before shouting the all-clear for the next person to follow.

Sammie stepped up, rifle slung over his back and shoulder for better balance.

"Keep a loose grip on that ropeline, Sammie," ordered Jake. "Only use it to guide yourself. Don't pull on it because it won't support you, understand!?"

"Yaas'suh, Mr. Jake."

"Keep your eyes on the log," said Alex behind him. "Ignore the water and anything in it. We have you covered from all angles now, okay?"

"Yaas'suh." With that Sammie walked ahead. Within less than a minute, he made it all the way across with no problems, never looking up once despite the company of a large alligator that swam under the log and popped its head up on either side of him. He looked like a professional acrobat, he was so steady. Nobody said a word until he made it to the conning tower. And then Jake, Rae, and Alex all broke out in applause.

Sammie climbed up into the bridge with Jake, unslung his rifle and provided cover. Only then did he exhale loudly.

Rae went next. She took it slowly and cautiously until she got spooked by a six-foot cottonmouth snake that swam parallel to the log not a foot away from her. Although she was wearing protective snake gaiters on her lower legs, it unnerved her so much that she lost her balance, flailed her arms, grabbed ahold of the rope, and then actually crouched down on her hands and knees to steady herself. Hyperventilating and almost paralyzed with fear, she stole a glance at the snake and watched in relief as it swam back to shore. It took her several more minutes and much encouragement from the others to even make it back to her feet again, let alone finish the log walk. When she arrived intact, the men cheered her accomplishment.

Alex was last and cockily strode across the log as if he were walking down the street. About halfway across, a massive snapping turtle climbed up on the log in front of him and faced his direction. Its enormous head and elongated snout extended to full length and then it opened its powerful jaws revealing a deep black hole down its throat. Alex froze.

He'd never seen a snapping turtle that big before. It looked well over three-feet long and had deep jagged ridges on the back of its black shell, with what looked like spikes along its edges. With thick feet and long sharp claws digging into the log, the damned thing looked immovable. A shot rang out striking the water right next to the turtle's head. It retracted and the beast slithered back into the pond, disappearing under water.

Up on the bridge, Sammie pulled up his rifle and chambered a new round. "Just wanted to scare him, Mr. Alex. They mean no harm."

Alex rolled his eyes. "Remember Gandalf versus Balrog in *Lord of the Rings*, Sammie? I thought the thing was going to rise up on its feet and eat me for a late night snack."

"Never saw the movie!"

Alex shook his head with a chuckle. "Never mind." He then continued forward at his same pace and made it across and up into the conning tower to join the others. He instantly demanded a shot of moonshine.

"Alright, listen up," barked Jake. "Here's the situation down inside best I can tell. It's hot, humid, smells like shit, still might have some poisonous gases down there, and looks to have standing water in places. Remember, there are bodies in there that have been decomposing for over 70 years. Either they'll have turned to goo or you'll find skeletons, I would imagine. Too many variants to know how far they've decomposed. And God knows what all, if anything, is still living down there in terms of bacteria. Keep your gloves on at all times. If you get cut, we need to disinfect it right away."

He then handed out protective breathing masks to the team while he continued going over the game plan. "I'm also worried about any lingering battery leakage such as chlorine gas, although it probably dissipated many years ago. I just don't want to chance it, ya know? You start feeling faint, get the hell out. This hatch has been venting for the last ten minutes so I'm thinking we're okay."

Heads nodded with nervousness.

"Since we didn't bring any breathing apparatus," continued Jake, "we need to get in and get out quickly. We need to do this in pairs, leaving two outside at all times in case of rescue. Two in, two out. Then we rotate as conditions warrant."

"Yeah, good idea," said Rae.

"So what's our goal?" asked Alex. "We do a quick recon, look for valuables, haul them out? That pretty much it?"

"Pretty much scouting it out, yup. Need to see its structural integrity, too. This is kinda like a treasure salvage operation right now. The historical significance can wait until later. Grab what you can. Stay close. Let's have Rae and I go in first as a pair."

"All yours, Mr. Jake," said Sammie, gesturing to the ladder down. "Pappy said it will be your discovery."

Jake watched Rae gulp hard. He took a deep breath himself.

Inside U-2370
Blackbeard Island, Georgia

Climbing down inside the tight confines of the conning tower, Jake now stood where Captain Werner Witte once used the periscope to spot his last target in the sinking of the destroyer escort USS *Frederick C. Davis* right before Germany surrendered. Jake immediately noticed more damage inside the heavily rusted metal shield wrapped around him. It, too, looked like Swiss cheese from the air attack. *No wonder the two American officers instantly lost their lives up here,* he thought.

Through the conning tower hatch, descending down the ladder to the next level, he finally entered the control room and stepped down onto the deck in a splash of rusty water. He could hear Rae just starting her climb down from above.

An uneasy feeling immediately swept over him. Duff's omen spoke in his head. *An iron coffin with a true skeleton crew inside. Trapped angry spirits that haven't been released.*

Jake slowly turned around, panning his headlamp.

Then screamed in horror.

Another Navy sailor stood before him in the same blue work shirt and dungarees as the previous two. His shirt was sweat-stained and streaked with grease. Except this man looked like a boneless zombie. His limbs were bent and broken and he was hunched over. His head was matted wet with blood and nearly twisted around. The dead sailor's black lifeless eyes met Jake's and his mouth fell agape. He then bellowed, "Get out!"

Jake's heart was in his throat and he screamed in terror again, stumbling backward. He tripped on something and fell to his ass in the water, bumping his head slightly against metal machinery – in the same spot Phoenix had clocked him.

"Jake! Jake," came screams from above on the ladder. He heard the metal clinking of Rae's hurried footsteps.

Moaning with renewed pain in his head, he turned to where the apparition stood.

It had disappeared.

On the deck plate where it stood lay a pile of decayed skeletal remains clumped together in deteriorated, moldy blue clothing and a pair of black leather boots that remarkably looked relatively new.

From his studies of the paperwork on the final mission of the sub and Duff's oral history with Captain Witte, Jake knew this corpse would be the chief engineer. His name was David Sloan, a convicted serial rapist of fellow submariners all throughout the war.

"David Sloan, I know you can hear me," said Jake in a firm voice raising his protective mask. "It's time for *you* to get out! There's a new crew taking over this sub. Your mission is over. Leave now!"

Across the control room, a small overhead lamp detached from the ceiling and crashed to the floor.

Guess you got the message, you bastard rapist, thought Jake.

"Jake! Jesus, what happened? Who are you talking to?" Rae said, stepping down into the control room, helping him to his feet.

Sammie and Alex shouted from above and Jake gave them the all-clear, that he had gotten spooked by a ghost again.

Jake pointed to the corpse in the corner. "That was the chief engineer. His apparition just appeared to me and point blank told me to 'get out'. They're going to be playing with us the whole time, Rae. We aren't the only ones down here. There's supposed to be two more bodies in the stern of the boat, and our guest of honor SS *Sturmbannführer* Franz Heidel up in the bow. Don't back down to them if they make an appearance."

"It's no wonder why Duff warned us."

"Yeah, it truly is an iron coffin," mumbled Jake. "But we're the new crew now. We've got to convince these spirits their mission is over and they can leave forever."

"Jake, remember when we did that paranormal investigation with the Savannah Ghost Research Society?" asked Rae.

"With Ryan Dunn, right? At that old mansion on Calhoun Square."

"Yeah, the famous 432 Abercorn Street. Remember when he told us that when bodies are lost or buried at a location that they act like an anchor keeping the spirit attached to it?"

Jake nodded, remembering quite well that special overnight, invitation-only event in historic Savannah. Jake and Rae had met author Ryan Dunn at a booksigning and they became good friends with him and his Savannah Ghost Research Society team. Soon they had been invited to one of Dunn's investigations.

The new owners of the old mansion on 432 Abercorn Street wanted to check things out before remodeling. It was already famous for a haunting that no one could prove, plus it hadn't been entered in over a decade. That night ended up scaring the living shit out of him and Rae, not unlike tonight's experiences. They encountered an aggressive apparition that ultimately drove the entire group from the house after one of the team members was attacked and cut across his cheek.

It was only after the remodeling crew came in several weeks later and discovered a shackled skeleton hidden in the wall in the cellar that the true story was revealed. It was determined to be a missing slave who served the owners back during the Civil War. Once the remains were removed and properly buried, the haunting ceased altogether.

"I think we need to remove their remains ASAP," said Rae. "It's the only way their angry spirits can detach from this place, just like Ryan said."

"Absolutely right," replied Jake. "I've got some trash bags in my pack. We can use those."

"We need to give them a proper burial at sea, too," added Rae. "They were U.S. Navy. It'd be appropriate."

"Part of me wants to feed them to the alligators," bitched Jake, taking off his pack and rummaging through it for the bags. "You wouldn't believe the crimes they committed from what I read about in the mission files."

"Haven't they suffered enough being stuck here for well over seventy years?" Rae countered. "Reliving that same trauma over and over again? It has to be mental torture."

"I know," Jake reluctantly agreed. "We gotta do the proper thing to expunge this vessel and free them. Let's you and I start with the chief engineer here and we'll get him out first. Then we can get the other two in the stern."

"On it," said Rae, grabbing a bag. She then took out her smartphone and clicked a few pictures. "We need to archive this first. Where he died. His condition. Sorry. Crime scene habits are taking over."

"Hey guys!" Jake shouted, looking up the ladder. "We're going to remove the bodies first. Send down a rope so you can haul them up."

"10-4," said Alex.

"Rae, put on some latex gloves from my pack and then put your work gloves over them. That'll give you the best protection. And then we'll toss our gloves later."

Within several minutes, they had Sloan's bagged body going up.

"Okay," said Jake. "Let's hit the stern for the next two bodies. We'll be looking for the radar operator. His name is Arthur Ricketts. And the man in charge of the operation, an OSS spy, the handler of the Nazi up in the bow they were transporting. His name is Frank Baker."

✵

Inside U-2370
Blackbeard Island, Georgia

Through the rectangular stern door and around one side of the huge rust-encased diesel engine block, Jake and Rae stepped through a tunnel of busted metal pipes, detached conduits, and nests of electrical wire. On the deck were piles of damaged sub equipment, broken boxes, and crates filled with seemingly valuable yet moldy paintings. They ignored the treasures.

Finally, in the very aft of the boat next to the toilet, they found the next two bodies. The Navy crewman was dressed as the others. The civilian was dressed in decayed khaki pants and an olive drab work shirt, even with black work boots still on. Both bodies had been laid out next to each other. They were no more than skeletons in soiled clothes with patches of dark leathery skin left over in a few places, including some hair on their heads.

"I can't believe how they look," said Jake, from behind his face mask. "Like mummified skeletons, if that makes sense." He stared at the bodies while squatting over them.

"I've seen a lot of decomposing bodies in my career," explained Rae, also masked as she bent down next to the corpses. Under her boonie hat, she wiped a sleeve across her sweaty forehead. "The condition you see here is what happens when the aerobic bacteria inside your body eats away from the inside out. The insides putrefy, turn gelatinous and eventually seep out of the body. When the air finally ran out down here, anaerobic bacteria probably consumed most of the rest of them."

Rae pulled out her smartphone again and tapped on the camera app to snap photos. "Plus, any insects that managed to get in here, too, would have feasted on them. But it looks like the outer skin, began to dry out, and you see how it is here, it becomes tough like leather. Mummified over the bones. It sure is nasty."

"You can say that again."

Suddenly, the screen on Rae's phone, and both her and Jake's headlamps all started to flicker.

Something caught the corner of Jake's eye. "Honey, don't move," he whispered. "There's two visitors standing behind us. Whatever you do, do *not* look back."

Her hand holding the phone immediately started shaking while her face blanched. "Oh God, oh God . . ." But then curiosity got the best of her and she hovered her thumb over the icon on her camera screen to give her a reverse image used to take selfies. She tapped it.

The camera now faced her.

Her mouth opened when she saw the two ghost figures of the submariner and the OSS agent standing behind her about four feet away. She tapped the screen and snapped a photo, but watched in slow motion horror as the agent lunged toward her in the screen.

A terrorizing wail emanated from her throat.

A force hit her in the back of the head, her phone flew from her grip.

The phone's screen went black. Both her headlamp and Jake's flickered simultaneously, then shut off, too. She screamed frantically again.

At the sudden darkness and his wife's screams, Jake couldn't help but bellow, too, in reaction.

The couple instantly groped for each other but only found dead air.

Fingernails then painfully dug into Rae's neck, and this time she utterly freaked out – quivering in spasms.

With banshee-like screaming, in pure survival mode, she ran for the only glimmer of light visible: the glow sticks way back in the control room. But in the sheer darkness, she slammed into Jake like a linebacker. He was pushed up against a wall of gears and wheels. And then something punched him hard in the gut, instantly knocking the wind out of him. He crumpled to his knees, clutching his stomach and gagging for air.

"Run, Jake!" She screamed, tripping over debris and banging against the long diesel engine block. Rae saw the stern bulkhead door and ducked to get through.

Her judgement was off and she smacked the top of her head under her hat against the top lip of the door. Seeing sparks from the impact and falling forward into the control room, she splashed onto the metal deck, scampered for the ladder, and climbed up as fast as she could.

Alex had already starting down the ladder when he heard the initial screams. He made it down to the control room just as Rae plowed through the open door. She frantically sideswiped him for her only escape, her face mask ripping off from the collision.

"Where's Jake?" he shouted as she climbed upwards.

"Engine room!" She cried out. "Ghosts!" With that, she was nearly up to the bridge. "Get him!"

Alex bent and lunged through the door, headlamp beam guiding him to the back of the boat.

Sammie was in a state of pure confusion up top as Rae hauled ass up the ladder. She ignored his pleas to stop and instead climbed over the bridge shield and started down the outside ladder.

He knew he had to look after her.

Rae wasted no time in jumping down to the base of the conning tower onto a clump of weeds. Her only goal was to get as far away from the U-boat as possible. She hopped onto the log and immediately started across. Unbeknownst to her, blood was pouring down her face from her head wound.

Sammie followed as best he could, his headlamp lighting the path on the log ahead of her in the hope she wouldn't fall in. He ended up slipping on the log himself and fell forward on his knees, but managed not to fall in the water.

Rae ran across the log bridge like she was a veteran lumberjack. Luckily, from both the moonlight and stray beams of Sammie's headlamp, she made it to the shoreline and collapsed in the tall grass.

Within seconds, Sammie was at her side.

Inside U-2370

Alex found Jake on his hands and knees gasping for air in the very back of the sub near two corpses. He bathed him in the beam of his light. In fact, he also noticed Rae's cell phone, its screen illuminated.

"Did Rae make it out?" asked a barely audible Jake.

"Yes. Up the ladder and out. She's fucking terrified. What happened?"

Jake pointed to the bodies. He rose and sat on his knees taking deep breaths. "Those two. Killed our lights. Attacked us. Punched me in the gut. Got the wind knocked outta me."

Alex helped Jake to his feet.

Jake snatched up Rae's phone and pocketed it. His headlamp suddenly flickered back to life and it shined down on the two bodies.

"Come on," he said. "We need to bag them and get them the hell outta here before they come back for another round." Jake wasted no time in scooping up the radar operator's remains while Alex held a trash bag.

Making quick work, they did the same with the OSS agent's body in a new bag, and then carried both back to the control room.

After shouting for Sammie and getting no response, both men double-stepped up the ladder with the bagged bodies in tow.

When they got up on the bridge, both Sammie and Rae were nowhere to be found. Fearing for their safety, Jake and Alex yelled out their names and panned their flashlights all around the pond.

A light beam blinked from the shoreline near the log bridge. "We're over here!" shouted Sammie.

"Is Rae okay?" yelled Jake.

"No, not really. She's having trouble breathing and has a big cut on her head. Bleeding pretty bad, but I think I can get it to stop."

"Oh, Jesus," Jake mumbled. "Okay, I'm coming over!" Jake shouted.

"Wait! Hold up," shouted Sammie. "Rae said to finish the job."

Jake grinned. *That's my girl.* "Tell her we'll get the rings and then we'll abort the mission."

The fearless Alex was already stepping back down the ladder into the conning tower. He glanced up at Jake. "Come on, dude. Let's go."

"Wait, just so you know, Heidel will be down there, too," said Jake. "He's supposed to be buried under a pile of mud in the torpedo room. I don't know what to expect. I'm just warning you."

Alex slid down the ladder. Jake followed and they regrouped in the control room. Jake took the lead through the bulkhead door entering the galley and crew quarters.

Rotted wood from the shattered galley cabinet lay in ankle-deep water on the heavily rusted deck plates. Moldy paper currency covered the walls. A deteriorated suitcase lay on a cot filled with more of the disintegrated paper money.

Fore of the crew quarters, behind a shredded curtain, Jake saw the torpedo room. He swallowed. As he slowly approached, his headlamp revealed a wide open tube door on his left. Deep inside, right where Duff said it would be, he spotted the rusted metal top and handle of the last ammo cylinder holding the remaining *Totenkopf* rings.

"Alex, see if you can fish that out of there," said Jake, pointing inside.

Jake then glanced to his right and saw the other torpedo tube, its door also open but filled with a seemingly solid brown cake. The hardened mud was filled with silver SS rings. The mud had also spilled onto the floor in front of it.

Protruding from the caked mud, Jake found the head of Franz Heidel. Hollow black eye sockets stared at him. His teeth-filled jaw had fallen open. A rusted mechanic's wrench lay halfway inside the smashed forehead of the Nazi SS officer. There wasn't any skin or hair left on the surface, nor any remains inside the eye holes, nose cavity, or mouth. Everything had been long been eaten away by bacteria. All that remained was a dirty greenish-yellow coating over the shiny white of the bone. It truly was a hollowed-out skull, yet apparently still attached to the spinal column. Also exposed was his scapula and left arm, but the radius and ulna bones of the lower arm were snapped off at the elbow.

"Heidel," whispered Jake, extracting the murder weapon from the skull. He tossed it on the deck behind him with a clang and a splash.

While Alex slid the remaining ammo can from the other torpedo tube and started unscrewing the lid, Jake fished out a trash bag and laid it on the floor next to Heidel's remains. He crouched down and placed his gloved hands around the skull to sever it from the neck when the temperature in the room suddenly dropped. A blast of cold air struck the men from behind. Goosebumps immediately formed on their arms. They turned and looked.

Standing there about three feet away, staring directly at Jake with fully-dilated black pupils, was a short man with wavy blonde hair wearing a freshly pressed black suit. His face was white with death. A gaping black hole in his forehead was caked with old blood. The figure frowned, threw his head back, and laughed loud in the most chilling other-worldly voice either man had ever heard in his life. The horrifying laugh echoed through the entire boat sending an ice cold jolt down both men's backs. It felt as if they were electrified in fear.

Wasting no time, Jake squeezed Heidel's skull between his hands and wrenched the head off its neck with a twist and a crunch.

Every remaining gauge with an intact glass face exploded all around them, showering the air with sharp shards. The men flinched and flung their arms over their heads for cover.

Their headlamp beams flicked off.

Darkness enveloped the pair like a heavy shroud.

The terrified men panted heavily anticipating an attack. The air grew warmer, and then just as sudden as they had gone out, their headlamps flickered back on.

Heidel's ghost had disappeared.

Inside the trash bag his skull went.

"Let's get the fuck outta here," Jake ordered.

❂

The Boneyard

Absorbing the first rays of daylight, the skeletal warriors of The Boneyard bid farewell to the exhausted quartet of explorers who dared enter the deep confines of the island they once guarded.

The Zodiac boat, with Sammie at the throttle, and now laden with four body bags filled with rocks and a container full of silver rings, sped due north into Sapelo Sound.

Over the deepest section, the team punctured the three bags of the Navy men and softly placed them in the water to fill up. With the rocks weighing them down, they let the bodies sink to their watery grave. All that was said for the burial at sea for the three Americans was, "Rest in peace," by Jake.

Next, Jake extracted SS Major Franz Heidel's grime-covered skull and jaw bone from its bag and cradled it with both hands. His plan was to drop the Nazi's head in the water, too. Instead, he sighed and started mumbling – more to himself than to anyone else.

"You know, the sea's just too good for you, Franz Heidel. You'll just be forgotten – another nameless coward who slaughtered unarmed innocents by the thousands." He looked up at the others in the boat as if pleading his case. "First it was the concentration camps, then the *Einsatzgruppen* death squads. This son-of-a-bitch harvested humans like a fucking crop. Hell, our own government even gave him a goddamn pass."

Rae shook her head in silence. This reminded her of a dark version of Hamlet speaking to Yorick's skull in the famous Shakespearian play.

"No one could oppose you," Jake said, addressing the skull again. "No one except for *Freemason* Werner Witte – your own countryman. He doled out the justice you deserved. Sorry, Heidel, I'm condemning your name to be *remembered*. No one will ever forget what you did after I'm done with you. The whole world will know your name as evil personified." Jake returned the remains to the bag. "Okay, we're done here. Take us back home, Captain Greenhall. This mission is over."

Ten minutes later they were docked at Greenhall Landing, unloading, and transferring gear to *Lizzie*.

29

ERHARDT HOFFMAN STOOD OVER NATHAN Kull's shoulder watching as the last of the financial transactions cleared on the master thief's brand new laptop computer screen. With the last $2 million of Kull's $10 million career gains going directly into the Fitzgerald, Georgia fallen police officer family's GoFundMe account, all of his secret numbered accounts had been completely pilfered. They were now spread out to various "charities" as Hoffman had explained. The older man then gently patted the younger seated man on his shoulder for a job well-done.

"Go on and finish your drink, Nathan," ordered Hoffman in his calm Charleston dialect. "I'll make you another." The thief never said a word. He simply lifted his glass and drained the rest of the cocktail, then placed it on the table next to a half-filled bottle of gin, a jug of tonic water, and a bucket of ice.

"Great job," praised Hoffman as if he were addressing a small child. Clutching the empty glass in his latex-gloved hands, he dropped several ice cubes in, then filled it half full of gin before topping it off with tonic. Unzipping his shirt pocket, he extracted a tiny plastic pouch with a white powder in it, labeled 'Devil's Breath.' Hoffman emptied the contents into the drink. After stirring it, he pushed the glass back in front of Kull.

"Drink half."

Kull complied again, as if he were a slave to Hoffman's every command, just as the drug was promised to function. It was given to him courtesy of Jake Tununda during their private conversation in his office last Friday. Against the wishes of his wife, Jake had secretly agreed with Hoffman to directly go after the thief-turned-killer rather than relying on the FBI to enact their prolonged process of limited justice. But Jake had been tied up in a separate project at the time and couldn't immediately help. Instead, he gave Hoffman the Devil's Breath and explained how it would work if he happened upon Kull's whereabouts.

Hoffman remembered Jake saying something profound that stuck with him. He said: *In life, you fight for the brothers you find worthy, for they are your home.*

Hoffman laid low, stewing in his moral dilemma, wondering if he had the balls to even act on his convictions. The tipping point came a few days later when Jake frantically told him that Kull had just stolen $3 million from his home. He advised Hoffman to go off the grid because Kull might be coming after him in Charleston.

A safe place doesn't exist in the real world, he remembered thinking at the time. He refused to live in fear, holed up in some remote cabin in the woods with paranoia infesting his mind. Instead, he decided to become a true social justice warrior and would secretly enter the lion's lair to confront the beast head-on.

After meticulous planning based on the location of Kull's residence, he caught a one-way ticket to Saint Lucia on an open-ended vacation. Flying into Hewanorra International Airport at Vieux Fort on the very southern tip of the island nation, he was then shuttled a mere one mile east to his lodgings on the coast.

Hoffman specifically booked a room at the luxurious Serenity at Coconut Bay resort because of the nearby proximity to Kull's Coconut Way residence not a half mile hike north through a nature preserve. He initiated surveillance of the thief's address while on walks, bike rides, and even using a rented ATV for tourists. He hit pay dirt on just his third day in country when he observed Kull in disguise as Frank Alan Mason leaving his home in an open top Jeep. Following on a rented bicycle, he tracked him not a mile away to *The Ugly Mug Grill & Stout.*

The Coconut Bay beach bar and restaurant was a non-descript local eatery sometimes frequented by tourists from the nearby resort. Dressed in a tie-dye t-shirt, straw hat and sunglasses, Hoffman grabbed an outdoor table overlooking the beach and ordered some local *Antilla* beer as he casually observed Kull eating dinner and watching TV inside at the small bar. An hour later, after hitting the men's room while passing by the bar, Hoffman overheard Kull saying he'd be back the next night for dinner, complaining that he hated cooking for himself and needed some company. The thief soon stumbled out drunk for the short drive back to his home.

That next night Hoffman was ready to pounce. He had arrived early after a short walk from his resort and took a table outside again.

After dinner, in the unlit parking lot, Hoffman flagged Kull down before he got into his Jeep. He addressed him as Frank Mason as if he knew him. Kull was confused, not recognizing the man. But it was too late. Closing in, Hoffman raised a handkerchief as if to sneeze and then blew powdered Devil's Breath into the thief's face.

The powerful active ingredient of burandanga, derived from the flower of the borrachero shrub common in the South American country of Columbia, took instant effect. Inhaling the powder, Kull's eyes immediately glazed over and he lost his balance. Hoffman grabbed his arm and propped him up. He said he'd give Mason a lift back home in his Jeep since he wasn't feeling well. Kull agreed wholeheartedly, giving up his keys as if they had been long time friends.

It was that easy.

At the thief's house, when asked, Kull also gave up the security code to deactivate the home monitoring system. He even revealed that there were no hidden security cameras in or around his house, jokingly remarking that he felt safe on Saint Lucia with just the basic system because he was hardly ever there. Inside, Hoffman mixed him a drink and added another dose of the tasteless, odorless drug. Kull drank as ordered.

Hoffman explained to a drugged-up Kull that he knew he was the master thief Phoenix, but he was there to protect him. That the FBI already knew his identity of Frank Mason and would soon show up to arrest him if he didn't do as he was told.

Kull bought the entire story, admitting he screwed up when he killed the cop in Georgia.

Hoffman convinced Kull to show him all of his financial assets. He was an open book. He gave up his most precious files that he had backed-up and downloaded off the Dark Web back onto his new laptop, passwords included. Hoffman said the FBI was going to seize everything and ordered him to transfer all of his money into a new list of numbered accounts. Kull followed the orders completely. Those transfers had already taken most of the night.

"Now I want you to show me the list of all your storage locker locations, the accounts, and access passcodes."

Kull slowly moved his hands over the laptop keyboard and went to work. Within seconds, a text document popped up listing five rental storage lockers located in New York City, Los Angeles, Savannah, London and the last, right there in Vieux Fort. Each location even included a list of inventory, which jobs his stolen items originated from, and their value.

Hoffman noticed on the Vieux Fort storage locker inventory two recently logged items: $3 million in U.S. dollars and a fake Van Gogh print – taken from Jake Tununda, Skidaway Island, GA. Hoffman frowned. *A fake Van Gogh print?*

"You are very organized, Nathan. Such detailed listings."

Kull looked up at Hoffman. His eyes were glazed over, pupils dilated like two black lifeless holes. "Thank you, Mr. Hoffman." Kull's words came out slow and slurred.

Hoffman produced a flash drive. "Copy that file onto this drive."

"Yes, sir. Not a problem." Again, Kull complied, attaching the tiny drive to the side port on his laptop, and duplicating the file.

"Tell me about the Van Gogh painting you took from Jake Tununda."

Kull frowned and crisscrossed his finger tips, staring into his laptop screen. "I should have wasted him, but I felt sorry for him. He refused to give it up. Needed it to pay a ransom to some Mexicans for hostages. I took his cash and took the painting any way. Fuck him. But he got the best of me. Gave me a taste of what it's like to be conned. Made a Giclée print of the original. I didn't know it was a fake until I was on my flight back here."

Hoffman smiled. The Tunundas brilliantly made a precautionary forgery of their valuable original painting. Smart people.

"Well, my friend. It looks like our precautionary steps are almost concluded." Hoffman pulled the flash drive and pocketed it.

"Now, if you would, please delete all of your Dark Web accounts you told me about and any digital assets within."

Kull logged-on to the underworld of the internet and killed his identity there, including all of his cloud back-up files.

"Drink the rest of your gin and tonic. It's good, isn't it?"

"It really is. I like it," said Kull, barely getting the words out. He drained his glass once again.

"Do you know how to erase the entire hard drive of your computer?"

"I sure do. Easy as pie."

"Good. Wipe it clean as if you worked for Hillary Clinton."

Kull smiled at the joke, then went to work. Soon they watched a progress bar slowly scroll across the screen wiping all of the files present on the laptop's hard drive. When it was finished Hoffman closed the laptop.

"Okay. You're doing great, Nathan. The last thing I'd like you to do is follow me outside to your pool for a swim. Come on. It'll be fun."

Hoffman grabbed the bottle of gin and led Kull out through a set of French doors to a tiled patio and inground pool. The lights were off, but a half-moon adequately lit the water's surface. A slight wind blew off the sea rustling the many trees that surrounded the property.

Kull walked very slowly, wavering from side to side under the effects of both excessive alcohol and the Devil's Breath. Hoffman held his arm to guide him out the doors. He looked and acted like a zombie, just as the stories about the legendary drug had described. Some called the drug an urban myth. Hoffman knew it was completely real.

"Don't be afraid, Nathan," Hoffman whispered. "Put your trust in me to guide and protect you."

He then extracted a handful of powerful prescription sleeping pills the emergency room doctor issued him after his hospitalization. One normally did the trick – he handed Kull fifteen of the pills and told him to swallow all of them with the rest of the gin. That he would fall asleep soon and his life would reach its pinnacle. Kull took the bottle of gin.

"Yes, Mr. Hoffman. The pinnacle of life is all I desire," slurred Kull, downing the pills and booze, spilling a few on the pool deck. He set the bottle down, but it tipped over and rolled into the pool.

Couldn't have planned it more perfectly, thought Hoffman. "Now take off all your clothes and enter the pool. It's time for a swim."

"Cool. This will be fun," said Kull. "Can't remember the last time I skinny dipped." Kull laughed but complied again, stripping completely naked. He entered the pool and splashed around, enjoying himself in the water. Hoffman backed off in the shadows to watch. And wait.

Kull's head flopped around on his shoulders as the overdose of sleeping pills and alcohol finally shut his system down. His eyes snapped shut and he wandered into the deep end of the pool. Slipping under water while losing consciousness, he started floating face down.

Under a steady stream of bubbles, his body slowly sank to the bottom of the pool and laid there unmoving. Hoffman walked up to the edge and watched for a couple of minutes.

Satisfied that Phoenix would never rise again, Hoffman carefully inspected the house for any trace evidence he may have left behind. He then fished Mona Lisa's reassembled phone from his pocket, powered it on, activated its Find My iPhone app, and placed it on top of the laptop. If the FBI was worth their salt, they'd instantly know of its whereabouts.

And who had drowned in the pool.

A quiet one-mile walk back to his luxury resort and he was back in his King-sized bed before midnight.

Early the next morning, he grabbed a taxi to Vieux Fort and gained access to the storage locker where he found a duffel bag full of crisp clean American bills. Also inside the bag of cash was a cylindrical leather case. It held the Giclée reproduction, except this canvas had been torn in half.

Hoffman packaged the duffel bag and fake painting in a cardboard shipping box he'd bought at the storage company, then dropped it off at a DHL Express, paying in cash for a guaranteed certified overnight delivery to *Tununda's Military Menagerie* in Savannah. The rest of the day he spent at his resort pool bar.

The following morning, he received a call on his burner from Jake Tununda.

"Hey brother, hanging in there? Just wanted to make sure you're okay."

"Never better. You get a package delivered to your shop this morning?"

There was a pause on the line. *"That was you?"*

"The bird who spoke in Devil's breath has been extinguished."

"Holy–"

"See you in a few days. I'm on vacation." Hoffman ended the call.

Hoffman stayed on the island three more days. He swam at the resort pool, sunbathed at the beach, received a massage at the spa, drank premium liquor, and feasted on fine dining, all the while checking the local newspaper for any word of Frank Mason's death.

Not a word, so he flew back home to Charleston.

The news hit Monday night when he'd gotten back to his home and checked online news outlets for the island. An article in the *Saint Lucia Times* broke the story:

The Royal Saint Lucia Police Force (RSLPF), in partnership with the United States Federal Bureau of Investigation (FBI), are investigating an apparent drowning accident in Vieux Fort that resulted in the death of one individual.

International businessman Frank Alan Mason, a 38-year-old Federation resident under the citizen by investment program, lost his life while swimming in his own pool at his Coconut Way residence in Coconut Bay Village. His corpse was discovered late Thursday night by visiting RSLPF officers who had been notified by the FBI in regards to an American fugitive named Nathan Kenneth Kull. Kull is wanted on multiple charges in relation to theft, kidnapping, and murder – most recently his killing of a police officer in the state of Georgia.

District Medical Officer Dr. Ronald O'Malley was summoned and pronounced Mason dead on the scene. According to a police statement, the scene was processed, and several items of evidential value were taken into police custody.

Alcohol and drugs were a contributing factor in the accident, according to a postmortem examination by Forensic Pathologist, Dr. Shirley Browne. Fingerprint and DNA analysis determined that Mason and Kull were one and the same person.

It is unknown at this time when the death occurred or how long the body had remained in the pool. Custom officials say that Mason returned to Saint Lucia last week on a private charter originating from Savannah, Georgia.

Mason has no known next of kin on file. His body is slated to be cremated.

Hoffman grinned. *The FBI always gets their man,* he thought with sarcasm.

30

STANDING ALONE IN FRONT OF A SQUARE, pedestal-style, 50" high exhibit case, its top third encased in tamper-proof tempered glass, bottom in a black finish, Jake Tununda remained motionless while looking at the priceless relic housed within. Illuminated with tiny accent lights, a glimmering life-sized skull sat atop a black silk cushion. It was an exact replica cast from SS *Sturmbannführer* Franz Heidel's skull retrieved from the wreck of U-2370, complete with his distinct cranial bone fusion embellishments and missing teeth.

Except this skull was completely made of solid silver, weighing in at an astonishing 64 pounds. The cast had been filled with silver melted down from thousands of SS *Totenkopf* rings originating from the U-boat wreck.

Jake stood three feet away, behind red velvet theater ropes and silver stanchions. He stared into the two painted black holes of the eye sockets. The bridge above the sockets were angled down by his commissioned artist to elicit a more evil-type expression apropos of the Nazi bastard it represented.

Deeply engraved on the polished forehead was the same Hoodoo vèvè graphical elements that appeared on *Doctor Blackbeard's Elixir of Life* moonshine label. However, Jake had his artist turn the double Xs into a true square and compasses configuration to honor the Freemasons. He didn't want the Mason's mark as subtle disguise. He wanted the world to know that Masonic warriors were the ones who took and branded this trophy.

Jake nodded unwittingly in deep satisfaction at the final result. Even the room it was housed in turned out perfectly and would surely get the public talking, especially when they found out where the silver used in the skull actually came from.

The display sat in what he named, the *Totenkopf Room*. Monitored with hidden surveillance cameras, it was now a highly secure vault worth millions of dollars, but its primary purpose was a reminder of one of the darkest episodes in human history.

This chamber was at the back of his old building, embedded within the original stone foundation, which had been built directly into the bluff behind River Street. It was the very last exhibit room after people made their way through his incredible, maze-like military artifact collection that spanned conflicts from the French and Indian War up to the War on Terror. The entire menagerie of rare weapons, uniforms, artifacts, and many other military treasures filled up the entire 15,000 square foot ground floor of his building. Jake spared not one penny in its high quality craftsmanship and materials. It was even the envy of some of the finest museums in Savannah.

Once visitors had reached the *Totenkopf Room*, there was only one way in and out: a heavy metal door. A limited number of people were allowed to enter at one time for a viewing session of 7 minutes. Upon entering, the interior walls, including the skull pedestal, were draped in black curtains.

The door was then closed and a flat screen display above the pedestal began an audio/visual presentation of the backstory of the SS and how they obtained their Death Head rings. At that point, the drapery on the walls rose to reveal thousands of the original *Totenkopf* rings behind accent-lit protective glass. The occupants would be surrounded by them.

The drapery over the pedestal display would then be lifted to reveal the shining, solid silver skull with the Masonic brand. Simultaneously, the presentation revealed the morbid story of SS *Sturmbannführer* Franz Heidel; the atrocities he and the Nazi party committed; how many innocents, including the Freemasons, were murdered under his command; how he was captured, turned into an asset under *Operation Paperclip*; and finally how he was smuggled onboard a surrendered German U-boat commandeered by a secret American crew to start a new life granted under the forgiveness of a secret corrupt cabal within our own federal government.

Without naming *Kapitänleutnant* Werner Witte or U-2370 specifically, the presentation finished when it was explained how one of the crewmen onboard – a Freemason – found out Heidel's true identity and enacted his form of justice for his war crimes.

When people exited the room, Jake wanted them in shock at the horrors men could bestow upon one another when political fervor turned into tyrannical suppression and then outright genocide. It was a warning he wanted them never to forget.

And it was all part of his brilliant marketing plan to put his menagerie on the map of military history collections worldwide.

The *Totenkopf Room* and the priceless silver skull itself were widely hyped in the national news media in the weeks preceding his grand opening. The news gained worldwide attention when he went public with the story behind the skull's true identity and how it was connected to *Operation Paperclip*.

Jake had released photos and video of a wrecked U-boat that he'd taken of U-2370 upon several return visits. He teased its existence without revealing its identity in order to force negotiations with the federal government, U.S. Navy, the State of Georgia, and the City of Savannah to ultimately salvage and rebuild the wreck. He insisted on it being a future museum to be docked right there on River Street in front of his building so people could eventually take a tour inside the vessel.

To back up his discovery, he released to the media redacted copies of the original documents found in the OSS agent's files pertaining to the Nazi that was being smuggled into the States. And he even went public with the Van Gogh painting he claimed was also being smuggled onboard.

On top of all that, Jake even teased that he knew where the famous horde of the rest of the SS *Totenkopf* rings was located, but that any expedition to search for them hinged on the Van Gogh painting being returned to Germany, and his team being compensated fairly for its discovery.

Jake's discoveries and revelations sent shockwaves through the world.

And now everyone queued around the block outside the menagerie's front entrance wanted to see the *Totenkopf Room* as a result.

Jake checked his watch. It was almost time to let them enter. But he had one more little ritual he wanted to perform before exiting the room and giving word to his employees to open the front door. He pulled out his iPhone, chose the Voice Memo app, and hit play on an edited file he had clipped from a long conversation.

It was cued to the moment of Duff's recording when he spoke of the forehead Hoodoo symbol on his moonshine skull label. He hit "play."

"You're exactly right, Jake. That mark has deeper meanings on so many different levels. We branded that Nazi motherfucker with the mark of the Masons to honor the tens of thousands of Freemasons who were murdered during the war. But for me personally, it was a way to remember that German soldier who saved my life in Italy. And for Witte, he said he wanted a special way to remember his act inside that sub to honor his father's death, while also acknowledging me for what I did for him in return. And just the fact it was placed on a skull of death, well, for us, it also meant resurrection. The start of a new life."

With a swig from his flask containing the *Elixir of Life*, Jake exited the room and met Rae, Becky, and his VIP guests Sammie and Duff waiting just outside. He shook hands with the two Greenhalls, thanked Becky for all her continued help, then hugged his wife.

"I'm all good," he whispered. "It's time. Let's open the door . . . and start a new chapter in life."

EPILOGUE

One year later
Grand Opening – Doctor Blackbeard's Distillery
Greenhall Landing
Sapelo Island, Georgia

DUFF RAISED HIS SKULL-SHAPED CRYSTAL SHOT glass filled with *Elixir of Life* moonshine and stood up with the help of a cane at the head of the long wooden farm table. Behind him, through a wide glass window, people could see the brand new, custom-made 300-gallon copper, brass, and wood still system. Someone turned the music off and the clinking of glasses could be heard. The beehive drone of some 150 special guests enjoying themselves while seated at similar tables in the new tasting and events room of *Doctor Blackbeard's Distillery* lodge, suddenly died down to a murmur.

Jars of moonshine were passed all around and every single person who'd showed up for the grand opening were now filling their own souvenir skull shot glasses in anticipation of what Duff Greenhall was about to say. An attending news reporter told her cameraman to start recording.

"I'ma gonna keep this short and sweet, because Lord knows I'm a ramblin' man," began Duff to much laughter as he addressed the seated crowd before him.

He stroked his gray beard as he spoke. "Y'all are literally standing on the ashes of a bygone era. As you now know, my old home burnt down well over a year ago, taking with it many memories of my loved ones. But it didn't take my family's foundation. That was preserved underground – as y'all have seen when you went downstairs and took the tour." Duff pointed to a door in the northeast corner of the lodge.

On the solid oak door was a large, elaborately carved rendition of the Doctor Blackbeard skull logo. The door had been placed in the same spot as the previous hidden wall door to lead down into the Spanish garrison. Cleo, the cat, lay on her side at the foot of the door.

"It's a foundation that has stood the test of time," Duff said. "Just like our Saltwater Geechee heritage present here. It has never crumbled since the day our ancestors were forced onto this island. Instead, that foundation has been built upon and strengthened by many caretakers over the years to keep our small community alive."

Heads nodded in the audience.

"Including fresh young minds, like my great grandson here, Mr. Sammie Greenhall, master distiller and founder of *Doctor Blackbeard's Distillery*. Sammie, stand up here with me. Come on now. Don't be shy."

The crowd clapped as Sammie stood up from the table and joined his Pappy. Cleo strutted over and rubbed up against his leg purring loudly. Sammie was dressed in denim overalls with a crisp white shirt underneath – the work uniform for his distillery. He was also sporting the beginnings of a black beard. Duff wrapped an arm around him.

"Sammie stood by my side while he was going through the worst time of his own life. He never wavered. Nuh, uh. He kept his strength."

Several women in the crowd repeated Duff's words like they were attending a church sermon.

"But now, pushing the *ripe* old age of 20, having brought this distillery back to life – *legally that is* . . ." Duff paused and lifted his gator tooth necklace over his head, held it out so all could see, then turned to Sammie. "He stands here now an upright man and Mason who has earned the coveted title that has been passed on for generations in our family. Sammie Greenhall, you are now Doctor Blackbeard." Duff placed the necklace over Sammie's head as everyone in the room clapped. The elder man grabbed his shot glass and held it high. Everyone in the audience mimicked his actions.

"Bottoms up, Doc!" Duff shouted. He downed his shot and slammed it on the table.

Sammie, in unison with the crowd, also shouted 'bottoms up.' The guests all drained their shots and hit the table just the same. Some people coughed, others howled, and many more licked their lips. The crowd then broke out into raucous applause as Sammie hugged his Pappy.

A tearful Duff soon held up his arms to gain their attention again. The crowd died down and he spoke. "Sammie has something big to announce. Sammie?"

"Hey y'all," said a smiling Sammie. "I-I-I'm not going to get all sentimental other than to say I love my Pappy and I'll never ever let him down. Now, what I'd like to announce is that we just entered into a huge new contract with a Southeast distribution company. Demand of *Doctor Blackbeard's Elixir of Life* is *through the roof* and I need to hire five new employees to fulfill orders. And Sapelo residents get first dibs for the jobs! That's all I've got to say."

Applause filled the lodge room again.

Once more, Duff quieted the crowd down. "Y'all get another refill now. I ain't done talking yet." More laughing ensued.

"I want to introduce to you another upright man and a fellow Masonic brother who, if it wasn't for him, this new distillery would've never have happened. Jake Tununda, come on and get your butt up here. And bring your shot glass, boy!"

Already well-known to everyone in the room, hoots and hollers went out as Jake rose from a nearby table. His wife Rae gave him a kiss. Marco D'Arata whacked him on his ass with his own cane. Becky Holden clapped loudly with a wide smile of bright white teeth. Alex Vann, who had recently been raised a Master Mason himself, bumped a fist with him, while his wife Marissa tipped her head and nodded. Lastly, Erhardt Hoffman stood up, shook hands, and embraced Jake.

Standing with Duff and Sammie, while someone filled his shot glass, Jake was all grins.

"Okay, okay, settle down now," Duff said. "Jake has some important news to announce." Duff and Sammie sat down to listen.

"First off, to Sammie, err, I mean, Doctor Blackbeard," said Jake with a wink. "I wish you and the people of Sapelo Island much success with your new distillery and keeping your heritage alive. You have one helluva moonshine with the *Elixir of Life!*" People gave shouts of approval.

"When you first stepped foot in my Savannah shop and placed that ring on my table, I didn't know what to think. But you ended up giving me an adventure of a lifetime. You and your Pappy, both. It was Duff Greenhall here who confided in me his deepest secrets. He's the one who gave me permission to officially *discover* the U-boat wreck that now sits right over there on Blackbeard Island."

Jake pointed north through the long row of display windows overlooking the bluff, salt marsh, and a brand new dock with many moored pleasure craft. Beyond was Blackbeard Island.

Gasps of shock rippled through the crowd. For the public, until that point, had no idea where the wreck was actually located along the Georgia coast. Chatter arose immediately. The news reporter started sending a text to her main office so their station could scoop the story.

"Indeed, that is one major announcement. Yes, the wreck of U-2370, a type twenty-three German electroboat, sits over there deep in the forest of Blackbeard Island. As we speak, U.S. Fish and Wildlife Service crews are cutting a road through the woods to get access to it. You'll learn much more in the days to come. Trust me, it'll be all over the news!"

The reporter looked up from her phone and Jake winked at her.

Vigorous clapping followed.

Jake held his hands up for silence. "More importantly, I'd like to announce *who* the captain of that German U-boat was. That's also been a long kept secret. With the blessing of his family, who came here all the way from New Ulm, Minnesota . . ." Jake paused to acknowledge a wide-eyed group at a nearby table.

"His name was *Kapitänleutnant* Werner Witte," announced Jake. "He was the sole survivor of the wreck on September 17, 1945 after Hurricane Homestead hit the island and literally swept the small U-boat inland. Now listen closely to what I'm going to say next." Jake paused for effect.

"Werner Witte was a prisoner of war who had already surrendered that same U-boat to our country many months before. He was then forced to command his own surrendered sub with an American crew assigned by the Office of Strategic Services – our modern day CIA – to transport, unbeknownst to him, mind you, a Nazi in disguise, back here to the U.S. But that Nazi died in the wreck."

Several people shook their heads, confused.

"That Nazi died at the hands of Captain Witte – once he found out who that man really was. That Nazi was none other than SS Major Franz Heidel. Yes, his silver skull is the one that now sits in my menagerie in the *Totenkopf Room*. He murdered thousands of Freemasons during the war, including – get this – Werner's own father, Otto."

More gasps from the crowd along with looks of shock.

"You see, Werner was also a Freemason. In secret. The Nazis never ever knew during his entire service throughout the war. He'd kept his foundation intact! And Werner wasn't going to let Heidel off that boat to start a new life after the war atrocities he'd committed against so many innocents."

The crowd went completely silent, on the edge of their seats. "Who found that U-boat wreck at the time in 1945?" continued Jake.

He placed a hand on Duff Greenhall's shoulder. "20-year old Army vet, Corporal Duff Greenhall did. While doing his Coast Guard patrol the very next morning after the hurricane."

The crowd buzzed again.

"As you know, Duff is also a Freemason, as are myself and many other men here in this room. And what do Freemasons do? We help a brother in need no matter if he was once our enemy, no matter the color of his skin, his politics, or his religion. For we believe in the good that man has to offer."

Jake saw many nodding heads.

"Duff found *Kapitänleutnant* Werner Witte inside that sub. He ultimately found him worthy as a man in need fearing for his life. Duff harbored and protected him as a fellow brother, in secrecy, under a new identity, or else he would have disappeared at the hands of our own government. The Greenhall family took him in." Jake paused again now, then looked over to the Witte family members, and one older man in particular.

"Werner left the island in 1956 and started his new life in Minnesota.

When he passed in 2003, his eldest son," said Jake with a tip of his head to the older Minnesotan, "Werner *Greenhall* Witte, contacted Duff and stated his father's wishes were to be buried on Sapelo Island. He was buried here in the Greenhall family cemetery, with his *Kriegsmarine* captain's hat on his head and a German Iron Cross to denote his service."

Werner Greenhall Witte nodded to Jake, tears falling from in his eyes.

Duff dropped his head, sobbing.

"Praise be the Lord!" A Sapelo woman shouted. Many others repeated her phrase.

Jake cleared his throat. "On behalf of the Werner Witte family, Duff Greenhall, and with the full support of the Federal government, State of Georgia, and City of Savannah, I am pleased to announce we've been given approval to raise U-2370 from Blackbeard Island. It will be refurbished and turned into a floating military museum docked on River Street and maintained in partnership by *Tununda's Military Menagerie* and the National Park Service."

Jake raised his skull shot glass and toasted, "To U-2370. Blackbeard's treasure has finally been found. Bottoms. Up!"

The crowd shot their whiskey again, then roared with applause.

THE END

FACT OR FICTION?

A breakdown of fact, fiction, and sources in order of the storyline.

Prologue: Unlike my first two books in the Tununda Mysteries series (*Crown of Serpents* and *Map of Thieves*), which re-enacted a true historical battlefield scene with real historical figures, the opening scene of *Skull of Disguises* is completely fictional.

However, having a German U-boat surrender to the U.S. Navy, and then be put back into service with an American crew might not be as far-fetched as one may think. This idea came from a real incident in 1941 when the British Royal Navy attacked and captured U-570, a Type VIIC U-boat, and put her back in service a month later with a Royal Navy crew under the name HMS *Graph*.

Having the "expendable" American crew made up of Navy convicts headed by an OSS agent under a secret program is an idea I emulated from the 1967 war classic *Dirty Dozen*. Having the U-boat wreck on Blackbeard Island, Georgia gave me the setting I desired.

U-2370: There was a real Type XXIII *Elektroboot* designated as U-2370 in the German *Kriegsmarine* during WWII. The technology and equipment descriptions of this *elektroboot* are based on research. The real U-2370 was launched in April 1945, but its service remains somewhat of a mystery. Some say it was never commissioned or even launched or that it was destroyed unfinished in its pillbox.

For me, this "miracle works" boat, full of state-of-the-art German engineering, was a prime candidate to create a storyline from. I needed a small submarine to make the journey all the way across the northern Atlantic to get to the North American seaboard to make the rest of my story fit – even though, according to war records, this particular type of U-boat never did. But with the help of larger refueling U-boats, a veteran captain in Werner Witte, and some creative licensing assigning it to *Gruppe Seewolf*, U-2370 was able to make that desperate journey at the end of the war.

U-2370's sister U-boat in the story, U-546, did exist and did sink the destroyer escort USS *Frederick C. Davis* (DE-136) late in the war. She was the last U.S. combat vessel to be lost by enemy fire in the Battle of the Atlantic. U-546 was subsequently sunk as described, its survivors were beaten and tortured during interrogation.

Portsmouth Naval Prison: This military prison did exist and was called the "Alcatraz of the East." It housed Navy and Marine Corps convicts and was located at the Portsmouth Naval Shipyard in Kittery, Maine.

Four German U-boats (U-805, U-873, U-1228, and U-234) that surrendered at the end of the war were towed to Portsmouth Naval Shipyard and their crews were housed in the prison. The crews did experience brutal conditions as described and were interrogated by the Office of Naval Intelligence. The commander of U-234, *Kapitänleutnant* Friedrich Steinhoff, was severely beaten by a Marine guard during interrogation. Two days later, in a Boston jail cell, he bled to death from a slit wrist, possibly inflicted by the broken lens of his sunglasses. The official cause of death was suicide, but that is still in dispute.

Doctor Blackbeard's Elixir of Life moonshine: I first heard about Sapelo moonshining from tour guide Stacey White, and then also reading of it in my treasured autographed copy of the late Cornelia Walker Bailey's memoir, *God, Dr. Buzzard, and the Bolito Man.* Bailey described how moonshining was a part of the culture of Saltwater Geechee, how everyone did it, and how some even made very powerful booze.

I chose the name Doctor Blackbeard to play, not only on the physical location of where the moonshine was distilled – at Raccoon Bluff on Blackbeard Creek – but as to who was actually making it, as well. In Bailey's book, she tells of Dr. Buzzard, a powerful Hoodoo root doctor. That root doctor always had moonshine to sell at his or her house. That 'shine attracted many people of all walks of life to come, sit, talk, and drink. White timber workers, fishermen, and lots of Scots-Irish visited Sapelo homes after a hard day's work. They got along harmoniously with their black counterparts while sipping moonshine. To me, that seemed apropos of the *Elixir of Life*.

And so, at a restaurant in Roswell, Georgia I tried a flight of moonshine for the first time in my life. And loved it! I then started "researching" moonshine, shall we say, having tried upwards of ten different potent brands. My research also included a tour of the *Dawsonville Moonshine Distillery* in Dawsonville, Georgia, the heart of moonshine country, where I learned the distillation process from Ken "Rocket Man" Martin. I also read an amazing book about the history of moonshine, called *Mountain Spirits* by Joseph Earl Dabney. I was even offered illegal moonshine by a fellow Georgia Freemason for $80 a jar. I turned him down, but soon may give it a "shot."

The *Skull of Disguises (Elixir of Life)* label design was my own. It is fictitious, of course, and provides symbolism that ties in with the storyline. The historical reasoning behind creating such a label (in my plot) – the poisoning deaths of forty blacks in Atlanta in 1951 – is true. Look up Fats Hardy, "the moonshine murderer." Historically, though, moonshine label designs or branded marks rarely occurred, at least that I know of.

Gullah-Geechee culture: I tried to be true to the history I learned of the Gullah-Geechee culture, language, and legacy, more specifically of the Saltwater Geechee on Sapelo Island. Sources included: *God, Dr. Buzzard, and the Bolito Man* by Cornelia Walker Bailey; the project *Drums and Shadows* conducted by Mary Granger; Buddy Sullivan's *Sapelo: People and Place on a Georgia Sea Island*; Pin Point Museum and staff interview; online documentaries, essays, and articles; personal interviews and island tours; and delving into the historical movie *Daughters of the Dust* by Julie Dash.

Phoenix and his cruise ship art heist: Compass Fine Art Gallery is a fictitious name based on the real art galleries that sell their wares on cruise ships all over the world. I visited one of these cruise ship art gallery auctions while on an Alaskan cruise with my wife. I'll refrain from naming the real company or the cruise line.

At the time, I was taken aback at how the so-called, valuable, one-of-a-kind original artworks were just laying about in various rooms with one or two employees present and an utter lack of security. After sipping free champagne, winning door prizes, and being schmoozed by the seemingly-knowledgeable staff, I totally got suckered into the auction process like so many naive art purchasers do. I never did bid on a piece of artwork because something seemed wildly amiss during the whole process. I'm glad I followed my gut because later I looked up the company and learned of the class action lawsuits, settlements out of court, long list of complaints over business practices, and many accusations of inauthentic art and blatant fraud. And so for all those thousands of people that got screwed over, I took fictitious revenge for them by sending in the legendary Phoenix.

Sapelo and Blackbeard Islands: With the exception of Greenhall Landing, everything described about the islands was based on either current news, historical sources, books, observations, or personal interviews. The Greenhall family estate is only meant as a fictitious portrayal of how one Saltwater Geechee family persevered and lived in Raccoon Bluff. There are no permanent residences left in the Bluff today, only one private seasonal lodge owned by several families.

On a long solo hike from Hog Hammock, I met James Austin, a well-mannered white teenager vacationing at that lodge. James and his younger brothers took me on their Polaris for a little adventure, showing me wreckage of a WWII P-40 fighter that had crashed during live-fire training early in the war, the pilot walking away at the time. James and I also briefly stood guard against a wild boar, he with rifle, me with pistol. James was part of the inspiration for my present-day, fictitious, independent, outdoorsy young black character, Sammie Greenhall, who lived all of his life on the Bluff.

On my visits to Sapelo Island, I took island tours; hiked the woods and beaches; explored abandoned homes, historical sites, and the Reynolds Mansion; conducted interviews; had cold beers and cigars at *The Trough*; drank Scotch with my "retreat" hostess Lucy Lea; was served food by *Lula's Kitchen*; played with feral cats; and I even helped extinguish a wind-blown, fast-moving brush fire I discovered threatening Behavior Cemetery. I'm just glad the Hell Hound let me in to fight the blaze. Note: I did ask 'leave.'

I visited Blackbeard Island only once, with photographer Michael Grafton. We boated over from his cottage on Shellman Bluff on a very hot

November day. We hiked; were swarmed endlessly by bugs; almost stepped on a cottonmouth snake; explored The Boneyard and the crematorium; and even got Grafton's boat stuck in the pluff mud at low tide for a few hours. That trip alone gave me great insight into the impenetrable dense brush of Blackbeard Island's interior, along with the north-south dune ridges and deep troughs. It's where I ultimately placed the wreck of U-2370 so it could be hidden for so many years.

Sammie and his uncle LeShaun Greenhall. Sammie is certainly the sympathetic character in this story. He's a tough, independent, intelligent young man emerging from the tragic loss of close family members while also transitioning into manhood. But he's treated as a slave by his guardian: his own uncle LeShaun "Buzzut" Greenhall. Sammie finally stands up for himself and his Pappy after enduring years of mental and physical abuse. The tipping point is when Buzzut tries to sell the coveted land that has been in the family estate since 1871 when their slave ancestor first purchased it as a freedman.

LeShaun Greenhall is the epitome of human garbage. Just a waste of oxygen. Origins for his character are derived from a South Carolina Gullah/Geechee lawyer named Horace Jones. This man was entrusted to take care of family matters for clients. Instead, he stole $600,000 from slave descendants who had owned property since the Civil War, land that was worth $10 million. He bilked another estate out of $150,000. He committed suicide before he could be convicted. One of his victims said, "Retribution is a universal law."

Buzzut's the main obstacle who Sammie, Pappy, and Jake must overcome. With a little help from the Boo Hag and some Liquid O, the "retribution" works out just fine.

One reader said this about Buzzut: "He's a nasty ass. A poor excuse for a human being." Scan the news on a daily basis and a Buzzut will always make an appearance, usually in a mug shot. I've been told many times that I create villains my readers love to hate. Buzzut fits this description perfectly. For my storyline, I turned this selfish piece of shit into a drug smuggler, a child abuser, an elder abuser, a financial leech, a thief, and a murderer. One who would single-handedly destroy his own family's name for personal gain.

Duff 'Pappy' Greenhall: This character was loosely based on two individuals: America's oldest living World War II veteran, Richard Overton, who is 112-years old at the time of this writing; and Allen Green (1907–1998) of Sapelo Island, one of the last holdouts of Raccoon Bluff. Green finally relocated to Hog Hammock in 1960 after R. J. Reynolds Jr. pressured him by threatening to cut off the roads to the north end of the island. Allen's unhappy removal from his ancestral roots and his loss of sense of place is symbolized in Duff Greenhall's struggle to preserve his own family's legacy.

Duff is a Saltwater Geechee, a root doctor, a legendary moonshiner, Prince Hall Mason, and a Buffalo Soldier.

The 92nd Division he served in during WWII was real. This segregated, all-black unit was the only one of its kind to see combat in Europe. Read *Black Warriors: The Buffalo Soldiers of World War II* by Ivan J. Houston.

The Buffalo Soldiers fought in northern Italy against the German Army along the Gothic Line high in the Apennine Mountains. The Sommocolonia, Italy battle did take place as described. Lieutenant John Fox did call in artillery on his own position killing over 100 German soldiers and allowing 18 Buffalo Soldier survivors to escape back to their lines. He was awarded the Congressional Medal of Honor, but not until many years later.

The battlefield act of the Freemason German soldier saving Corporal Duff Greenhall from execution during that battle was fictitious. The idea, however, came from another true WWII Masonic story given to me by fellow Mason Jason Dailey. He said this: "A brother at a lodge I visited told me about his grandfather, who was a WWII vet, and how he and another soldier had been captured by the Germans. They were placed on their knees to be executed. He was about to get shot and gave the words of distress, as well as the man next to him, and their lives were spared by an officer. They were taken aside by the officer who asked them how they knew the words, and they told him they were Masons. Under the dark of night, they were fed a hearty meal in a small room, and taken to a spot where they could escape easily without capture. The irony is, of course, Freemasonry was banned in

Germany, and the officer was also a Mason, but his life was spared because his name was not on a list."

During the war, many German Freemasons were placed in concentration camps with an inverted red triangle badge sewn onto their prisoner uniforms. This denoted they were political prisoners. Ultimately, they were murdered along with everyone else considered a "deplorable" in the eyes of the Nazis. Note: Hillary Clinton needs to choose her words more wisely when describing fellow American citizens.

Some 80,000 Freemasons alone were said to be executed during the war. Didn't matter if you were a law-abiding German citizen or a decorated war veteran. If you didn't toe the Nazi Party line, you were a dead man.

And so, because a German soldier saved the life of Duff Greenhall in the heat of battle is why I had Duff save the life of Werner Witte inside the U-boat once he found out he, too, was a Mason. Especially, after what Witte did to SS Major Heidel. Duff wanted to reciprocate on that core belief in brotherly love.

Regarding that tenet of Masonic obligation, versus loyalty to a government or an army, this quote sums it up perfectly: "We were here (the Masons), before this was here (the United States). My loyalty lies with the Freemasons, not the United States Army. My fraternity is older than the United States of America. If I see an enemy on the battlefield throw up a grand hailing sign, I don't give a damn what orders I'm under, he gets a pass. I ain't dropping the hammer on him." – *Freemason Dan Leger, repeating the words of an older Mason in lodge.*

German U-Boat Captain Werner Witte as a Freemason: The notion of a WWII German U-boat captain being a Freemason came from an interview with one of my Masonic brothers in Savannah. His name is Dan Leger, better known as 'Savannah Dan,' former U.S. Army MP, former law enforcement officer, and now one of the best historical tour guides in Savannah. Dan is the same character that Jake Tununda briefly meets in Chippewa Square in *Map of Thieves*.

During our lunch together at *The Olde Pink House*, where I indulged in shrimp and grits, Dan told me of a WWII story he'd heard from an older

Mason. The story went like this: an American merchant ship captain (a Freemason) was under attack by a surfaced German U-boat. He and the U-boat captain were looking at each other through binoculars. As a last act of desperation, the American gave the grand hail sign of distress. The German U-boat captain, also a Freemason, albeit secretly, recognized the sign and immediately ordered his crew to dive. He let the American vessel go, saying to his crew, "we'll do no more hunting today."

This humanitarian battlefield act between enemies is another amazing story in Freemasonry's rich history. It gets to the core tenet of brotherly love and loyalty, choosing respite for a man of the fraternity over obligations to a government, army or navy. That scene, in my mind's eye, was the seed I needed to create my Masonic character of the U-boat captain.

It's also worth noting that Witte, living a secret life in the United States as a former prisoner of war, was based on a true story I found about an escaped German POW who evaded capture for over 40 years. His name was Georg Gärtner. He took the alias of Dennis F. Whiles, obtained a Social Security card in that name, and lived a normal life until, at the age of 64, he revealed his identity. Although being on the FBI's most wanted list, he was never charged with a crime.

Operation Overcast/Paperclip. This secret government program to smuggle Nazi human assets into the United States as "intellectual reparations" did exist. Originally dubbed *Operation Overcast,* it was authorized in May 1945 by the Joint Intelligence Objectives Agency, a subcommittee of the Pentagon's Joint Chiefs of Staff. They did so without the knowledge of President Truman at the time. Truman found out in September 1946 and officially approved the program with the explicit order to exclude anyone "to have been a member of the Nazi party and more than a nominal participant in its activities, or an active supporter of Nazi militarism." However, intelligence operatives running the operation "bleached" the Nazi backgrounds of those human assets; gave them clearance to work in the States; and falsified their employment histories. The project was renamed *Operation Paperclip,* after the paperclips attached to their personnel files. The program was not made public until 1973, with most information surrounding it still classified as secret.

Thousands of scientists, engineers, technicians, and intelligence agents along with some of the most vile Nazi criminals in the war, were exfiltrated and given a new life in service to the United States government. Notable, if not infamous, names included: Reinhard Gehlen, Klaus Barbie, Otto von Bolschwing, Otto Skorzeny, Georg Rickhey, Wernher von Braun, Hermann Oberth, Hubertus Strughold, and Arthur Rudolph, among many others.

SS Sturmbannführer Franz Heidel. He is the personification of evil in this story and an example of who our government let into our country under *Operation Overcast/Paperclip.* He was based on the many concentration camp *Totenkopfverbände* commanders in the war, as well as the *Einsatzgruppen* death squads. With the exception of a very few, they all got away with murder. I wasn't about to let Heidel get off that U-boat once Witte found out his true identity and what he'd done to so many Freemasons.

SS Totenkopf Rings. All mentions of this ring, including the secret hidden horde at Castle Wewelsburg, are true. It is said that if that horde, estimated from 9,000 to 14,000 rings, is found it could be worth up to $95 million in silver. SS *Totenkopf* rings are a highly prized World War II relic in militaria collector circles. They range from $7,000 to $11,000 depending on condition, but with proper provenance of a ring bearer's name, their worth can go up dramatically. For example, visit www.totenkopfring.eu, where you'll see SS *Oberst-Gruppenführer* Josef "Sepp" Dietrich's 1933 ring priced at $235,500.

Monuments Men corrupt truck team. The corrupt, black market U.S. Army truck team assigned to the woefully understaffed Monuments, Fine Arts, and Archives program (MFA&A) at the end of the war is one of those 'could-have-beens.' My gang of thieves was based on a document I read titled, *Plunder and Restitution* (December 2000), specifically, in Chapter 4 under the subhead: *Security Issues, Problems in the Field.*

These guard units were essentially contractors entrusted with the protection, collection, and transportation of valuable treasure caches to MFA&A collection points. But, as noted in the report, those guard units were all too often looting the items they were supposed to protect, and then shipping the treasures back to the States uninspected by U.S. Customs.

Another factor contributing to this military gang of thieves came from the book, *Nazi Gold*, authored in 1984 by investigative journalists Jan Sayer and Douglas Botting. Dubbed the "Biggest Robbery in History," the story goes in-depth about how more than $2.5 billion in gold, currency, and jewels hoarded by the Nazis simply disappeared in the chaos of 1945.

Erhardt Hoffmann. This famed German militaria expert is fictitious, but his parents' background is based on my good friend and fellow Mason Robert Soderstrom's parents. Just as described, his father was a U.S. Army officer during WWII and his mother was a member of the Hitler Youth. Hoffman also is loosely based on fellow Freemason Mike F. Morris, a noted military collector/dealer and author of *Sacking Aladdin's Cave: Plundering Göring's Nazi War Trophies.*

Hitler's pistol and Göring's baton backstory. Except for my three paragraphs describing how the sergeant had his loot smuggled to Bermuda and then sent Harris Neck, the incredible story of how Hitler's pistol ended up at the West Point Museum is all true. Google: "Hitler's Lost Treasure. Where Is It Now?" by Ron Laytner. Göring's baton story is also true and based on U.S. Army historical records.

Hell Hounds, Boo Hags, and ghosts. Who really knows? I tend to lean toward these entities or spirits really existing. The stories of a Hell Hound and a Boo Hag on Sapelo are prevalent enough with the Geechee, but I came up with the hag's ancient Guale and Spanish backstory. The name Yahoodi came from when my father scared the shit out of me when I was a kid, naming the bogeyman Yahoodi. As for ghosts, I did consult with the real Ryan Dunn of his Savannah Ghost Research Society for the U-boat scenes. I met fellow author Ryan Dunn at a booksigning in Savannah where I was promoting my *Haunted Savannah Illustrated Map.*

R. J. "Dick" Reynolds Jr. With slight embellishments to fit the plot, I stayed true to Reynolds's past. A highly accomplished man, in my opinion. Some hated him, some loved him. I learned about Reynolds on my first visit to Sapelo after seeing his old mansion. I then read two biographies: *The Gilded Leaf* written by his son Patrick Reynolds, and *Kid Carolina* by Heidi Schnakenberg, from both of which I derived much information. The Reynolds Mansion scene and history is all described accurately.

Drones. Major package delivery companies are already testing drones in their business systems. And just after I wrote this book I learned of a start-up called Volans-i, whose drones have a 500-mile range carrying 20-pound loads at speeds up to 200 miles-per-hour. They can even land on ships sailing at sea. It's just a matter of time until the cartels obtain this technology and smuggle large amounts of drugs, if they aren't already doing it now. But using the combination of container ships and narco-drones was something I came up with in my own "criminal" mind.

Saint Lucia. Wanna get away? That's what Nathan Kull does under his 'legal' alias identity as Frank Alan Mason. The government's Citizenship-by-Investment program is real. By simply making a real estate investment in a government-approved real estate project, with a minimum of $300,000, a high net-worth individual can become a lifetime citizen.

After passing a criminal background check, you are issued an official biometric passport. No visit in person, nor interview, nor residency required before or even after you gain your passport. There is no personal income tax, no wealth tax, and no inheritance taxes.

My wife and I visited Vieux Fort, Saint Lucia. We stayed at the luxurious Serenity at Coconut Bay resort just as Erhardt Hoffman did, and even had an *Antilla* beer at *The Ugly Mug Grill & Stout*.

The three master thieves and con men Nathan Kull named himself after are real individuals: Frank Abagnale, Alan Golder, and Bill Mason. Read their stories and you'll know where Phoenix originates . . . and perhaps how he may just rise again. *Wink.*

ACKNOWLEDGEMENTS

First and foremost, many thanks to the scores of readers who loved my first two books in the series. You demanded another, and again, after much research and writing, and juggling of my other business interests, I'm glad I pulled this one off. Really enjoyed producing this story. Best one yet!

Continuing in my series theme of Native American history and sacred lands, I chose a unique group of Native *African*-Americans for this book: Gullah/Geechee slave descendants. Specifically, I focused on a dwindling community of Saltwater Geechee on Sapelo Island, GA. I'm not even sure what first drew me to Sapelo, but once I started learning the history of the island, I completely immersed myself in uncovering more of the past. A major start to that inquiry was reading the late Cornelia Walker Bailey's book, *God, Dr. Buzzard, and the Bolito Man*.

Of course I need to mention Buddy Sullivan and his wealth of historical publications, including his most recent tome: *Sapelo: People and Place on a Georgia Sea Island*. A thank you to longtime Sapelo resident Lucy Lea for her grand tour of the entire island and Reynolds Mansion; and to Stacey White for her South End tour and sharing memories of moonshining. Shout outs to James Austin for showing me the WWII plane wreckage – and tracking a wild boar; to Fellow Mason Rodney Jones, a law enforcement instructor with the Georgia DNR; to Stephanie Chewning, DNR Naturalist at the Reynolds Mansion; to Jim Beckemyer, former U.S. Coast Guard DOG unit; to photographer Michael Grafton for staying at his Shellman Bluff cottage and boating over to and exploring Blackbeard Island; and lastly Captain Wild Bill for his history of Blackbeard Island and for turning me onto the book *Shadow Divers,* about a sunken U-boat discovery.

Speaking of U-boat research, another great book I read was *Hitler's U-Boat: the Secret Menace* by David Mason. That was followed by an entertaining work of historical fiction based on a sunken U-boat off Tybee Island, titled *No Enemy But Time* by Savannah native William C. Harris, Jr.; and of course the grandmaster of adventure fiction Clive Cussler and his Fargo Adventure novel, *Spartan Gold,* featuring a midget German

U-boat in a Maryland swamp. I'd be remiss if I didn't mention the website www.uboat.net, created by Gudmundur Helgason, the "Bible" for U-boat enthusiasts. Another fantastic resource was the private Facebook group "U-Boats" of some 3,500 members. From that group alone I need to thank Bob Goodwin, Zdenek Zidon Vacek, Mike Sivocha, Jerry Mason, Brad Golding, and Kyle Hutcheson for their feedback and critique. The greatest resource of all was touring U-505, a Type IXC U-boat captured by the U.S. Navy in 1944. It sits in the Chicago Museum of Science and Industry in an amazing exhibit that every U-boat enthusiast must visit.

A thank you to all my Masonic brothers who helped me out on various topics: Brothers Dan Leger, Robert Soderstrom, James and Jim Rowell, Danny Wofford, Dean Kennedy, Shawn Weldon, and Jason Dailey.

A gracious thank you to the following people for offering your expertise: author Rick Reed, former detective for his personal story; author Gavin Reese, law enforcement officer; author Kent Holloway, medical forensics examiner; Debbie Farley Marsh, registered nurse; Shepherd Stewart, forensics insight; Andy Watkins, former U.S. Army captain and police officer for investigative techniques and his personal stories; Jean Louis Rheault for his personal story; A.D. Kent for engine killing tip; Brian Lord for his personal story; Jerry Pelusio for real estate legal questions; Alison Cope Emann for her list of WWII treasures; Ryan Dunn, Savannah Ghost Research Society; and Kim Armistead for her colorful Southern sayings.

Much appreciation to all my beta test readers: especially my wife and best friend Laura Karpovage; Freemason brothers Billy Gould, Tim Yarbrough, and Dr. H. Craig Holoboski; long time fans Gene Conrad and Paula Howard; meticulous proofreader Linda S. LeCroy; and to new fan, good friend, and fellow relic hunter Robert Brian Miller.

Lastly, a special thank you to my editor Michael Brewster. He's been another long time fan of the series and did a wonderful job with developmental and copy editing to improve the narrative as a whole. Michael also was my go-to guy for any mathematical questions I had, namely how many skull rings could fit into a German ammo container, and also how much a solid silver human-sized skull would weigh: 64 lbs. Go figure.

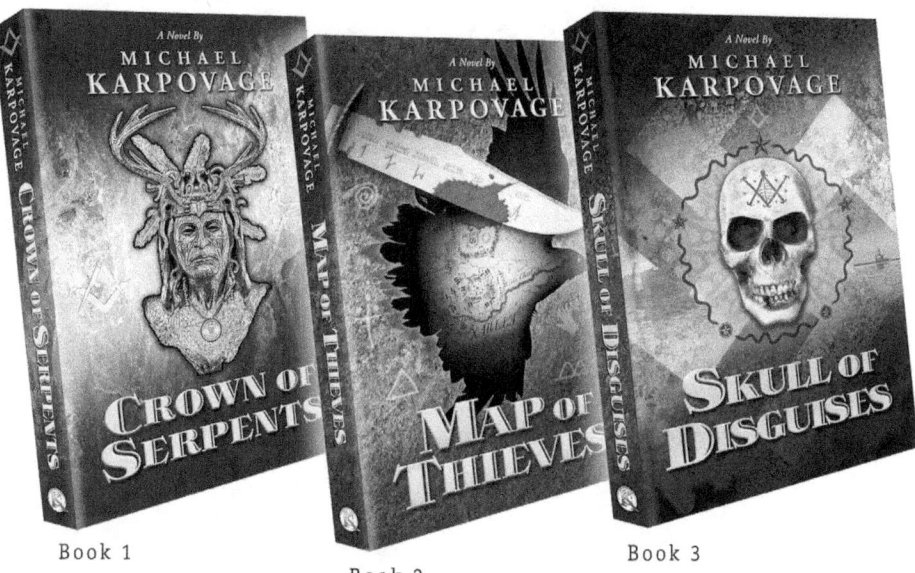